When the Day is Done

ALEXANDRA AYRES

When the Day is Done
Copyright © 2026 by Alexandra Ayres

All rights reserved.

No part of this publication may be reproduced, stored in a retrieval system, or transmitted in any form or by any means, electronic, mechanical, photocopying, recording, or otherwise, without the prior written permission from the author, except in the case of brief quotations embodied in critical reviews and certain other noncommercial uses permitted by copyright law.

This is a work of fiction. Names, characters, places, and incidents either are the product of the author's imagination or are used fictitiously. Any resemblance to actual persons, living or dead, events, or locales is entirely coincidental.

First Edition: March 2026

Published by Northern Creek Press LLC
northerncreekpress.com

979-8-9919800-4-3 (Paperback)

Cover Design by Mel D. Designs
Editing by Made Me Blush Books and Simply Write
Proofreading by English Proper Editing Services

For a full list of content warnings, please visit:
alexandraayres.com/content-warnings

*To the darling readers who took a chance on me
and love this series as fiercely as I do—
This one is especially for you.*

LUCY

Ever since I can remember, I've wanted kids. I'd pictured myself with a small hand in mine long before I ever pictured myself in a wedding dress or climbing career ladders or whatever adulthood was supposed to look like. Maybe it comes from growing up as the youngest of three, always orbiting around my older brothers with their scraped knees, loud games, and bigger-than-life energy. Our house was chaotic in the best way, and being wrapped up in that noise made me crave a future filled with the same kind of love.

I never thought much of it then. It was simply part of who I was.

I was twenty-four when the pain started getting worse. Those sharp, twisting aches that made me double over or curl on my side through the night. I told myself it was normal. Women were built to endure, right? And for a long time, I did just that. Endured.

It wasn't until the afternoon I found myself perched on an exam table in one of those crinkly paper gowns that everything I'd imagined for my future tilted off its axis.

The doctor was kind enough. She walked me through the details, the numbers, the what-ifs and maybes. With each one of her carefully chosen words, something I'd always taken for granted shifted from a given into a question mark.

I nodded, thanked her, and scheduled a follow-up. I think I even smiled.

The crying inevitably came later.

It wasn't grief for children I might never have, because that was the key word—*might*. It was, however, grief for the version of myself who had believed something so deeply, so wholeheartedly, without ever imagining I'd have to fight for it.

But here's the part I didn't understand back then...

A diagnosis doesn't close a door. It just changes the path.

one

LUCY

The bell jingles as the café door swings open. I spin, coffee pot in one hand, half eaten scones on a plate teetering in the other. I narrowly dodge a toddler who has decided the aisle between the tables is a runway. The espresso machine hisses and one of the baristas mutters something about "mutiny" while wrestling with the grinder.

It's chaos, and I love it. Thistle & Spoon isn't just a café, but also a piece of my heart and a piece of Mum's, too. She built this place from nothing, pouring her soul into every cozy corner, every battered book tucked onto the shelves. And now it's mine.

Juliette strolls in, calm as a Sunday morning, tote slung over her shoulder, and stops dead. Her eyes sweep the room, twinkling with amusement. "Did someone declare war on this place?"

I drop the scones onto the counter. "You'd know all about that, Mrs. Mum-of-Twins Extraordinaire."

She laughs. "At least my little terrors are at home with

Knox today. I swear your brother thought twin girls would be a breeze."

"Knox has always been overly confident," I say, wiping my hands on my apron. "He doesn't do reality checks unless reality hits him square in the face."

Juliette moved here to Scotland from the States when she started dating my oldest brother, Knox. Now they're married with two girls, Maisie and Keira. After Juliette moved here, it wasn't long before her best friend, Bree, ended up with my other brother Callan. Now she's future sister-in-law number two.

I never imagined my hard-headed brothers settling down, but somehow these women have softened them in ways I didn't think possible. Watching them all pair off so easily, like it was written in the stars, makes me so happy for them. Jules and Bree are the sisters I never had. At the same time, though...I'm a little restless. My brothers found love that crossed oceans, and I can't even decide if I want to give the guy down the road a proper chance.

The thought barely settles before Juliette slides onto a stool at the counter, instantly making herself at home. "Speaking of MacKenzie men and their delusions, have you heard from Callan and Bree?"

I roll my eyes. "Callan texted this morning. According to him, Bree has decided they need to taste test every wedding cake in Scotland before they commit."

"That sounds like Callan's idea, not Bree's."

"Oh, it absolutely was." I grin, pouring her a cup of coffee without asking.

"This is such a cute idea!"

I glance up and catch the sparkle in her eye as she studies the stack of flyers beside the till.

"*Kids' night at Thistle & Spoon*," she reads aloud. "*Stories, snacks, and stargazing. Every child leaves with a homemade treat and memories to keep.* Lucy, this is exactly what we need."

I nod, a flutter of excitement and nervousness mingling in my chest. "I've been thinking about it for ages. The town has plenty for the grown-ups, but the wee ones deserve their own special night, too."

"I'd love to bring the twins. Do you think ten months is too young?"

My heart melts at the thought of my nieces. "Are you joking? They'd be our guests of honor. I can't believe how fast they're growing."

"Too fast," Juliette sighs. "They're starting to pull themselves up on everything. Knox caught Maisie trying to climb a bookshelf yesterday."

I laugh, already imagining the twins crawling around, their matching rompers bunching at the knees. "I was hoping they could come. I've got a special corner planned with sensory toys and those soft picture books they love. I also found the sweetest little star-shaped teething biscuit recipe."

"You've thought of everything. The parents will adore you for this."

"I just want to create something special, you know?" I say, fiddling with the edge of the flyer.

Something lasting. Something that matters.

It might be silly to care this much about a kids' night at a café, but when the doctor's explanation of my endometriosis is still lodged in the back of my mind with warnings about lower odds, you start searching for other places to pour all that hope.

So, I'm trying to make this a place where kids will laugh and grow. Somewhere my heart can live, even if the family I dreamed about stays just that. A dream.

I push the thought away before it can get its claws in too deep.

"Everything okay, Lou?" Juliette's voice breaks through my thoughts.

I look up quickly, pasting on a smile. "Aye, just thinking about all the details."

Juliette studies me with those perceptive eyes of hers. She has this way of seeing right through people and is one of the few people who knows what I've been dealing with. "You know you can talk to me about anything, anytime, right?"

I busy my hands, straightening the flyers into a too-perfect stack. "I'm all right," I say, a little too quickly.

Juliette doesn't push. She just watches me with that quiet patience she's so good at, her hands cupped around her mug.

I clear my throat and force a smile. "Anyway, I was thinking we could set up a cookie decorating table."

Juliette gives me that soft, knowing smile of hers that tells me she sees right through the pivot but loves me enough to leave me be. "That sounds perfect."

I latch onto the topic like a lifeline, because right now it's easier to be just the girl who loves her café and her town, and not the girl who's terrified her life might never look the way she always dreamed.

"Are you volunteering as the cookie supervisor?" I ask, trying to sound brighter than I feel. "The twins can eat the rejects."

Juliette lets out a genuine laugh. "Knox will thank you for that. He's already convinced they're going to be master chefs by age three."

"MacKenzie delusions strike again," I say, and we both giggle, the sound chasing the tension out of my shoulders for a heartbeat.

I let my gaze wander around the café. The mismatched

chairs, the worn wooden tables that have seen a thousand first dates, heartbreaks, and celebrations.

It's not perfect. Nothing ever is. What it is, though, is alive, messy, full, and golden in its own way. Just like life, just like family, just like this small corner of the world I'm lucky enough to call mine.

two

AIDAN

The last two weeks have been a blur of twelve-hour shifts, endless solitude, and weather that chews you up and spits you out. The grind's become second nature over the years, and fatigue hardly even registers anymore. Just part of the deal. The work's relentless, but that's the life I chose. Right now, I'm counting down the days until I can get the hell off this rig.

I moved closer to my mum recently. She downsized into a smaller house in a quieter town, and since she's the one who looks after Isla when I'm working out here, it made sense for us to follow. Our new place is only ten minutes from her and thank god for that. I couldn't do this without her.

It's getting harder every day, though. Isla's growing up too fast, and I hate missing it. Every giggle I don't hear, every scraped knee I don't patch up—it digs under my skin. The two weeks I'll be at home coming up is something, at least. Seeing her face again is what keeps me going.

A sharp clang of metal drags me from my thoughts. The wind howls, thick with oil and salt spray. My jacket might as well be tissue paper for all the protection it offers, but I pull it tighter anyway, scowling at the chill.

"Oi, Aidan!" Jack's voice cuts through the hum of machinery, barely audible. "We've got a situation with pump three. Need your eyes on it."

I nod, glad for the distraction. Jack's been my closest mate since we started working on the rig together eight years ago. He usually does a decent job of keeping my mind off things, but as I make my way across the slick deck, my mind wanders back to Isla. Has she grown taller in the couple weeks I've been gone? Will she still want to play our silly make-believe games, or is she starting to outgrow them?

The pump's usual hum is off, replaced by a faint stutter in its rhythm that tugs me back to the deck. I crouch low, hands already moving to check the seals and pressure gauges. The salt in the air stings my eyes, forcing me to squint at the readouts. The numbers blur for a moment, but I focus, trying to make sense of them. Something's definitely off.

"Partial blockage," I shout over the noise. "Must be debris in the intake. We'll need to shut it down and flush it out."

Jack gives me a quick nod, already reaching for his radio to call in the maintenance crew. While we wait, I lean against the railing, my eyes scanning the endless stretch of gray sea. The waves are choppy today, rougher than usual. It's a brutal reminder of just how small we are out here.

The crew arrives, and we get to work. It's a messy job, but it keeps my hands busy, my mind occupied. As we're elbow-deep in grease and saltwater, Jack breaks the silence.

"So, how's the wee lass of yours doing?" he asks, his voice muffled by the noise.

I can't help but smile, even as I fight with a stubborn bolt. "Growing like a weed. She'll be starting school soon."

Jack whistles low. "Time flies, aye? Seems like just yesterday she was a newborn."

The reminder sends a pang through my chest. I've missed so much already. "Aye," I grumble, "it does."

"Thanks for the assist," Jack says, clapping me on the shoulder. "You heading to the mess after this?"

I shake my head. "Nah. Turning in early. Got a chopper to catch in the morning."

"Right. Back to the real world," he says with a grin before heading off.

I don't linger. The rig's steel corridors are quieter this late in the shift, but the thrum of machinery never really fades. Back in my cabin, I strip off my gear, tossing them in a heap. I sit on the edge of the bunk, letting out a long breath.

The compact space feels even smaller tonight, almost suffocating after two weeks out here. The North Sea doesn't offer much comfort. Just cold, noise, and harsh work. It's a tough routine, but at least it's predictable. The world back home? That's a different beast altogether.

I glance at the duffel bag in the corner, already half packed. Two weeks off isn't a holiday. It's a list of things that need doing. House repairs. Bills to sort. My mum's got a few updates on Isla for me, no doubt. She's great, from what I hear. Happy. Stubborn as hell, though I'll admit, she gets that from me.

The updates never come easy, though. They're reminders that while I'm away, she's out there growing up without me, and every time I come home, it feels like I have to earn my way back into her world. Prove I'm more than the man who passes through with apologies. She's got her own opinions, her own routines. By the time we find our rhythm again, it's usually time for me to leave.

I can't help wondering if one day she'll stop letting me back in at all.

For now, there's no use stewing on it. Tomorrow, the chopper's my ticket off this floating hunk of steel. I'll have two weeks back onshore, which isn't exactly rest, but it's a change of scenery. That's good enough for now.

three

LUCY

"What can I help with, boss?"

I turn to my left, and there's Poppy, always ready to jump in. She's tying her apron with that no-nonsense look of hers, sleeves pushed up to her elbows, glasses perched just a little crooked on her button nose. A few rebellious curls escape from the messy bun she's tried to wrangle them into, framing her round face.

"Would you mind giving me a hand with these cookies?" I ask, glancing back at the dough. "I've still got a tray to finish cutting out, and these are for kids' night tomorrow."

My hands are coated in a light dusting of flour, trails of it creeping up my arms. The kitchen air is thick, mingling with the sweet, almost intoxicating scent of butter and sugar that permanently sticks to every surface.

"This is just the test batch," I say, lifting a star-shaped cutter and pressing it into the dough with a little extra care, making sure each edge is sharp and clean. "I want to make sure they're perfect. The kids deserve the good stuff."

"Of course!" Poppy slides up beside me, already grabbing a

heart-shaped cutter from the nearby tray. "These smell incredible already. What's the secret ingredient this time?"

"A bit of honey and a dash of cinnamon," I reply as I add another star to the tray. "Thought we'd try something new for the wee ones."

As we work side by side, the rhythmic click of cookie cutters pressing into the dough is almost meditative. The kitchen is my sanctuary, humming with a warmth that goes beyond the heat of the ovens.

"If you've got this for a bit, I'm going to head back up front to make sure Michael doesn't need help with anything," I say, wiping my hands on my apron.

"Sure thing, I've got this." She doesn't miss a beat as she presses another heart-shaped cutter into the dough with a little extra flourish.

I wash my hands quickly, and as I step out into the shop, the familiar buzz of activity greets me. Before I can properly take in the scene, a loud clattering noise erupts from the back, echoing through the space. My head snaps toward the sound.

"Ach! Sorry, Lou!" I turn to see one of our regulars kneeling on the floor, surrounded by the debris of a broken mug.

"No worries, Shane," I call back. "We'll get that cleaned up, and I'll grab you another one."

I glance over at Michael, who's already starting to head to the back for a broom. "Would you mind taking care of that? I'll hold down the fort up here."

He nods without a word, and I return my focus to the counter, making sure everything is running as it should. The usual sounds of laughter, clinking cups, and the soft hiss of the espresso machine surround me, but then there's something else. A low, deep rumble of a voice I don't recognize drifts in from outside, and my head lifts to the front window like it's been tugged by a string. And then I see him.

He's...a lot.

Tall, broad shouldered, and soaked from the rain like the universe just dropped him off here gift-wrapped in storm clouds and brooding energy. His damp jacket clings to his frame as he steps through the threshold like he's not entirely convinced he wants to be indoors. The cold air follows him in, curling around my ankles.

He doesn't look at anyone. Just heads straight to the counter with a look that says *don't start with me*, and for some reason, I really, really want to start with him.

He steps up to the counter, his gray eyes sweeping the menu. A tiny crease tugs between his brows—focused, unaware he's already caught my attention. He has lines around his eyes, but not in a tired way. More in a...been through it kind of way. Mid-thirties, maybe? A full decade older than me, if I had to guess. He's not the buttoned-up, office job kind of thirty something, though. No... This guy looks like he builds things with his hands and breaks them when he's mad.

I press my palm flat against the counter to ground myself and clear my throat. "Welcome in! What can I get you?"

His eyes snap to mine, and I forget how to breathe.

"Coffee. Black. To go."

Each word lands with weight, like conversation is a currency he's not willing to spend. Still, there's something in the way he says it, something rough around the edges that scrapes against my skin and leaves a mark.

I nod, already moving. "Coming right up."

As I turn, I feel his eyes on me. Not a glance, not a casual once-over. This is full-on attention. It prickles along the back of my neck, curling low in my stomach in a way that feels both wrong and wildly right.

I set the cup down in front of him. "On the house," I say, a little breathless. "Looks like you could use it."

For a second, he doesn't move. Doesn't blink. Just lifts those stormy gray eyes to mine and quirks a brow.

"I...sorry. You don't look *bad* or anything. Just...tired, maybe? And...damp?"

Oh god, I'm just digging this hole deeper. I'm usually fantastic with small talk. Why does he have me so flustered?

He finally offers a subtle nod, putting me out of my misery before he says, "Thanks."

That's it. No smile. Just his rough, deep voice twisting through my insides like smoke. That voice is doing...inconvenient things to me.

He wraps both hands around the takeaway cup, his focus dropping to the swirl of steam rising from the lid. I linger long enough to feel silly about it until I realize I'm just standing there like I forgot how to be a functioning human.

"Right. Well, enjoy!" I blurt, my voice pitching higher than I want it to, cheeks heating. *Smooth, Lou. Olympic-level grace, right there.*

He turns as if he's going to walk out, then comes to a halt. His attention snags on the stack of flyers by the till, colorful and slightly crooked.

His eyes narrow slightly, and he reaches for one with a hesitant hand. "Can I take one?"

"Oh! Absolutely!" I yank the top flyer off the pile with perhaps a bit more enthusiasm than necessary. The corner catches on the rest, and a few of the flyers flutter to the floor like confetti. "Here," I add quickly, pressing the flyer into his hand before dropping to my knees to scoop up the mess.

By the time I straighten, he's already studying the flyer, his rough fingers tracing the edges of the paper. For a split second, I let myself really look at him. His dark hair peeks out from under a beanie, just enough to hint at the unruly waves beneath. The scruff on his jaw is a few days old, adding to the rugged charm that practically radiates off him.

Just when I think I've let myself stare a little too long, he moves again. A slight tilt of his head, like he's genuinely interested in the flyer. He glances up at me, voice quieter this time, and I don't know if I'm imagining it or if there's something softer in his tone.

"Kids' night?"

"Yep." My brain's still struggling to catch up, but at least my voice doesn't crack this time. "First one's tomorrow. Should be fun. I mean, for the kids. And, uh, hopefully the adults, too."

He gives a small nod before tucking the flyer into his jacket pocket, mumbling a quick thanks before heading for the door.

The door swings shut behind him, letting in a sharp gust of winter air, and I exhale slowly, realizing I'd been holding my breath the entire time.

"Who was *that*?" Michael asks, appearing at my side with a broom in hand.

"I'm not sure," I murmur, my eyes still locked on the door, as if expecting him to walk back in at any moment.

"Looked like he'd just stepped out of one of those Highland adventure novels," he chuckles, leaning on the broom with a smirk. "You know, the ones with the brooding hero on the cover?"

A blush creeps up my neck, warmth spreading across my cheeks as I quickly turn away, pretending to be busy with wiping down the counter. "Oh, hush. He was just a customer."

Even as I say it, I know it's not true. There was...*something* about him. Something in the way he carried himself, in the intensity of his gaze, that made him stand out.

I shake my head, trying to push the thoughts of him out of my mind. "How are we doing on pastries?"

"We're running low on scones," Michael replies, his eyes

still twinkling with that roguish amusement. "I'll go grab some from the kitchen."

I nod, but even as he walks away, I'm still replaying that brief, heart-skipping encounter. His stormy eyes, that low, gravelly voice...

I take a deep breath and straighten my shoulders. I've got a shop to run. What I don't have is time to swoon over some guy with a killer jawline and a mysterious air. I grab a tray of pastries, forcing myself to stop thinking about the way he looked at me, the way he made everything else in the room feel a little...off. No more distractions. Just get back to work.

The afternoon rush hits like a wave, and I'm instantly pulled back into the familiar chaos of taking orders, steaming milk, and pouring lattes with the ease of muscle memory. My hands move faster than my brain can keep up, and before long, I'm floating in the rhythm of it all.

Thoughts of the gruff stranger are pushed to the back of my mind, tucked away where they won't distract me. For now, anyway.

As the last customer shuffles out and the café door clicks shut, I flip the sign to *Closed* and let out a tired sigh, the weight of the day settling on my shoulders. The café lights glow against the frosted windows, while outside the January sky is slipping toward night, all shadows and cold.

I wipe down the tables, stack a few mugs, and lock up. Routine. Easy. Then I tug my scarf tighter around my neck and push into the crisp air, cheeks instantly stinging from the chill. The walk home isn't long, and I know every step by heart. My flat's just a few streets over, tucked into one of those new builds. Two bedrooms, nothing flashy. But it's mine. It's close enough that I can roll out of bed and into the café when I need to.

I reach my front door and fumble with the keys for a moment, the usual clumsiness of the end of a long day taking over. Finally, I push it open and am greeted by a rush of warmth, along with the faint scent of lavender lingering in the air. Dropping my bag by the door, I kick off my shoes and let out a deep sigh, already imagining how good it's going to feel to sink into the sofa and let the day slip away.

I pause for a moment, staring at the empty space around me. I think I need to get a cat or something. The thought's been nagging at me more and more lately, especially on nights like this when the silence in my flat feels louder than anything.

You'd think, after spending my entire day surrounded by people, chatting with regulars, greeting new faces, and hearing snippets of conversations, I'd crave the quiet. But it's the opposite.

The emptiness of the place seems to echo. No sense of another presence here. Just me.

Lonely. There, I've said it. It's the word I keep dodging, but it's the truth. Maybe a little ball of fur with a penchant for getting into mischief is exactly what I need to fill the space, to add a little commotion to the quiet.

I shake the thought off, mentally rolling my eyes at myself, and head to the kitchen instead, hoping the task of making something to eat will distract me. I yank open the fridge, only to be greeted by the sad reality of leftovers and half-empty containers. My stomach grumbles in protest. I really need to go shopping.

Sighing, I pull out some cheese and bread, hoping I can at

least make it a decent snack. As the pan heats up, my phone buzzes from the counter. It's a text from Callan.

Callan: Lou, you free this weekend? Thinking of having a family dinner.

I love it when we get everyone together. The café keeps me busy, but there's never a good excuse to skip family time.

Me: Sounds great! I'll be there. Need me to bring anything?

Callan: Just yourself. And cookies ;)

Me: As if I wasn't going to already.

I can practically see his grin through the screen, and it makes me shake my head as I set my phone down. Classic Callan, always thinking about sweets. Not that I'm much different. I flip my sandwich in the pan, realizing I'm smiling, too. The weekend can't come fast enough. Noise, commotion, family—it's exactly what I need.

LUCY

Sleep came easily last night, and I wake up before my alarm, the early morning light already sneaking through the shades. I've grown accustomed to these peaceful, quiet mornings after years of early starts.

After a quick, hot shower, I towel off and stand in front of my closet, eyes scanning for something cozy but practical. I settle on my favorite pair of well-worn jeans, soft and snug in all the right places, and a powder-blue sweater that's like a hug in fabric form. I pull it over my head, smoothing out the fabric with a quick flick of my hands before stepping into my boots.

I glance at the clock, then quickly wring out my hair, still damp from the shower. I twist the wet strands into a loose knot at the back of my head, securing it with a few pins. Not the fanciest, but it'll keep the hair out of my face for the day.

Grabbing my keys and bag, I head out into the brisk morning air. The sky is still tinged with pink, the sun just beginning to stretch its golden fingers over the horizon. I inhale deeply, savoring the tranquility of the early hour before the world fully wakes up.

As I round the corner to the café, I spot a familiar figure hunched by the door, his hands tucked into the pockets of his coat. It's Mr. Wilson, one of our regulars. He's always here early, but today...it's even earlier than usual. I can't help but smile at the sight. He's as dependable as my morning coffee

"Morning, Mr. Wilson," I call out. "You're out and about early today."

He turns, a weary smile creasing his weathered face. "Aye, lass. Couldn't sleep. Thought I'd come down and see if you'd let an old man warm his bones a wee bit early."

I can't help but smile back, the warmth of his words melting away some of the early morning chill. "Of course. Come on in."

He gives an appreciative nod, shuffling past me into the café. I follow him inside, flicking on the lights and turning on the espresso machine. As Mr. Wilson settles into his usual seat by the window, I start on his coffee, already thinking about my to-do list for tonight.

I know most folks would probably say I'm putting in too much effort for something so simple. Decorating cookies, reading books, just a little kids' night. But it's special to *me*. I've always loved the sound of laughter echoing through the café, the excited chatter of little ones discovering new things, and the way they can make even the dullest afternoons feel full of life. It's the kind of magic I wish I could bottle and keep for myself.

I've always imagined having a family of my own, raising kids who'd grow up in this space I love, surrounded by the same coziness and joy I try to offer every day. It doesn't matter how much I dream about it, though. Because as it turns out, life doesn't always line up the way you picture it.

I'm only twenty-five, and it's not like it's entirely impossible for me someday, but the doctors have made it clear that it will be difficult. It's harder to accept than I'd like to admit. Harder still to look at families with their children, laughing and living, and knowing that I might not have that for myself.

So, I focus on the joy I get from the little ones that do come into the café. Their faces lighting up with excitement as they discover new flavors, new friends, new little bits of happiness. Some days, it's harder than others. The truth is, I'd give anything to be the one baking cookies for my own kids, reading bedtime stories, and sharing serene mornings like these. It's a longing that pulls at me, always there, just beneath the surface. It doesn't matter how many times I tell myself I'll be okay—how it's just not meant to be—because that longing never really goes away.

So, I do what I can, which is putting in the effort to ensure tonight is something special. Just because I might not have it for myself doesn't mean I can't create it for someone else.

As I hand Mr. Wilson his steaming cup of coffee, the weight of that ache mixes with something bittersweet. I blink it away just as the bell above the door chimes, signaling another early bird.

I take a deep breath, pushing the hushed thoughts aside. Another day. Another chance to create something comforting for someone who needs it.

"I think we're all set," Poppy remarks as I add the final touches to the cookie table.

We've been closed for a couple of hours, but in just a few minutes, the doors will open again for the evening's event.

In the corner of the café, I've arranged a long table, its surface covered in wax paper. Bright, vibrant icing in every shade imaginable sit in bowls alongside colorful sprinkles, with freshly baked cookies waiting for small hands to decorate. Tiny chairs circle the space, perfectly sized for little legs.

On the opposite side, nestled by the bookshelves that line the walls, I've set up a cozy reading nook. A soft circle of cushions sprawls across the floor, inviting little ones to curl up with a book, stacks of well-loved children's stories ready to be read.

The plan is simple. Let the kids unleash their creativity on the cookies, then gather them in the corner for a story as they nibble on their sugary masterpieces.

And, of course, coffee is ready and waiting for the grown-ups.

I raise my hand to swipe at the beads of sweat gathering on my forehead, pausing to take in the scene. With my hands on my hips, I give the setup a once-over, nodding in approval. "Yep, this looks perfect. We're all set."

A sudden knock on the door makes me freeze. "What the—"

I can't even finish the thought before the whole MacKenzie circus barrels through the door. Callan's the first one through, of course, carrying Maisie under his arm like a squirming sack of potatoes while Keira clings to Knox. Bree and Juliette are right on their heels.

A helpless laugh breaks free. "What...exactly are you doing?"

"We thought you could use reinforcements," Callan says. "Early reinforcements."

Bree grins as she steps up beside him. "He insisted we shouldn't wait in the car like normal people."

"We're not normal people," Callan declares. "We're efficient. And helpful. And incredibly good-looking."

I snort. "Ridiculous. All of you."

"Oh! Before I forget," Bree exclaims, digging into her oversized tote. "I brought you something."

She pulls out a package wrapped in colorful tissue paper. I take it from her hands, feeling the weight of something solid inside.

"What's this for?" I ask, already tearing into the wrapping.

"Just a little congratulations for putting this whole thing together. I know how hard you've been working."

The tissue paper falls away to reveal a ceramic mug. I turn it over in my hands and burst out laughing when I see the front. It's adorned with a cartoon sheep wearing oversized glasses, and underneath in swoopy lettering, *I'm just here for the BAAA-rista*.

"For your collection," Bree says, grinning. "I saw it and immediately thought of you."

"It's perfect." I have dozens of mugs lining the shelves in my flat. Some quirky, some elegant, all with memories attached. "I'll give it a place of honor."

Juliette steps over to give me a quick squeeze. "Put us to work. What do you need help with?"

Callan hands Maisie off to Knox and claps his hands once, all business. "Right. Where do you want your chaos squad? Point us toward a job before the children unionize."

"Well...the hot chocolate table needs some finishing touches. And someone needs to greet families when they get here."

"Done," Bree says, already moving. She nudges Callan with her shoulder. "Come on, chaos commander."

"And what about these wee monsters?" Knox asks, jiggling both twins in his arms, making them squeal with delight. "They've been talking about decorating cookies all day."

I can't help but laugh. "They've been talking, have they? At ten months old?"

"Well," Juliette corrects with a smile, "it was more like excited babbling whenever we mentioned coming to see Auntie Lou."

"Well, then," I say, setting the mug down on the counter before reaching for Keira who's already stretching her arms toward me, "I think these two deserve the VIP treatment. Let's get some cookies before everyone else gets here."

"You sure?" Juliette asks.

"They're MacKenzies," I say with a wink. "And my nieces. Special privileges apply."

I lead them over to the cookie decorating station, where I've already prepared a separate little area with two high chairs.

The twins get settled and in no time at all they both have frosting on their hands, their shirts, their cheeks. It's everywhere. They're perfect.

I'm wiping Maisie's fingers when she decides she'd rather be held, so I scoop her up in one arm, her sticky hand patting my shoulder and leaving a little smear of pink behind. I don't even care.

A small stampede of footsteps pounds up to the door, and then the bell chimes as I look over and spot the first cluster of families.

Within minutes, the café is buzzing with the sound of excited little voices. Families trickle in, bundled in coats, shaking off the winter chill as they make their way to the cookie table. Kids dash for the brightly colored icing and sprinkles, hands already coated in sugar before they've even started. Parents linger near the hot chocolate station, chatting and sipping coffee as they keep an eye on their little decorators.

Just as the first batch of cookies begins to take shape, the door chimes again. I glance up, my heart skipping a beat as a familiar figure steps inside—this time with a little girl clutching his hand.

She can't be more than four or five, her wide eyes drinking in the festive setup, cheeks flushed from the cold. Her tiny fingers tighten around his as she takes in the world one cautious step at a time.

But it's not her presence that throws me.

It's all him. Again.

He seems…less intimidating now, like the gruffness I'd first noticed wasn't the whole picture. His hard expression eases as he kneels to whisper something to the girl, and she nods, her lips twitching into the smallest smile.

I swallow, trying to process the sudden, unexpected pull low in my stomach.

The hat he wore yesterday hid what I now see is dark hair, almost black, tousled in that effortlessly messy way that makes it look like he just rolled out of bed. A few strands fall across his forehead as he speaks to the little girl, his posture relaxed yet protective.

His presence seems to take up space without trying, and he moves with confidence while staying acutely aware of everything around him. Like he's always watching, always reading the room.

I steal another glance, just as his lips twitch into the faintest hint of a smile at something she says.

And that's my cue to stop staring. Quickly. Before I get caught like an absolute idiot.

It's not often a new face strolls into the café, and I probably should've introduced myself properly yesterday. I clear my throat, straighten my shoulders, and make my way over.

"Welcome! I'm so glad you could make it," I say, shifting Maisie a little higher on my hip. My voice stays bright, even though my stomach flutters nervously. "I'm Lucy. And who is this little cookie expert?"

The girl tilts her head up at me, her dark gray eyes

sparkling with confidence. They're so much like his, I can't help but assume they're related—she's probably his daughter. A halo of wild chestnut curls frames her face.

"I'm Isla," she announces. "And I'm here to make the *best* cookies ever. I'm really good at it."

I laugh at her enthusiasm, the way her excitement all but vibrates in the air. The man watches with a half-smile, amusement tugging at his mouth while his eyes soften in a way that's hard to miss.

"It's so nice to meet you, Isla! And I'm sorry, I don't think I caught your name?" I say, glancing up at him.

His eyes catch mine, and for a second, the air shifts. The steadiness in his gaze unsettles me, like he's seeing layers I don't usually let anyone near.

"Aidan," he says, voice rough and low as it sends a sudden shiver down my spine. "Aidan Reid."

I repeat his name without thinking, testing the sound of it. "Aidan." It suits him. Strong. Uncomplicated.

Shaking it off, I gesture toward the setup. "Well, I'm so glad you're here. We've got a cookie decorating station over there," I point toward the long table, "and later, we'll have story time in the reading nook."

At the mention of cookies, Isla's whole face lights up. "Can we go now?" she asks, already tugging at Aidan's hand, her impatience barely contained.

A ghost of a smile tugs at his lips as he glances down at his daughter. "Aye, little storm. Lead the way."

They take a few steps toward the table, but Isla suddenly stops and spins back to me, her eyes squinting with suspicion.

"Are you a grown-up?" she asks, tilting her head. "You're pretty, and you don't look old. Not like him." She jabs a thumb at her dad with zero hesitation. "And that's a cute baby. Is she yours? What's her name?"

Aidan groans. "Isla."

I laugh. "That's a lot of questions. Let's see if I can answer them." I crouch down to her level, Maisie still snug on my hip. "I am a grown-up. Just a newer one, I guess. And this is my niece. Her name is Maisie."

At the sound of her name, Maisie coos softly and Isla giggles. "How old is she?"

"She'll be one in just a couple months."

"How old are you?" she asks, because of course she does.

"Twenty-five," I say, then glance up at her dad with a grin. "Ancient, I know."

Isla looks between us, clearly trying to puzzle out what that means. "Daddy's thirty-five," she announces.

"Is that old?" I ask her.

She narrows her eyes at him dramatically. "He groans when he gets off the couch."

I burst out laughing. "Well, that settles it."

Aidan just shakes his head as he lets Isla drag him toward the cookie table. The gentleness in his gaze now is a startling contrast to the unreadable man I met yesterday.

I can't explain why he keeps snagging my attention or why my pulse flutters every time his eyes catch mine. I'm usually very cautious when it comes to new faces. Friendly, of course, but mindful, nonetheless. I don't fling my trust at the nearest charming smile. I wait. I watch. I let people show their true colors in their own time.

Aidan... He throws that right out the window. I've already flipped ahead to the parts that make my heart race, and there's no use pretending I haven't.

I can't say I've felt a pull like this before. The men I've dated in the past have always been safe choices. Familiar. Friends who'd been around for years, so there was never any guesswork. Just stable, comfortable companionship.

Aidan's a mystery. The way he's all rough edges and abrupt words…until he's with his daughter, evidently. Then, he softens, like she's the only thing in the world that matters. It's in his eyes. In the slight shift in his voice when he speaks to her. In the way she looks up at him, unshaken, certain that he'll always be there.

There's a part of me that wants to understand him, to peel back the layers and see what's underneath. But that doesn't mean I should.

AIDAN

There's a tug in my chest the second our eyes meet, and I know better than to feed it.

Lucy's smile is warm and open, as if she's got all the time in the world for a stranger, and it throws me off. Makes my boots feel heavier on the floor, my body registering the danger before my brain does.

She's the kind of woman who softens a room just by being in it and makes you forget, for half a second, that life's not soft at all.

And I don't like that. Not one bit.

She's got this comfortable, easy way about her and for one stupid heartbeat, I wonder if she'd try to make space for me, too. I almost laugh at the thought because god knows I don't belong in places like this.

It was her eyes that caught me yesterday when I stopped in. The most vivid green I've ever seen. Big. Barely guarded. Eyes that tell you everything she's thinking, whether she means to or not. It made me itchy.

Her hair had been a mess, pulled back in some haphazard

knot, wisps everywhere, but somehow it worked. When she'd spotted me standing there, her expression shifted. There was a flash of uncertainty before she smiled again, all gentle yet curious, like she wasn't sure what kind of animal she was dealing with.

She was right to wonder. I'm shit at putting people at ease, and I'm not looking for connections or interested in smooth voices, lingering looks, or hands that reach out when they shouldn't.

I will say, she's damn beautiful. Even I'm not blind enough to deny that, but she's too young for me. Too kind. Too everything I don't have the time or the heart for.

Besides, the only reason I'm here tonight is Isla. This is our new start, and I owe it to her to make it stick. She's already been through enough and deserves a place to belong. She deserves friends and laughter and a little softness in a world that can be sharp as hell.

Me? I'll stand at the edges and watch her world grow from a safe distance.

"Look!" Isla tugs at my sleeve, her voice buzzing with excitement. "It's a star cookie, but I—" she pauses. "I think it needs more sprinkles."

I glance down at her, at the way her whole face lights up, and the knot in my chest loosens. She's so damn happy here. That's all I've ever wanted for her.

"It looks great, love, "I say. "But you're right. Definitely needs more sprinkles."

I look up just in time to catch Lucy observing Isla, that same smile on her face she's had all night. She watches Isla like it's second nature, like she genuinely cares. It catches me off guard again, because people don't just act like that.

A few minutes ago, I'd been standing back, pretending to check my phone, and I'd seen her hand her niece off to who I assume is the little girl's mother. Even from a distance, I couldn't miss the way her whole body relaxed as she leaned in, the careful tilt of her head, the tiny squeeze of her fingers as she made sure the baby was secure.

I had chastised myself immediately for noticing those little details. It wasn't my business, and yet, I couldn't look away.

Isla huffs as if this is the most critical decision of her life, bringing me back to the present. Just then, Lucy moves. She tucks a strand of hair behind her ear, smooths her hands over her apron, and catches my gaze. There's a question in her eyes, unspoken but clear.

I give a small nod.

She doesn't hesitate. Just lifts the container of sprinkles from the far end of the table and makes her way over, rolling her sleeves up as she walks. She stops beside Isla, close enough that I catch the faint scent of vanilla and lavender.

"I couldn't help but overhear," she says. "Does the little artist need more sprinkles for her masterpiece?"

You'd think Lucy just handed Isla the moon with the way her eyes widen. "Yes, please!" she chirps, thrusting her cookie forward.

Lucy kneels beside her, moving with an effortless kind of grace I catch myself noticing. She hands over the sprinkle shaker, wrapping Isla's small fingers around it. "There you go. Just a little at a time, like this."

Isla's whole body tenses with focus, her tongue peeking out at the corner of her mouth as she carefully shakes out the sprinkles. She's taking this so seriously, and I know for a fact she thinks the fate of the world rests on getting every sprinkle just right.

Lucy glances up at me, curiosity flickering in her eyes. Or is it interest? I can't pin it down, and that alone puts me on edge.

"There," Lucy says. "Now it's perfect, don't you think?"

Isla holds up her cookie like the priceless artifact it is. "It's the prettiest star in the whole galaxy!"

I huff a quiet laugh, shaking my head as I take in her absolute certainty. "No doubt about it, kid. You nailed it."

Lucy stands, brushing off her knees, and for a second, everything slows. She's close now, too close. The air carries that hint of vanilla again, subtle but impossible to ignore. It's a hell of a thing to notice, especially when she's looking at Isla like the mess she's making is something worth admiring. Like she matters.

Damn it, that hits harder than I want it to.

"Are you two new to the area?" she asks, breaking the silence.

It takes me a beat before I realize she's asking me a question. I hesitate, feeling the instinct to pull back, to keep my distance like I always have. Before I can decide how to answer, Isla's voice rings out, completely unaware of my internal battle.

"We just moved here!" she announces, face bright with excitement. "Daddy says we're gonna stay for a long time."

Lucy's eyes shift back to mine. "Is that so?" she asks. "Well, welcome to our little corner of the Highlands. I hope you'll both feel at home here."

I shove my hands into my jacket pockets to hide the tension, giving a quick nod. "Thanks." I clear my throat, the words coming out rougher than I want them to.

Lucy doesn't flinch or seem put off by the coarse edge in my tone. If anything, her smile only grows, the care in her eyes unmistakable as she tucks a loose strand of hair behind her ear that immediately falls back to her cheek. I'm painfully aware of the fact that I want to reach out and tuck that stray strand of hair back myself.

"If you ever need anything, I'm always here," she says

lightly. "Well, except for Sundays and Mondays. Other than that, you know where to find me."

I stare at her for a beat too long, trying to figure out her angle. People don't just offer help like that without wanting something in return, except her eyes are nothing but honest.

"Right. I'll keep that in mind," I say, the words coming out flat.

Asshole.

Lucy nods before she moves to help another child. It's hard not to admire her ease, the natural way she connects with everyone around her. But damn, it's almost *too* much. She's the kind of sweet that would normally make me roll my eyes or mutter something under my breath. But with her, it doesn't seem fake. She's not doing it for show. It's just her. Pure sugar.

It should annoy the hell out of me. And maybe it does, just a little. Still...I can't tear my eyes away.

I finally turn my attention back to Isla, who's now deep in conversation with a freckle-faced boy about the merits of different cookie shapes, her hands gesturing wildly as she talks.

This is a side of her I haven't seen in a while, and it's bittersweet. She's happy. Carefree. I find myself always wanting to wrap her up, protect her from the world and all the ways it can let you down. Yet I know I can't do that forever. She has to find her own way, even if it scares the shit out of me.

My gaze drifts back to Lucy, almost against my will. She's in the middle of it all, her laughter ringing out as she moves from child to child, offering encouragement and praise in equal measure.

I can't help but feel out of place. An intruder in a world that doesn't quite belong to me.

six

LUCY

I'm wiped out but also so incredibly satisfied. Looking around at the mess of cookie crumbs, frosting smears, and sprinkles scattered across the floor, I can't help but grin. Tonight was a total win.

Bree grabs a damp cloth, tossing a teasing glance toward Callan as he eats another cookie.

"What?" he protests around a mouthful of red icing. "Quality control doesn't just do itself, you know."

Bree cackles. "You say that, but I've watched you eat at least seven of those."

He winks, never breaking eye contact with Bree as he licks a stripe of frosting from his knuckle.

Knox leans against the counter with his arms crossed, raising an unimpressed brow. "You two are getting dangerously close to weird territory. I suggest you take...wherever this is going elsewhere."

Callan just grins, grabbing Bree by the waist and spinning her in a circle. By the way Bree shrieks and laughs, you can tell there's nothing else that exists for her in that moment. They orbit each other without even trying. I love that for them.

Juliette watches them goof off with a fond, slightly exhausted smile with the twins perched on each hip. Then she turns to me. "These two are going to crash hard as soon as we get them in the car." Maisie's already rubbing her eyes, and Keira has her whole fist crammed into her mouth, a sure sign she's moments from a meltdown.

Knox fumbles for the diaper bag, taking Juliette's cue, but he keeps glancing at the twins with awe, like he can't believe they're real. Knox and Juliette have always moved together in a seamless rhythm. They have the kind of partnership I've always dreamed of.

I keep telling myself I'm fine with how things worked out… or rather, with how they didn't. But tonight, with the twins' sleepy faces pressed against Juliette's shoulders, the ache sneaks back in.

My last relationship fizzled in a slow, painful way. We'd been together for a year when I eventually had the doctor's visit that gave me all the answers I didn't want to hear. I told him about the numbers and the odds. He tried to act like it didn't matter, but the shift in our relationship was palpable. Date nights turned into takeaway and TV. His hand, once always in mine, became a casual brush on the shoulder, then nothing at all. I knew he was running the risk calculations in his head, weighing a relationship with me against the big family he'd mapped out for himself. I wasn't the safe choice anymore.

When he finally left, it was with a sheepish apology, some half-hearted line about *different futures*. I remember standing in the doorway after he drove off, feeling stupid for being surprised. I'd seen the retreat happening in real time.

What stung most wasn't losing him. It was the way he'd

looked at me near the end, as though I was already a disappointment.

Since then, romance has felt like walking barefoot over thin ice. I've gotten into the habit of pretending I'm not listening for cracks, but they always eventually make themselves known.

We say our goodbyes before Juliette wrangles the twins into their coats. Knox lingers with her by the door, holding it open as a bitter wind snakes in. I watch them bundle the girls into the car with their tiny hats pulled down over their ears, identical chubby faces peeking out from around fleece. They wave, headlights swinging past the café windows as they drive off.

Inside, it's just the three of us. Callan's stacking chairs, and Bree is scrubbing down the tables with a vengeance. I'm gathering sticky spatulas and empty sprinkle jars when Bree sidles up beside me.

"All right, spill," she whispers. "You spent the whole night giving googly eyes to some guy."

I freeze, every muscle in my body locking up as I scramble to mask the rush of heat flooding my face. I know exactly who she means, but I'm not about to admit it. "Which guy? I chatted with a lot of people tonight."

"You can't fool me, Lucy." Bree smirks, folding her arms as she raises a brow. "I could tell you were getting all flustered from across the room."

"I was not!" I protest, but even I can hear the faint crack in my voice.

She shoots me a knowing look. "Uh-huh, and I'm the Queen of Scotland."

I groan, grabbing the nearest trash bag and pretending to focus on something, anything, to avoid her amused stare.

Bree leans in closer, her grin growing wider. "You know, Cal and I could do some recon for you. Figure out what Mr.

Tall, Dark, and Grumpy actually likes, besides brooding in corners. See if he's single?"

Of course she lands the one question I absolutely am *not* asking. Not out loud, anyway. Inside, I've been pathetically wondering if he's married or not. I'm not giving Bree and Callan that kind of ammunition.

Callan flashes a wicked grin, playing along. "Plot twist: He loves puppies and long walks on the beach."

"Goodnight!" I blurt, tossing the trash bag over my shoulder with far more force than necessary. "I'm going home before this turns into an actual roast."

Bree waves innocently. "Fine, fine. But we're not done with this conversation, you smitten kitten!"

They're ridiculous, but unfortunately, they're also not wrong. That's what makes it even worse.

seven

AIDAN

"That was so much fun." Isla's sleepy voice drifts through the quiet room, her face still lit with the excitement from the night, even if the rest of her is sinking into the softness of the covers. She's got her stuffed bunny clutched tight against her chest.

"Yeah?" I drop onto the edge of her bed, brushing a loose curl from her face. "You had fun decorating cookies, huh?"

"Mmhmm." She nods, her curls bouncing with the motion. "And Lucy said mine was the prettiest one she'd ever seen. Did you see her smile, Daddy? She has a really pretty smile."

I grunt, feeling that tightness in my chest. "Yeah, she seems nice," I mutter, hoping that's enough to shut this down.

"Daddy," she whines, dragging the word out in that singsong tone that means I'm not getting off easy. "Can we go back again soon? Please?"

I hesitate, my gaze shifting to the small window. "We'll see," I finally say, standing up and tucking the blankets tighter around her.

"Good night, Daddy," she mumbles, eyes already drifting shut.

"Night, love," I whisper, flicking off the light and easing the door shut behind me.

I head downstairs, running a hand through my hair and letting out a frustrated sigh. Innocent people like Lucy don't belong in my world. But hell if she doesn't make me wish things could be different.

I need a drink. A strong one.

I make my way to the kitchen, the old hardwood creaking beneath my weight. The whisky bottle's there on the counter, just waiting. I pour a heavy splash into a tumbler, the amber liquid sloshing as it fills.

I take a sip, relishing that familiar burn as it slides down my throat. No matter how much I try to focus on the warmth spreading through me, though, Lucy's smile keeps playing behind my eyes. The way she looked at Isla, that kindness in her gaze... It stirred something I thought I buried years ago.

I swirl the whisky in my glass, watching the liquid catch the light. Another sip. What am I even doing? I came here for a fresh start, to give Isla some stability. Not to pine after the first beautiful woman I saw.

I exhale sharply, slamming the glass down harder than I mean to. I rub the back of my neck, glancing at the clock. I should probably head to bed.

As I climb the stairs, I already know sleep will be a losing battle. That smile has itself lodged somewhere it doesn't belong, and I've got no fucking clue how to get rid of it.

THE NEXT MORNING, I'm bleary-eyed and irritable, trying to pour Isla's cereal without spilling it everywhere. She's still buzzing from last night, chattering away with endless energy, while I grunt out half-hearted responses, just trying to keep my head from splitting.

"Daddy, can we go to Lucy's café today?" Isla asks, her spoon clinking against the bowl.

I wince at the sound. "Not today, sweetheart. Daddy's got work to do."

Her face falls, and the guilt hits me. But what choice do I have? This house needs too much work. Two weeks isn't gonna cut it. It's more of a construction site than a home right now.

The kitchen faucet's still dripping, and the draft creeping through the windows isn't letting up. It's as if the house itself is daring me to crack, testing how much I can take before I break. And maybe I deserve it. Maybe all this frustration is mine to own for dragging Isla into a life where I'm always too busy, always fixing things, always chasing something just out of reach.

"Daddy?" Her small voice breaks through the noise in my head, her hand tugging at the hem of my shirt. "Maybe another time?"

Her hopeful tone twists the knife in my gut. I crouch down to her level. "Yeah, love. We'll go soon."

The way her face lights up shouldn't feel like a victory, but it does.

"Besides, Nana is going to stop by today," I remind her, watching her eyes widen with excitement.

"I forgot!" She squeals, bouncing in her seat. "Can I show her my new drawings?"

"I'm sure Nana would love that."

Right on cue, there's a knock at the door. Isla bolts from her chair, nearly sending her cereal flying in her rush.

"Nana!" Isla cries, throwing herself into my mother's arms.

"There's my little sunshine," Mum says, lifting Isla up and showering her with kisses. She glances over Isla's head at me. "Aidan, you look like you've been dragged through a hedge backward."

I grunt in response. "Thanks."

I finish off my lukewarm coffee as I listen to Isla's animated chatter, showing off her latest work of art she's added to her ever-growing gallery on the fridge.

A familiar ache hits me deep. This is how it should be. Surrounded by family, loved, and being doted on. Not stuck in a half-finished house with a father who's barely keeping his head above water.

"And this one," Isla says, pointing to a colorful blob that might be a cat, or a very misshapen horse, "is Fluffy. The cat I want."

Ah. So it is a cat.

Wait.

"The cat you...want?" I wince.

"Aye," she says matter-of-factly. "Every princess needs a cat."

"Every princess needs a...cat," I repeat, still trying to wrap my head around it.

She lets out a sigh, one of those exasperated ones no four-year-old should be capable of. "Isn't that what I said?"

I glance over at Mum, hoping she'll throw me a lifeline here, but I couldn't be more wrong. She's doubled over in laughter, practically in stitches. Great.

"Oh, this is payback, dear," Mum gasps between breaths, wiping her eyes. "It's like watching you thirty years ago. Minus the princess thing."

This kills me. Isla asking for all the normal things I can't give her. A pet, a real home, the kind of stability every kid deserves. I doubt Mum's keen on us carting a cat back and forth to her place every two weeks, but even if she didn't mind, it's not fair to the damn animal.

This isn't the first time I've realized my job just doesn't work for us anymore. It was tough when Isla was a baby, but the money was decent, and her mother was still around. For a while, anyway. Long enough to fool myself into thinking it might all work out. Except now it's just the two of us.

Fuck. I need to get out of my head. There's work to be done, and it sure as hell won't magically finish itself while I sit here feeling sorry for myself.

I glance at the list I scrawled on a scrap of paper earlier—patch the hole in the living room wall, finish painting Isla's room, replace the leaky kitchen tap.

"I'm gonna get to work," I mutter more to myself than anyone else.

I head straight to Isla's room first. I promised her a pink room, her *princess castle*, and I intend to make good on that.

As I lay out the drop cloth and pop open the paint can, Isla's giggles float up the stairs, followed by a loud thud. "Everything all right down there?" I call out.

"We're building a fort!" Isla yells back.

The sound of her laughter cuts through the heaviness in my chest. The house might not be perfect yet, but it's a start for both of us.

I'm finishing the second coat of paint when Isla pads into the room, her favorite stuffed rabbit clutched in one hand. She plops down on the drop cloth, careful not to touch the wet walls, and tilts her head to look up at me.

"Daddy, can we invite Miss Lucy over?"

The question throws me. I glance down, wiping paint off my hands. "Why would we do that?"

"She's nice," Isla says, as if it's the most obvious thing in the world. "And she said we could ask her for anything. Remember?"

"Lucy's got her own things to do," I say. "She's busy running the café."

Isla doesn't look convinced. "But I like her. And I think she likes you."

I huff out a laugh. "Isla, just because someone's nice doesn't mean—"

"She smiled at you," she interrupts, as if that's all the proof she needs.

I shake my head, trying not to let the heat creep into my face. "Go on, love. You've got fort-building to finish."

As she skips out of the room, I lean back on my heels, staring at the now pink walls. Invite Lucy over? What kind of idea was that?

I haven't let a woman close to us *ever*. Haven't even looked at one, honestly. What's the point? It's not like I've got time for dating with my schedule. Two weeks on the rig, two weeks home, trying to make up for lost time with my daughter. That's my focus. That's all I've got room for.

Besides, the last time I let someone in, it damn near destroyed me. Isla's mum left a mark I'll probably never get rid of. That same mark is on Isla, too, even if she's too young to remember. I can't risk that again.

So, no. I'm not letting my mind drift into unrealistic fantasies of someone new stepping into our world. I'm silencing that thought before it ever even starts.

LUCY

I'm leaning against the windowsill of my childhood home. The sun is sinking lower, painting the sky in shades of gold and pink, while the hills beyond glow in the warm light. The scent of something roasted and hearty wafts in from the kitchen.

Mum's laughter spills out from somewhere behind me, followed by the clatter of plates and Dad's teasing reply. Not my biological dad—he passed away when I was just a baby—but the only dad I've ever known. He's been here for as long as I can remember. To me, he's just Dad.

This is cozy. It's home.

And yet, my heart aches as I watch the sun dip. The air is charged, and my heart picks up speed. It's like I'm waiting for something, but I just...don't know what.

"Lass, are you staring out that window again?" Dad calls, his voice abrupt but wrapped in affection. "Come eat before Callan helps himself to your plate!"

I huff a quiet laugh and pull myself away from the window.

"I'm coming!" I shout back, casting one last glance at the horizon.

Whatever I'm hoping for can wait. Dinner, apparently, cannot.

I wander into the kitchen, and the heat hits me first, along with that mouthwatering mix of roasted lamb and rosemary. Mum's at the stove, cheeks pink from the heat, completely absorbed in the simmering pots. Dad's at the counter, carving the meat with that careful, patient precision he always has. Then there's Callan, already at the table, blue eyes gleaming with mischief as he attempts to snag a roll.

"Oi, hands off," I scold, swatting his arm. "Some of us haven't even sat down yet. And in case you've forgotten, there are actual babies in this family now. They get priority."

He smirks, tearing the roll in half. "Pretty sure they don't even have teeth yet."

As if summoned, the front door bursts open, Knox's voice booming through the house. "Sorry we're late. Someone had to change twice before we left the house."

Juliette trails behind him, both twins balanced on her hips, her hair in a loose braid that's already fraying.

"Don't blame me," she says with a tired laugh, gently readjusting Maisie—always the bold one—as she tugs at Juliette's earring. "They both have a wicked arm for flinging food."

Knox leans over to kiss her temple before gently prying a squirming Keira from her arms.

Mum abandons her pots with a squeal, rushing over to scoop Maisie straight out of Juliette's arms. "Hello, my darlings," she coos.

Callan leans back in his chair. "Here we thought family dinners were loud before."

Bree rolls her eyes as she slides into the seat beside him. "As if you're not the loudest one in the room."

The room hums to life with clinking cutlery, overlapping voices, the twins babbling. Mum keeps darting around to make sure everyone's plates are full, Dad pretends to grumble about something, and Juliette manages to snag two rolls at once, cheeks puffed out in triumph.

I sit back, soaking it all in. The chaos. The laughter. The way Knox never strays far from Juliette, always with a hand at her back or ready to swoop in when one baby gets restless. He's so attuned to her.

Callan cracks another joke that sends Bree into hysterics, and for a moment, the whole table erupts, voices tumbling over each other. It's messy, loud, and utterly brimming with love.

"Earth to Lucy." Bree's voice slices clean through my trance, and I blink, snapping back to reality. "You're awfully quiet tonight. Everything all right?"

Her smirk says everything I don't want her to say out loud. She hasn't forgotten the conversation I dodged the other day.

All eyes are on me. "Oh, aye. Just…thinking," I say, flashing a small smile in an attempt to ease the sudden attention.

"Dangerous pastime, that," Callan quips, leaning back with that smug smirk of his that practically screams trouble. "Wouldn't be thinking about Mr. Tall, Dark, and Grumpy, would you?"

The flush creeping up my neck and onto my cheeks betrays me instantly. No matter how hard I try to keep my expression neutral, it's clear as day. "That's ridiculous," I say with a flustered laugh, reaching for the breadbasket for a distraction. "I was thinking about dessert, actually. Mum's sticky toffee pudding is far more interesting than…him."

Callan arches a brow, clearly unconvinced, while Juliette struggles to hide a knowing smile behind her hand. Even Knox looks up from his plate with mild curiosity, and that's all it takes to make my cheeks burn hotter.

"I mean, honestly," I continue, trying to sound casual, "what's there to think about? He's just...a customer. And a new neighbor. And he's great with his daughter, but that's neither here nor there!" I add quickly, my voice pitching up a little more than I intend. "Nothing to overthink, right?"

Callan lets out a low whistle, and Juliette's gaze softens. I press my lips together, determined not to let Callan get under my skin. If there's anything he's good at, though, it's the way he knows exactly how to hit a nerve.

"I just think people deserve the benefit of the doubt, that's all," I say firmly, trying to sound confident, clasping my hands in front of me in an attempt to hide my nervous energy. "Not everyone can be as effortlessly charming as *you*, Callan."

That earns a laugh from Juliette and Mum, who's busy setting another dish on the table. "All right, leave her be," Mum says, shaking her head but smiling all the same.

I don't know why I'm being so defensive. It's not like Callan's wrong. Aidan has been creeping into my thoughts more than I'd like. But admitting that, even to myself, feels like stepping onto shaky ground.

How can someone I barely know get under my skin like this? I don't even know him beyond the gruff demeanor and broodiness, and the way his eyes soften when he looks at his daughter. Yet my thoughts are tangled together in a confusing knot. None of this makes sense. I'm not the kind of person who gets flustered over someone I hardly know, yet here I am, cheeks blazing and heart racing like I've just run up the hills outside. I feel...out of control. I don't like it one bit.

I've got no idea what to do about it, if anything at all. All I know is that the few times Aidan's eyes landed on me, I was acutely aware of my rapid heartbeat, the way the air felt a little too warm, and how my thoughts scattered like confetti.

WHEN THE DAY IS DONE

What is it about him? Why does it feel like there's something *more?*

LUCY

The last few days have flown past in a blur, each one spilling into the next before I even get a chance to catch my breath. The café's been busier than usual, tables full, orders piling up, the clatter of cups and chatter blending into a comforting chaos. I'm not complaining, though. Not even a little. There's something about the constant motion, the smell of fresh coffee and baked goods, the tiny moments of connection with regulars and strangers alike that makes me feel alive, even on the days that start before the sun.

I'm tucked behind the counter with my tablet, handling the not so glamorous part of café life, checking inventory and what needs to be reordered before next week, when the door chimes. I glance up just as Aidan walks in, Isla's small hand clasped tightly in his. He moves like he's carrying the world on his shoulders but trying not to crush her with it.

"Good morning," I say, my voice a little too chipper for how early it is. There it is again. That little flutter in my chest I'm trying so hard to ignore. "What can I get you both today?"

Aidan gives me a curt nod, his eyes meeting mine for the

briefest of seconds before his attention shifts down to his daughter. "Black coffee and a hot chocolate, please."

I catch Isla eyeing the fresh cinnamon buns in the display case. "Daddy, can we please get one of those?" Her voice is a sweet little plea.

Aidan's brow furrows just enough that it's obvious he's weighing his options. For a moment, I almost expect him to say no. Then he looks down at Isla, her wide eyes full of hope, and I catch the moment his tough exterior cracks just a little.

"All right," he sighs, giving in with a reluctant smile. "We can share one."

"Great choice." I shoot a wink in Isla's direction. "Sit wherever you'd like. I'll bring everything to your table when it's ready."

Isla's chestnut curls bounce with each step as she skips toward a table, her little shoes tapping the floor. Mid-stride, she spins around, beaming at me. "Thank you, Miss Lucy!" she calls before turning back to her dad with a giggle.

As I prepare their order, I can't help but steal a few glances in their direction. Isla is in full storyteller mode, her small hands waving around wildly as she recounts whatever adventure she's on about today. Aidan listens intently, his stormy eyes focused completely on her. Every now and then, the corners of his mouth twitch, the faintest almost-smile pulling at his lips, but it's gone as quickly as it appears.

Balancing the mugs and plate on a tray, I make my way over to their table. Isla's eyes dance with delight as I set everything down, her small hands already reaching out.

"Careful, this is hot," I caution, sliding the mug of hot chocolate closer to her. She nods, blowing on it with exaggerated puffs, her brows knit in concentration.

Aidan's fingers graze mine as he takes his coffee, and lightning strikes straight through my veins. His eyes catch mine, and for a single, suspended heartbeat, everything else disappears—the café, the noise, even time itself.

I jerk my hand back, cheeks burning. I force my eyes elsewhere, but it's useless. My heart is already tripping over itself, and the ghost of his touch lingers on my skin.

I clear my throat, my voice coming out a little more strained than I intend. "Apologies in advance for the sugar rush she's about to get, Dad," I joke, hoping the teasing tone will mask how flustered I feel.

His expression shifts. Firm and unreadable, like always. He's not much for extras, I've noticed. No wasted words or unnecessary reactions. Just the bare minimum.

When he shrugs, it's not dismissive. Just enough to tell me he's heard me. "That's all right. I think she's earned it." His voice softens a fraction, smoothness pushing in around the rough edges.

I steal another glance at him, brief enough that I think maybe he won't notice. But he's already looking at me.

Our eyes meet again, and for a heartbeat, that usual wall around him seems thinner. There's something else there...suspicion? I'm not sure, but I find myself wanting to know exactly what it is.

"Well, I'll let you two enjoy," I say, taking a step back instead. "Just holler if you need anything."

I've only just turned when Isla's voice rings out. "Miss Lucy, wait!"

I glance over my shoulder and see bright eyes and cheeks smudged with icing.

"Do you want to hear about the fairy I saw in the garden yesterday?" Isla asks, bouncing in her seat as if the story might just burst out of her if she holds it in too long.

"Oh, Isla," Aidan starts. "I'm sure Miss Lucy is busy—"

"Not at all," I interrupt. "I'd love to hear about it. Was it a big fairy or a tiny one?"

Isla beams. "Tiny! Smaller than my pinky." She holds up her little finger. "It had sparkly wings and a shiny dress, and it flew *right* past the trees."

I crouch beside their table. "That sounds *so* magical. Did the fairy say anything to you?"

Her eyes go wide. "No," she whispers, "but I think it winked at me." She leans in, glancing at her dad. "Daddy says he's not sure fairies come out in the winter, but I know what I saw."

I sneak a glance at Aidan, expecting another patient sigh or maybe the ghost of a smirk. But he's just watching inquisitively.

I lean in a little closer, dropping my own voice to a whisper. "Well," I say, giving Isla a knowing look, "I think sometimes daddies don't always see the magic right in front of them. Us girls, though? We're special."

I wink, and Isla dissolves into giggles before she takes a careful sip of her hot chocolate. "We *are* special, aren't we?"

I smile, straightening up and smoothing my hand over my apron. "Definitely. Now, you finish your treats and keep an eye out. If that fairy comes back, I expect a full report."

As I turn back to the counter, I can't help but catch Aidan's gaze one more time. He offers me a slight nod, the barest hint of an *actual* smile tugging at the corner of his mouth.

Is he always so composed and carefully in control? What's made him hold the world at arm's length?

I wonder what he'd look like if he *really* smiled. Maybe it's selfish, but I ache to see it. Just once, so I can stop wondering if he's ever truly happy.

I go back to my work, pushing thoughts of Aidan out of my mind. The café is bustling, and there's plenty to keep me occupied. I lose myself in the familiar rhythm of brewing coffee, plating pastries, and chatting with regulars.

By the time the morning rush slows, I glance up just in time to see Aidan gathering their things. Isla's on the move, hopping down from her chair with that boundless energy only kids seem to have.

"Miss Lucy," she calls out. "The cimma...cimman...cinnamon bun was the best ever!"

I laugh, leaning on the counter. "I'm so glad you liked it."

She beams up at me. "It was so yummy! I'm gonna ask Daddy for another one next time."

Just then, Aidan appears behind her, his footsteps heavy. He places a gentle hand on Isla's shoulder, the touch surprisingly tender. "Come on, little storm. We've got to get going."

His gaze lingers on Isla for a moment longer before he looks up at me. He shifts his weight from one foot to the other, then rubs the back of his neck, a gesture so human and unguarded that it feels almost out of place coming from him.

"Uh, thank you. For entertaining her story." He pauses. "She's got quite the imagination."

The words are simple enough, but there's a hesitance in his tone, as if he's not entirely comfortable with this exchange. He shifts again, the muscles in his jaw tightening just slightly, a spark of his usual gruffness hovering beneath the surface.

I offer him a warm smile, hoping to ease the tension between us. "No problem at all. I love seeing the world through a child's eyes. It's a breath of fresh air."

A brief silence hangs in the air, and I can practically see him wrestling with what to say next. His lips part, then close again, like the words he wants to share are caught somewhere between his mind and his mouth. Watching him grapple with that vulnerability is oddly endearing.

Before the silence stretches too long, I speak up, giving him a bit of an out. "Well, I hope I see you two again soon. Next week I'm making my special blueberry scones."

He glances at Isla, then back to me, and I catch a hint of something softer as it curves his lips. "Might have to stop by for those."

"We'll come!" Isla chimes in. "I *love* blueberry scones."

For a moment, Aidan's gaze locks onto mine, and I swear the world around us pauses again. His voice drops, quieter and steadier this time. "Guess we'll see you then."

His words land gently but leave my heart fluttering, a warm rush spreading through me. My reply slips out softly. "See you then."

As they walk away, I catch myself staring, a smile stretching across my face before I can stop it. There's a delicate hairline crack in that seemingly impenetrable façade of his. I wonder what might be waiting on the other side.

ten

AIDAN

What the hell was I thinking back there?
Flirting.

The word leaves a bitter taste in my mouth. I'm no lovesick kid, but the way she smiles at me, like there's something worth seeing beneath the surface, disarms me. And her voice, so soft and calm while she looked at my daughter with the same adoration I do? Damn it, she's practically angelic. All innocence and dark hair that I know would feel smooth as silk between my fingers. The way I could ruin her, leave her trembling, undone...*fuck.*

It's been too damn long, and my mind is spiraling. Attraction like this is a dangerous game for someone like me. It's been four years since I've been with anyone. Four years of cold showers and falling asleep to the company of my own right hand. Now my mind's conjuring images I have no business entertaining—Lucy beneath me, her hair splayed across my pillow, those innocent eyes clouding with pleasure as I—

"Do you think she'll make some extra scones for us?" Isla

pipes up from the backseat, cutting through my inappropriate thoughts like a bucket of ice water.

Thank Christ.

"Maybe."

Or maybe I'll just steer clear of the café altogether and save myself the trouble. Mum can take her instead. I don't need to get tangled up in anything, and I've got more than enough on my plate between the long weeks offshore and raising Isla. It's predictable. Controlled. Safe. Just the way I like it.

But the image of Lucy's smile lighting up her face like a damn sunrise won't leave my thoughts. The way her cheeks flushed under my gaze, like she was unsure how to handle my attention but didn't mind having it at all. It made me want to... smile? Say something that could keep her talking just a bit longer?

Ridiculous.

I rub my hand over my face, scowling at the notion. I can't let her sweetness get under my skin. It's like stepping too close to a fire just to feel its heat. She could burn me down without even trying. My life, my focus, my very self, all at risk of being consumed.

And yet, every fiber of my being wants to step closer, anyway.

eleven

LUCY

Sunday. *Finally.* My favorite day of the week.

I genuinely love my work, but there's something undeniably magical about Sundays. It's the calm before the chaos and a perfect excuse to slow down and just breathe.

I usually start with a mental list of everything I need. A quick grocery run, maybe a stop at the farmers' market for fresh blooms to brighten up the flat, and then some time in the kitchen to prep for the week ahead.

I like slipping into the grocery store before most people have even put on real pants. There's something strangely soothing about the silence, a handbasket, and the power of choosing produce no one else has pawed at yet.

I'm lost in my own head, scanning the pile of avocados when I spot the perfect one. Just as I reach, my hand collides with another larger, calloused one.

"Oh!" I jerk back so fast I nearly fumble my basket. "Sorry, you go ahead."

It's the spark that shoots through me when that foreign hand brushes against mine that stops me in my tracks. It's quick, like a static shock, yet strong enough to send a wave of heat up my arm. My breath catches as I glance up, and there they are—those slate gray eyes I've been trying not to think about, staring back at me.

Aidan's brows lift slightly, and for a second, I catch the same flicker of surprise that's coursing through me cross his face. What are the chances?

Well…I guess in a town this small, the odds are actually pretty decent. Still, of all the people I could have bumped into while grabbing milk and bread, it had to be him? This broody, gorgeous guy who completely rattles me?

I'm caught between wanting to say something clever and pretending I didn't just feel that undeniable spark when his hand brushed against mine. But if I'm being honest, my brain isn't exactly firing on all cylinders right now.

"Lucy." My name on his lips in that deep voice leaves me momentarily breathless.

I manage to force a smile even though my heart is doing somersaults in my chest. "Hi! Fancy meeting you here."

He quirks a brow, his gaze darting to the avocado we were reaching for, then back to me. There's a trace of amusement in his eyes.

I laugh nervously, tucking a strand of hair behind my ear as if that could somehow calm the heat creeping up my cheeks. "Great minds, right?"

He picks up the avocado, turning it over in his hand before offering it to me. "You take it."

Our fingers brush again as I reach for it, and it's like my whole body is suddenly hyperaware. The touch is brief, hardly even a graze, but my skin hums like it's been charged. "Thanks," I say softly.

I glance around, searching for Isla to ease the tension. "Oh, hey. Where's your shadow?"

The question slips out casually, but inside, I'm spiraling. This isn't like me. I can chat up a stranger or banter with a grumpy regular at the café without missing a beat. Instead, I'm a puddle of nerves, all because of one infuriatingly handsome man who completely throws me off balance.

"She's with my mum. I can't get any actual shopping done when she's with me."

I wonder where Isla's mum is. Maybe he *is* single? A tiny, reckless spark flares in my chest at the thought...then I immediately scold myself for it. For all I know he has a wife at home and he's letting her sleep in. Or a partner working an early shift. Or some complicated custody arrangement that is most definitely none of my business.

"I can imagine," I say, letting the words come out light. My gaze flicks ever so quickly to his left hand. Bare. No band. No tan line. Nothing obvious.

It doesn't prove anything, but it nudges the possibility a fraction closer.

He shifts his weight, and I can't stop myself from noticing how his henley stretches across his broad shoulders, sleeves pushed up just enough to reveal strong, tattooed forearms.

I nod, trying to ignore the flutter in my stomach. "It's nice you have family around to help," I continue, realizing I'm still clutching the avocado like it's made of gold. "Um, thanks again for this."

He shrugs, his eyes never leaving mine. "It's just an avocado."

"Right," I laugh nervously. "Of course." I drop it into my basket, searching for something else to say. "So, um, what else are you shopping for?"

He nods toward his cart. "Just the basics. Isla goes through cereal like it's her job."

Talking about his daughter seems to bring a gentler look to

his face, and I find myself smiling. "She's adorable. How old is she?"

"Four," he replies with a hint of pride in his voice.

"That's such a fun age."

He chuckles softly, the sound warm and unexpected. "Fun, sure. Exhausting, too. She's got more energy than I know what to do with."

That's the most I've heard him say at once. "Sounds like you've got your hands full."

"You have no idea." His eyes hold mine for a beat too long, then, as if remembering where we are, he straightens. "I should probably finish up before Isla realizes I'm gone."

"Of course," I say quickly. As he turns to leave, I look for something better to say. "And hey...don't forget to grab the good cereal. You know, the kind with marshmallows."

That was...dumb.

He pauses mid-stride, briefly turning his head with a grin. A *real* grin. "Noted."

It's a small thing, but the warmth in his smile lingers long after he walks away, leaving me standing there like a fool with an avocado and a heart that won't stop racing.

Jeez. Pull yourself together, Lucy. He's just a guy...albeit one with mesmerizing eyes, a voice that could melt butter, and an indisputable tenderness when it comes to his daughter.

I give my head a slight shake, as if that could dispel the haze of attraction clinging to me. There's a shopping list to finish, but as I move through the fluorescent lit aisles, my eyes keep searching for that tall silhouette among the shelves.

This isn't like me at all.

My last boyfriend, Owen, had pressed shirts and every single one of our dates scheduled. He worked at the bank and could tell me exactly where he'd be ten years from now. Again, safe, but never thrilling.

Nothing like the way Aidan makes me breathless, which terrifies me because that has *never* happened before.

As I'm turning around the corner to the dairy section, my foot catches and I almost collide with a shopping cart. "Oh, I'm so sorry!"

I freeze when I see who's behind it.

Aidan raises a brow. "We've got to stop meeting like this."

"I swear I'm not following you."

"Shame," he murmurs, so quietly I'm not sure I heard him correctly.

"Right. Well, I'll, uh, let you get back to your shopping."

He gives a small nod as he pushes his cart away.

I watch him go, my feet suddenly feeling like they're stuck in wet cement. In a rush to make my escape, I grab a carton of milk off the shelf...and promptly knock over a stack of yogurt cups. They tumble to the floor with a crash, and I stand there for a moment, horrified.

"Nice one," I mutter to myself, crouching down to scoop up the mess. The yogurt cups are scattered *everywhere*. I swear, if the floor could open up and swallow me whole, I'd dive right in without hesitation.

Then I hear it.

A deep, husky laugh—*Aidan's* laugh—drifts over from a few aisles away, and I freeze, my hands hovering over the mess. The sound vibrates through the air, and I realize I've never wanted to hear a sound more in my life.

I'M CURLED up on my couch later in the evening, and I've decided I am indeed getting a cat this week. It'll be nice to have another living being in this house to help me redirect my thoughts.

Right now, the memory of Aidan's touch lingers like an echo against my skin that I can't shake. At first, I thought I'd imagined it, my mind spinning tales of what could be, but when it happened again, it sent my heart racing.

I want more than just fleeting moments, which is ridiculous. Completely irresponsible, especially when I come with fine print and future complications. I don't need another man deciding I'm not worth the gamble because my body doesn't cooperate with his five-year plan.

I exhale, pressing my fingertips to my temples.

Maybe it's time to call Juliette. She has this uncanny ability to sort me out before I spiral into a full existential crisis.

And right now? I'm teetering awfully close to the edge.

twelve

LUCY

Winter's finally loosening its grip as we approach the end of February, the snow retreating one stubborn patch at a time. The air still bites a little, but the glimpses of brown grass hint that spring is coming.

I'm elbow deep in pastry flour when the bell above the door jingles. Glancing up, I spot Aileen bundled in her signature tartan scarf. Her silver hair catches the morning light as she makes her way to the counter. She's newer to town, but talking to her is like talking to someone you've known for ages.

"Lucy, dear," she calls. "Got a moment for an old woman?"

"For you, Aileen? Always." I wipe my hands on my apron and slide around the counter. "The usual?"

"Aye, but I'm not just here for your heavenly scones today. I've got a special request for someone with your particular talents."

I pour her tea—Earl Grey, splash of milk, no sugar—and slide it across the counter. "I'm all ears."

"Do you ever take custom orders? My granddaughter's

birthday is in a couple weeks, and I'd love to have you make her cake. Your stuff is to die for."

"I've made a few custom cakes over the years," I admit, feeling a flutter of excitement at the thought. "I used to do quite a bit more baking like that before I took over running the café full time."

The words bring back memories of late nights in my kitchen, experimenting with flavors and decorations, the satisfaction of creating something unique and beautiful. It's been ages since I've had the time to really dive into a project like that.

"Is that so?" Aileen's eyes twinkle. "Then I've come to the right place. Would you have time for something special? Nothing too elaborate, mind you."

"I'd absolutely love to," I say. "It would be nice to stretch those muscles again, honestly."

She beams at me, reaching across the counter to squeeze my hand. "Oh, wonderful! I knew you were the right person to ask."

"Tell me about your granddaughter," I say, pulling out my notebook from beneath the counter. "What flavors does she like? Any hobbies or interests?"

"She's turning five," Aileen says, her eyes crinkling at the corners. "Wee Isla is absolutely obsessed with fairies. Can't get enough of them. Her father—my son—built her a little fairy house for Christmas last year. It's quite elaborate, with miniature furniture and everything."

My heart stops.

"Wait—did you say Isla?" I set my pen down slowly, trying to keep my voice casual even as my pulse picks up. "Dark curly hair?"

"That's the one. I know Aidan's brought her here a couple times."

The pieces snap together in my mind like a puzzle finally making sense. Aileen. *Reid.* The grumpy, gorgeous man who's been occupying far too much of my thoughts lately isn't just some random single dad who wandered into my café—he's Aileen's son.

"Isla's absolutely delightful," I say, working to keep my voice steady. "She told me all about seeing a fairy in the garden."

Aileen laughs. "Oh, that girl has quite the imagination! Aidan was just as wild and full of stories when he was her age. Don't let that tough exterior fool you. He's got a soft heart."

I bite my lip, trying not to reveal just how interested I am in learning more about Aidan. "I've noticed that already," I say with a smile, picking up my pen again. "So...fairies, then? I can definitely work with that."

I'm trying to focus on my notes, but the image of gruff, serious Aidan meticulously painting fairy doors makes admiration bloom in my chest.

I press on. "So, what flavors does she like? Chocolate? Vanilla?"

"Strawberry," she says decidedly. "She's mad for anything strawberry."

I jot that down, my mind already spinning with ideas. "And when would you need it?"

"Her birthday's March first. It's a Sunday, but I know you're off that day so I could come get it a day early?"

I shake my head. "That's okay. I want it to be fresh. I could drop it off to you that Sunday if you'd like. I know you don't live too far."

"Oh, that would be lovely. You don't mind?"

"It's no trouble at all." Aileen studies me as I jot down her address. "I'm excited to do something special for Isla."

"You're an angel," she says. "I'm sure Aidan will appreciate it, too."

My cheeks flush. "Oh, well, I'm just happy to help."

We talk pricing and chat for a while longer before a few more customers come in. As she gathers her belongings to leave, I can't help the swirl of emotions churning inside me. Aidan is Aileen's son. It makes perfect sense now. They have the same gray eyes. How did I not see it before?

I lean against the counter, my mind racing. This changes things, doesn't it? Or maybe it doesn't change anything at all. I'm not even sure what "things" I'm referring to, because there aren't any "things" between Aidan and me to change in the first place.

I've just volunteered to personally deliver a birthday cake to what's bound to be a full-blown family gathering. What on earth was I thinking?

"You're overthinking this," I mutter to myself as I wipe down the counter with perhaps more vigor than necessary. *It's just a cake. For a child.*

And an excuse to see her dad again.

No.

I press my palms to my cheeks and blow out a frustrated breath. *Focus, Lucy.* Cake. Child. Delivery. Not daydreams about Aidan.

Dang it.

thirteen

AIDAN

I got back from work yesterday just in time for Isla's birthday. I glance at the clock and mentally curse. It's just after noon. I'd meant to leave earlier, but when you're responsible for a kid who insists on wearing mismatched socks and combing her hair with a fork, well...time slips away faster than I'd like to admit.

"All right, kiddo, let's get you in the car. You're going to be late for your own party," I call to Isla, who's stumbling around as she tries to put on her own shoes. She's twisting her right shoe onto her left foot, tongue sticking out in concentration.

I sigh, crouching down to help. "Wrong foot, love."

"I can do it myself," she insists, yanking the shoe off with surprising force. Her bottom lip juts out, that stubborn determination flashing in her eyes. The same look her mother used to get.

I hold my hands up in surrender. "All right, all right. But we need to hurry."

She's five today. *Five.* How did that happen so fast? It feels like yesterday I was holding this tiny human in my arms, trying to figure out how to be responsible for someone other than myself. Now she's all fire and independence.

She's starting school later this year, and I'm thrilled for her, but I also want to press pause and keep her like this, small and determined and impossibly fierce.

She's growing up too fast, and every step she takes away from my arms is a reminder that time doesn't wait.

A tug on my sleeve breaks through the spiral in my head.

"I'm ready!"

She stands beside me, purple tutu fluffed to maximum volume. Shirt askew but proudly chosen. Shoes miraculously on the correct feet this time.

"See? I did it myself."

I swallow around the lump in my throat and force a smile. "You look beautiful, love."

Her grin widens. "I know."

And just like that, I'm reaching for my keys, trying not to think about how many more *I did it myself* moments are coming.

"Come on then," I tell her, holding the door open. "Let's go celebrate my big girl."

My mum's house is bright and warm when we arrive. Isla bolts ahead of me as soon as I push the door open, her tutu bouncing with every step.

"Nana!" she shrieks, launching herself at my mother who's waiting with open arms.

"There's the birthday girl!" Mum exclaims. "Look how beautiful you are!"

I hang back, taking in the scene. The living room is transformed with pink and purple streamers, balloons floating against the ceiling. A handmade banner spelling out "Happy Birthday Isla" stretches across one wall.

"You're late," Aunt Margaret calls from the kitchen doorway.

"Blame the fashion show," I say, nodding toward Isla.

She laughs. "Well, she looks absolutely perfect, so it was worth it."

I'm about to respond when Isla calls out, "Uncle Jack!"

I turn abruptly, my eyes widening as I spot Jack leaning against the wall by the fireplace with the same shit-eating grin he always wears.

"Well, if it isn't my favorite little troublemaker."

Isla darts over, looping her arms around his neck as soon as he crouches. He lifts her effortlessly, spinning her once before setting her down with a gentle thump before ruffling her curls.

"Well, look what the tide dragged in," I say, crossing the room to clasp his hand.

He pulls me into a quick embrace, thumping my back. "Couldn't miss the little princess's big day, could I?"

A familiar face is a welcome sight. Jack's been there through the worst of it—the endless shifts, those first brutal months of single parenthood when I had no bloody idea what I was doing.

"You should've told me you were coming."

"And miss the look on your face? Not a chance," Jack laughs, then lowers his voice. "How's the new place working out?"

I shrug, watching as Isla twirls for my mum. "Getting there. Still feels temporary sometimes."

"Aye, I know that feeling." His eyes follow mine to Isla. "She seems happy, though."

"She is," I agree. "Found a café in town she likes. Made a few friends at the park, too."

Jack nods, a knowing look crossing his face. "And what about you? Still no...connections?"

I shoot him a warning glance. "Don't start."

"What? Just asking how you're settling in."

"I'm fine," I say firmly. "Got the house, got work, got her. That's all I need."

The doorbell rings, its chime cutting through the chatter. Mum's head snaps up.

"That'll be the cake," she says with a strange little smile that makes me suspicious. "Aidan, be a dear and answer that, would you?"

I frown but head for the door. When I pull it open, I nearly stop breathing.

Lucy's standing on the doorstep, a large white box balanced carefully in her hands. Her dark hair is loose today, falling in soft waves. She's wearing a sand-colored sweater that brings out the green in her eyes, and for a second, I just stare.

"Hi," she says, her voice soft. "Special delivery."

"You're...delivering the cake?"

"I am." She shifts the box slightly. "Your mum ordered it. For Isla."

"Right," I finally manage. "Come in."

"Actually, would you mind taking this?" She gestures toward the box. "Keep it as level as possible until you put it down. I just need to run to my car to grab something."

I take the box from her as gently as possible, waiting by the door until she returns with a bright pink gift bag overflowing with glittery tissue paper.

"You didn't need to get her anything," I tell her.

"Psh. Of course I did. I'll take any excuse to go shopping for a little girl. It's so much fun."

I hum in response, trying not to jostle the cake box as I lead her through the house.

"Lucy!" Isla's voice cuts through the chatter as she spots her, her face lighting up. She practically flies across the room, tutu fluttering behind her.

"Happy birthday, Isla," Lucy beams, kneeling to meet my daughter at eye level, the gift bag held out. "I brought you something special."

Isla's eyes widen to saucers. "For me?"

"Of course."

Something unfamiliar twists in my chest as I watch them together. Lucy treats Isla like she's precious, not just humoring her the way adults sometimes do with children.

Just like that, something cracks open where I've spent years welding the pieces shut. It's like the hinges of a door I swore would stay closed giving way. I try to slam it back shut, but it's too damn late.

Allowing myself to feel anything for Lucy is reckless and stupid. She's just being kind, but...the way she looks at Isla, like she matters just for existing, isn't something I can ignore.

"Aidan, the cake," my mother reminds me.

"Right." I carefully set the box on the dining table where Mum's already laid out plates and napkins. As I lift the lid, there's a collective gasp.

The cake is...unreal. It's shaped like a fairy garden, with tiny mushroom houses nestled among what looks like a forest. In the center sits a fairy, wings dusted with glitter. The attention to detail is astonishing.

Isla gasps, pressing her hands to her cheeks.

My eyes lift to find Lucy, who's watching Isla's reaction with barely contained delight.

"You made this?" I ask her.

She nods, a faint blush coloring her cheeks. "I used to do more custom work years ago. It was fun to get back into it."

"It's incredible. You're talented," I tell her honestly. "Thank you."

Surprise glimmers in her eyes before she smiles. "You're welcome."

Lucy stands next to me for a moment, watching Isla as she inspects the cake from every angle. She shifts close enough that I feel her warmth. It's just a subtle shift of air, the brush of her sleeve near mine, but it hits me all the same.

Suddenly, I have this urge to slide an arm around her waist and pull her in, feel her settle there. The thought blindsides me. I haven't even wanted something like that in a long time.

I clear my throat, forcing my hands to stay where they are, clamped uselessly at my sides.

She swallows, eyes flicking up to mine as if she feels the shift, too. Then she steps back, the space she leaves behind cooling far too quickly.

"I should, um…I should get going," she says quietly. "Let you get back to the party."

"Are you sure you can't stay, Lucy?" Mum asks. "You're more than welcome."

Lucy offers a soft smile. "I'm actually heading over to my parents' place in a bit. I appreciate it, though."

Before anyone can say more, Isla barrels forward, wrapping her arms around Lucy's legs. "Thank you for my cake."

Lucy lowers and tucks a curl behind Isla's ear. "You're very welcome, sweetheart. Happy birthday."

Isla beams, then dashes back as quickly as she appeared.

"I'll walk you out," I say.

Lucy nods. "Sure."

We head for the door together, side by side, her shoulder

brushing my arm. It's the smallest touch, one you could chalk up to the narrow hallway, but it lights me up.

I open the door for her, the early March air cool against the overheated house.

Lucy pauses at the threshold, turning to face me. The sunlight catches in her hair, turning it almost amber. I'm painfully aware of how close we're standing, the doorway forcing us into each other's space. Her gaze meets mine.

"Thanks again for the cake," I say, my voice rough. "Isla will remember this for a long time."

"It was my pleasure," she replies. She takes half a step back, but her eyes stay locked on mine.

Her eyes flick to my lips for just a fraction of a second, and my heart hammers against my ribs. I find myself swaying forward, just slightly. My fingers twitch at my side, resisting the urge to brush the stray hair the wind has blown across her face. A sudden gust catches us, sending that loose strand dancing across her cheek. I tighten my fist to stop myself from reaching out. It would be so easy to tuck it behind her ear, to let my fingers graze her skin. The impulse is overwhelming, foreign, and terrifying all at once.

"I haven't seen you and Isla in the café in a while," she says almost timidly, tucking the lock of hair away herself.

"Offshore work," I mutter, shoving my hands into my pockets where they can't betray me. "Oil rigs. I'm usually gone a few weeks at a time."

Her eyes soften a fraction, but there's no pity there. "Well, maybe I'll see you both at the café sometime this week?"

It sounds like a question, but it's phrased like she wants me to say yes. My throat goes dry, and I nod before I can overthink it.

"Aye, we'll stop by."

Her smile blooms slowly, lighting up her entire face. I don't know when it happened, but I'm already halfway gone over her lips and her smile.

That kind of wanting will ruin a man.

"I really should get going," she says softly.

I step back. "Right. Drive safe."

She gives a small, tentative smile that makes my chest ache. "Enjoy the party. Tell Isla I hope she loves her present."

I watch as she walks to her car. Only when she pulls away do I realize I'm still standing in the doorway like an idiot, letting all the heat out of the house.

When I finally turn around, Jack's standing there with a smirk that makes me want to punch him.

"Well, well, well," he drawls, crossing his arms over his chest. "That was quite the goodbye. Thought you might follow her to her car like a lost puppy."

I brush past him, jaw clenched. "Shut it."

"I haven't seen that look on your face since...actually, I don't think I've ever seen that look." He falls into step beside me, lowering his voice. "Correct me if I'm wrong, but was that actual human interest I detected?"

"It's called being polite," I mutter, heading back toward the living room. "She brought a cake for my daughter."

Jack snorts. Isla saves me by squealing about presents, and the attention shifts right back where it belongs—on her. I spend the next few minutes watching her tear into colorful packages, her face lighting up with each new discovery. And somewhere in the back of my mind, Lucy presses against my thoughts, sparking a pull I can't—and don't want to—ignore.

AIDAN

I agreed to have a drink with Jack after Isla's party. I'm three fingers of whisky into the night when he brings up Lucy again. The pub's noise is barely a buffer. Just enough to keep our conversation private, not so much that I can use it as an excuse to shut him up.

"All I'm saying," Jack says, "is that I've never heard you speak about a woman, never mind look at one. Not since—"

"Are we still on this? It's been hours." I knock back the rest of my drink, savoring the burn as it slides down my throat.

"Hours during which you've checked your phone exactly seventeen times." He raises his brows. "Did she text you?"

"No," I grumble. What he doesn't know is that I check my phone every couple minutes to make sure Mum hasn't tried to reach me since she's watching Isla right now. It has nothing to do with a woman. "We barely know each other."

Jack signals the bartender for another round. "So, you're telling me the pretty café owner who hand-delivered a fairy cake isn't on your mind at all."

The bartender slides fresh drinks in front of us. I take mine immediately, needing something to do with my hands.

"Look," I say finally, "even if I was interested—which I'm not saying I am—it's complicated."

"How? You're single."

"I'm gone for weeks at a time, Jack. That's not exactly relationship material. How's that been working out for you?"

He winces in response as I swirl the amber liquid in my glass.

"And I've got Isla to think about."

His expression softens. "Isla seemed to like her well enough."

"That's part of the problem."

"You know what your actual problem is?"

I fight the urge to smirk. "Please, enlighten me."

"You've convinced yourself that being alone is safer." He leans in, suddenly serious. "But mate, I've seen you these past few years. That wall you've built isn't keeping you safe. It's just keeping you lonely."

He thinks he's got me figured out. Shit, maybe he does, but I'm not about to let him have that satisfaction. Loneliness isn't something you confess out loud.

I drag a hand over my jaw, clearing my throat. "That's one theory."

Jack's right, and I bloody hate it. What pisses me off even more is that I can't stop thinking about her.

"Another theory," I mutter, "is that you're a pain in my arse who should mind his own damn business."

Jack laughs, completely unfazed. "Someone's got to look out for you. God knows you won't do it yourself." He pauses for a beat. "Look, I'm not saying rush into anything. Just...consider the possibility."

I shift uncomfortably on my barstool, staring down at my glass. "You done with the lecture now?"

"For tonight. No promises about tomorrow."

The whisky's starting to take the edge off. My mind wanders where it isn't supposed to, like the way Lucy's eyes crease at the corners when she laughs, or the soft shift in her voice when she talks to Isla.

"She's probably not interested, anyway," I mutter, more to myself than to Jack.

He snorts. "Right. That's why she couldn't take her eyes off you."

Damn him. The problem isn't whether she's interested or not. The problem is that I'm actually considering it. As much as I hate admitting Jack's right, I hate even more that some part of me is starting to hope.

LUCY

The first bite of spring always tastes the sweetest. It makes you forget the damp chill of winter ever existed with the sun bright, the breeze warm, the world suddenly too full of possibility to keep up with.

It's town festival day. The local businesses line up with their booths, the streets fill with music and laughter, and everyone comes out for a good time. Poppy was supposed to help me set up, but she's come down with something, leaving me to do the heavy lifting solo.

I grip the edge of the folding table and haul it toward its spot. It's heavier than I remember, the weight of it digging into my arms and making the muscles in my neck strain in protest.

I've got a good stretch ahead of me if I want to get everything set up before the crowd starts rolling in. Callan and Knox said they'd come help once they get their own booth for the distillery sorted down the street, but apparently, that's its own kind of chaos.

I finally manage to wrestle the table into place and take a step back to assess what needs to be set up. It's not much, just a few baskets of pastries and cookies to display. I've been baking since dawn. Strawberry tarts, lemon scones, chocolate chip cookies still slightly warm from the oven. The makeshift banner I made flutters in the breeze, the words "Thistle & Spoon" threatening to tear away from the flimsy tape holding them in place.

Just as I'm setting out the first tray of pastries, a gust of wind tears through the street, sending napkins flying and knocking over the stack of paper cups I just arranged. I lunge for them, nearly toppling the display in the process.

"Come on," I mutter, trying to anchor everything down while simultaneously reaching for the flyaway napkins. My fingers brush against one just as another gust sends it spiraling farther away.

The wind picks up again, stronger this time, and I watch in horror as my carefully arranged sign starts to peel away from the front of the table. I dart forward, trying to catch it before it takes flight, but my elbow knocks against the tray of scones, sending them sliding precariously close to the edge.

"No, no, no." I make a desperate grab for both the sign and the tray. The wind has other plans, though, whipping the sign free and sending it tumbling down the street like a wayward kite.

"Perfect," I mutter, blowing a loose strand of hair from my face.

That's exactly when the tower of cardboard boxes I'd stacked behind the table decides to join the chaos, toppling over and spilling the packaged pastries across the pavement. My heart sinks as I watch my morning's work scatter on the ground.

I drop to my knees, frantically gathering what I can salvage. Thank god a few baked goods landed on the stray napkins but the rest…It's an absolute crime scene. My fingers work quickly, scooping up the less damaged goods and trying to arrange them back on the trays. The festival officially starts in fifteen minutes, and I'm nowhere near ready.

"Need a hand?"

The low voice slices right through my flustered spiral. I glance up to find Aidan towering in front of me, broad shoulders framed by the sun like some kind of reluctant, brooding hero. He's wearing a navy T-shirt that fits unfairly well. It's snug across his chest and tight around his tattooed biceps that I'd bet good money he doesn't show off on purpose. His jeans are worn and faded, and there's a little scuff of stubble along his jaw, catching the light as he squints down at me.

The look on his face lands somewhere between amused and mildly exasperated, like I'm a walking storm he's half tempted to get caught in.

"Oh! I—" I push a lock of hair out of my face, painfully aware of how much of a mess I must look. Hair falling out of place, cheeks flushed, pastry carnage at my feet. "I mean, yes. Please. If you don't mind."

He doesn't say anything, just lowers himself into a crouch beside me, jeans pulling tight across his thighs as he starts collecting the scattered scones with care. His hands—goodness, his strong, capable hands—move with a surprising gentleness.

My stomach does a little fluttery thing that I pretend not to feel.

"Wind's causing you grief?" he says, his voice low enough that only I can hear it over the bustle around us.

I let out a breathless laugh. "That obvious?"

He glances over, lips tugging up at one corner. There's a small dimple that appears when he does that. It's subtle, but there.

"Just a bit," he says, eyes dragging over me in a way that doesn't feel unkind. Just...observant. Noting every flyaway hair, every smudge of flour I probably didn't catch. Not judging. Just seeing.

I move to straighten the crate again, trying not to focus on how close he is. He smells like clean soap and cedar and the last bit of night air before the sun comes up. It fills my lungs, mixing with the buttery sweetness of the pastries, making my brain go a little hazy.

My eyes linger on the curve of his mouth, the way the tendons in his forearms flex as he steadies the napkin beneath the stack. He's...impossibly handsome. I just pray he doesn't notice the heat creeping up my neck every time I look in his direction.

"Where's Isla today?" I ask, hoping my voice sounds steadier than it feels.

"With my mum just down the street," he replies, standing up with some rescued pastries. "I saw you battling your table."

I nod. "It's just...one of those days." I gesture toward the desserts on the table still teetering dangerously close to disaster.

He follows my gaze, and then without asking, starts helping me arrange everything.

"I owe you one," I say, my hands still moving in a little flurry of action. "Really didn't expect to end up alone with this, but..." I shrug. "I'll survive."

Aidan places the last tray of scones at the front of the display. The festival crowd streams past us, but somehow, it feels like we're in our own little bubble.

"I've got time," he says simply, his gray eyes meeting mine. "Isla's busy making flower crowns with my mum. She'll be busy for the next hour, at the minimum."

"Well, in that case, would you mind helping me get this banner back up? It seems determined to fly away today."

He nods, reaching for the sign I'd rescued from halfway down the street. Our fingers brush as he takes it from me, and that same spark I felt in the grocery store jolts through me again. I quickly turn away, searching for tape in my apron pocket.

"Here," I say, pulling out a roll. "If we can secure it better this time, maybe it'll stay put."

Aidan takes the tape without a word, making quick work of securing the banner to the front of the table. He's methodical, making sure each corner is reinforced against the persistent breeze.

"Thanks," I say, mesmerized by the efficiency of his movements, the concentration in his expression. "You're good at this."

He glances up briefly. "I'm used to it. Everything needs to be secure when you're out at sea."

I nod, trying to imagine what that life must be like. Weeks away from home, surrounded by nothing but water and steel. It explains the weathered look about him, that slight hardness around his eyes.

"Must be tough," I venture, arranging the last of the cookies on their tray. "Being away from Isla for so long."

His hands pause for just a moment, and I worry I've overstepped. Then he continues, his voice a little rougher than before.

"It is. But it's provided well for us. And she's got my mum." He secures the last corner of the banner. "It's just how it is."

There's a finality to his words that makes my heart ache. I busy myself with the display, not wanting him to see the emotion I'm sure is written all over my face.

After a beat, Aidan steps back, his eyes scanning the table. "Looks good."

"It would have been a disaster without your help."

A comfortable silence settles between us as we stand back to admire our handiwork. The wind has calmed a bit, and the pastries now sit safely displayed, the banner secure against any future gusts.

"So...which is your favorite?" I ask. "I'm setting one aside as payment for your heroic rescue."

His gaze flicks up from the pastries to me, eyes crinkling slightly at the corners. Not a full smile—it seems he never gives those out freely—but close enough to make my heart skip. "Don't need payment for lending a hand."

"Well, I insist," I say, sweeping my hand toward the slightly pathetic, but now stable, array of scones and cookies. "Baker's honor."

He glances at the display, and for a second, I think he might deflect again. He surprises me by pointing to a lemon scone. "If there's any of those left at the end of the day, I'll take one."

I grin. "Excellent choice. My secret recipe."

"Secret, huh? What makes it special?"

"If I told you, it wouldn't be a secret anymore," I tease. The corner of his mouth twitches up again, just a fraction.

For a heartbeat, the world blurs around us. He watches me with guarded yet curious eyes.

Then, because apparently fate has a wicked sense of humor, a gust of wind kicks up again, sending a stack of paper cups skittering across the pavement.

"Bloody hell—" I lunge for them, but Aidan moves at the same time. We collide. My shoulder knocks against his chest. One of his hands grabs my waist to support me.

Everything stops.

His touch is too careful to be casual, too protective to be nothing. We both go still, the air between us yanked tight. His hand doesn't fall. If anything, it settles more firmly at my waist.

I can feel every inch of him, solid and *so close*. His gaze drops to my mouth, and the world narrows to that single, impossible inch between us.

He leans in just enough that I feel the whisper of his breath against my cheek, the promise of something we're both seconds from falling into.

A burst of noise—someone shouting—snaps the moment. His hand falls from my waist before he steps back.

"Sorry," he breathes, rough and unsteady.

"It's okay," I murmur, still rooted to the spot, crumpled cups forgotten. Because all I can really feel is the ghost of his palm on my waist and the space where his mouth almost touched mine.

"I should probably check on Isla."

"Right." I nod, trying to look composed even as my pulse is still tripping over itself. "Thanks again. For the help."

"Of course." He gives me one last look before turning to walk back toward the crowd, his shoulders tense, hands shoved in his pockets.

I'm left standing in a tangle of wind-wrecked treats and paper cups, feeling the pull of something between us that he won't...or can't, admit.

The rest of the morning passes quickly enough. Customers come and go, the festival swells with laughter and music, and I keep busy, though my mind drifts to Aidan more than I'd like to admit. Every time the crowd shifts, I catch myself looking for him.

"You're staring again," Callan says, appearing at my side with that knowing smirk of his.

I nearly jump out of my skin. "I'm not staring at anything," I protest, turning to face him with what I hope is an innocent expression.

"Sure you're not," he drawls, crossing his arms over his chest. "And I'm not your brother who's known you your entire life."

I roll my eyes, busying my hands with rearranging the few remaining pastries. "Don't you have your own booth to run?"

"Bree's handling it with Knox." He leans against the table, his eyes scanning the crowd before landing back on me with a grin. "So, when did this happen?"

"When did what happen?" I ask, though the heat creeping up my neck betrays me.

"You. Him." Callan gestures vaguely toward where Aidan had disappeared. "The whole blushing schoolgirl routine."

"I am not—" I start, then catch myself. "There's nothing happening. He just helped me set up the booth."

"Uh-huh." Callan's eyes dance with amusement. "That's why you've been watching the crowd like a hawk for the last hour."

I shake my head, fighting a smile. "You're impossible."

"And you're transparent," he counters, snagging one of the last cookies from the display.

Before I can respond, there's a commotion at the edge of the crowd. I look up to see Isla breaking free from her grandmother's grasp, darting through the festival-goers with surprising speed for someone so small. She's wearing a lopsided flower crown, petals already falling loose around her curls.

"Miss Lucy!" she calls, her face alight with excitement as she races toward the booth.

My heart swells with joy at the sight of her, and I crouch down just in time to catch her as she launches herself at me.

"Whoa there!" I laugh, bracing her as she nearly topples us both over. "Careful, or you'll send all our pastries flying again."

"Look what I made!" She thrusts a second flower crown toward me, this one even more precarious than the one on her head, with daisies and buttercups woven haphazardly through twisted stems. "It's for you."

"For me?" I press a hand to my chest, genuinely touched. "It's beautiful, Isla."

She beams, bouncing on her toes. "Put it on!"

I lower my head, and she places the crown on my hair with all the seriousness of a royal coronation.

"How do I look?" I ask, straightening up.

"Like a princess," she declares.

Callan laughs beside me, and I shoot him a warning glance before turning back to Isla. My pulse kicks up when I see Aidan approaching, his hands still tucked into his pockets but with something almost like a smile tugging at his lips.

"Look!" Isla squeals, launching herself at his legs. "A flower crown for me, one for Miss Lucy, and one for Nana."

Aidan scoops her up with one easy motion, settling her on his hip. His eyes linger on mine, and I resist the urge to fidget under his gaze.

"Beautiful," he says quietly, and the simple compliment sends heat blooming across my cheeks.

Beside me, Callan clears his throat loudly. "I should get back to Bree," he announces, not even trying to hide his smirk. "She'll be wondering where I've gone." He gives Aidan a brief nod before shooting me a look that clearly says we'll be discussing this later.

Once he's gone, I turn my attention back to Aidan and Isla. "How's the festival treating you so far?"

"Good," Aidan replies, gesturing to the bustling crowd around us. "Isla's won just about every game she's tried."

"Did not," Isla protests. "I didn't win the ring toss."

"Only because your arms aren't long enough yet," Aidan says, his voice softening as he adjusts her on his hip. "Give it a few years."

This tiny glimpse into their relationship makes my heart swell. "Well, I've still got a few lemon scones left if anyone's interested?" I offer, already reaching for the pastry I'd set aside earlier.

"Me!" Isla's hand shoots up, nearly toppling her flower crown in the process.

Aidan sets her down gently, his eyes meeting mine over her head. "What do we say, Isla?"

"Please, Miss Lucy," she chirps.

"Yes, of course," I say, handing Isla a scone wrapped in a napkin. "Careful, it might crumble a bit."

I grab the other scone I'd saved and offer it to Aidan. "For your heroic table rescue earlier."

His fingers brush against mine as he takes it, sending that familiar spark dancing up my arm. "Thanks," he says, his voice low enough that only I can hear it. Then he turns to Isla. "We really need to find your nana before she spends any more money on you."

Isla mumbles in acknowledgement through a mouthful of crumbs before they both offer a wave goodbye. We don't really know each other beyond a handful of shared smiles and a few messy, thrown together moments. And yet, it stings as I watch them walk in the opposite direction.

The festival winds down as the day stretches into late afternoon, and the crowd thins as families head home with painted faces and pockets full of trinkets. I'm packing up the last of my supplies, carefully folding the tablecloth and stacking the empty trays, when I sense someone watching me.

I glance up, expecting to see Callan ready with another teasing comment, but instead, it's Aidan. He's standing just a few feet away.

"Hey," I say softly.

He shifts his weight, and our eyes meet for the barest second before he looks away. "Thought you might need help packing up."

A warm flutter sparks in my chest, but I tamp it down. "I think I've got it," I say, forcing the words out steadily. "Thank you, though."

For a second, I think he's going to turn and leave. Instead, he steps forward, reaching for one of the heavier boxes. "Let me at least carry this to your car."

I hesitate, my pride warring with practicality. The box *is* heavy, and my car is parked at the far end of the lot. "If you're sure..."

He nods, lifting the box with ease.

We walk in silence as we make our way toward the parking area. The setting sun casts long shadows across the pavement, painting everything in soft gold and amber. I'm acutely aware of his presence beside me and the careful distance he maintains between us.

"Your brother?" he asks suddenly.

I glance over, surprised to hear him speak. "The one at the booth earlier? Yeah, that's Callan."

He adjusts his grip on the box. "How many of you are there?"

"Three of us," I reply, fishing my keys from my pocket as we approach my car. "Knox, Callan, and me. I'm the youngest."

"They both live around here?"

"Yeah, they actually run our family distillery. You might have seen their booth."

He dips his chin, a hint of recognition crossing his face. I unlock the trunk, and he sets the box inside, careful not to jostle it.

"Thanks," I say, closing the trunk.

He lingers, one hand resting on the car, his eyes fixed on some point in the distance. "I wanted to thank you again," he says finally. "For earlier. For the last couple months, really, and for being so friendly with Isla."

I shake my head, leaning back against the car. "You don't need to thank me for that. She's a loveable little girl."

Aidan doesn't move at first. Doesn't even blink. Just stands there with that intense, unreadable expression that always makes me feel like I've been caught looking too closely.

"Maybe not," he says finally, voice rougher than before. "But I felt like I should, anyway."

That cracks me wide open, because I'm fairly certain Aidan doesn't offer up pieces of himself often. If ever.

"This isn't easy for me," he starts, eyes meeting mine for a second. "Having Isla get attached to people."

I watch his throat move as he swallows, his jaw clenched tight. He's not looking at me now. He's looking somewhere past me, like it's easier to face the empty sky.

"Because of your job?"

"Partly." He runs a hand through his hair. "Isla's mum left when she was only a few months old."

A breath punches from my lungs. "Aidan...I'm so sorry."

He shakes his head. "I'm not telling you this for sympathy. I just..." He exhales, long and slow. "I want you to know that Isla forms attachments quickly, and I'm doing everything I can to make sure she doesn't get hurt."

His words land like a blow. They're honest but devastating.

In that one moment, I see more than the gruff exterior or the tired father doing his best. I see the man who's been holding everything together with his bare hands and a thin thread of control, terrified that if he lets one thing slip, the whole thing will collapse.

I nod, my throat too tight to speak. My heart's already spilling all over the place.

"Thank you for telling me," I whisper, because it's all I can manage.

His eyes come back to mine, maybe searching for doubt or judgment. What he'll find is understanding.

"I should get her home," he says quietly.

"Of course." I tuck my hands into my sleeves, suddenly chilled. "I'll see you around?"

He hesitates for just a breath, and then the corner of his mouth lifts into the smallest smile. "Aye," he murmurs. "See you, Lucy. Soon."

Then he walks away, officially taking a piece of my heart with him before I even realize I've handed it over.

sixteen

AIDAN

The sun has just risen over the hills when Isla barrels into the kitchen, all energy and pink cheeks. She clutches her stuffed rabbit tight against her chest, determination set into her jaw that makes me brace for whatever she's about to ask me.

"Can Lucy come hiking with us today?"

The question lands like a punch I didn't see coming. Right in the ribs.

I rinse out my coffee mug a little harder than necessary, watching the water swirl down the drain instead of looking at my daughter. "Probably not today, kiddo."

She plants herself in between me and the sink. "She likes outside stuff. She said so."

I rub a hand over the back of my neck, dragging out the silence. Long enough that she huffs and stomps away toward the door, muttering something about dads being "no fun."

Christ.

I brace both hands on the counter and let my head hang for a second, breathing through the churn in my chest. It's not that I don't want Lucy there. Hell, that's the fucking problem.

I do.

I want her laughter echoing off the trees, her eyes squinting up at the sun. I want the way she looks at my daughter to be something I don't have to give up at the end of the day.

None of that changes the fact that wanting things has never gone too well for me. It's easier to keep our world small. Just me and Isla and the life we've patched together out of broken things.

Except now there's this bright-eyed, messy-haired woman who smells like vanilla and feels like the first deep breath I've taken in years.

Before I can fully talk myself out of it, Isla's already halfway into her boots.

"Where are you going, little storm?" I ask, even though I know damn well what she's up to.

"To ask Lucy!" she chirps in her singsong voice.

I shake my head, pressing my thumb and forefinger to my eyes like maybe that'll stave off the brewing headache. "Isla, we can't just show up—"

She's already tugging the front door open, cool spring air blasting through the house.

"Isla!" I snap, my voice sharper than I intend. She freezes, one foot already out the door. "Get back here. Now."

Her bottom lip juts out in that stubborn little pout she gets from her mother. "But Daddy—"

"No buts." I cross the room in three long strides and shut the door behind me. "You don't open the door and go off without me. Not safe."

Her little shoulders slump, the fight draining out of her. "I just want Lucy to come," she mumbles, voice so small it breaks my heart.

I bend down to her level, trying to gentle my voice. "I know, kiddo. But Lucy might be busy. She has a café to run, remember? And we can't just show up at her door without warning."

"It's Sunday. She said she doesn't work on Sundays. We could call her," Isla suggests, perking up again.

"I don't have her number," I say, relieved to have a practical reason to shut this down. But Isla's nothing if not persistent.

"Nana does! She and Lucy talk about flowers and stuff."

Of course they do.

I scrub a hand over my jaw, feeling the day-old stubble catch against my palm. The smart thing to do would be to dig in. Hold the line. Tell Isla no, tell myself no.

Then I look at Isla with her eyes shining with that wild, innocent hope, and the words die in my throat.

It's just a hike. Just a couple hours in the woods. Not a forever thing.

And yet, I know better than anyone that Isla doesn't separate things out like that. She doesn't draw lines between *now* and *always*.

Damn it.

It's selfish, but right now, with Isla practically vibrating beside me, her small hand tugging at mine and her face lit up, it feels like one of those rare moments when life isn't taking something away from me. It's offering something, and for once...I don't want to be the guy who walks away from that.

"All right," I sigh. "I'll ask Nana for her number. But," I lift a finger, "no promises. Lucy might have plans today."

Isla nods vigorously. "She won't. I know she won't."

Her confidence is blinding. The way she believes in people so easily guts me. Sometimes I look at her and wonder how on earth she still sees the world as a place that gives. A place where people stay.

I fish my phone from my pocket, thumbing through the

contacts until I find Mum. The phone rings three times before she picks up.

"Aidan? Is everything all right?"

"Fine, Mum," I say, watching Isla dash up the stairs, presumably to pick out her hiking clothes. "Listen, do you have Lucy's number? From the café?"

There's a pause on the other end, and I can practically hear the smile spreading across her face. "Sweet Lucy MacKenzie? Why, yes, I do. We were just talking about flower arrangements for the spring festival last week." I catch the knowing lilt in her voice, and I silently curse myself.

"It's nothing like that," I mutter. "Isla wants to invite her hiking with us today."

"Oh?" The single syllable carries a weight of questions I'm not ready to answer. "Well, isn't that lovely. Just a moment, let me find it."

Papers shuffle on the other end, and then Mum's back, rattling off a number that I quickly jot down on the back of an old receipt.

"Thanks," I say, eager to end the conversation before she can start in with the questions I just know are hovering on the tip of her tongue.

"Aidan." Her voice softens. "It's good to see you reaching out. Both of you."

I grunt noncommittally, not sure what to say to that. "Talk to you later, Mum."

I hang up and stare at the numbers. This feels like crossing some invisible line where I'm about to invite trouble into our carefully balanced world. Still, it doesn't change the fact that the thought of Lucy's smile makes my chest ache in a way that's not entirely unpleasant.

I dial before I can talk myself out of it.

The phone rings once. Twice. Three times.

My thumb hovers over the *end call* button. This was a bad idea. She's probably still asleep, or busy. I should hang up. I *will* hang up. Then—

"Hello?"

Her voice. Soft, familiar, a little sleepy, but not annoyed. I freeze for a second, caught off guard by how much relief floods through me.

"Lucy. It's Aidan." I pause, swallowing down the sudden sandpaper in my throat. "Did I wake you?"

"Aidan? No, not at all. Is everything okay?"

What is it with everyone assuming something must be wrong?

I clear my throat. "Yeah, everything's fine. I, uh—"

Jesus. I sound like I'm fifteen again and calling some girl's landline to ask her to the school dance.

I scratch the back of my neck, eyes fixed on the far side of the room like it's going to give me a better line. "Isla and I are heading up the ridge trail today. She, uh... She asked if you'd want to come with us."

There's a beat of silence. Then another, and that's when the doubt kicks in. I should've just texted. Or probably kept my damn mouth shut and never called in the first place.

"Would that be okay? Do you want me to come?"

Her question lands softly in my ear. I press my thumb to my brow, pacing slowly across the kitchen floor while my brain scrambles for the safest answer. The one that won't give anything away.

The truth pushes harder than my pride does.

"Aye," I manage. "I...yeah, I'd like it if you could come."

A beat. Then her breath catches. "I'd love to."

Just three words, and suddenly, I'm standing up straighter.

"What time were you thinking?" she asks.

"Can we pick you up in an hour?"

"That's perfect. I'll text you my address."

We hang up, but my pulse is doing something fucking *weird*, and I don't know what the hell to do with that, so I shove it deep and walk it off.

At the foot of the stairs, Isla's already dressed in her purple hiking outfit, beaming up at me.

"Did she say yes?"

I nod once. "She's in."

She fist pumps the air, and damn it, I feel the grin tugging at my mouth before I can stop it.

I don't know what the hell I'm doing.

She said yes, and god help me, I wanted her to.

seventeen

LUCY

What if it's weird?

That's the question looping in my head as I pace around my flat, my hiking boots squeaking against the laminate floor. What if it's awkward? Stilted? What if we run out of things to say halfway up the trail and end up spending the rest of the day pretending not to notice?

I'm good with people. I've built a career out of smiling and small talk and knowing when someone needs an extra drizzle of honey in their tea. But this isn't that. This is *him*.

A rumble of tires on gravel cuts through my spiral. I dart to the window just as Aidan's truck pulls up outside. My stomach gives one of those traitorous little flips that makes me question if I've eaten or just swallowed a live bird.

Bag. Door. Go.

I force myself to move before I can start overthinking again.

When I step outside, he's already out of the truck. Sunlight catches the edges of his broad frame, haloing him in gold like some blue-collar god.

He gives me a nod—his version of a greeting—and I can't help but notice the slight softness in his expression today.

"Morning," Aidan says, his voice a low rumble that slides easily into the quiet hush of the morning.

"Morning!" I chirp back, my nerves buzzing just under my skin. I'm just stepping up to the truck when a high-pitched voice bursts through the glass.

"Miss Lucy!"

Isla's face appears in the back window. "We're going hiking!"

Aidan moves to open the door for me, and I catch the ghost of a smile tugging at his mouth. He's probably been up since sunrise, wrestled his kid into socks, and still remembered to hold the door open. Chivalrous. Unfairly attractive.

I climb in, turning in my seat to look at Isla. "You're going to love it. There's this little spot by the loch where the view will knock your socks off."

Her eyes go wide. "Will there be fish? What about birds? Will there be bears? Do you have snacks?"

The questions tumble out of her in a joyful stream, and I answer as best I can, smiling so hard it makes my cheeks ache. She's a little firework in a booster seat, and something about the way she looks at me like I know every secret in the world makes something in my chest pinch, then bloom.

"Ready?" Aidan asks.

"Absolutely."

We ease onto the road and Isla's voice bubbles up again immediately. She doesn't leave space for nerves with the way she chatters about everything and nothing. Asking if I like peanut butter on toast—yes. If I've ever seen a deer up close—once. And whether flowers grow better when you sing to them—jury's still out, but I say yes to keep the magic alive.

She's a one girl welcome wagon, barreling through any

potential uncomfortable silence with enough enthusiasm that makes it impossible not to smile.

Every few minutes, I catch Aidan sneaking a look my way. It's like he's waiting to see if I'll get tired of the noise, or if the nonstop chatter will wear thin.

As if. I'm soaking up every second.

He doesn't say much, but I can tell he's listening. His hands firm on the wheel, his jaw a little less tight than usual. Isla's energy seems to settle something in him, too.

Then she launches into an animated tale about a rainbow-feathered bird she swears she saw once "in real life, not in a book," complete with hand gestures and dramatic reenactments.

I glance over just in time to catch another pull at the corner of Aidan's mouth. Still not a full-blown smile exactly, but I'm starting to think I might see it soon.

None of this is awkward like I feared it might be. Not even close. It's...easy. Natural.

The road snakes through the hills, the morning light casting golden highlights over the endless stretch of heather. The view never fails to catch me off guard, no matter how many times I drive through.

"Wow," Isla whispers from the backseat, her nose pressed against the window. "It's so pretty."

I turn just enough to catch her expression—wide-eyed wonder, pure and unfiltered. "Just wait until you see the loch," I say, smiling. "On days like today, you can see the sky in it."

As we pull into a gravel turnout at the edge of the trailhead, Isla's excitement ramps up to near combustible levels.

Aidan catches her eyes in the rearview mirror, lifting a brow in that *dad* way of his, but there's nothing stern in his expression. If anything, it's soft. Playful. The version of Aidan that isn't all guarded silence and protective walls.

I want to see more of that version. I want to be the reason it surfaces, but rather than stew on that thought, I unbuckle and pretend like my heart isn't doing stupid things just from watching him parent his kid.

"Remember the rules, Isla," he says. "Stay where we can see you, and no running off."

"I know, *Da*," she sasses back, her enthusiasm undimmed. "Can we go now? Please?"

He nods, and we climb out of the truck. The air is cool and clean, laced with pine and damp earth. I open Isla's door, reaching in just as she wriggles out of her seatbelt, all uncoordinated limbs and boundless energy.

"Hold on, I've got you." I scoop her up before she can launch herself into the air. She giggles the second her boots hit the ground.

I crouch instinctively, tugging her jacket straight and brushing her hair out of her face like I've done it a hundred times before. It's only when I rise that I notice Aidan standing a few steps away, motionless.

His gaze is fixed on me, brows drawn, lips parted. He looks...surprised.

Crap. I didn't think. I just moved. Did I step over some invisible line?

"I—" I start, but he shakes his head almost immediately, the tension draining from his shoulders. And then it happens.

A smile. Not wide, but real. It's like the sun breaking through clouds.

"Thank you," he says quietly. His gaze lingers for a moment, taking in what I just did in a way that feels more profound than I anticipated.

I try to hold his gaze, but it's too much. Too tender. I look down, not because I'm unsure, but because I'm *too* sure.

Don't read into it, I tell myself.

Ha.

Too late.

Before either of us can say another word, a small hand slips into mine.

"Come on!" Isla chirps, tugging me toward the trailhead. "Are there birds here? What about squirrels? Do you think we'll see a fox?"

Her sweet voice is full of wonder, and just like that, the moment passes, tucked away between heartbeats.

I let her lead me forward, the warmth of her hand still in mine. Aidan falls into step beside us, his usual stoic expression absent as he watches his daughter eventually skip ahead, pointing out every interesting rock and flower she spots.

"Isla, remember what I said," he calls out as she starts to veer off the path.

"I know!" she shouts back.

There's something so endearing about witnessing this gruff, guarded man transform into a patient, attentive father. I've had glimpses, but it's a side of him I hadn't fully grasped until now.

"She's got a lot of energy," I say, casting a sidelong glance at Aidan.

He nods, eyes trained on her. "Aye, that she does."

His hands stay tucked in his pockets, broad shoulders slightly hunched against the morning chill. I keep pace beside him, all too aware of the space between us. It isn't much, just a few inches of cool air, but it might as well be a canyon. I want to close it. I want to feel the brush of his knuckles against mine. His fingers curling around my hand.

He doesn't reach for me, though, so I tuck my own hands deeper into my coat, pretending I'm not hoping. Pretending my chest doesn't ache a little.

I sneak another glance at him, and it's silly how much I

wish he'd look back. Just to meet my eyes and let me believe, for one second, that maybe he wants to reach for me, too.

Isla's chatter floats ahead of us, her voice bright against the backdrop of the wind. I do my best to focus on her excitement, laughing as she asks if bears roam around here. "No bears, just the occasional sheep!" I reply, but my thoughts keep drifting back to the space between Aidan and me.

I stifle a sigh. Maybe I'm overthinking it. I'm fairly certain this is just who Aidan is. Very careful, quiet, always keeping his cards tucked close.

That tiny flutter of hope beneath my skin won't settle, and yet...I get it.

We're here with Isla. That's the priority. She's Aidan's whole world wrapped up in tiny legs scrambling over roots and endless questions. I don't want to pull focus or tilt the delicate balance he's worked so hard to protect. Today should be carefree and untouched by the complicated tangle of adult feelings.

So I keep my smile in place and my steps light, even as my fingers itch with the need to reach for something that isn't mine to take.

The trees begin to thin ahead of us, the trail opening just enough to reveal glints of water shimmering in the morning sun. Isla lets out a delighted gasp, skipping ahead to press closer to the view.

"I can see it!" Isla's eyes are wide with wonder as she inches toward the water lapping gently at the rocky shore. "Can we go closer?"

"We can, but you've got to hold my hand," Aidan replies. He extends his arm, and Isla grabs onto him, her tiny fingers disappearing into his larger grip.

I hang back for a moment, letting the distance stretch so I can take them in.

Isla's tugging him toward the edge of the loch with all her

might. Aidan's as alert as ever, watching the ground and every step she takes, a silent sentry in jeans and worn boots.

It's not just protective—it's instinctive, and it unravels me a little more every time I see it.

The way he moves beside her. The way he crouches without hesitation to steady her as she leans toward the water. The way his hand lands lightly on her back, fingers splayed like a shield. There's something fiercely masculine about it, all rough edges tempered by tenderness, and it hits me right in the heart.

"Come see, Lucy. The water's so cold!" Isla calls.

Aidan lifts his head, eyes meeting mine, and for a second, I forget how to breathe.

There's a softness there, tucked behind the usual restraint. I see it. I *feel* it. Then he turns back to Isla, grounding her with a quiet word as she squeals and dips her fingers into the loch.

The breeze drifts over me as I make my way toward them. Isla beams up at me, cheeks flushed.

"Touch it," she urges, pointing eagerly at the water.

I crouch down to dip my fingers in, and the cold bites, sending a jolt that makes me laugh in surprise. "Wow, you weren't kidding!" I shake the water from my hand as Isla bursts into giggles.

Aidan chuckles low under his breath, and the sound hits me somewhere embarrassingly deep. I want to hear it again, just to feel it ripple through me like that.

"It's a loch," he says dryly, one corner of his mouth lifting. "It's always cold."

"Can we find rocks to skip?" Isla asks.

Aidan nods. "If you can find some flat ones."

Without missing a beat, she bolts toward a pile of stones near the shore, sorting through them. The sheer determination in her tiny frame makes me laugh.

"She's got the right idea," I say, rising to my feet and brushing off my jeans.

Aidan watches her movements for a moment before turning his focus back to me. "She likes you, you know."

"I like her, too," I manage, a little breathless from how close he's standing. "Her dad's not half bad, either."

That earns me a crooked grin. "Is that so?"

I shrug, feigning nonchalance even as my heart does somersaults. "Aye. Don't let it go to your head."

"Too late," he murmurs.

A flush creeps up my neck, but before I can respond, Isla comes bounding back, her hands overflowing with stones.

Aidan crouches down to her level, examining the rocks with exaggerated seriousness. "Well done, lass. These look perfect for skipping."

I catch myself staring as he patiently demonstrates, suddenly feeling like I'm on the outside, watching something that's so personal between them. The bond they share is undeniable, and it makes me wonder if I could ever find my place within it. Just then, Aidan's gaze darts in my direction. I quickly look away, redirecting my attention to Isla's animated chatter instead.

Even as I try to shift my focus, I feel his pull. It's not the kind of thing you can ignore, and in that moment, I realize just how much I want to be a part of it.

"Lucy, come try!" Isla's voice rings out, as if she can read my thoughts.

I glance over at her as Aidan looks up, too, a faint smirk dancing on his lips as he watches me.

I hesitate for a moment, then shrug. "Why not?"

I move toward the water's edge, squatting down to pick up a smooth, flat stone. I've done this a million times as a kid, but definitely not recently. I take a breath, steadying my hand.

I flick my wrist, and the stone glides effortlessly across the water, skipping three, four times before sinking.

Isla's jaw drops. "Whoa."

Aidan's expression shifts to one of amusement. "Not bad at all."

"I grew up with two older brothers who insisted they were rock skipping champions," I tell them. "Naturally, I couldn't let them win without a fight. We'd spend hours slinging stones into the creek behind our house, each of us claiming victory even when none of us could agree who actually won."

I choose another rock from the pile and send it flying. It skips another four times—maybe even five if I count generously—before vanishing beneath the surface with a satisfying plunk.

Isla gasps. "You're so good."

"Looks like someone's giving me a run for my money," Aidan says, casting a glance my way.

I peek back at him, and for a second, the world narrows to just his eyes on mine. The echo of laughter still hanging between us. The loch glittering like glass behind him.

I never did beat my brothers at skipping stones, but standing here with him, watching the ripples spread wide across the water, it kind of feels like I've won.

eighteen
AIDAN

I lean against a nearby tree, arms crossed, watching Isla by the water's edge. She's close enough that I can keep an eye on her but far enough that I have a moment to think. Not that my thoughts are playing nice.

Lucy kneels a few feet away, turning a flat stone over in her hand, the sunlight catching in her hair. She looks so at ease, like she's made for this place.

I shift my gaze to the hills, trying to ground myself. This was supposed to be a simple outing. But with her here...it's anything but straightforward.

"It looks like Isla is having a good time," Lucy's soft voice pulls me from my thoughts. I hadn't even noticed her come up beside me.

When I glance down at her, I'm struck by how small she is next to me. The top of her head barely brushes my shoulder, and yet, she somehow fills any space she's in more than anyone I've ever known. It's her presence. She doesn't need to take up much room to leave a mark.

It's always her eyes that really get to me, though. They're

not just expressive. They *speak*. Every time I catch her gaze, it feels like they're sharing a story, a secret. Right now, they're so bright, so damn happy, that it sends a tightness through my chest.

I nod, forcing my tone to stay even. "She loves anything with water. Always has."

She tilts her head, watching me. There's something in her gaze, something too warm, too understanding. I don't know what to do with it.

"You're a really good dad," she says gently.

The words land like a punch to the gut. I look away, jaw tightening. "I just do what I can."

She doesn't respond right away, just keeps studying me like she's trying to decide whether to push or let it go.

"Still," she says after a moment, "it shows."

The silence that follows isn't uncomfortable, but it's heavy. Too heavy and filled with unspoken thoughts I'm not ready to voice.

She hasn't asked for details about Isla's mum yet, which surprises me. I half expected her to, the way anyone else would. But she hasn't said a word. Not once.

Most people would've pried by now. It's a natural question, one I've answered a hundred times. Lucy just…lets me be. I don't know what to make of it. I almost want to tell her everything just to get it out of my system. At the same time, I'm relieved she hasn't asked. Some things are easier left buried.

That's the thing, though. *She* makes me want to dig them up.

I shift my weight, the rough tree bark biting into my shoulder. Before I can dwell on it further, a splash and a delighted squeal pull my attention back to Isla. I snap my gaze to her, relief flooding through me at the distraction. She's grinning, clearly having the time of her life.

"Daddy, look!" she calls out, holding up a dripping stone. "I found a sparkly one!"

I force a grin, anything to push the weight of the moment between me and Lucy aside. "That's a good one, love. Nice find."

The heavy thoughts can wait. Right now, there's nothing more important than Isla's laughter carrying over the water, the pure joy lighting up her face as she darts through the shallows. Her world is small and simple and safe, made up of smooth stones and cold water and the comfort of people who love her.

She comes barreling toward us, breathless and holding a glinting stone high.

Then she veers—not to me, but Lucy.

Lucy lowers to meet her, her voice enthusiastic as she leans in to examine the stone like it's the most important thing in the world. Isla beams, soaking it up like sunlight.

I'm frozen. Watching.

It shouldn't matter. It's just a kid with a rock. Just a woman being kind.

But it *does* matter because that space, those little, sparkling moments of wonder and closeness, have always been mine. Me and Isla, weathering the storms. Just us. And now Lucy's standing in the middle of it, and it doesn't feel wrong at all.

I swallow hard, hands shoved deep into my pockets to stop myself from fidgeting. I force a breath.

This is what I was worried about. Not just me falling for someone, but Isla, too. She looks at Lucy as if she trusts her. It's happening too fast, and I'm fucking terrified that this could be real. That I could want it enough to forget all the ways things fall apart or that Isla could start to depend on her. If Lucy ever decides to walk away, what then?

What happens when Isla turns to show her another sparkly stone and Lucy's not there to see it?

Isla continues to chatter about the rock. It's sweet. So damn innocent, but she's too young to know what it means to let people in. She hasn't learned that people can leave you even when they swear they won't. They don't mean to hurt you, but they do, anyway.

And sometimes, they just stop showing up.

I step forward, trying to shove the wariness and fear somewhere deep and unreachable. Lucy is anything but a threat, and I won't let my own damage shape the way Isla loves people.

Christ, this is hard. I'm losing control, but I'm the one who invited someone into our world. I opened a door and didn't think about how I'd close it if I had to.

Because that's the thing. I *did* open it. *I* let her in.

I did it because some reckless, aching part of me wondered if maybe, this time, it could be different. I knew it wouldn't be easy, but I didn't expect it to hurt like hell, either.

In the end, I'm the one who's going to keep opening the door. I'm the one who'll let her come back until her laugh becomes part of our story.

All I can do now is hope that she's not just passing through.

nineteen

LUCY

The walk back to the car is quieter. Isla skips ahead, humming to herself and blissfully unaware while I trail behind, stealing glances at Aidan.

He's not looking at me.

His jaw is clenched so tight, grinding back whatever's on his mind. It could be nothing. Maybe it's just end-of-day fatigue. Or maybe...it's me.

I thought we'd been having a good time. There were smiles. Laughter. That moment by the water, where it felt like something had shifted. I thought I could sense that he wanted more by the way he looked at me, except now he's miles away, and I don't know how to bridge the gap without making it worse.

Did I misread the whole day? Was I too much? Too present, too eager, too in it?

I want to grab his hand, force the words out, ask him what's wrong, but I also don't want to push him further into whatever shell he's retreating into. So, I just keep walking, heart sinking with every step, wishing he'd look at me the way he did earlier.

This was probably a bad idea. I never meant to cross a line.

I just didn't realize it was there until I was already on the other side of it.

"Aidan," I start softly, not wanting Isla to overhear. "I hope I didn't overstep. I know this is your time with Isla, and I—"

He cuts me off with a terse shake of his head. "It's fine."

Judging by the way his gaze slides away instead of meeting mine, it doesn't seem fine. His tone is controlled in that way people get when they're trying to put distance between you without saying it outright.

"You didn't do anything," he adds, his voice still clipped.

I flinch. It's subtle, just a small shift in my posture, but he notices. His storm cloud eyes finally come back to mine, the muscle in his jaw ticking.

Still, he doesn't try to explain or soften the edges. Just leaves the words hanging there between us.

I swallow hard, pressing the burn in my chest into something smaller, something more manageable. *This isn't about me.* It's what I tell myself as I look away. This is his daughter, his world. I'm just orbiting it, and I have to respect that. Even if it hurts a bit. Or a lot.

"Okay." I force a small smile that feels like it might crack. "If you're sure."

We continue walking in silence. Isla hums ahead of us, hopping over roots and stones like this is still just a perfect day. Then, just before we reach the car, Aidan stops short.

"Lucy," he says, finally turning to me. "I'm not... I'm not good at this."

I look up at him, heart thrumming. "At what?"

He exhales slowly. His eyes meet mine, and for once, they don't look away. "Letting people in."

And there it is. Not an invitation. Not quite a warning, either. Just the truth.

I wait, holding my breath, afraid to break whatever fragile

thread of honesty that's making him open up. My heart beats faster, but I keep quiet, letting the silence stretch, needing him to keep going.

"If it's all right," he finally continues, "I'll see if I can drop Isla off with my mum for a bit. I'd like to, uh...have some time. With you."

He shifts his weight, rubbing the back of his neck as if he's not sure how to handle what he just said. It's clear he's out of his depth with his guard down. It's vulnerable. Unexpected. And kind of ridiculously charming.

Here's the thing about me, though. When I get nervous, I laugh. Not a cute, contained little giggle. No, it's breathless, irrepressible, mortifying laughter. It's not a choice. It just... happens.

And this? Aidan, after shutting down and shutting me out, suddenly offering time alone? My brain short-circuits. My heart skips a beat. My stomach does a backflip. Then, I laugh.

It starts as a tiny huff, bubbling up, unstoppable. A full-blown hoot tumbles out of me. I slap a hand over my mouth, but it's too late.

Aidan's brows pull together, his head tilting slightly. His gaze drops to my mouth, eyes searching, probably wondering if I'm laughing *at* him.

"Sorry!" I manage between gasps, wiping tears from my eyes. "I'm not laughing at you. I just... I do this when I get nervous."

He blinks, processing, before his mouth tugs into that slow, reluctant smile I've started to crave. His shoulders ease just a little, and the heaviness between us vanishes.

"Should I consider that a *maybe* to spending some time with me?" he asks dryly.

Just like that, I can breathe again. I should probably be

concerned that a mere half smile from him feels like the only thing I need to exist, but...well, here we are.

I take a deep breath, attempting to quell the laughter still threatening to bubble over. "Aye, you can consider it a maybe," I tease.

"I'll take it."

Just then, Isla comes bounding back to us. "Daddy, can we get ice cream?"

He winces. "Not today, love. How about you go spend some time with Nana instead?"

"Oh, yes! She'll get me ice cream!"

Aidan rolls his eyes, even though there's nothing but affection in his gaze.

"I think you're outnumbered," I joke.

He shakes his head. "Don't remind me."

We approach the truck, and Isla scrambles into her seat. Aidan is quick, already there, guiding her and clicking the straps into place.

"Not too tight?" he asks, his voice softening as he checks the fit.

"Nope! Perfect," she chirps, swinging her feet and beaming up at him.

He slides into the driver's seat, adjusting the rearview mirror and glancing at Isla as she launches into a monologue about the merits of sprinkles versus chocolate sauce.

Aidan drives with one hand on the wheel, the other resting casually on the center console. Though his eyes are fixed on the road ahead, I catch the faintest twitch of his lips every now and then, the smallest sign that he's tuned into every word Isla is saying.

His mum's house looks like it always smells of roses and fresh laundry. All stone walls and flowerpots, with ivy climbing one side. Isla's already halfway out of her seat before we're in park, her fingers fumbling at the buckle as I roll down my window.

"Well, hello there!" Aileen calls, stepping onto the path with open arms.

Aidan gets out of the truck and has barely set Isla down on her feet before she launches herself into her grandmother's embrace. "Daddy says you'll get me ice cream!"

Her gaze lifts to Aidan with a smirk. "Did he now?"

Aidan shrugs, and there's something boyish in the way he does it. "She negotiated better terms than I could offer."

"Mmm," she hums, clearly amused, and then her gaze slides to me.

"Hello there, Lucy."

I tuck a piece of hair behind my ear, suddenly feeling like a teenager being sized up for intentions I haven't even fully admitted to myself. Which is absurd. It's not like that.

Except maybe it is. A little.

I've known Aidan's mum for a while now. She comes into the café from time to time, but showing up *with* Aidan like this is...new.

I give her a wave from the truck before Isla starts chattering away about ice cream. Aidan ruffles her hair before she dashes inside, then heads back toward me. He gets in the truck but doesn't move to drive just yet. He sits there, forearms balanced on the steering wheel, eyes fixed on something in the distance. His knuckles flex white then relax as he stares straight ahead.

"I'm sorry," he says finally, voice rough like he had to drag the words up from somewhere deep. "For earlier. At the loch."

I study his profile, the strong line of his jaw, the slight furrow between his brows.

"You don't have to apologize."

"I do." He turns to face me then, and the rawness in his expression steals my breath. "You deserve that much."

His hand slides off the steering wheel, hovering in the space between us before settling on mine, finally gifting me the contact I've been craving all day. His palm is warm, calloused in places that tell stories of hard work and long days.

"Seeing you with Isla... The way she looks at you," he starts, then pauses, searching for words. "It's a lot."

My heart drops. "Too much?"

He shakes his head slowly. "No. That's the problem."

His thumb moves over my knuckles, an absentminded back and forth that seems to ground him, and somehow me along with him. Nothing has ever felt so *right*.

AIDAN

Her hand in mine is everything, and yet, it isn't enough. Every inch of me wants to trace the line of her arm, to feel her pressed closer.

I tighten my grip just slightly, testing the boundary. She doesn't pull away.

Every sense is keyed to her—the soft press of her hand, the faint scent of vanilla. I steal a glance, letting my eyes linger, memorizing the curve of her smile, the tilt of her jaw.

We've been silent since I started driving, but I haven't felt the need to speak. It's been...comfortable.

When Lucy finally speaks, her voice is careful. "So, um... where are we going?"

Oh, shit. That probably would've been good to mention before now.

"Sorry," I say quickly, clearing my throat. "I really didn't have a plan. I thought we could head to my place?"

As soon as the words are out, they sit there between us, too open-ended. What if she thinks that's arrogant?

She turns to look at me, but I don't dare look back. My

heart is doing that uneven, off-beat thing it does when I feel too much while trying to feel nothing at all.

Fuck, I'm making a mess of this.

"It's nothing fancy," I add quickly, trying to keep my tone even. "Just quieter than town. Easier to talk."

She nods slowly. "Okay."

This whole thing is messy, and I know it. I've spent years keeping things neat, keeping people out. Now here I am, inviting her in, because I can't seem to help myself?

"You don't have to," I say before I can stop myself. "If it's too much—"

"Aidan," she cuts in, a playful lilt in her voice. "Are you always this nervous when you invite a girl over to see your... what? Record collection? Fishing trophies?"

Her eyes sparkle with mischief, and the tension in my chest eases slightly.

"I don't have either of those things," I admit, the corner of my mouth tugging upward. "I'm not some mysterious bloke with hidden collections," I add, trying to ignore the way her teasing makes me feel lighter. "Just a normal house. Probably a lot more kid's toys than you're expecting."

"I beg to differ on the mysterious part, but I'm looking forward to seeing it," she says before tightening her fingers around mine.

I keep my eyes on the road, following the familiar curves through the hills, but then I look over and immediately wish I hadn't.

Her shirt clings to her chest under her unzipped jacket, and I catch the slow rise and fall of her breaths.

Heat punches low in my gut, enough that I shift in my seat, trying to ease the pressure building in my jeans. My grip on the wheel tightens, knuckles whitening.

She has no idea what she does to me. Or how close I am to

missing a turn because my cock's reacting faster than my common sense.

She bites her lip while lost in her own thoughts. It's the third time today, and every damn time, it chips away at my restraint. Doesn't matter that it's probably just something she does without thinking. My body doesn't care. My mind sure as hell doesn't care. All I can focus on is the shape of her mouth, soft and flushed and so damn tempting it's bordering on cruel.

If I grip the wheel any tighter, it's going to snap. I'm trying like hell to ground myself in anything other than the image of her lips caught between her teeth. The things I'd do if I let myself close the space between us... To lean over. To taste her. To lose myself for one goddamn second.

She doesn't know how close I am to unraveling.

We're finally rolling to a stop as I pull into the driveway. One hand eases off the wheel, but the other stays tightly clasped in hers.

"We're here," I say.

When I turn to her, it hits me all over again. God, she's beautiful. Her hair falls loose above her shoulders, catching the late afternoon light like it's made for it. The way she's looking at me now—open, patient, a little nervous—makes me want to pull her closer and find out if she tastes as sweet as she looks.

"What is it?" she asks, her voice barely above a whisper.

I want to trace the curve of her cheek with my knuckles just to see if she'd lean into it like I'm dying for her to. But I don't, because if I start, I won't stop. It wouldn't be fair to either of us.

"Nothing," I mutter, dragging my gaze away. "Just...come on in."

I reluctantly let go of her hand to climb out of the truck, rounding the hood to meet her as she steps down.

I place a hand at the small of her back as we make our way to the porch. The garden's a bit wild, overgrown in spots where

I haven't had time to tame it, but there's something about the way Lucy looks at it that makes me see it differently.

"It's lovely," she says, her eyes sweeping over the climbing roses and unruly hedges.

"It's a work in progress," I correct her, fishing my keys from my pocket.

The lock sticks a bit, and I have to jiggle the key before the door swings open. I step aside to let her in. "It's not much," I mutter. "But it's home."

She steps inside, and all I can do is watch her.

Her gaze drifts slowly across the room, taking in the worn leather couch, the coffee table cluttered with Isla's crayons and paper scraps, the framed photos lined up with a kind of crooked pride along the mantle. She lingers on one of Isla beaming, curls everywhere, watermelon juice staining her cheeks from last summer.

"It's really nice, Aidan," she says. "Lived in. Homey."

I don't know what to do with that, or with the way she's standing here, in my space, fitting into it so perfectly.

She moves farther into the room, fingertips trailing over the back of the couch. I track the movement, every inch, heat curling low in my stomach that has nothing to do with lust and everything to do with how goddamn vulnerable this feels.

"Can I get you something to drink?" I ask. "Water? Tea?"

She turns to face me, a polite smile playing at her lips. "Tea would be nice, thank you."

"Milk? Sugar?" I ask, already half turned toward the kitchen.

"Just a splash of milk," she says.

I nod, walking through the house. The moment the kettle's on, I brace my palms against the counter, bowing my head for a second. *Breathe.* Get it together. It's just tea. Just a woman standing in my living room who somehow makes it feel smaller and fuller at the same time.

By the time I return with two steaming mugs in hand, she's drifted toward the mantle, fingers grazing the edge of a framed photo. Her head tilts slightly as she studies it.

"She was the most beautiful baby," she says softly, eyes fixed on a photo of Isla with chubby cheeks and a sun hat two sizes too big. "She has your eyes. It's one of the first things I noticed."

I hand her the mug, and she takes it gently, both hands cradling the ceramic. Her fingers absently trace the handle.

I clear my throat, just to break the silence. "She was a handful. Even back then. Hated naps. Loved throwing food."

Her eyes lift to mine, and her lips twitch like she's fighting a smile before she steps away from the mantle, lowering herself onto the couch.

I hesitate long enough for her to notice. Then I follow, easing down onto the opposite end, leaving more space than necessary between us.

"I don't bite, you know," she teases. "I'm not really sure what's going on with *you* today, but I can say with certainty, that won't be a problem."

That pulls a laugh out of me. "I'll keep that in mind."

The couch creaks softly as she shifts, curling one leg beneath her. She's still watching me, but she doesn't press. She just sips her tea and waits.

It's time for me to say something. The words are right there, but they get stuck somewhere between my lungs and my throat. Once they're out, there's no taking them back.

"Look, I..." I exhale sharply, shaking my head. "I'm not good at talking. Or any of it, really."

She takes another slow sip of her tea, watching me over the

rim. "Mmhmm," she hums, finally lowering the mug. "You've mentioned that."

I nod, swallowing hard. "Aye. I don't know where to start."

She leans forward slightly, the movement bringing her a breath closer, and a hint of vanilla reaches me, mingling with the scent of tea. "Start with what you're thinking right now."

I study her for a moment, caught between wanting to bolt and wanting to stay. I really *don't* know how to do this.

"I think I'm going to mess this up," I admit, the words rough. "Whatever this is."

She nods slowly, her eyes never leaving mine. "And what do you think *this* is?"

The question hangs between us, loaded with possibilities I'm not sure I'm ready to face. "I don't know," I admit. I'm choosing to be honest, even if it makes me sound like a coward. "I just know it feels different when you're around."

Her head tilts, just a little. "Different how?"

I exhale slowly. "When you're with us, me and Isla...things feel lighter. Like maybe everything isn't such a mess."

Her brows lift slightly, not in shock, more like she didn't expect me to say it out loud. Hell, I didn't expect me to say it out loud.

"I've spent so long keeping our world small," I continue, the words coming easier now. "Just me and Isla against everything else. It made sense to keep it that way." I meet her gaze, allowing myself to really look at her. "Now I'm starting to think that maybe we're missing something. That maybe having people like you in our lives wouldn't be such a bad thing."

Her smile spreads slowly, lighting up her face as she sets her mug down on the coffee table. "I'd like that," she says softly. "Being in your lives, I mean."

My hand rests on the couch between us, and I'm acutely

aware of how close her fingers are to mine. Just a few inches of worn leather separating us.

"You know," she continues, "when I first met you, I thought you were just..." She pauses, searching for the right word.

"Difficult?" I offer with a wry smile.

She laughs. "I was going to say *reserved*, but sure, difficult works, too."

I can't help but chuckle at that. "Fair enough."

The teasing light in her gaze softens into something more serious. "Then I saw you with Isla, and I saw a different side of you. You looked at her like she's your whole world, Aidan. So patient with her, even when she's driving you crazy." She pauses. "It made me want to know that version of you more."

The words land between us with a weight that makes it hard to breathe.

"I'm not..."

I'm not...what. Not good? Not ready? Not enough? I don't even know what I'm trying to say.

Lucy's expression remains open in that way that makes it hard to look at her and even harder to look away. She doesn't rush in to patch the silence.

I let out a breath that scrapes its way out of my chest. "I don't always get it right," I finally say. "With her. With any of it."

Her mouth curves into a small smile. "No one does."

I'm not sure who the hell I thought I was fooling by pretending I hadn't already made the decision that I want to try this with her.

I've spent so long trying not to need things for myself. But this? Her? I want to know what it looks like to let her in. And not just around the edges, not just in the cracks when I'm too tired to hold it all together. I want the whole thing.

So instead of reaching for all the heavy shit again, I lean

into the one thing I haven't let myself have in a while. Curiosity.

"So," I say, "tell me something I don't know about Lucy MacKenzie."

A soft chuckle escapes her lips. "Okay," she says, leaning forward just slightly. "Here's one. I can't ride a bike."

"You're joking."

Her grin only widens. "Nope," she says, shaking her head, "I never learned. Knox and Callan tried to teach me once when I was a kid, but I fell and broke my wrist. I swore I'd never get on one again, and I stuck to it."

A low chuckle rumbles from my chest, and for a second, the sound surprises me, but it feels good. "You run a whole café by yourself, but you're scared of a bike?"

She rolls her eyes. "It's not about fear. It's about principles. Besides, I'm perfectly content walking everywhere."

"So, you've never taken a road trip on a bike, then? Experienced the wind in your hair, the freedom of the open road?" I lean back into the couch, finding myself more relaxed than I've been all day.

"I've managed to experience plenty of freedom without risking life and limb, thank you very much." She smirks at me. "Your turn. Tell me something I don't know about Aidan."

I take a slow sip of tea, buying myself a second to think. Not because I don't have answers, but because I don't have the kind you give when someone's looking at you like that. Like they might actually care what you say.

"I can play the guitar," I offer. "Or I used to, anyway."

Her eyebrows lift, and her whole face brightens. "Really? I wouldn't have pegged you for a musician."

"I'm not." I huff a laugh. "Just something I picked up in school. I played around with it for a few years but haven't touched it much since Isla came along."

"Do you still have one?"

I nod toward the hallway. "In the closet somewhere. Gathering dust."

"You should play for Isla sometime. I bet she'd love it."

I nod again, slower this time. "Maybe."

I've thought about it. I just haven't had the time, or hell, maybe the permission to want something that small and personal for myself.

"You should play me something," she says, nudging her foot against mine lightly. "Maybe not tonight. But sometime."

I raise a brow. "And what would I play? Some soft acoustic ballad to sweep you off your feet?"

"I mean, if you have one in your repertoire, I wouldn't complain."

"I'm more of a 'poorly tuned strings' kind of guy," I deadpan.

"Oh, be still my heart." She leans back dramatically, hand over her chest. "Next you'll tell me you sing off-key, too."

"I do," I say without missing a beat. "You've been warned."

She laughs, head tipping back, and the sound hits me square in the chest. God, she's something else.

"You're ruining the fantasy, you know," she teases, eyes dancing.

"Good," I mutter, leaning back into the cushions beside her. "You don't want to build up expectations I'll never live up to."

"Oh, Aidan." She shakes her head. "You don't even know, do you?"

"Know what?"

Her eyes catch mine, steady and sure. "You've already far surpassed any expectations I had."

twenty-one
LUCY

We've been talking for hours, drifting from easy, surface-level conversation to the corners of his world he doesn't usually invite anyone into. The only time we stopped was when my stomach growled loud enough to make both of us laugh, and we realized it was time to order food before I embarrassed myself further.

Somewhere between the laughs and eating, I learn his middle name is Hamish—delivered with a reluctant shrug because he was half embarrassed to share it. As if Janet is any better.

Then he drops a detail that sticks. As a kid, his mum used to call him "Aidy-Pie." It's absurdly sweet, and I catch myself smiling before I can stop it. The way his eyes flicker with something almost shy makes me want to catalog every little thing about him.

I notice the stack of books on the end table after that—old Scottish poetry, spines worn soft. He tells me he always cleans his glasses twice before reading, a habit he can't break. I tuck that detail away, too.

Somewhere in the soft hush of the evening, I realize I'm already holding onto these pieces of him that don't need loud declarations. To me, it's these little moments that matter the most.

"Can I ask you something?" I finally say as we're winding down. "You don't have to answer if you don't want to."

He gives me a wary look, but nods.

I take a deep breath, gathering my courage. "What happened with Isla's mother?"

The question hangs in the air between us, heavy and unavoidable. Aidan's expression shifts immediately.

For a moment, I don't think he's going to answer. His eyes darken, focusing on some distant point beyond me, and I can almost see the walls rebuilding themselves brick by brick.

"I'm sorry," I say quickly. "I shouldn't have asked that. You don't have to—"

"No," he interrupts. "It's all right."

He leans forward, elbows resting on his knees, hands clasped together. When he finally speaks, each word seems carefully measured.

"Her name is Emily." A muscle in his jaw twitches. "Our relationship moved fast. She got pregnant after only a few months together."

I stay perfectly still, afraid that any movement might make him stop.

"We tried to make it work, but she didn't want this life. Didn't want the responsibility. Said she wasn't cut out for it."

My throat tightens, and my vision blurs as tears well in my eyes. I blink rapidly, trying to hold them back, but one escapes, sliding down my cheek before I can catch it.

"She really just...left?" My voice breaks on the last word.

I can't fathom walking away from that beautiful little girl

with her wild curls and endless questions. From Aidan, who clearly gives everything he has to being a good father.

There are so many people who would give anything to have what she did. People like *me*.

Aidan's eyes snap to my face, catching that single, stubborn tear. "Some people aren't meant for this kind of life," he says, his voice carefully controlled.

I shake my head, the ache spilling over. "That doesn't make it okay."

"No," he agrees. "It doesn't."

He shifts beside me, closing the distance, and suddenly, I'm caught in the heat radiating off him. His hand moves slowly, hesitant, asking permission without words. Then his thumb brushes the tear away, so light it steals my breath.

"You're crying for us," he says, a quiet kind of wonder threading through the roughness in his voice.

I lean into his touch before I even realize I'm doing it. "Of course I am."

His palm cups my cheek now, and I can feel a slight tremor in his fingers. "Lucy…"

His eyes drop down to my lips, and the whole world shrinks. Breathing feels like a stranger, and every instinct screams at me to close the space that's been hovering for too long.

Before the doubt claws its way in, I lean in, closing the last inch, and press my lips to his.

For one heart-stopping moment, he freezes, and I'm afraid I've made a terrible mistake. My heart clenches, bracing for the rejection that I'm sure is coming. Then his hand slides from my cheek to the back of my neck, pulling me closer with an urgency that ignites a wildfire inside me.

His lips are softer than I imagined, but the kiss itself is anything but gentle. It's hungry and desperate, like he's been starved for this and I'm the first taste of something that finally fills him. His mouth moves against mine with a fevered need.

His hand tangles in my hair, tugging me closer. I fold into him without thinking, meeting the heat of his mouth as the kiss deepens. A sigh escapes me, and the moment it slips free, he smiles against my lips. A satisfied curve that tells me he heard every ounce of want in it.

I slide my hands to his chest, feeling the rapid beat of his heart beneath my fingertips, the hard, comforting rhythm that only amplifies my own racing pulse. I could get lost in the way his mouth moves against mine, in the way everything else falls away—the noise, the world, everything that's not this.

When we break apart, both of us breathless, his forehead rests against mine.

"I've wanted to do that for a while now," he confesses, his voice a low rumble that vibrates through me.

I smile, running my fingers through the short hair at the nape of his neck. "Me, too."

He pulls back, his gaze searching mine. "This changes things."

"I know," I whisper, because I do. This isn't just about us. There's Isla to consider, and all the hurdles that come with letting someone new into their carefully constructed world.

"If this goes wrong—" he starts, but I reach up, pressing my fingers gently against his lips, stopping the words before they can form.

"Don't," I whisper. "We don't have to figure it all out right now."

His eyes hold mine. There's a battle waging inside him—fear warring with something that looks dangerously like hope.

"I'm not going anywhere, Aidan," I say softly. "Not unless you want me to. And I promise to be so careful where Isla is concerned."

He takes my hand, pulling it away from his lips but not letting go. His thumb traces slow circles against my palm, sending tingles up my arm.

"I'm thirty-five years old, Lucy."

"Okay?"

"You're...twenty-five."

"I am," I say, still not seeing the issue.

He lets out a heavy breath. "That's ten years between us. When you were finishing university, I was changing nappies and working double shifts."

There's a spark of frustration flaming inside me. After the way he just kissed me like I was as essential as the breaths he takes, he's hung up on birth years?

"Is that supposed to matter to me?"

"Shouldn't it?" His thumb stills against my palm. "I'm at a different stage in life. I've got the baggage to prove it. You deserve someone who—"

"No," I interrupt, my voice firm. "I deserve someone who makes me happy. Aidan, I'm not some naive girl who doesn't know what she wants," I continue, shifting closer. "I run my own business. I make my own decisions. And I'm choosing to be here."

He searches my face, and I let him see everything. The certainty, the want, the stubborn determination that runs through every MacKenzie that's ever walked this earth.

"Fucking hell, Lucy. I couldn't stay away if I tried."

Then he leans in again, lips meeting mine with a softness that catches me off guard. He tastes like fresh mint from the tea he was drinking, cool and grounding against the heat of our kiss.

This one isn't desperate like before. It's slower, deeper, his lips coaxing mine open with a slow sweep of his tongue teasing against mine. When we part, the room spins just a little, and

I'm dizzy with it. His fingers trace the curve of my jaw, light as a whisper.

"I should get you home," he murmurs, but he doesn't move.

"Probably," I reply, even though my body leans toward him. "Or...I could stay a little longer."

His eyes gleam with something dark that I can feel more than see. For a heartbeat, I think he's going to kiss me again. Instead, he stands slowly and reaches for my hand.

"Come on," he says.

I take it, letting him pull me to my feet. He leads me through the living room to a back door I hadn't noticed before. When he opens it, cool night air rushes in, and we step out onto a small wooden deck. The night sky stretches above us, a canvas of deep blue scattered with stars that seem close enough to touch. The moon hangs low, casting silver light across the yard and the trees beyond.

"Oh," I breathe, taking in the view. "This is beautiful."

Aidan stands beside me, his shoulder grazing mine. "It's why I bought this place."

I lean against the railing, tilting my head back to take in the vastness above us. "I can see why."

He hums low in his throat. Out here, everything slows. The questions I haven't dared ask don't feel so loud anymore.

"You ever bring anyone else out here?" I tease.

He lets out a quiet breath that might be a laugh. "No. I like the quiet. Doesn't usually make sense to share it."

"What about now?" I ask, my voice catching just a little.

His mouth curves into a near dangerous smirk. Then, slow and sure, he lifts his hand, brushing a loose strand of hair behind my ear. His fingers trail down, skimming the side of my neck, making me shiver.

He steps closer, crowding my space until my back meets the railing and he's all I can see. I let myself take him in, savoring every detail. The surprising length of his lashes, the small scar just above his brow that I must have missed before, the way his gray eyes are dimmer now, like the calm after a storm rather than the storm itself.

His hands settle on the railing, caging me in. "What do *you* think?"

I blink up at him, brain scrambling. *What do I think?*

I think my heart's somewhere in my throat, because I can't remember what I asked him. Not with his body so close that I could count the freckles dusting the bridge of his nose if I wasn't too busy staring at his mouth.

"What..." I start, then stop, because I honestly can't remember what we were talking about.

Aidan's smile widens before his mouth finds mine again. His lips move over mine with aching patience, drawing out every heartbeat, every breath. It's like he wants to make sure I feel it everywhere. And I do. God, I do.

His hand cradles the back of my neck while his thumb grazes just beneath my jaw, coaxing me closer.

The stars could be spinning above us and I wouldn't know. There's only him, his steady hands, his steady heart, and the way he kisses me like staying away was never an option at all.

twenty-two
LUCY

I'm lying in bed after Aidan dropped me off, the ghost of our kiss still dancing on my lips. The warmth lingers, a sweet burn that ignites my skin every time I think of it. His breath had mingled with mine, testing the waters, gauging whether I'd pull away. But I didn't. I couldn't.

I've never felt anything like that before. Not the heat, the intensity, and definitely not the way my heart seemed to sync with his. Every inch of me seemed to melt into him, falling into something intoxicating that felt too good to resist.

I've obviously been kissed before. Some were good, some not so much. Aidan's kiss, though... It was a revelation. No one's ever made me feel like that. Not even *close*.

I roll over, bury my face in the pillow, and try to calm the emotions swirling inside me, but it's useless. Every time I close my eyes, I see Aidan's face, feel the roughness of his stubble against my cheek, smell the faint scent of sea salt and something woodsy that clings to him.

I'm jolted awake by a sharp knock at the door. For a second, I just lay there, blinking into the dim light, disoriented and clinging to the remnants of sleep. The knock comes again, firmer this time, and I groan.

Who on earth would be here this early?

A quick glance at the clock on my dresser tells me it's not early at all. Ten o'clock? Oh no. I bolt upright, panic setting in. I was supposed to meet Bree an hour ago. I haven't slept this late...ever.

"Lucy, are you alive in there?" Bree calls, her voice cutting through the fog of my grogginess.

"Just a second!" I manage to shout back. I scramble out of bed, adrenaline kicking in as I throw on a robe, trying to appear somewhat presentable. My fingers fumble through my tangled hair, wincing at the knots that formed overnight.

When I finally swing the door open, there's Bree, arms crossed and one eyebrow raised. "Well, well, well," she says, giving me a once-over with a sly grin. "Someone had a late night."

"I'm so sorry, Bree. I completely overslept."

She waves off my apology, pushing past me into the room with an air of confidence that she always has. "I'm not here to judge your punctuality. What I am here for," she says, spinning around to face me, her smirk widening, "is to find out what—or should I say who—has you sleeping so late."

I groan, shutting the door behind her. "It's nothing like that."

Her eyes narrow, mischief dancing in them as she crosses

her arms, leaning against the back of a chair. "Mmhmm. That blush on your face says otherwise."

"It's not what you think," I insist, hoping she'll drop it. The last thing I want is to dissect what happened between Aidan and me like it's some kind of puzzle to solve.

I've never been the type to share details about things like this. It's not that I'm ashamed or anything. It's just...personal. Bree is always so open about these things, so casual in the way she talks about feelings and attraction. I envy the way she can make it all sound so simple. It's never been like that for me.

"Oh, honey." She tilts her head, her expression turning far too curious for my liking. "You don't even have to tell me. I already know that look. You've got *swept off my feet* written all over you."

I open my mouth to protest, but she's on a roll now, pacing the room. "Let me guess. Tall, dark, and brooding?"

"Bree," I warn, but she ignores me, plowing ahead.

She claps her hands together triumphantly. "Knew it. Spill. What happened?"

I bury my face in my hands, torn between exasperation and the tiniest urge to laugh. "You're impossible, you know that?"

"And you're stalling," she shoots back, plopping onto the edge of the couch as if she has all the time in the world. "So? Did he finally make a move? Or did you?"

"It was just a kiss," I mumble, but even as the words leave my lips, the memory of last night sends a thrill coursing through me. "Or three."

Bree gasps. "Just a kiss? Kisses with a man like that are never just anything."

I roll my eyes. As relentless as Bree can be, she's not wrong. Last night wasn't just a kiss.

I let out a sigh and sink into the seat beside her. "Fine. You're right. It was..." I trail off, searching for the right words.

How do I even begin to capture what Aidan did to me? The electric spark, the magnetic pull, the way it felt like he was everywhere all at once, and the ache that remains, even hours later?

Her expression softens, her voice turning gentler. "That good, huh?"

I nod. "I've never felt anything like it. It was like everything just stopped. Like nothing else mattered."

She doesn't laugh or tease me this time, just gives me a knowing smile.

It's short-lived, because then her eyes light up with mischief. "Was there tongue? Did he use his hands? Oh! Did he do that thing where he cups your face?"

"Bree!" My cheeks burn hotter. "I'm not going to give you a play-by-play."

Her lips press together, forming an exaggerated pout. "You're no fun. But fine, keep your steamy secrets," she teases. "Seriously, though, good for you. Mr. Tall, Dark, and Grumpy is..." She pauses, fanning herself theatrically and pretending to swoon.

I can't help but laugh, grabbing a pillow and tossing it in her direction. "I can't even with you."

"What?" She dodges easily, her grin widening. "I'm just saying. If I were you, I'd need a moment to recover, too. That man is scorching."

"His name is Aidan, by the way."

"Aidan," she repeats, testing the name. "Suits him. When are you seeing him again?"

That's the question, isn't it? The one that's been looping through my head since the moment he walked me to my door last night. Since his hand lingered on mine as if he had more to say but swallowed it down instead.

I finally have his number, but there was no talk of what comes next. No promises. No plans.

That's the part I keep circling back to over and over because Aidan doesn't strike me as the kind of man who does things halfway.

I don't even know how to start this. Do I text him first? Wait for him to reach out? Would he even want me to?

"I...don't know," I admit.

Her eyebrows shoot up. "You didn't make plans? Lucy MacKenzie, have I taught you nothing? This is dating 101. Secure the next encounter before the first one ends."

I huff out a breath. "It's not that simple. He's...guarded. He has a daughter. Plus, he works offshore for weeks at a time. It's a lot."

Bree tilts her head, considering. "So, what you're saying is, he's an emotionally unavailable part-time mermaid with baggage?"

I give her a look, but she just grins.

"Look," she continues. "Complicated doesn't mean bad. It just means you need to figure out if it's worth it."

Wanting someone has never been the hard part. It's everything that comes after. The expectations. The uncertainty. The possibility of getting it wrong.

And Aidan... He isn't something I can take lightly.

twenty-three
AIDAN

I keep saying it, but two weeks at home is never enough. I'm always trying to shove a lifetime's worth of living into fourteen days that slip through my fingers faster than I can catch them. There's always something with this damn house—an old creaky floor, a window that won't shut, pipes that think it's funny to leak when it rains. I'm constantly knee-deep in repairs, fixing up what's broken, trying to make this place solid. Something for Isla that she can count on. It almost seems useless, because every time I fix something, another thing falls apart. It's like the damn place is telling me I'm not around enough. Not doing enough.

And then there's Lucy. I don't know how the hell she managed it, but she slipped right into the middle of my world like she'd always been here. That day with her last week turned into me finding excuses to text her, and she's popped over here a few evenings after work. Nothing serious, just hanging out for an hour or so, her laugh filling the house whenever Isla says something ridiculous, her smile patient when I'm trying too hard to be tough.

Sometimes, it's like she's the only thing that lets me breathe, like she's the calm in the middle of all this chaos. She's got this way of making me feel like maybe I'm doing something right for once.

Tomorrow, I'm back to work. Yet here I am, up in the attic trying to patch up another leak before the storm hits. The thick, dusty air settles in my lungs, the musty smell of old wood sticking to my skin. Sweat trickles along my temple as I fight this beam that clearly has a personal problem with me. Frustration flares, but I crush it and stay at it.

Then Isla's giggles drift up from the lower level, bright and sweet, spilling through the floorboards, tangled up with Lucy's softer laugh. The sound slips right past my defenses, making the tension in my shoulders loosen.

Having Lucy here is strange sometimes, but nice, too. Too nice if I'm being honest with myself. I keep waiting for the moment when she realizes it's too much and decides she's had enough. But she hasn't pulled away. She's still here, laughing with Isla, wanting to be a part of this.

That's what scares the hell out of me. I don't want to start leaning on or depending on her, but there's no ignoring how damn good it is to have her here.

Tomorrow, Isla will miss me, but she's used to that. She's learned how to deal with me being gone. But Lucy? Hell, I don't know how this thing works with her. How long is she going to keep showing up and finding something in us worth sticking around for when I'm gone all the time?

The thought of Lucy slipping away nearly knocks the wind out of me. I shove the notion down and force my focus back to what I'm working on. That's the only thing that's ever made sense, anyway. Fix what's in front of me, do my part, and hope to god it'll be enough this time.

I'm so deep in my head that I almost don't hear the creak of the attic stairs. Lucy pops up through the trapdoor.

"Thought you might need a break," she says, lifting a thermos. "I made some tea."

I set the hammer down and swipe the back of my hand across my brow, smearing sweat and sawdust together. I probably look rough, sweat soaked and grime streaked. "Thanks," I mumble.

She makes her way across the attic, careful with each step, weaving around the stacks of old boxes and forgotten furniture. When she finally reaches me, she hands over the thermos, her fingers skimming mine just long enough to send a sharp jolt through me.

"You look like you've been through a war up here."

I crack the lid open, the steam carrying the tea's scent into the stale air. "Feels like it," I mutter, taking a sip. The warmth settles low in my stomach, but it's got nothing on the heat rising the second I realize she's still looking at me.

Her gaze lingers at first, almost like she doesn't mean to get caught. Yet she doesn't look away. Her cheeks go a little pink, and she tucks a loose strand of hair away as her eyes drift over the sweat clinging to my skin, the dust smudged across my forearm.

She tilts her head, offering a small, uncertain smile. "You, um… You clean up nice, I bet. Not that you need to. I just mean…" Her words knot together, and she bites her lip. "It suits you. The whole…hardworking thing."

I lift a brow, sip my tea, and let a smirk tug at my mouth. Watching her scramble for footing is kind of cute.

"I'll have you know, I clean up just fine."

She laughs softly, and the sound echoes in the cramped space, making everything feel a little less dusty, a little less worn. "I don't doubt it for a second."

I take another sip, watching her over the rim of the thermos. She looks out of place up here, too bright for all this darkness.

Lucy shifts her weight, her fingers fidgeting with the hem of her shirt. "So...you'll be gone for three weeks this time?"

I nod, setting the thermos down on a nearby box. "Yeah. Longer rotation."

She doesn't say anything for a moment, just looks at me with those eyes that see too much. Then, "We'll miss you."

She reaches up, brushing a bit of dust from my shoulder, her touch lingering for a moment before she pulls back. I stare at the empty space where her hand was, and I hate how much I already miss it.

"Lucy," I rasp, but she's already stepping back, her hand falling casually to her side.

"You better finish up before the rain starts."

Just like that, she's gone, and I'm left standing here with my heart pounding and no idea what to do with the ache she's left in her wake.

Lucy...Jesus. She's been chipping away at my resolve, bit by bit. I don't know what this is between us because we haven't put a name to it. All I know is my hands itch to touch her when she's close, her smile makes something in my chest crack open, and that three weeks away from her is going to feel like a lifetime.

I finish up just as the first drops of rain start to tap against the roof. By the time I head downstairs, everything I didn't want to feel is shoved back into its box.

I round the corner into the living room, and whatever calm I thought I had scatters.

Lucy's sitting on the floor, legs folded beneath her, surrounded by a sea of colored pencils and half-finished drawings. Isla's hunched over, her face scrunched in fierce concentration as she drags a crayon across the page. Lucy leans in close and points at something on the paper, her voice full of gentle praise.

Fuck, if that doesn't make me want her even more.

I stand there for a moment, frozen, just watching them. Lucy's hair falls in soft waves around her face as she bends over the drawing, and for a split second, all I want to do is reach out and run my fingers through it. Then she looks up, catches my eye, and that smile—*god*, that smile—grows even wider.

"Daddy!" Isla squeals. "I made you something!"

"Did you now? What is it?"

She thrusts the paper toward me, beaming with pride. "It's for when you're on the big boat. So you don't forget us."

I move closer, squatting down beside them, desperate to hide the way those words tear me apart from the inside out. I look at the picture of three stick figures Isla's holding out. One's tall with spiky hair—me, I guess. One's small with pigtails—Isla. The third one is right in the middle, with shoulder-length, chestnut hair.

"That's Lucy," Isla says, pointing at the middle one. "I put her there so she can hold both our hands at the same time."

My heart skips a beat, and I look over at Lucy. Her cheeks are flushed, a little embarrassed, but I catch the way her lips tug up into the smile she's trying to hide.

"It's beautiful, love." I clear my throat, trying to pull myself together. "Why don't you go wash up for dinner? I'll help Lucy clean up here."

She nods, and before I can even blink, she's up and off, dashing toward the bathroom. The sound of her little feet fades, and it's just me and Lucy in the room. I glance over at her, and she's already picking up the mess.

"I'm sorry about that," I say quietly, reaching for a stray pencil. "The drawing, I mean. I don't want you to feel—"

"Don't," Lucy interrupts, her hand coming to rest on mine. "Please don't apologize. It's... It's really sweet."

I swallow hard, trying to find the right words. "I don't want you to feel pressured. This situation is complicated."

She shifts closer, her knee brushing against mine. My pulse picks up again, and I have to fight the urge to close the space between us. "I know that, Aidan. I'm not here because I think it's going to be easy. I'm here because I want to be." She pauses, her eyes searching mine. "And complicated doesn't have to mean impossible."

I find myself leaning in, pulled toward her like I'm caught in a current. Her lips part slightly, eyes flitting to mine, then to my mouth. The air between us crackles with something dangerous.

"I can't reach the soap!" Isla's voice calls from the bathroom.

I close my eyes, take a deep breath, and when I open them, Lucy's looking at me with a smirk on her lips. "Go," she says, but there's a longing in her gaze that holds me for a second longer. "I've got this."

I make my way to the bathroom to find Isla struggling on her tiptoes, her arms stretched up high, but she's not quite tall enough. I pass the bottle to her, making sure she gets a good lather, watching as her hands work under the water.

I zone out a bit as she scrubs away, humming a tune to herself. Tomorrow, I'll be back on the rig, and I'll miss this. I'll miss her little hands, the sound of her laughter bouncing off the walls, the way she looks at me like I'm everything she needs. I'm already bracing myself for the emptiness that comes with leaving.

I force my jaw to relax, keep my face neutral, but inside, it's a damn storm. I can't keep pretending it's all fine when it's absolutely fucking *not*.

"All done," Isla announces, holding up her dripping hands for inspection.

I grab a towel to dry her hands, focusing on the simple task to distract myself. "Good job, sweetheart. Listen, about tomorrow—"

"I know, Daddy," she cuts in, her eyes serious. "You have to go to work on the big boat."

I pull her into a tight embrace, breathing in the scent of her shampoo. I squeeze her a little tighter. "I'll miss you. I'll be back before you know it."

She hugs me back with all the strength she can muster before pulling away, looking up at me with those wide eyes. "Can I have a hug when you come back?"

I can't help but laugh, brushing my lips over the top of her head. "Of course. You can have all the hugs you want."

She grins with a big, goofy smile that makes everything feel a little less heavy.

LUCY

I've gotten used to slipping out early when dinner's over. It's the polite thing to do, right? Giving Aidan and Isla space before their bedtime routine, not making things weird. But tonight, as my hand reaches for my coat, Aidan calling my name stops me cold. There's a little tug in my chest, and I know it's because this will be the last time I see him for three whole weeks. My heart does that little drop thing.

I take a slow breath, trying to keep everything in place and to not show how much I don't want to go. I turn around, keeping my fingers on the sleeve of my coat, and glance at him.

"You don't have to go yet."

My stomach twists a little. I want to stay, but I don't want to overstay my welcome, either. I pull my coat closer to me and hesitate, chewing on the inside of my cheek. "Are you sure? I don't want to intrude on your last night together before you leave."

His hand drifts to the back of his neck, fingers catching in his hair in that endearing way he probably doesn't realize he does. I've learned the gesture well by now—his nerves are slipping through.

His eyes meet mine for a split second before quickly darting away. "You're not intruding, lass." His voice is low, tender. "I'd like you to stay. If you want to, that is."

"I'd love to," I say before I even really think about it. My hands are already moving to hang my coat back up, making the decision for me.

For a split second, relief flashes across Aidan's face. It's so quick, so subtle, but it's there. He nods, his lips curling up just a little at the corner. "Good." His voice clears, a little husky. "I thought maybe we could watch a movie with Isla if you're up for it."

"Sounds perfect." I follow him into the living room where Isla's already sprawled across the couch, her bunny clutched close to her chest. Her legs swing lazily in the air with not a care in the world.

"Lucy's staying for movie night," Aidan announces.

Isla's face lights up. "Yay! Can we watch the one with the talking dogs?"

I glance at Aidan, catching the smallest roll of his eyes. The little shift in his expression makes me laugh. "Aye, fine," he grumbles, sinking into the armchair with a sigh. I know it's all for show, though. He's not fooling me for a second.

As the movie starts, I slide onto the couch beside Isla, who immediately curls into my side. Aidan stays where he is, sprawled out in his armchair, his broad shoulders slouched just enough to look casual, but I know he's still tuned in to everything around him.

When our eyes meet, there's a spark of amusement in his gaze, and I can almost hear the silent thought. *You don't have to sit so far away.*

The movie plays on, but I find myself stealing glances at him without meaning to. The soft flicker of the screen casts shadows across his face, highlighting the sharp, chiseled line of his jaw and the slight curve of his lips. Every time our eyes meet, the world slows down for a moment.

Halfway through the movie, Isla's body grows heavy against mine. Her head starts to droop as she fights sleep, her soft breaths slowing with each passing second.

"Mission accomplished," Aidan muses.

I chuckle softly, careful not to disturb her. My fingers instinctively smooth the hair out of her face. "She fought it hard, didn't she?"

He nods, his eyes softening. "Aye, she always does when I'm leaving. Thinks if she stays awake, morning won't come."

I can't help but feel the ache in my own chest, realizing how much this separation must hurt him, too.

"I'll take her up," Aidan mutters, pushing himself up from the armchair. He gently scoops Isla up into his arms. She stirs just slightly, mumbling something incoherent as she shifts. Just as quickly, she settles back against him. He moves toward the stairs with a quiet tenderness that makes my heart squeeze. It's a simple act, but the care in the way he holds her, the way he *always* holds her, says more than any words could.

"Be right back," he whispers.

I nod, watching as he disappears up the stairs with her. The movie continues playing, but I'm not watching anymore. My mind keeps drifting to the fact that after tonight, I won't see him for almost a month.

I really like him. He's gruff, often quiet, and sometimes impossible to read. Then there's this softness that slips through the cracks sometimes. Rare, unguarded moments when he lets his walls down, even if it's just for a second.

I hear his footfalls on the stairs before I see him, and my stomach does that flutter thing again. I straighten up on the couch, suddenly unsure where to put my hands. Should I leave now?

When Aidan appears beside me, he pauses for a moment. The soft lamplight catches the angles of his face, and I notice the slight furrow between his brows.

"She went down okay?" I ask, just to break the silence.

He nods, running a hand through his hair. "Aye."

"I should get going," I sigh, forcing myself to my feet.

"Stay."

The word lands between us like a spark. My heart thuds in my chest, too loud, too fast. I glance back at him, his eyes dark and intense in the dim light. It's just one word. One simple word, but it feels like he's opened a doorway I never thought he would, or maybe even one I never expected to walk through.

"Aidan..." I start, but I don't know how to finish. Don't know what I'm warning him about or what I'm asking for.

He takes a step closer, and suddenly, I'm acutely aware of the hum of the refrigerator in the kitchen, the way his eyes have darkened to the color of a storm-tossed sea. I look down, way too aware of how long it's been since his mouth was on mine. I'm pretending I'm not aching for it, but neither of us has dared to do too much in front of Isla. Not even a stolen kiss.

"Lucy, please," he murmurs, his voice low and rough. He lifts his hand, his calloused fingers gently tilting my chin up until I have no choice but to meet his gaze. "I want you to stay."

I swallow hard, knees shaky. It's as if I'm sixteen again, nervous and wild and completely undone by one boy's attention. Only he's not a boy. He's all man, all presence, and the way he's looking at me makes heat trail up my spine.

"I..." I start, but the words crumble as his thumb traces over my bottom lip.

He leans in. His mouth brushes mine, barely there, more breath than kiss. A whisper. A question. It steals every ounce of logic I've got left.

I give in.

I give in to his warmth. To the way his lips linger, patient and tentative like he's not sure if he's allowed to want this as badly as I do. We're both trying not to cross a line we've already obliterated.

He pulls back just a fraction. His brow furrows, the only sign of uncertainty. If he's giving me space to make a choice, I don't need it. I already know what I want.

I reach up, my fingers sliding into his hair, pulling him back down to me. This time, there's nothing tentative about the kiss. It's all heat and need and everything we've both been holding back for too long. His arms wrap around my waist, drawing me closer until I'm pressed against the solid planes of his body.

"I want to stay," I whisper against his lips, the words falling out before I can overthink them. I know what staying means tonight, and I want it. All of it.

"Are you sure?"

I nod. "Yes."

Relief and desire flash in his eyes before he captures my mouth again. The kiss deepens, his tongue sliding against mine, and a soft sound escapes me. His hands tighten at my waist in response.

His lips trail a path along my jaw, down to the curve of my neck. I shiver.

That's when it hits me. I'm not just interested in Aidan… I've already fallen. Harder than I've ever fallen for anyone.

I wasn't supposed to crash into these feelings this hard, this fast. What if he leaves tomorrow and realizes this was all a mistake? Three weeks is a long time to think, to reconsider, to build walls back up. Aidan has walls like a fortress, and I've only just begun to see behind them.

Then Aidan's hands slide up along my sides, his thumbs grazing the underside of my breasts, and suddenly, all my worries scatter.

twenty-five
LUCY

"Lucy, I need you to understand something." His voice is rough, scraped raw at the edges, his hands fixed at my waist. I nod, scarcely breathing, the pressure in my chest so tight it feels like my ribs are about to crack open.

His eyes search mine, and whatever he finds there makes his jaw flex. "I've been trying to go slow," he says, quiet now, his thumbs brushing slow circles into my hips. "But once I have you like this, I won't be able to pretend it's anything less."

I swallow, but it does nothing to ease the dryness in my throat. "I know," I whisper, my voice so small it nearly disappears in the space between us. "I don't want you to pretend."

His hand slides up my back, spreading wide between my shoulder blades, drawing me flush against the heat of his chest. The air between us collapses.

His lips brush the edge of my jaw, just once. "You still sure?"

"Yes," I breathe, no hesitation. "Please."

That's all it takes.

His mouth finds mine with all the reverence in the world. It's like he's memorizing every part of me, like he's waited so long, and now that he has me, he's going to take his time. His kiss is deep and claiming, but careful.

"Upstairs," he commands.

When I nod, he takes my hand, lacing his fingers through mine. He leads me toward the staircase, each step causing the wooden stairs to creak beneath our weight, the sound impossibly loud in the quiet house. I'm painfully aware of Isla sleeping just down the hall, and Aidan seems to sense my thoughts.

"She sleeps like the dead," he whispers, squeezing my hand reassuringly. "Nothing wakes her."

His bedroom at the top of the stairs is simple. A large bed with dark sheets and a dresser, but I don't have time to notice anything else as he guides me inside, closing the door with a soft click. He doesn't immediately reach for me. Instead, he stands there, eyes drinking me in.

When he finally moves, it's with purpose. His hands cup my face, thumbs stroking my cheeks as he leans down to kiss me, softly at first, then with growing intensity.

"I need to see you," he murmurs against my lips, fingers finding the hem of my sweater.

I nod, lifting my arms as he slowly pulls the fabric over my head. The cool air kisses my skin, and I fight the urge to cover myself. His eyes grow impossibly darker as his fingers trace the edge of my collarbone.

"You're so soft everywhere," he marvels, almost to himself, brushing his knuckles over the dip between my breasts. "Sweet girl. Been driving me out of my mind."

He takes his time tracing the lace edge of my bra. I shiver under his touch, my body responding to his attentive exploration. His deft hands slide to my back, and the clasp of my bra gives way under his fingers. My breath hitches with a flutter of nerves, yet the sure pressure of his hands on my body makes me trust I'm exactly where I'm supposed to be.

He gently removes the last barrier between his gaze and my bare skin, his eyes holding mine for a heartbeat before dropping.

"Fuck...Lucy," he breathes, his voice a low rumble that vibrates through me. "You're beautiful. I want to take my time with you. Is that all right?"

I nod, unable to find my voice as his calloused fingers trace a path down to the curve of my breast. The contrast between his rough hands and gentle touch is incredible.

"Tell me what you like," he commands softly, his thumb brushing across my nipple. "I need to hear you say it."

"I like your hands on me," I whisper, my voice trembling slightly. "Everywhere."

His mouth curves into a satisfied smile. "Good girl." He lowers his head, pressing his lips to the hollow of my throat. "And here?" His teeth graze my skin lightly.

"Yes," I gasp, my head tipping back in surrender, baring my neck to him without a second thought.

If I seem composed on the outside, it's a lie. Because inside...I'm unraveling.

Good girl.

When he says it again, it doesn't feel patronizing or soft. It feels earned. It makes me feel seen and wanted and powerful all at once. Like giving in is the strongest thing I've ever done.

"Your pulse is racing," he murmurs against my skin. "Your heart's beating so fast." His palm spreads flat against my chest, feeling the erratic thrum beneath my breast.

His eyes find mine, watching my reactions carefully as he

continues to explore. "I want to feel every part of you," he says, his voice deep and assured. "Want to learn what makes you tremble." His hand slides down my stomach, stopping at the waistband of my jeans before he quirks his brow in a silent question.

I nod, and his fingers work the button of my jeans with deliberate slowness.

He eases them down my hips, his knuckles grazing my skin as he does. When I stand before him in just my underwear, he takes a step back, eyes roaming over me with such intensity that I can almost feel his gaze like a physical touch.

"Look at you." His voice is thick with admiration. "Perfect."

I'm so exposed, but the hunger and appreciation in his eyes melts the shame right off my skin.

"Come here," he says, his voice a gentle command.

I step toward him without hesitation, drawn by the gravity of his words. He's still fully dressed, and I reach for the buttons of his shirt with trembling fingers.

He covers my hands with his. "Let me."

He guides me backward until the backs of my knees meet the bed, then lowers me down. I sink into the mattress, my breath caught somewhere in my throat as he straightens and reaches for the buttons of his shirt.

One by one, they come undone, giving me time to take it in. And I do. I can't *not*.

Tanned skin comes into view first, then the dark lines of ink sprawling across his chest and down his arms. Some of it is bold and sharp, some faded with time, but all of it...is him. Real. Raw. Beautiful.

"I didn't know you had all this," I whisper.

His eyes meet mine, something unreadable glinting there. "No one's seen them in a long time."

He shrugs the shirt off fully, and I swear the room tilts.

Because it's not just the tattoos or the way he's built—strong, solid, every inch of him carved and inked with stories I want to learn. It's the trust in the way he lets me look.

"See something you like?" he asks, a hint of amusement in his voice.

I bite my lip, nodding silently, too overwhelmed to form words.

When he's down to just his boxers, he moves over me, the mattress dipping beneath his weight as I lie on my back. He hovers above, his arms braced on either side of my head, his eyes locked on mine. The intensity of his gaze makes me shiver.

"Cold?" he asks, his voice a low rumble that I can feel in my chest.

I shake my head. "No. Just...nervous."

His expression softens, and he lowers himself to his forearms, his face inches from mine. "We can stop anytime," he says, his thumb tracing the curve of my cheek. "Just say the word."

"I don't want to stop," I whisper, my hands finding courage as they slide up his arms, feeling the hard muscle beneath warm skin. "I want you."

A groan escapes him. "Say it again," he commands softly, his lips brushing against mine. "Tell me what you want, Lucy."

Heat floods my cheeks, but his unwavering gaze holds mine. "I want you, Aidan," I repeat, my voice steadier now. "All of you."

"Good girl," he praises, his words sending another shiver of pleasure through me. His lips find mine again, capturing them in a kiss that steals my breath.

His lips trail down my neck, each kiss deliberate and precise, mapping every inch of my skin. "Tell me if anything doesn't feel good," he says against my collarbone.

I nod, unable to form words as his mouth continues its

journey downward. I'm fairly certain nothing he does could ever feel anything but right.

When his lips close around my nipple, a gasp escapes me, my back arching instinctively.

He smiles against my skin, the satisfaction written all over his face enough to send my pulse into a frantic beat.

"I want to hear every sound you make. Don't ever hold back with me."

His words strike something deep inside me. I let go, allowing my body to do what it needs, no longer trying to hold back. Soft sighs escape me, quiet moans slipping from my lips, each one a reflection of how he makes me feel—alive, wanted, and completely his.

It's like I'm uncoiling, shedding layers I didn't even realize I was still holding onto. His touch and his words give me the permission to be just *me*.

His hand slips between us, fingers trailing down my stomach. When he reaches the lace edge of my underwear, he pauses, his eyes finding mine in the dim light.

I nod, breathless. "Please."

His fingers dip beneath the fabric, and I gasp at the first touch, my hips rising to meet him. He watches my face intently, reading every spark of pleasure, learning what makes me sigh, what makes me tremble.

"There she is," he murmurs approvingly when he finds the spot that makes me arch against him. "So responsive for me."

I close my eyes, overwhelmed by the sensations coursing through me, but his voice calls me back.

"Keep those pretty eyes on me," he orders softly. "I want to see you."

I force my eyes open. His eyes never leave mine as his fingers work their magic, building a pressure inside me that threatens to shatter me completely.

"You're so beautiful like this," he says, his voice thick with desire. The words wash over me, and I can't help the way my body responds, arching into his touch, seeking more.

His fingers move with deliberate precision, drawing circles that make my breath hitch and my thoughts scatter. I'm trembling now, my hands clutching at his shoulders, anchoring me as pleasure builds in waves.

"Aidan," I gasp as I feel myself approaching the edge.

"That's it," he encourages, his eyes darkening as he watches me unravel. "Let go for me."

When it hits, it's an overwhelming rush that crashes through me, leaving me breathless and shaking. He holds me through it, his lips pressing soft kisses to my temple, my cheek, the corner of my mouth as I come down slowly.

Before I can catch my breath, he's moving again, sliding my underwear down my legs and discarding them somewhere on the floor. The cool air brushes against my heated skin, but then he's there, his body covering mine.

"Fuck," he rasps. "I need to be inside of you."

I nod, my hands sliding down his chest to the waistband of his boxers. He kicks them off, and my stomach flips at the sight. He's long and thick, rigid with unrestrained need.

He shifts then, muscles flexing as he reaches into the bedside drawer for a condom. He rolls the condom on with ease, then positions himself between my thighs.

He hesitates for just a moment, his weight balanced on his forearms above me.

"Lucy," he says, voice rough as gravel. "It's... It's been a long time for me."

The confession catches me off guard. Just a second ago he was this confident man who seemed so sure of every touch. I reach up, cupping his face in my hands, feeling the scratch of stubble against my palms.

"For me, too," I whisper, and it's true. More than that, though... It's never felt this important.

He lowers his head, pressing his forehead to mine, breathing me in.

"I don't want to rush this," he murmurs. "I want to make it good for you."

I slide my hands into his hair, pulling him down for a kiss that tells him everything words can't. When we break apart, I'm breathless.

"You already are," I assure him.

He slowly pushes forward, the pressure making me gasp. He stills immediately.

"Okay?" he asks, concern etching his features.

"Yes," I breathe. "Don't stop."

He continues, inch by inch, giving me time to adjust to the feeling of him. When he's fully seated, he pauses, his breath coming in short bursts.

"You feel incredible," he groans, his voice hoarse with the effort of holding back.

I wrap my legs around his waist, urging him closer. "Move, Aidan," I whisper against his lips. "Please."

He begins to rock against me, his movements slow and careful at first. His eyes never leave mine, watching every reaction, adjusting his rhythm to match my responses.

My hands slide up his back, feeling his muscles tense beneath my fingertips. His pace remains unhurried, the slow drag and push creating a building tension that has me arching beneath him. But his control is slipping—I see it in the tightening of his jaw, the flexing of his muscles as he holds himself back.

"More," I whisper, encouraged by the desire darkening his eyes. "I won't break."

A flash of raw hunger breaks through his careful control.

His hips snap forward with sudden force, and a surprised cry tears from my throat.

"Like that?" he growls, his voice barely recognizable.

"Yes," I breathe, digging my fingers into his shoulders. "Don't hold back. I want all of you."

The last thread of his restraint snaps. His movements become deeper, faster, more urgent. His breathing turns ragged against my neck, and I can feel him trembling with the effort to not completely let go.

I cradle his face in my hands, forcing him to look at me. "Please, I want it all," I tell him. "I want to see you lose control."

His rhythm falters for just a second, surprise spreading across his face. "Fuck, Lucy," he groans.

I want to know that I can break through those carefully constructed walls. My nails dig into his shoulders as I pull him closer, urging him deeper.

His movements become harder, more demanding, as he finally surrenders to what we both need. The headboard knocks against the wall, and I'm vaguely aware I should be quieter, but I can't hold back the sounds he's drawing from me.

"That's it," he urges, one hand sliding beneath me to lift my hips higher. "Take it all."

The change in angle hits something deep inside me that makes stars burst behind my eyelids. I whimper his name as pleasure coils tighter, threatening to snap.

"I'm—fuck. I'm so close. Come for me, beautiful. Now."

His demand pushes me over the edge, and I shatter beneath him. He watches me fall apart, his eyes never leaving my face, drinking in every gasp and moan.

Just as I start to come down, his rhythm falters. With a deep groan, he follows me over the edge, burying his face in my neck as he finds his release.

For several moments, we stay like that, our bodies still joined, his weight pressing me into the mattress in the most comforting way. His breathing gradually slows as he presses gentle kisses to the curve of my shoulder.

He finally lifts his head, brushing a strand of hair from my face, his touch impossibly tender. "I didn't hurt you, did I?"

"No." I smile. "That was...everything."

A sigh escapes him as he carefully withdraws, leaving me feeling oddly empty. The mattress dips as he rises, moving with purpose toward the bathroom. I watch him go, unable to tear my eyes away from the broad expanse of his back, the defined muscles shifting beneath inked skin as he walks. The moonlight filtering through the curtains traces the contours of his body, highlighting the strength in his shoulders, the narrowing at his waist, the firm curve of his backside.

He's beautiful in a way that's all hard angles and power. Not polished or perfect, but real.

When he returns, his eyes find mine in the low light, searching, though I'm not sure what he's looking for.

He slides back beside me, his warmth immediately enveloping me. He hesitates, then tugs me close, curling his arm around my waist like he's afraid I might change my mind. My cheek finds the solid wall of his chest.

He exhales against my hair. "You don't have to stay, but I'd like it if you did."

Coming from him, it's a piece of him handed over. It's not just an ask—it's a confession. He doesn't ask for much, if anything. I don't think he knows how to want out loud. But he wants this. Me. Here. With him.

I could tell him I was planning to stay all along. I could tease him or say something light to break the weight of the moment. But I don't. I just press my face closer to his chest, breathing him in, and let my hand slide over his side.

"I want to stay."

He doesn't say anything, but he tightens his hold on me. His thumb draws soft circles into my hip like he's grounding himself with the feel of me. There's nothing rushed or messy here. Just skin against skin and hearts that are finally starting to speak the same language.

twenty-six
AIDAN

The soft creak of the mattress stirs me, pulling me from my haze of sleep. Isla might sleep like the dead, but I don't. Not ever since she was born.

I keep my eyes closed, but I can feel Lucy moving beside me, trying not to shake the air around her. She's always so damn sweet, even now, tiptoeing around not wanting to disturb a moment of peace. What she doesn't get is that *she's* the peace.

I crack one eye open just as she swings her legs off the side of the bed. Her back catches the light, pale and soft against the shadows. Her hair's a wreck, wild strands falling across her neck, and there's a red mark on her shoulder, a reminder of where I left my hand while we slept. She doesn't look like she's been up all night. She looks like the damn sunrise. Beautiful, without even trying.

"You sneaking out on me, lass?" I tease, my voice rough with sleep.

She jumps, head spinning around to meet my eyes. Her cheeks flush, a soft pink creeping up to her ears. "I didn't mean to wake you," she whispers, hands twisting in her lap.

I push myself up onto one elbow, a lazy grin tugging at my lips. "You think I'd let you slip out of here without a proper good morning?"

Before she can say anything, I reach for her. My fingers find her wrist, just firm enough to pull her back toward me. Her soft, airy laugh hits me right in the chest.

She slinks back under the covers, and my hands move over her, my lips trailing against her skin, nothing rushed.

I've spent so long pretending I didn't need this. The heat of someone's body pressed close. The way a woman feels wrapped around me, pulling me under, reminding me I'm alive. I thought I'd trained it out of myself, buried the hunger so deep it couldn't surface. Now she's here, and I'm desperate for more. Exactly what I was afraid of.

"I need to get home to change before work," she sighs. "And I'm sure you don't want Isla to see me sneaking out of your room."

She's not wrong. I'm not about to explain this shit to a five-year-old, and yet, the thought of leaving for weeks without being inside her again? That doesn't sit right. I can't do it.

My lips brush lightly against her neck. "Let me have you one more time." I'm begging without wanting to admit it. "I can be quick."

Probably too quick, considering it took every ounce of willpower I had not to explode the second I was inside her last night.

She laughs again, and damn it, I swear I'd give up anything just to hear that sound every day for the rest of my life.

What the fuck?

I'll think on that later, because right now, her perfectly round tits are pressed up against me, and my dick is so hard it hurts. I need the memory of how she feels to get me through the next few weeks.

"Please," she whispers, and that's all I need.

We're lying side by side, her face nuzzled against my chest as I push in slowly. Her tight, wet heat grips me, and I bite back a groan, teeth gritted to keep from losing it right there.

"Fuck, Lucy," I groan. My hand rests on her ass as I move in and out at a leisurely pace. Her skin is smooth to the touch as I trail my fingers up her spine, tilting her head up so I can taste her sweet mouth.

My tongue sweeps over the seam of her lips, and she moans in response. I'm dying to flip her over and take her until she's screaming. But at the same time, I'm struck by how perfect this is. Her soft curves pressed against me, her warmth seeping into my skin, the quiet little whimpers she makes with each thrust. It's driving me mad.

I'd hardly consider myself to be the gentle type, but with Lucy, I find myself wanting to take my time, to savor every moment, every sound she makes. Her nails dig into my shoulders as I thrust deeper, her body arching to meet mine.

"Aidan..." she breathes, and the way she says my name, like it's something valuable, nearly undoes me.

I capture her lips, swallowing her moans as I pick up the pace, driving into her with more force. Her leg wraps around my waist, pulling me closer, deeper. She clenches around my cock like a vise, and it feels too fucking good. I'm going to have to pull out before I can give her what she needs, because I forgot a damn condom.

I want to hear her gasps over and over again. She's tightening around me, her body tensing. She's close. I slip my hand between us, finding that sweet spot that makes her tremble.

"Come for me," I whisper against her ear. "One more time, lass."

She buries her face in my neck, muffling her cries as she

comes undone. I hold her tight against me, feeling her pulse around my cock. It's too much. Too fucking good.

"I need to pull out," I groan, voice ragged. My hips jerk into her without meaning to. I can feel it building—every nerve screaming, every muscle coiled tight. I'm right on the edge, and I know if I push a second longer, I'll lose it completely.

"No..." she breathes. "I'm on birth control. Please don't. Don't pull out. I don't want you to."

Goddamn it. I'm trying to be a halfway decent human being here and then she goes and says that.

That's all it takes. I thrust deep one last time, holding her tight as pure lightning shoots down my spine. My body shudders against hers as I empty myself inside her.

For a few moments, there's nothing but our frayed breaths mingling in the quiet room. I keep my arms locked around her, savoring the way her body molds perfectly against mine. Like she was made just for me.

Eventually, Lucy stirs and lifts her head. Her green eyes are hazy with satisfaction that makes my chest ache in a way I'm still not ready to examine too closely. That wasn't just sex, though, and that scares the hell out of me.

The sound of tiny feet skittering down the hallway slams into the moment like a wrecking ball. Lucy's eyes go wide, panic flashing across her face. I'm up before I even think about it, throwing myself out of bed and grabbing the nearest pair of sweatpants off the floor. Lucy's already yanking the covers over her head, vanishing beneath the sheets.

"Daddy?" Isla's sleepy voice comes from the other side of the door, followed by a soft knock.

"Just a minute, love," I call back, my voice steadier than I feel. My adrenaline's kicking in hard. I throw on a T-shirt and glance back at Lucy. She's tucked herself up in the duvet, only her wide eyes peeking out, looking both mortified and amused.

I open the door just enough to slip through, making sure to close it behind me with a little more force than necessary. Isla stands there, all messy hair and princess pajamas, rubbing her eyes.

"What's up, little storm?" I ask. "It's still a bit early, aye?"

She looks up at me, her bottom lip wobbling just a bit. "I had a bad dream," she mumbles. "Can I sleep with you?"

My heart stutters. I want to pull her right into my arms, let her crawl under the covers and fall asleep with me. But shit, not with Lucy in there.

I drop to one knee, meeting her at eye level. "How about we go downstairs, and I'll make you some hot chocolate?" I suggest. "Then we can snuggle on the couch and watch cartoons until it's time for breakfast. Sound good?"

She nods, her eyes lighting up at the mention of hot chocolate. I scoop her up, her small arms instantly wrapping around my neck, her face buried in my shoulder. As I carry her downstairs, I can't help but think about Lucy in my bed. I hope she understands.

I set Isla down on the couch once we're in the living room, wrapping her in a blanket and putting on her favorite cartoon. Her expression already looks lighter, bad dream forgotten.

"Hot chocolate coming right up," I say, ruffling her hair before heading to the kitchen.

As the milk heats up on the stove, my thoughts keep drifting back upstairs to Lucy. I can picture her there, all tangled up in my duvet, hiding like she's trying to melt into the bed. I can't help but huff a quiet laugh. I'm going to have to figure this out without making things more awkward than they already are.

I carry the hot chocolate to the couch, setting it down in front of Isla. She flashes me a grin. "Thanks, Daddy."

"Anything for you." I lean down to kiss the top of her head. "I'll be right back. Just going to check on something."

She doesn't even look up, already lost in the colorful chaos of the cartoon. I slip away, my steps soft as I make my way back upstairs.

When I reach the bedroom, I ease the door open, slipping inside without a sound. Lucy's sitting on the edge of the bed, fully dressed now. Her hair's still a mess, and her face is caught between embarrassment and something else, like she doesn't know whether to laugh or keep hiding.

"How's Isla?" she asks, her voice barely audible.

"She's fine," I say, keeping my voice low. "Hot chocolate and cartoons work miracles."

She nods, offering me a soft smile. "I should go," she says, standing up, a little reluctant. "I really do need to get home and change before work."

I know she's right, but I hate it at the same time. "I'll walk you out."

We move silently down the stairs, careful to keep our steps quiet. At the front door, I hesitate. My hand lingers on the handle, not sure of what to say.

She solves the problem for me, rising on her tiptoes and leaning in to press a soft kiss to my cheek.

"Have a safe trip," she whispers. "I'll...see you when you get back?"

I know I'm an ass for not defining whatever this is with her before I leave, especially after last night. It's suddenly hitting me that this isn't like the other times I've left for a rotation. Before, it was just Isla I was leaving behind. My little girl who I'd kiss goodbye and promise to call, whose drawings I'd tuck into my bag to tape up in my bunk. That was hard enough.

Now there's Lucy. Lucy with her soft skin and quiet laugh and the way she fits against me like she was made to be there.

Lucy, who I just had in my bed, and somehow, I think, snuck into the parts of me I've kept locked down for years.

I'm leaving her, too.

I swallow hard, nodding. "Yeah. I'll call you while I'm gone."

I want to say more, but the words jam in my throat. What am I supposed to tell her? That I'm already dreading the empty bunk on the rig? That I'll be counting down the days until I can touch her again?

Her eyes search mine for a second, like she's looking for some kind of confirmation or clue that I mean it. Finally, she nods, her smile a little sad before she slips through the door. Her chestnut hair catches the morning light, and I can't take my eyes off her. As she reaches her car, she turns and gives a small wave. I raise my hand in return, feeling something twist painfully in my chest.

I close the door quietly behind me, pressing my forehead against the cool wood. I let out a long, slow breath. The house feels emptier now. Colder.

Three weeks is going to be brutal.

There's no going back to pretending I don't want this. The way she handled Isla showing up, the way she didn't bolt the second things got complicated—it's more than I ever thought I could ask for.

For now, though, I have to push all that aside. My job is simple today. Be Dad. Make pancakes. Watch cartoons. Hold my daughter tight before I leave.

twenty-seven
LUCY

I'm in Knox's loud kitchen, surrounded by people who love me. I'm here, but...not here.

Aidan said he'd call.

Not *maybe*. He said it like a promise, and stupid, hopeful me believed him. A full week of zero communication has settled in my stomach like a lead weight I can't shake off, no matter how many times I try to tell myself I'm fine.

No call. No messages. Not even a simple "hey, talk soon" text. Just silence. Cold and loud and echoing in all the spaces he left behind.

I keep telling myself he's busy. That it's a rig, a godforsaken, floating tin can in the middle of the North Sea. Bad signal. Long shifts. Time slipping away easier out there. That's all.

It doesn't matter how hard I try to stay rational. The same dreaded thought keeps circling back.

What if he changed his mind?

What if all that tenderness, all that heat and honesty he poured into me that night, wasn't what I thought it was? What if it was temporary? Convenient?

My stomach twists, that sour pit of doubt hollowing me out in quiet little bites. I hate how easily my mind goes there. How quickly I can go from trusting to spiraling. I don't want to be *that* girl—the needy one, the overthinker, the one who's too much. But I'm unraveling by the minute.

I pick up my phone again. No notifications. My fingers hover over his name, then retreat. What am I even supposed to say? *Hey, just checking if you've ghosted me? Hope you're well either way!*

I shove my phone into the back pocket of my jeans with a frustrated huff. I'm being dramatic. Or...maybe I'm just scared. Because the truth is, I wanted this. Him. I let myself hope.

My skin prickles with awareness as I feel Callan's gaze on me. His brow furrows and his lips twist downward as if he's noticed something in me he doesn't like. I try to smile, stretch my mouth into something close enough to pass for a grin, hoping he buys it.

He doesn't.

My family's everything to me, but I can't handle any more teasing about my love life today.

I turn my focus back to pressing the dough into the tart pan, my fingers working mechanically, smoothing it down in practiced movements. Normally, this is the part I look forward to—getting lost in the rhythm of baking and the way it calms me, with the kitchen filled with the comforting sounds of laughter and chatter in the next room. But tonight, the dough is heavy, like a weight in my hands instead of something to shape. Every press is a chore, and my mind spins in endless loops of thoughts I can't seem to outrun.

I don't even notice Bree until she's right there, standing at my side. She leans against the counter, her blue eyes locked on me with that familiar intensity, piecing together the words I'm not saying.

"You know, Lou, if you keep frowning like that, your face might stay that way," she teases.

"Oh, it's nothing," I say with a dismissive wave. "It's just... you know the cat I got? Marmalade? Total nightmare. Keeps knocking everything over in my flat at night. I haven't slept properly in days."

The lie tumbles out so easily I almost believe it myself, but instead of the expected chuckle, Bree steps closer, and her voice softens. "Hey, whatever's going on, I'm here. So is Jules. You know that, right?"

I don't have a lot of close friends. Bree and Juliette are really the only ones I trust to share what's on my mind, to vent when it gets too heavy, or ask for advice when I'm unsure. When I took over the café years ago, I threw myself into it and became the rock everyone else could lean on, the reliable hand in a world that felt like it was always spinning. Somewhere along the way, I let my own support system slip through my fingers. It felt easier to just take care of everyone else, to be the one with the answers, the one who always had it together. Slowly, it became second nature to handle things on my own.

I take a breath and try to steady myself, not wanting to let the weight of it all spill out too quickly. "I'm just...waiting," I murmur, low enough that no one else can overhear. "I've been seeing Aidan for the past few weeks. He's away at work, and he said he'd call, but it's been a week. Not a word."

The pressure in my chest builds again. I exhale, letting some of it go. "I feel like I'm stuck in limbo." My voice cracks at the end, and I'm grateful it's quiet enough that no one else can hear it.

Bree studies me with that knowing look people only earn the hard way. "You're in deep, huh?"

"Mmhmm." I focus back on the dough in my hands, my fingers pressing into it with more force than necessary.

She tilts her head. It's her signature move right before she's about to share some nugget of wisdom.

"I'll let you in on a little secret," she says, her voice dropping to a quieter, almost conspiratorial tone. "Men? They're clueless sometimes. I mean, sure, they think they know what they're doing, but half the time, they're just not paying attention."

I glance up at her, raising a brow, but she meets my gaze with that unshakable look of hers.

"Sometimes they need time to figure things out," she continues. "And sometimes they're just not thinking at all. You know, with everything going on in his world—his job, the stress, his daughter—he might not even realize that you're sitting here, waiting for a call. Or that you're hurt because he hasn't followed through like he said he would."

Her shoulders lift in a casual shrug, the motion somehow making it seem like maybe it's not as complicated as I'm making it out to be.

I chew on her words, letting them settle slowly. I stare down at the tart I'm still trying to finish, my fingers still.

Bree doesn't let the silence stretch too long. "Don't be afraid to tell him what you want. Lay it out. Sometimes, it's gotta be black and white, no gray area. Otherwise, you're just setting yourself up for more of this...confusion."

I nod. I've been so caught up in my own thoughts and fears that I haven't considered the possibility that Aidan might be just as lost as I am.

"You're right," I say, looking over at her with a grateful smile. "I guess I've been expecting him to just...know."

She grins, nudging my shoulder. "That's your first mistake, Lou. Men aren't exactly known for their psychic abilities."

I can't help but laugh, a weight lifting off my shoulders, the knot in my stomach loosening just a bit. "I guess I've been afraid of pushing too hard, you know? I don't want to scare him off."

She rolls her eyes, but there's affection in the gesture. "If he's worth your time, he'll listen. And if he doesn't step up, well, there are plenty of other grumpy men on oil rigs."

I laugh again, shaking my head. "Let's not get ahead of ourselves. I actually like this one. Thank you, though," I continue. "For talking through that with me."

Bree snorts, crossing her arms and leaning back against the counter. "Girl, I'm going to be pissed if you keep holding stuff back like this. Juliette's already going to be mad that we had no idea you were dating the guy."

"Aye," I laugh. "Noted."

Her finger jabs the air in my direction. "And next time," she continues, shaking her finger for emphasis, "don't make me play referee, okay? You've got to give us more of a heads-up before you go all 'silent sufferer' mode."

Just then, Knox pokes his head into the kitchen. "Hey, you two gossiping hens, are we eating tonight or what?"

"Keep your kilt on!" Bree quips, winking at me. "We're almost done here."

Just as I slide the tart into the oven, my phone buzzes in the back pocket of my jeans.

My fingers are suddenly useless as I fumble for it, nearly knocking the oven mitt to the floor in my scramble, but when I glance at the screen, my heart skips.

I look up, breath caught in my throat. Bree's brows lift in question, but she reads the answer on my face before I say a word.

Her expression softens. She nudges the oven shut behind me and gives a little wave of her hand. "Go," she mouths. "Take it."

I dart into the hallway, heart kicking up as the kitchen

noise fades behind me. Relief hits first, like I can finally breathe, but it tangles with a rush of nerves and a flicker of excitement that makes my steps too fast. I answer the second I'm out of earshot.

"Hello?" My voice comes out in a whisper.

There's a beat of silence. A quiet exhale. Then, "Hey, Lucy."

It's only two words, but the sound of his voice knocks the air right out of me. Deep, rough, and achingly familiar. My eyes sting, stupidly, my body finally catching up to everything my heart's been holding in.

"I'm sorry," he says. "Things got complicated out here. I didn't mean to go quiet."

I lean back against the wall, my free hand fidgeting with the hem of my shirt, the fabric twisting between my fingers. Bree's words echo in my mind, urging me to be direct, to stop letting things fester in silence.

"I was worried," I admit softly.

The silence on the other end drags. When he finally speaks, his voice is remorseful. "I should've called sooner."

I nod, even though he can't see me. "I just...I started to wonder if you'd changed your mind. If I'd made all of it up in my head." My lungs squeeze, the words catching. "Mostly, I didn't know if you were safe."

"No, Lucy. God, no." His response is immediate, adamant. "I'm okay, and you haven't misread a thing."

I let out a breath I didn't realize I'd been holding. "Okay."

"I'm so fucking bad at this," he continues, the frustration in his tone clear now. "Especially when I'm out here. I haven't stopped thinking about you. I didn't mean to make you doubt that."

I close my eyes, letting those words settle.

"I missed your voice," I admit.

He groans. "Don't say that unless you want me on the next damn chopper off this rig."

A soft laugh escapes me. "I happen to know of two ladies who wouldn't complain."

"Don't tempt me," he grumbles, but there's a hint of a smile in it now. "I'd jump into the North Sea if it got me home faster."

I huff out a laugh, pressing my palm against my chest as if I can suppress the fluttering inside. We can joke all we want, but the fact is, we still have a lot of important stuff to talk about.

"Aidan?"

"Yeah," he says. "I'm here."

I chew on the inside of my cheek, mulling over my words. "I don't need constant texts or hour-long calls. I know you're busy out there, but if we're doing this—whatever this is—we need to talk when you get back. Like, *really* talk. About what we want, or if we're even trying for something here."

Wow. Go me. I actually said it.

Sure, I know I'm going to replay this conversation in my mind a thousand times and second-guess every word and every pause, wondering if I sounded too eager or too cold, too forward or not enough. What I do know, though, is I can actually breathe without feeling like I'm suffocating on my own thoughts.

"Aye. You're right," he says, his voice low and earnest. "But Lucy? That night with you... It wasn't nothing. And I'm so fucking sorry I made you feel like it was."

Relief floods through me, easing the raw edges of my nerves. I hadn't realized how much I'd been holding on to until his words allowed me to exhale. He's not exactly the type to bare his feelings easily, so hearing him say that is a surprise in the best possible way. My heart's pounding so loudly in my chest, I swear it's echoing down the hallway.

"Wow," I say, blinking up at the ceiling like it might help hold back the sudden rush of tears. "Sounds like you might actually...miss me or something."

There's a pause, and then he groans. "Jesus, you're gonna make me say it?"

A grin tugs at my lips. "Say what?"

"I miss you," he mutters. "I've been missing you every damn day since I left."

I bite down on my smile. "I'm glad you called. I needed to hear that."

He pauses for a beat before he responds. "I'm glad you're okay, Lucy."

I feel so much lighter now. Then, a thought strikes me.

"You know, I'm always happy to take Isla for a little adventure while you're gone," I suggest. "Maybe go for a walk in the park or hit up the zoo. Give your mum a bit of a break."

There's a brief pause on the other end. "She'd love that," he says. "And Mum, too. She's been doing a lot. More than I probably realize."

"Just say the word," I tell him. "No pressure. I'll make it something good."

"I'll message my mum tomorrow," he says. "I should go. We've got a situation with one of the pumps that needs sorting."

"Of course," I say quickly. "Go. Be safe."

"I will. And Lucy?"

"Hm?"

"I'll call again. Soon. I promise."

This time, I know he'll be calling.

twenty-eight
LUCY

Aidan's finally home today after what has been the longest three weeks of my life. I haven't texted or called to ask to see him, even though I want to. *God*, I want to. He needs some time with Isla first, though. I know how much it kills him to miss even the smallest things, like her new favorite song and the funny way she says mermaid. That little voice of hers is everything to him.

So instead, I bake.

Two pies. One unnecessarily complicated. One safe and familiar. There's flour on my elbows, sugar under my nails, and I'm just trying not to watch the clock.

It's fine. This is fine. He's home, and that's what matters.

And yet, every time my phone buzzes, my breath catches for a second.

I'm so lost in my own head that I almost don't hear the light knock at my door. When it comes again, a little more insistent this time, I frown.

I wipe my hands on the dish towel, wiping my forehead

with the back of my wrist as I make my way to the door. When I pull it open, my heart nearly stops.

Aidan stands there, looking exhausted but somehow more handsome than ever. His hair is slightly damp as if he's just showered, and there's a hint of stubble along his jaw. What actually catches me off guard is the bouquet of white peonies in his hands—massive, full blooms that look impossibly soft against his calloused fingers.

"Surprise," he says, voice gravel-deep and making my knees wobble.

Then I notice Isla peeking out from behind his legs, beaming. She's holding a single peony that looks comically large in her hands.

"We brought you flowers!" she announces proudly. "Daddy said they're your favorite and that ladies like surprises."

My heart lurches, awe and ache colliding in my chest. My first instinct is to throw my arms around him, press my mouth to his, and tell him exactly how much I've missed him.

Instead, I crouch down to Isla's level, a smile stretching across my face as I reach for the flower in her outstretched hand.

"Ladies *do* like surprises," I say softly, glancing up at Aidan. "Especially ones like this."

I take the single peony from her small hands, careful not to crush the delicate petals. "It's absolutely perfect. Thank you, sweetheart."

When I stand, Aidan's eyes lock with mine.

"These are beautiful," I say, nodding to the bouquet he's still holding. "How did you know they were my favorite?"

Aidan shifts his weight, a hint of color creeping up his neck. "I noticed you always have fresh ones on the counter at the café," he says. "White peonies in that blue vase. Every time I've come in, they're there."

My heart flips. He noticed. All those times he came into the café with Isla, sitting at that corner table by the window, he was paying attention to details I didn't think anyone cared about.

"You're observant," I tell him, unable to keep the smile from my face.

"When it matters," he admits, finally extending the bouquet toward me.

I take them, our fingers brushing in the exchange. Even that brief contact sends electricity racing up my arm.

"Thank you... I thought you'd be spending time with Isla tonight. Not that I'm not glad you're here. I most definitely am."

"We have been. All day. But someone..." he shoots her a teasing side-eye, "wouldn't stop asking when we could come see Lucy."

Isla beams up at me, proud and entirely unbothered by the implication. "Daddy missed you, too," she says, matter-of-factly. "He said so."

Aidan's cheeks flush, and he clears his throat. "Looks like you're baking."

"I sure am. Some pies with way too much sugar." I shoot a wink in Isla's direction. "I could definitely use an assistant."

"Think you wanna help?" Aidan asks her. "Might be a good idea to wash those sticky hands first."

She doesn't hesitate. "Yes! Where's the sink?"

I point toward the hallway. "Bathroom's that second door just there."

She bolts, and the moment she rounds the corner, Aidan turns back to me.

He doesn't waste a second before stepping forward and pressing his lips to mine. It's not a soft, tentative kiss. Hardly a *hello*.

It's powerful and full of heat, and I'm breathless before I

even register what's happening. I gasp, and he takes it as the invitation it is, his lips parting to deepen the kiss. His free hand finds my waist, pulling me closer, pressing me against his solid chest. The peonies brush against my shoulder as he shifts, his tongue sweeping in slow, deliberate strokes that make my head spin.

I melt into him, my free hand sliding up his chest, feeling the steady thrum of his heartbeat beneath my palm. It's been three weeks of nothing but his voice through the phone, and now he's here, solid and real and—

The patter of small feet echoes down the hallway. Aidan pulls back swiftly, his breathing ragged as he puts a respectable distance between us. His eyes hold mine for one heated moment before he composes himself, running a hand through his hair just as Isla bounces back into the room.

"My hands are super clean," she announces, holding them up for inspection. "See? No germs."

I smooth down my shirt with my free hand and try to control my breathing. "Perfect timing. I was just about to put the filling in the pie crust."

We head to the kitchen, and I set the bouquet on the counter. "These need water. Would you mind grabbing me a vase from the cabinet above the sink?"

While Aidan searches for the vase, I pull a stool over so Isla can reach the counter. "We're making cherry pie, which means we need to mix these cherries with sugar and a little bit of this special powder that makes everything thicken up." Her eyes widen with excitement as I hand her a wooden spoon. "Just stir everything together, nice and gentle."

Aidan retrieves a glass vase from the cabinet and fills it with water. His movements are careful as he unwraps the peonies, trimming the stems with scissors I didn't even see him find.

There's something mesmerizing about watching his large, rough hands handle something so delicate with such care.

He arranges the flowers, adjusting them with surprising attention to detail, making sure each bloom has its place. When he's satisfied, he sets them on the counter near the window where the afternoon light catches the ivory petals.

Then he leans against the counter, arms crossed, watching us with an amused expression. "Be careful with that spoon. Remember what happened with the pasta sauce at home?"

"I'll be super careful," Isla promises, gripping the utensil with determination.

I measure out the cornstarch and sugar, adding them to the bowl of cherries. "Okay, now we mix it all together."

Isla attacks the task with enthusiasm, stirring so vigorously that cherry juice splashes up from the bowl.

"Whoa there," I laugh, placing my hand over hers to slow her down. "Like this, see? Gentle circles."

She nods, trying to mimic my movements, but her enthusiasm can't be contained. As she dips the spoon back into the mixture, her elbow knocks against the bowl, sending it teetering toward the edge of the counter.

"Isla—" Aidan lunges forward, but he's a second too late.

The bowl tips over, sending a crimson wave of cherry filling cascading down the front of his clean shirt. It splashes across his chest and drips down onto his jeans, leaving him looking like something from a horror movie.

We all freeze. Isla's mouth forms a perfect O of shock, her eyes wide with horror. Aidan stands there, arms outstretched, cherry juice dripping from his fingertips onto my kitchen floor.

Then Isla giggles. It starts small, a tiny sound that bubbles up from her chest, and then it grows until she's doubled over, clutching her stomach.

"Daddy looks like a monster!" she howls, pointing at the red stains spreading across his shirt.

I press my lips together, trying desperately to maintain my composure, but it's impossible. A snort escapes me, then another until I'm laughing, too, tears forming at the corners of my eyes.

Aidan looks down at himself, then back at us. His eyes narrow.

"Glad I could provide today's entertainment," he mutters dryly, though the twitch at the corner of his mouth gives him away.

I'm wheezing at this point. "I'm so sorry," I say, breathless through my laughter, grabbing the nearest dish towel. "Here, let me—"

"Don't." He lifts a hand, his palm sticky and glistening with pie filling. "If you touch me, you're going down with me."

"Is that a threat?" I ask, my voice still quivering with laughter. I hold the dish towel out as a peace offering, staying just out of his reach.

He takes a predatory step forward. "Consider it a promise, lass."

Isla's still giggling, perched on her stool and watching us with bright, curious eyes. "Lucy's gonna get all sticky, too!"

"Not if I can help it," I say, backing away slowly, the towel clutched to my chest.

Aidan glances down at his ruined shirt, then back at me, his eyes darkening with mischief. "Come here, Lucy," he says. "Don't you want a hug?"

"Don't you dare!" I laugh, retreating until my back hits the refrigerator. "You're dripping all over my floor!"

A wicked grin spreads across his face as he lunges forward, impossibly quick. Before I can dodge, he's on me, strong arms wrapping around my waist and lifting me clean off the floor in one fluid motion. I squeal as he spins me around, pressing his cherry-covered torso against me, the sticky sweetness soaking through my apron.

"Aidan!" I shriek, squirming in his grip as my feet dangle helplessly above the ground. His laughter rumbles deep in his chest, vibrating against me as he holds me.

Isla's giggles fill the kitchen as she claps her hands. "You match!"

"That was the plan," Aidan murmurs against my ear, his voice low enough that only I can hear. He sets me down slowly, his hands lingering at my waist.

I look down at my previously flour-dusted apron, now sporting a perfect cherry-red imprint of his chest. "You're terrible," I say, trying to sound stern despite my smile.

I manage to point toward the hallway, tears of laughter threatening at the corners of my eyes. "Bathroom. Clean towels under the sink. Try not to drip all the way there."

He exhales through his nose, the sound a mix between a grunt and chuckle, and steps carefully around the cherry massacre splattered across my kitchen floor.

Before he disappears, he turns to Isla. "You. Do not move. No more disasters while I'm gone."

The second Aidan vanishes down the hall, I survey the disaster zone that used to be my kitchen and shake my head, still fighting back giggles. "Well, this is quite the mess we've made, isn't it?"

Isla gives a slow nod, as if she's passing judgment on the chaos herself.

I reach behind to untie my apron strings, slipping the cherry-stained fabric over my head, pleasantly surprised to find my T-shirt and jeans completely unscathed beneath.

"Look at that," I say, holding up the ruined apron. "My clothes survived the cherry bomb, after all."

Isla's eyes widen. "Whoa. It's like magic."

"That's what a good apron does," I tell her, tossing the soiled fabric into the sink to deal with later. "Now, how about we clean up this mess before your dad comes back?"

"I'll help!" Isla volunteers, already sliding off her stool.

I grab a roll of paper towels and hand her a few sheets. "Careful not to get it on your pretty shirt."

She nods with all the solemnity of a kid on a very important mission.

"Lucy?" she says after a moment.

"Yeah?"

She pauses mid-wipe. "Do you like my daddy?"

"I...yes, I do. He's a good friend."

She considers my answer before she says, "He smiles more when you're around."

My heart squeezes in my chest, and I'm not sure what to say. How do you respond to a child's innocent observation that cuts straight to the heart of everything?

"That's... That's nice to hear," I manage.

"Are you his girlfriend?" she asks, eyes bright with curiosity.

I nearly choke. "I, um—"

"Isla." Aidan's voice slides into the room. He's leaning in the doorway, white T-shirt clinging to his frame, the stained flannel hanging over his arm. His eyes catch mine, and there's amusement there, or the faintest thread of panic. It's hard to tell.

She spots him and beams, already halfway across the kitchen. Then, mid-run, she screeches to a halt. "You have a cat!"

Before I can answer, she's off like a shot, barreling toward the corner of the living room where Marmalade is lazily grooming her paw on the back of the chair. The orange cat lifts her head just in time to assess the incoming hurricane and, miraculously, doesn't bolt. Instead, she blinks as Isla throws herself down beside her.

"Her name's Marmalade," I say. "I got her a few weeks ago."

Aidan huffs a quiet laugh beside me, but his eyes are still on Isla, who's now gently stroking Marmalade's back as if she's the most precious creature to ever exist.

"She's so soft," Isla breathes, face pressed into pale orange fur. Marmalade, to her credit, just flicks her tail and lets it happen.

"She's got the attitude of a grumpy old librarian," I tell her, leaning a little closer to Aidan without meaning to. "She's good company, though. Follows me around like a shadow. Sleeps right on my chest."

Isla seems to be lost in her own world with the cat. Then Aidan speaks.

"She asks a lot of questions. Always has. Doesn't miss much, either. I heard what she asked you."

I nod, swallowing. "I didn't know what to say."

"You don't owe her, or me, an answer."

"Aidan..."

"I haven't exactly made things clear," he admits. His voice drops, low enough that only I can hear. "I've been thinking about what we said on the phone. About figuring out what this is."

I glance over at Isla, still completely absorbed with the cat, then back to him. "And?" I whisper.

His eyes hold mine. "And I want to try. I want to give this a real chance." He hesitates, then adds, "But I need you to know, I'm scared shitless."

I blink, not expecting the honesty or the way it latches onto something deep inside me—because I'm scared, too. "Of what?"

"Of screwing it up. Of pulling you into something messy when I don't have all the pieces figured out yet." He looks at me like he's bracing for me to pull away. "For Isla."

My chest tightens with the best kind of ache. This is the part of him he doesn't let most people see.

"You know what I think?" I say, my voice light but steady. "I think you're overthinking this."

He arches an eyebrow, clearly not expecting that response. "Am I?"

"Mmhmm." I take a step closer, my fingers trailing down his arm until they find his hand. "I think you're standing in my kitchen with cherry pie filling all over your clothes, worried about things we can figure out together."

The corner of his mouth twitches. "That simple, huh?"

"No," I admit, giving his hand a gentle squeeze. "But maybe it doesn't have to be as complicated as we're making it." I glance over at Isla, still entranced by Marmalade, then back to Aidan. "I like you. I absolutely adore Isla. The rest... We can work it out as we go."

His eyes soften, the tension in his shoulders easing slightly. "You're not scared?"

"Terrified," I whisper with a smile. "But I'd rather be terrified *with* you."

Aidan doesn't say anything at first. He just looks at me, and I feel it everywhere. Then, quietly, "Okay. We're doing this, then."

I nod, heart thudding. "Yeah. We are."

He exhales like he's been holding it for years. Then he lifts our joined hands and presses a kiss to my knuckles.

"I'm gonna mess up," he warns.

"Same," I say. "Probably in spectacular fashion."

"At least we've got good cleanup practice."

A tiny giggle bubbles up from the living room, and we both

turn to find Isla lying on her back now, Marmalade perched squarely on her belly. She's talking to her in a hushed voice.

I lean my head on Aidan's shoulder. He lets it rest there, his cheek brushing the top of my hair.

"So..." I lift my head. "What's the policy on kissing your girlfriend in her kitchen?"

"Strongly encouraged."

He dips his head toward mine, just enough to keep it subtle. If we're quick and quiet, we might just get away with it.

His lips brush mine, soft and tasting faintly of cherry, when—

"Daddy!"

We spring apart like guilty teenagers caught in the back row of a movie theater.

Isla is sitting upright now, Marmalade still sprawled lazily across her lap. She points an accusatory finger, eyes wide with scandalized delight. "You were kissing!"

Aidan clears his throat and straightens up. "Just a little one."

Isla sighs. "Ugh, grown-ups. Next time you should tell me first."

He raises a brow. "Tell you?"

"So I can close my eyes," she huffs before I hear her mutter, "*grown-ups.*"

Aidan's hand finds mine again, his thumb stroking along my knuckles.

I lean in and whisper, "Sorry about that. Guess we'll have to work on our stealth."

"It's okay," he says. "I just need to talk to her about what this means."

"You think she'll be okay?"

He nods, squeezing my hand. "I think she'll be more than okay."

twenty-nine
AIDAN

There's applesauce on my kitchen table.

Not a lot, just a little smear of it left behind from breakfast, a glint of sun catching in the sticky residue. Isla's crouched beside her chair, using a sparkly hairbrush to detangle her doll's synthetic curls, entirely unaware that I'm bracing for one of the most important conversations of my life.

I clear my throat. "Hey, little storm."

She looks up immediately. "Yeah?"

"Can you come sit with me for a sec?" I pat the chair beside mine.

She considers it with one last tug on the doll's hair, then she clambers up.

I take a breath. "Remember last night? When you asked Lucy if she was my girlfriend?"

"I saw you kiss."

"Yeah," I say, chuckling under my breath. "You did."

She swings her feet under the table, winding up to a question, but waits.

"I wanted to talk to you about that. About me and Lucy." I

rest my forearms on the table and lean in a little, dropping my voice. "We like each other. And we're going to be spending more time together. Probably with you, too. If that ever feels weird or if you have questions, I always want you to tell me, okay?"

She frowns, thoughtful. "Like if I feel yucky about it?"

"Exactly."

She nods slowly. "I don't feel yucky."

My heart cracks open a little. "That's good. You like Lucy?"

"She makes the best toast. With the swirly butter."

"Swirly butter, huh? That's serious business."

Isla grins, then goes quiet for a beat. "She talks to me like I'm big. Not like I'm little."

I swallow. "Yeah?"

"And you laugh more when she's here."

That lands hard, right in the center of my chest. Kids don't bother with polite lies. They say what they see.

And what she sees...is me, lighter.

There were nights—god, *years*—when I was worried I'd never figure this out. That no matter how much love I gave her, it wouldn't be enough to make up for the pieces we didn't have. For what she lost before she could even remember it.

And now here we are.

It's not like I'm not scared shitless. I'm terrified of what it means to let someone in and build something that could fall apart. To ask Isla to open her heart and then have it broken by an adult who's supposed to stick around is big.

And then I think about last night with cherry pie filling everywhere, Lucy's hand in mine, and the way she looked at both of us like we belonged there.

We already let her in. All that's left is the name for it.

I press a kiss to the top of Isla's head.

"Okay," I say quietly. "So maybe Lucy's going to be around a lot more."

Isla considers this for a moment, her small face scrunching in concentration. "Like a sleepover?"

I nearly choke on air. "Well, not exactly. At least not right away."

"But maybe someday?" Her eyes are wide and hopeful, and I'm struck by how easily children adapt, how readily they make room for new people in their hearts when adults spend years building walls and constantly checking for weak spots.

"Maybe someday," I agree, treading carefully. "For now, we're just going to spend time together. The three of us. Would you like that?"

She nods enthusiastically. "Can we go to her house again? I want to play with Marmalade."

I huff out a low laugh. "I think that can be arranged."

LUCY

Three months have slipped by since that night at my place, and in that time, we've established a new dynamic. Things are different now, but better.

Aidan's opened up to me in ways I never expected. It's not always with words, but it's in the way he looks at me. The moments when he lets his guard slip, just a little, and I catch a glimpse of the man underneath all that rough exterior. Like when I make him laugh that deep, husky sound, or when I see that spark in his eyes that only shows up when he's around people he trusts. Or the way he showed up a few weeks ago when I was horribly sick, antibiotics hardly keeping me upright. He and Isla came over multiple times, checking in, making sure I was okay until I finally started to feel human again.

And Isla. She's become my sunshine. I never thought I'd feel this connected to someone else's child, but she makes me feel like I matter to her. Like I'm someone she needs. It's in the little things, like the way she reaches for my hand when we're walking, how her giggle bubbles up over something silly I say, or that shy little smile she gives me after I tell her how amazing her drawing is. Every time she does something like that, it's like my heart grows a little, stretching just enough to make room for her.

I'm just so...happy. I love the way Aidan holds me, even when he acts like it's no big deal. Like it's just a casual thing, but I can feel the weight of his arms around me, the quiet strength in the way he pulls me close, as if he's saying everything without saying anything at all. I love the way he is with Isla and how he makes sure she's always taken care of.

It's not casual anymore, which is why the guilt has started to creep up in the quieter moments. It's the unspoken thing I keep tucking behind smiles and late-night kisses and stories read aloud from Isla's favorite picture books. I haven't told him I may not be able to have kids, because saying it makes it real again. And saying it might make him rethink all of this.

Maybe he'll say it doesn't matter, and maybe he'll mean it. There's also the alternative that he won't. It's the *unknowns* that silence me.

Aidan is *so* good at being a dad. I know for a fact he'd be amazing again, if he ever wanted to. I can picture him kneeling beside a crib, brushing hair out of the way for some tiny version of him, kissing foreheads and rubbing backs until the crying stops. He was made for that kind of love.

I might not ever be able to give him that.

So I pretend like it's still new and we're still figuring things out. But every time I pack an overnight bag or fold one of Isla's shirts because it slipped into my laundry, I feel us creeping closer to the moment when I can't *not* say it anymore.

Tonight might be the night, because he's looking at me like he sees everything. If I don't tell him soon, I'll be lying every time I let him touch me and allow him to think I'm all in.

I help Aidan tuck Isla in, watching as he pulls the covers up to her chin and presses a kiss to her forehead. She's already drifting off, eyelids heavy from the busy day we spent at the park. Her stuffed bunny is close to her, and her breathing has slowed to that peaceful rhythm that comes right before sleep.

"Goodnight, sweet girl," I whisper, smoothing a hand over her wild curls.

"Night, Lucy," she mumbles.

Aidan and I slip out of her room, leaving the door cracked just enough to let a sliver of hallway light spill in. He takes my hand as we head downstairs, his thumb tracing absent patterns against my skin. It's these little touches that undo me, the casual intimacy that's become our normal.

In the living room, he pulls me down beside him on the couch, his arm sliding around my shoulders. I curl into his side, breathing in his familiar scent—sea salt and something that's uniquely Aidan.

"You're quiet tonight," he murmurs.

I nod, trying to swallow past the lump in my throat. My heart pounds so hard I'm sure he can feel it.

"I need to tell you something, if that's okay?" I finally ask, pulling away slightly so I can see his face.

His brows knit together, concern immediately darkening his eyes. "What is it?"

I take a deep breath, my hands suddenly trembling. I clasp them together in my lap to still them.

"I've been wanting to tell you for a while now, but I wasn't sure how." My voice sounds fragile to my own ears. "I had some health issues a while ago."

His expression softens, his whole posture easing, but he doesn't interrupt.

"The doctors explained that I have endometriosis, and it can affect fertility," I continue, my throat tightening. "Not always, and not in the same way for everyone. They told me that getting pregnant might be more complicated for me. Not necessarily impossible, just...uncertain."

My fingers curl against each other, a faint tremor running through them. "They couldn't give me a clear percentage or guarantee either way. It's more...a middle ground. A lot of unknowns, which has been really upsetting for me. I've always wanted to be a mother more than anything."

I force myself to meet his eyes, searching for any sign of disappointment or regret. He's quiet for a long moment, his expression unreadable. My stomach drops, anxiety clawing its way up my throat.

"I know this changes things," I continue, looking back down to my lap. "And I understand if you need to think about what this means for us. You're already an amazing father, and I wouldn't want to take away your chance to have more children if that's something you want."

His brows furrow deeper, and he reaches for my hands, stilling their nervous movement.

"Lucy," he says, his voice low and steady. "Look at me."

I lift my gaze to his, blinking back the tears that threaten to spill over.

"Is that what you've been worried about? That I'd walk away because of this?"

I nod, swallowing hard. "It's why my last relationship ended. And the way you are with Isla... It's one of the things I..." I catch myself before saying *love about you.*

"It's so incredibly special," I continue. "I wouldn't want to take away the possibility of you having that again."

His expression shifts, something between disbelief and tenderness crossing his features. His hand reaches up to cup my cheek, his thumb brushing away a tear I didn't realize had fallen.

"Baby," he says, his voice rough with emotion. "I already

have a daughter. A perfect, beautiful little girl who means everything to me. I'm not with you because I'm looking for someone to give me more children."

"But you might want that someday," I whisper. "And I might not be able to give that to you."

"Might not," he emphasizes. "Not can't. Even if it *was* can't..." He takes a deep breath, his eyes never leaving mine. "I'm here for you. Not for what your body can or can't do."

His words wrap around my heart, squeezing until I can barely breathe. I've been carrying this fear for so long it's fused to my bones, stitched into every hopeful glance I let myself steal when he's not looking. I've been bracing for disappointment, for the moment his sympathy turns into pity, or worse, distance.

"I'm not going anywhere, Lucy."

I sob.

Not a quiet, graceful tear slipping down my cheek, but a whole-body kind of cry. It tears out of me like a dam breaking open.

It's everything I've been holding in—all the fears and doubts and moments of grief when I'd allowed myself to imagine what might never be. It's the memory of sitting in that sterile doctor's office alone, the weight of possibilities shrinking with each clinical word. It's every time I watched a mother with her child and felt that hollow ache.

I'm crying because he didn't even hesitate. Didn't pull away or try to let me down easy. I've spent so long preparing for rejection that I never prepared for acceptance.

"I'm sorry," I hiccup through my tears, embarrassed by how completely I've fallen apart. "I just—I thought you'd—"

"That I'd what?" Aidan asks, his voice impossibly gentle. "Leave?"

I nod against him, unable to form words. The thump of his heart grounds me as his fingers thread through my hair.

"I'm not him, love," he says simply. "And it sounds like he was a fucking idiot."

His bluntness startles a laugh out of me. "You're not disappointed?"

"Disappointed?" He looks genuinely confused. "Lucy, if anything, I'm disappointed in myself for ever making you feel like you couldn't tell me sooner."

Who says that? Who thinks like that? How can he sit here looking at me like I've handed him something precious, not something broken?

"It was never you, Aidan. I just...needed to work through it on my end, I guess."

I feel like I can finally breathe. The weight that's been pressing down on me lifts so suddenly I'm dizzy with relief.

I want to look into those steady eyes of his and spill the entire truth I'm holding in, but I don't. Not because I'm afraid he won't say it back, but because whatever this is between us already feels real enough to hold me together. This is the kind of love that doesn't need declarations to exist.

He doesn't need the words yet. He's been showing me their shape all along.

So I stay tucked against him, my tears soaking into his shirt, letting my heartbeat speak its own language. When his hand slides up to cradle the back of my neck and his lips brush the top of my head, I know he hears me. He already knows.

I'm in love with him.

thirty-one
LUCY

Aidan and Isla are coming with me for dinner with my family tonight. As excited as I am, there's still this flutter of nerves that won't quit. This is another little shift in the landscape between us. We're taking this thing and making it more solid. I can't wait for them to meet everyone.

I check the time on my phone for the fourth time in as many minutes. It's only five-fifteen—we're nowhere near late yet.

"You sure this sweater looks all right?" Aidan asks, stepping out of the bathroom. His hair is still damp from the shower, and he's wearing a dark blue sweater that brings out the gray in his eyes. He runs a hand through his hair, his expression betraying just a hint of uncertainty.

He seems nervous...and it's ridiculously adorable. He's usually all firm hands and broody stares, but here he stands looking to me for approval like he actually needs to hear me say it.

"You look *dashing*," I tease. "They're going to love you. Both of you."

"It's Knox I'm worried about," he mutters, tugging at the sleeve of his sweater. "The way you talk about him, sounds like he'd try to snap me in half if I looked at you wrong."

I laugh, crossing the room to loop my arms around his waist. "He's protective, not homicidal. And he's actually a big teddy bear, but never tell him I said that. Besides, once he sees how you are with Isla, he'll be fine."

Aidan frowns, his hand moving to rub the back of his neck. "It's not just that." His voice drops lower. "I'm ten years older than you, Lucy. Your brothers will take one look at me and think I'm too old for their little sister. And what about your dad? Christ."

I pull back slightly, studying his face. There's genuine worry in his eyes, something I haven't seen since those early days when he was so afraid of letting me get too close.

"That's what's been bothering you? Our age difference?"

He runs a hand through his damp hair, making it stand up slightly. "When they see us together, that's the first thing they'll notice. Their beautiful, full of life daughter and sister with some older guy."

"First of all," I say, reaching up to smooth his hair back down, "you're not 'some older guy.' You're the man who makes me happier than I've been in a long time."

His expression softens a little, but I can tell he's not convinced.

"And second," I continue, "my family isn't going to care about a number."

"Do you think they'll ask about it?"

"Knowing my dad, yes. Not for any malicious reason, though. They'll ask about everything. That's what families do."

He exhales. "I just don't want them to think I'm taking advantage of you."

"Aidan Reid, listen to me. My family knows me. They

know I don't do anything I don't want to do." I smile softly. "The only thing they'll care about is how you treat me, how you are as a father, and who you are as a person."

Aidan's mouth quirks up at one corner, not quite a smile but close.

"Daddy!" Isla calls from down the hall, breaking the moment. "I can't find my sparkly shoes!"

Aidan clears his throat. "Coming."

Before he turns to go, the worry melts from his eyes. His hands cup my face, then his mouth is on mine. His kiss isn't careful like our usual ones with Isla nearby. This is raw and claiming. I gasp against his mouth, surprised by the sudden intensity, and he takes advantage, his tongue sliding against mine.

My back hits the wall as he presses closer. His fingers thread through my hair, cradling the back of my head as he angles me exactly how he wants me. A soft sound escapes my throat when he nips at my bottom lip, and I feel him smile against my mouth.

When he finally pulls back, we're both breathing hard.

"What was that for?" I whisper.

"Just getting it out of my system before I have to be on my best behavior," Aidan murmurs, his voice a low rumble.

"Daddy!" Isla calls again, more insistent this time.

Aidan pulls away with a sigh. "Duty calls."

THE DRIVE OVER TO MY PARENTS' house is filled with Isla's chatter from the backseat, asking a hundred questions about who she'll meet and if my parents' house is big and whether they might have a cat like mine. Her excitement helps diffuse the nervous tension radiating from Aidan beside me. He keeps both hands firmly on the steering wheel, his jaw set in that way it gets when he's trying to hold himself together.

I place my hand on his thigh. "They're going to love you both."

He gives me a quick glance, the corner of his mouth lifting in what might be a smile if he weren't so tense. "I'll take your word for it."

When we pull up to my parents' home, Isla gasps from the backseat. "It looks like a castle!"

I laugh, and we get out of the car. The old stone house isn't quite a castle, but with its weathered walls and the way it sits nestled against the rolling hills, I can see how it might look that way to a child.

The front door swings open before I can even knock, and there's my mother, her face lighting up at the sight of us. Her gaze immediately drops to Isla.

"Well, hello there!" she says, her voice warm as honey. "You must be Isla."

Isla beams up at her. "Are you Lucy's mum?"

"I am, indeed. You can call me Sam." She bends down slightly, extending her hand to Isla, who takes it with surprising formality and gives it a little shake.

Mum straightens and turns her attention to Aidan. "And you must be Aidan. It's lovely to finally meet you."

"The pleasure's mine."

Mum doesn't hesitate, wrapping Aidan in a hug. I catch the momentary stiffness in his shoulders before he relaxes, returning her embrace with careful politeness.

"Come in, come in," she says, ushering us through the door. "Everyone's in the living room."

I lace my fingers through Aidan's, feeling the tension in his fingers. He's trying so hard to appear calm, but I know better. His eyes dart around, taking in the family photos lining the hallway, the worn comfort of our family home.

"This is beautiful," he admires, and I can tell he means it.

We follow Mum into the living room. Dad's standing by the fireplace, a glass of whisky in hand, and he turns as we enter. His eyes crinkle when he sees me, but I can feel his appraising gaze as it shifts to Aidan and Isla.

"There she is," Dad says, setting down his glass and opening his arms to me.

I step into his embrace, breathing in the familiar scent of wood smoke and that spicy aftershave he's worn for as long as I can remember. "Hi, Dad."

When we pull apart, he looks past me to Aidan, who's standing tall with Isla partially hidden behind his legs, her small fingers clutching the fabric of his jeans.

"Paul," my father says, extending his hand. His voice carries that gentle authority that's always been his signature.

"Aidan Reid," Aidan replies, his grip firm as they shake hands. "Thank you for having us."

Dad nods. "We've been looking forward to it. Lucy speaks very highly of you both."

"Daddy," Isla whispers. "Can I go see the babies?"

My eyes drift to the couch where Bree and Juliette are sitting with the twins. The girls are tiny, perfect little mirrors of one another, their soft giggles filling the room.

Aidan's attention flickers to Isla. "Of course."

Isla approaches cautiously as Juliette beckons her over. "Would you like to sit next to me and say hello?"

Isla nods eagerly, climbing up onto the couch. Aidan relaxes beside me as Isla is welcomed into the fold.

I turn to see Callan striding into the room, his face lighting up when he sees me. Behind him is Knox, whose eyes immediately narrow when they land on Aidan.

"Lou!" Callan sweeps me into a bear hug, lifting me off my feet. "Thought you'd never get here."

"We're right on time," I laugh as he sets me down. "Callan, Knox, this is Aidan. And that's Isla over there, making friends with the twins."

Callan's eyes shift to Aidan before he breaks into a wide grin. He claps Aidan on the shoulder with enough force to make a lesser man stumble. "Welcome to the madhouse, mate."

Knox finally steps forward to shake Aidan's hand. His grip looks firmer than necessary. "Knox. Nice to meet you."

"Knox, play nice!" Juliette calls from the couch.

"Yeah," Bree adds. "Don't break him yet. I haven't even gotten a chance to interrogate him."

I let out a laugh, feeling some of the tension lift from my shoulders. I slip my hand back into Aidan's, giving it a squeeze.

"Don't worry," I whisper, leaning closer to him. "That's Bree's way of saying she likes you."

Aidan doesn't look entirely convinced, but his mouth quirks up at one corner.

"Dinner's almost ready," Mum calls from the doorway.

As everyone starts moving toward the dining room, I notice Isla still perched on the couch beside Juliette, completely entranced by the twins. Her small face is alight with wonder as one of the babies grabs her finger.

The pride in Aidan's eyes as he watches her makes my heart swell.

Dinner goes well with easy conversation. Once the plates are cleared, Isla abandons her chair at the table in favor of playing in the living room with the twins.

Everything seems to be falling into place. My family's warming up to Aidan, and he's more than holding his own. True to form, my dad can't let the question I've been waiting for go unasked now that it's only adults at the table. "So, Aidan, you're quite a bit older than Lucy, aye?"

My heart skips a beat, and suddenly, the room shrinks. A knot forms in my stomach. I quickly glance at Aidan again, but he's not reacting the way I thought he might. No tension in his jaw, no shift in his posture. He was waiting for this.

The words hang there, awkward, like they always do when my dad asks something everyone else sidesteps. Aidan reaches for my hand under the table, and his voice when he answers is astonishingly sure.

"Ten years, yes," Aidan says, his thumb brushing over my knuckles. Callan's watching us with interest while Knox's gaze is more scrutinizing.

"And you work on the rigs?" Dad asks, leaning back in his chair.

"Aye, North Sea. Two weeks on, two weeks off. Been doing it for eight years now."

Dad nods thoughtfully. "That's a tough schedule. Especially with a young daughter."

"It is," Aidan agrees. "But it provides well for us, and I get proper time with her when I'm home."

I squeeze his hand under the table, grateful for his candid responses. He's not defensive or apologetic. Just honest.

"And how do you manage the time apart?" Dad continues. "With Lucy, I mean."

I open my mouth to intervene, but Aidan beats me to it.

"It's a challenge," Aidan replies. "But I've been lucky. Lucy's incredibly understanding about my schedule. We make the most of the time we have together."

I feel a rush of warmth at his words, at the way he speaks about us with such certainty. There's no hesitation, no awkwardness in how he claims our relationship in front of my family.

"And what about long term?" Dad presses, swirling his whisky.

"I've been thinking about that," Aidan admits. "There are some local positions I've been looking at. Less money, but home every night." His eyes find mine. "Seems like a fair trade."

My heart skips. This is the first I'm hearing about this. He's been thinking about a job change? For us?

"Good man," Dad says with an approving nod, and I release the breath I didn't realize I was holding.

Knox clears his throat. "And Isla? How's she handling all this?"

"She adores Lucy," Aidan answers simply. "And Lucy's amazing with her."

I could cry. I want to cry. My heart is full in a way I didn't even know was possible. I want to lean over, in front of everyone, and kiss him. Right now. I want him to feel what I feel, to know that every ounce of me is right here, entirely his.

I love him. I love him so much it hurts.

"SWOON." Bree fans herself. "Tell me I'm not the only one melting right now."

I can't help the laugh that slips out. Even with her teasing, there's a warmth in her eyes that makes me smile. Bree is Callan's match in the way they always cut through discomfort with humor.

"You're glowing, Lucy," she adds, grinning at me.

I shake my head. "I'm just...happy."

"And you should be," Bree says, softer now.

"Well, looks like you're stuck with her now, mate." Callan smirks. "I mean, if she's got you feeling all soft and gooey inside, there's no turning back."

Aidan gives him an amused look, but he doesn't miss a beat. "I can live with that."

Knox clears his throat, drawing Aidan's attention. "Speaking of being stuck with her," he says, his voice deceptively casual, "you should know that if you ever hurt her, there's a whole lot of us who know exactly how to make sure no one finds your body."

"Knox!" Juliette gasps, her hand flying out to smack his shoulder with shocking force. "For god's sake!"

Aidan, to my complete surprise, just chuckles. "I'd expect nothing less," he says, looking over his shoulder to where Isla is still playing with the twins. "I'd do the same for Isla."

Knox gives a small nod, seeming to accept his response.

I glance at Aidan again, my hand still firmly clasped in his, and an irrepressible smile spreads across my face. Whatever comes next, whatever storms we might face, I know we've already found something worth holding onto.

thirty-two
LUCY

I've been on cloud nine since that dinner with my family. Aidan left for another rotation shortly after that, and I'll always miss him when he's gone, but everything is as perfect as it could be.

It's mid-July, warm and golden, and I'm completely lost in thought as I stand at the shore of the loch. Isla is skipping around in her little world, her laughter carrying across the water as she hunts for the perfect skipping stones.

This has become our thing when Aidan's away. Our little routine.

"Look, Lucy," she calls out, holding up a flat, smooth pebble with a triumphant grin. "This one's gonna go far!"

I watch her carefully as she winds up and releases the stone with all the enthusiasm her small arms can muster. It skips once, twice, three times, before finally sinking beneath the surface. Isla's eyes light up as she turns to me, her face shining with pride.

"Did you see that?"

"I did see!" I laugh, giving her a high-five. "You're getting really good at that."

She grins before running off to find another perfect stone. I love spending time with her, but I miss Aidan. We've talked on the phone, but it's not the same. I even find myself missing his brooding silence.

I glance at my watch, taken aback by the time. I hardly noticed the sun dipping lower.

"Isla, sweetie, we should get you home," I say, pulling my thoughts back to the present. "Your nana is going to be there soon. She's going to stay with you tonight since I have to be up early for work tomorrow."

She lets out a small groan, but there's no actual fight in it. She drops the stones she'd been collecting with a sigh, and without another word, follows me to the car.

She skips ahead of me, her feet leaving footprints in the damp earth, and it hits me again how real this is. I haven't moved in with them or anything, but I have been staying over with Isla more often to help Aidan out and give his mum some rest.

Isla chatters nonstop in the backseat, her words tumbling out faster than I can comprehend. I catch her in the rearview mirror and can't help smiling—her cheeks are rosy, curls wild and untamed, each bounce of her head radiating pure joy.

We pull into the driveway, and I cut the engine, taking a last glance at her. "Let's get inside and cleaned up before your nana gets here."

She nods eagerly and lets me help her out of the car. Her little hand brushes mine as we walk up the path, and I hear her gasp.

"Lucy, look!" she exclaims, her finger shooting straight ahead, pointing toward the porch.

I follow her gaze, and my heart skips a beat. There's Aidan, leaning against the railing in his usual worn jeans and dark sweater. His hair's a little tousled, wind-touched, and it makes me want to reach out and smooth it. But it's his smile that catches my attention.

"Daddy!" Isla squeals, and before I can even blink, she's running full speed toward him. Aidan drops to one knee, arms wide, as she leaps into them.

"There's my wee lass." He lifts her off the ground and spins her in circles until she squeals even louder. "Did you miss me?"

"So much!"

I hang back a few steps, giving them their space. I let my gaze drift back to him, and when our eyes meet over Isla's head, my heart skips again. There's an unusual spark in his eyes today.

His voice is a little lower as he gently lowers Isla to the ground. "Surprise."

"Hey you." I close the gap between us. "I didn't expect you back so soon." My voice catches just a little. I feel like I could cry from relief. I don't know why I'm feeling so overwhelmed.

His hand comes to rest on the small of my back, pulling me gently into him. I tilt my face up to meet his while Isla's excited chatter fades into the background as she runs into the house.

His hand rises to cradle my face, his thumb tracing the curve of my cheekbone. "I couldn't wait any longer," he mutters before his lips brush mine with the softest kiss. "I missed you."

"I missed you, too. But can you just…leave work like that?"

He pulls back just enough, but his eyes stay locked on mine. "I'm done with it, Lucy," he says. "I got that local job." And then, like it's nothing at all, "I'm home for good."

My world tilts sideways.

"What?" The word comes out barely above a whisper. I'm afraid if I say it too loud, I'll wake up from whatever dream this is.

His thumb continues its gentle path along my cheekbone. "I can't keep leaving you and Isla."

Tears spring to my eyes before I can stop them. Joy. Relief. I swallow hard, my breath shaky, trying to hold it together, but then he's already pulling me close, wrapping me up in his arms. He knows exactly what I need.

"You okay?" he asks softly as his lips press against my hair.

I nod against his chest, letting out a breathy laugh. "More than okay. I just... I can't believe it."

His arms tighten around me. "I was going crazy out there, Lucy. It was time."

Isla's voice rings out from the living room. "Daddy, Lucy, are you coming inside or what?"

"Come on," he says with a gentle smile as he takes my hand and guides me toward the door. "I'll tell you all about it."

I follow him inside, still trying to wrap my head around it. My heart can't quite catch up to my thoughts.

Isla bounces around us as we step into the living room. "Daddy, can we have pizza for dinner? Please?" She tugs on his sleeve with wide, pleading eyes.

Aidan chuckles, a sound that always seems to calm something inside me. He reaches down to ruffle her hair. "Aye, we can have pizza. Why don't you go wash up while I order?"

She darts off, disappearing down the hall. Aidan turns back to me, and without a word, he takes my hand again, leading me toward the couch. He sits, pulling me down onto his lap.

"I know this was quick," he admits. "But being away, missing so much of Isla's life, missing you... It wasn't working anymore."

My heart thuds as I wait for him to say more, his thumb tracing slow circles on the back of my hand.

"The life I want isn't on some rig in the middle of the sea. It's here, with Isla...and with you."

Something breaks inside me at his words. It's like a dam bursting, sudden and overwhelming. Tears spring to my eyes before I can stop them, streaming down my face in hot, uncontrollable waves.

"Lucy?" Aidan's voice shifts, concern etching his features as his hands come up to frame my face. "What's wrong?"

I try to speak, but a sob escapes instead. I press my palm against my mouth, trying to hold back the flood, but it's useless. The emotions are too big, too raw, like they're being ripped straight from my chest.

"I-I'm sorry," I manage between gasps. "I'm just so happy." Another sob cuts me off, and I shake my head helplessly.

His eyes crinkle at the corners as he watches me fall apart in his arms. Instead of trying to stop my tears, he just pulls me closer, his hand cupping the back of my head.

"Look at you," he says with a small shake of his head. "Crying because I'm staying." His thumb brushes away a tear from my cheek, and there's something so tender in the gesture it only makes me cry harder.

"I know," I hiccup, trying to catch my breath. "I'm a mess."

"You're perfect," he says, his voice dropping to that low rumble that always makes my heart skip. "Do you have any idea how much I love you?"

My breath catches in my throat as I stare at him. Did he just...?

"What did you say?" I whisper.

His eyes don't waver from mine. "I said I love you, Lucy MacKenzie. I've loved you since that night with the cherry pie all over your kitchen."

I let out a watery laugh, my hands trembling as they find his wrists, holding on.

"I love how you care for Isla like she's your own," he continues, his eyes never leaving mine. "I love how you look at me. I love that you never push, but you never back down, either."

His forehead presses against mine, his breath warm against my lips. "I love that you're stubborn as hell when it matters. That you've made room for us in your life when you didn't have to."

My lips are on his before another word can leave his mouth, kissing him with every ounce of hope I've been holding onto.

"I love you, too," I whisper against his lips. "I love you *so* much."

He kisses me back with equal fervor, his hands tangling in my hair. All the fear, all the uncertainty I've been carrying just melts away. This is real. He's here, he's staying, and he loves *me*.

When we finally break apart, both of us breathing hard, I can't stop the smile that spreads across my face. It's so wide it actually hurts.

I laugh, resting my head on his chest just as Isla comes running back into the living room.

"Why are you crying, Lucy?" she asks.

I quickly swipe at my eyes. "Oh, sweet girl, these are happy tears." I wipe my eyes one last time. "Sometimes grown-ups cry when they're really, really happy."

Isla looks between Aidan and me, her brows furrowing in thought. "Are you happy because Daddy's home?"

"That's part of it, but your daddy just told me some really good news." I meet Aidan's gaze, my heart swelling. "He's going to be home a lot more now."

Her eyes widen, the realization hitting her in an instant. "Really? You're not going away anymore?"

"That's right, love. I'll be here every day now."

Isla's eyes sparkle with pure joy. Without missing a beat,

she throws herself on top of us. "Yay! We can go to the park, have movie nights, make pancakes on the weekend—"

Aidan chuckles. "Aye, we can do all those things and more. I promise." He presses a kiss to the top of her head. In that moment, I see a future I didn't dare dream of before. Lazy Sunday mornings, family dinners, bedtime stories with the three of us snuggled together.

"And you'll be here, too. Right, Lucy?" Isla asks. "You'll stay with us?"

The question is so innocent and pure, but it catches me off guard. The weight of her words, the *implication* behind them, settles heavily on my chest. I glance up at Aidan, unsure how to respond. His eyes meet mine, and I catch a flicker of uncertainty there, too. It's not like we've had a chance to talk about how this changes things, or if it does.

Finally, Aidan breaks the silence. "Lucy will be here," he says. "As much as she wants to be."

I feel tears prick at my eyes again. "I'd love to be here," I tell Isla, reaching out to smooth a stray piece of hair from her face. "If that's okay with you?"

Her face lights up instantly. "Yes! Can you stay forever?"

I laugh softly. "Well, let's start with me being here more often and see how it goes, okay?"

Her head bobs up and down. "Okay. Can we have pizza now?"

I can't help but marvel at how, one second, she's asking if I can stay forever, and the next, she's laser-focused on pizza as if that's the most pressing matter in the world. Kids really do keep you humble.

"All right," Aidan chuckles, giving Isla's shoulder a gentle squeeze. "I'll order the pizza. Why don't you go pick out a movie for us to watch while we eat?"

She dashes off to search through her pile of movies while

Aidan pulls me to my feet, his hand sliding into mine as he leads me toward the kitchen.

Once we're out of earshot, he turns to me, his face growing serious. The playful smile from earlier fades, and I can see the weight of his words hanging between us, waiting to be said.

"I hope you know I meant what I said," he begins. "I want you here, as much as you're comfortable with."

My heart swells at his words, but there's something vulnerable in his eyes that makes me step closer. I reach up to cup his face, feeling the rough texture of his stubble beneath my palms.

"I know you meant it," I whisper.

His shoulders relax, tension I didn't even realize he was carrying melting away. "Good," he says simply, but the relief in his voice is unmistakable.

His eyes drop to my mouth, darkening in a way I've come to recognize. "Fuck, I missed you." He backs me up until I'm pressed against the counter. "I plan on showing you exactly how much once Isla's in bed tonight."

My breath catches in my throat as his hands find my hips, fingers digging in just enough to make me shiver.

"Oh?" I manage, my voice embarrassingly breathless. "And how do you plan on doing that?"

He leans in, his lips brushing against my ear. "I'm going to take my time with you tonight." His voice drops to that rough, gravelly tone that makes heat pool low in my stomach. "I want to hear those little sounds you make when I touch you just right."

I swallow hard, feeling my face flush. "Aidan..."

"I'm going to make you blush just like you are now." His teeth graze my earlobe before he pulls back, his hands lingering on my hips before dropping to his sides. "Now, cheese or pepperoni?"

thirty-three
LUCY

I breathe him in, savoring the faint trace of sea salt that always lingers on his skin, wondering if it will always be there or if one day it'll fade. Isla's tucked in bed, the house is quiet, and we're curled up on the couch.

"I'm sorry we don't get much time alone," Aidan says quietly.

I tilt my head up from his shoulder. "Don't apologize. I love every second with you, whether we're alone or not."

His lips twitch, amusement dancing in his stormy eyes. "Aye, but I wouldn't mind a bit more time where we don't have to worry about tiny ears overhearing things they shouldn't."

Heat prickles up my neck, memories flashing through my mind of whispered confessions, rough hands, and the way his voice turns molten when he tells me exactly what he wants. And how I never hesitate to give it to him.

I swallow, trying to ignore the way my pulse kicks up. "Well," I murmur, letting my fingers trace absent patterns against his chest, "when you put it like that, I wouldn't mind an evening with you, either."

"Just an evening? I'd need at least a full day to do everything I have in mind."

Heat coils low in my stomach, and before I can stop myself, I drag a teasing finger up his thigh. "Well, can I get a little preview tonight?"

He huffs a low laugh, but the sound turns into something rougher. "That's a bit forward, lass." His voice drops, turning to pure sin. "But fuck yes you can. Head upstairs and get ready for me. I'll be up soon."

A sharp pulse of need shoots through me, and I scramble to my feet, nearly tripping in my rush. My heart is hammering as I climb the stairs, each step sending a new wave of anticipation through me. My skin hums, tingling with the kind of energy that makes my breath come short, goosebumps rising despite the heat of the house.

I'm still getting used to this version of me that comes alive under his hands. Even now, I can feel him like a phantom touch, setting every nerve ending on fire before he's even laid a finger on me.

I fumble with the buttons of my shirt. Each piece of clothing that slips from my body only heightens the thrill coursing through me. By the time I perch on the edge of the bed, my skin is flushed, my breath uneven.

Every creak of the floorboards downstairs makes me jump. I picture him taking the stairs two at a time, his jaw set with that delicious determination, driven by the same urgency I'm feeling.

The soft click of the door pulls my breath out of me. Aidan's there, framed in the hallway light, broad shoulders just catching the glow. His eyes lock on mine.

"Goddamn," he exhales. "You're...unreal."

His gaze drags over me, slow and deliberate, leaving no inch of bare skin unacknowledged. I'm exposed, yes, but powerful, too. I could ask him for anything right now, and he'd give it to me.

He finally stalks toward me, shedding his clothes along the way. My pulse pounds as, inch by inch, he reveals his broad shoulders, the sculpted lines of his chest, and the strength coiled beneath his skin.

He stops in front of me, his warm, calloused hand cradling my cheek, tilting my face up to meet his gaze. His eyes, dark and hungry, lock onto mine as he leans in, his lips brushing the shell of my ear.

"You like it when I tell you what to do, don't you?" His voice is a low rumble against my skin, sending shivers down my spine.

I nod, not trusting my voice.

"Words, Lucy," he commands softly. "I need to hear you say it."

"Yes," I breathe. "I like it."

His lips curve into a smile against my neck. "Good girl."

Those two simple words make my entire body flush with heat. He knows exactly what they do to me, how they make me melt.

He lays me back onto the bed, his body following mine until I'm pinned beneath his weight.

"I've been thinking about this for weeks," he admits, his mouth trailing down my throat. "Couldn't focus on a damn thing."

His hands slide down my sides, gripping my hips as he flips me over. My breath catches as I find myself pressed against the mattress, his chest a warm wall against my back. His fingers tangle in my hair, gently tilting my head back.

"I want you like this," he growls, his voice rough with need.

I gasp as his other hand slides between my thighs, finding me already wet and ready for him. "Please," I whisper.

He releases my hair to grip my hips, positioning me on my hands and knees before him. The mattress dips as he moves behind me. He's hard against me, pressing into the curve of my backside. My entire body is on fire, desperate for him.

"Aidan," I whimper, pushing back against him, silently begging.

He chuckles. "So impatient." His teeth graze my shoulder, just hard enough to make me gasp.

When he finally pushes inside me, I have to bury my face in the pillow to muffle my cry.

He fills me completely, stretching me in the best way. His hand climbs up my spine, then tangles in my hair, tugging just enough to arch my back.

"Look at you," he groans, his voice strained with the effort of holding back. "So perfect for me."

When he starts to move, it's with measured control that contradicts the tension coiled in his body. Each thrust is deep and purposeful, drawing soft moans from my lips.

"That's it," he encourages. "Let me hear those pretty little sounds."

"Aidan," I gasp, his name falling from my lips like a prayer. "Harder."

His grip on my hips tightens. "Look at me," he commands, his voice rough. "Turn your head and look at me, Lucy."

I do as he asks, twisting to meet his gaze over my shoulder. The sight of him nearly undoes me, his face flushed with desire, jaw clenched, eyes burning into mine. His rhythm intensifies, each thrust more demanding than the last. The sound of skin against skin fills the room, punctuated by my breathless moans and his deep groans.

"You're so beautiful like this," he praises, his hand slipping around to cup my breast, thumb brushing over my nipple. "Taking me so well."

When his fingers roll the sensitive peak between them, the sensation travels like lightning straight to my core. The sudden jolt of pleasure is so intense, so unexpected, that I cry out his name as everything inside me shatters. My body tenses, trembling as my orgasm crashes through me, leaving me gasping and clutching desperately at the sheets beneath me.

"That's it," Aidan growls, his voice thick with satisfaction. "So responsive for me."

He doesn't slow his pace, driving into me as I quiver around him, prolonging my pleasure until I'm whimpering, overwhelmed by sensation. His rhythm becomes more erratic as he chases his own release.

"Lucy," he groans, the sound raw and primal.

I push back against him, wanting to feel every inch, wanting to be the reason he loses control.

With a final, powerful thrust, he stills, his body shuddering against mine as he finds his release. His forehead drops to my shoulder, his breath hot against my skin as pleasure ripples through him. Every pulse of his cock sends aftershocks through my already sensitive body. His arms tighten around me as his body trembles against mine, his chest heaving with ragged breaths as he empties himself completely.

"Fuck," he groans.

He gently eases us both down onto the mattress. He doesn't pull away immediately, keeping me pressed against him as our heartbeats gradually slow. His arms wrap around me, one hand splayed possessively across my stomach.

"You okay?" he asks against my hair, his voice soft with concern.

I nod, too blissed out to form words.

He presses a gentle kiss to my shoulder, his lips lingering against my skin. I feel him smile, that rare, unguarded curve of his mouth that I've come to treasure.

"I missed this," I whisper, my voice still a little shaky. I shift slightly, turning in his arms until we're face to face. In the soft glow of the bedside lamp, the usual storm in his eyes calms to gentle waves. I trace my fingers along the stubble on his jaw, marveling at how this gruff, guarded man can look at me with such tenderness.

"What?" he asks, catching my hand and pressing a kiss to my palm.

"Nothing," I say, but I can't help the smile that spreads across my face. "Just...happy."

"I like seeing you like this," he mumbles against my skin. "All soft and satisfied."

He presses his lips to my wrist before he trails his lips higher, pressing gentle kisses along the inside of my arm. Each touch sends little sparks through me, reawakening nerves I thought were thoroughly spent.

"I think I could get used to this," I admit softly. "You coming home to me every night."

His eyes darken at my words, something possessive flashing in their depths right before he flips me onto my back. I feel him growing hard again, the evidence of his renewed desire pressing insistently against my thigh.

"Already?" I whisper, unable to keep the pleased surprise from my voice.

"Can you blame me?" His voice is a low rumble that I feel more than hear. "Fuck, I need to taste you."

I arch against him as his lips travel lower, his stubble creating a delicious friction against my sensitive skin. When his mouth closes around my nipple, I gasp, my back bowing off the bed. His tongue swirls around the hardened peak before he sucks harder.

"Aidan," I gasp, straining against his hold.

He cups both breasts, kneading the soft flesh as he moves to give attention to my other nipple. The contrast between his rough palms and the wet heat of his mouth makes me dizzy with want as I thread my fingers through his hair.

"These gorgeous tits fill my hands perfectly," he groans. "Made for me."

A needy whimper escapes my throat at his words. His hand shifts between us, and my breath catches when I realize he's gripping himself, stroking his length while his mouth continues its sweet torture on my breast. I find myself watching him through heavy-lidded eyes.

"I've never watched a man touch himself like that before," I say, my eyes fixed on his hand wrapped around his rigid length. The words slip out before I can stop them, heat rushing to my cheeks at my own admission.

Aidan moves slowly. "No?"

I shake my head, swallowing hard. "No. It's... I like watching you."

He shifts, positioning himself so I have a better view.

"Watch, then," he says. "Watch how hard you make me."

My breath catches as his hand begins to move again, stroking from base to tip with unhurried movements. I'm transfixed by the way his muscles tense, the flex of his forearm, the way his jaw clenches when he twists his wrist just so.

He leans down to take my nipple between his lips again.

"You're going to kill me," I mumble.

He chuckles against my skin, the vibration sending shivers through me. "Not before I make you come again."

His pace quickens, his hand pumping with more urgency as he switches to my other breast. I can't tear my eyes away from the hypnotic rhythm of his hand, the way his jaw works as he sucks me harder, the dark hunger in his eyes when they meet mine.

His mouth never leaves my breast as his hand abandons his

own pleasure to give me mine. His fingers slide between my thighs, instantly finding my clit. The dual sensation of his hot mouth laving my nipple while his fingers work in tight, deliberate circles is overwhelming.

"Oh god," I gasp, my hips bucking against his hand.

He increases the pressure, the rhythm perfect as he alternates between firm strokes and featherlight touches. All while his tongue flicks across my hardened peak in the same maddening pattern.

The pleasure builds rapidly, coiling tighter with each pass of his fingers. My breathing becomes ragged, my entire body tensing as I climb higher.

When he sucks harder and flicks his finger just right, the tension snaps. I shatter completely, crying out his name as waves of pleasure crash through me. My body arches off the bed, but he holds me steady, guiding me through each pulsing aftershock.

"Oh, fuck, Lucy—" Aidan's voice breaks into a guttural groan, dragging my eyes open just in time to see his face contort with pleasure. He still hasn't moved his hand back to stroke himself, but he's coming anyway, his release spilling across my stomach in hot pulses. His body shudders as he watches his own cum coat my skin.

I can't look away.

"Jesus...Christ," he pants, chest heaving as he braces himself above me. "Just watching you makes me fucking lose it."

His hand finally moves to grasp himself, fingers wrapping around his still-hard length. I watch, mesmerized, as he strokes slowly, drawing out the last pulses of his orgasm. His hand moves in long, deliberate pulls, coaxing a few more spurts across my skin.

Pride surges through me. I did this to him. I made him lose control.

When he's finally spent, he collapses beside me. His arm drapes possessively across my waist, careful to avoid the mess on my stomach. I turn to look at him, taking in the flush on his cheeks, the slight sheen of sweat on his brow.

"That's never happened before," he admits. "You have no fucking idea what you do to me."

I reach for him, threading my fingers through the hair at the nape of his neck and pulling him down into a kiss that's slow and deep. He responds immediately, his lips soft against mine.

"I think I've got a pretty good idea," I whisper against his lips, tasting the smile that flickers there.

"Let me clean you up."

He slips out of bed and comes back with a warm, damp cloth. The way he moves is filled with care as he gently swipes my skin.

When he's done, he tosses it into the hamper, then tugs me into him, my back pressed to his chest, his legs tangling with mine. I lie there wrapped up in him, skin clean but nerves still sparking, and wonder what the hell just happened. Not the sex. I mean, yes, that too...but *this*. The way he took care of me after. I think I liked that more than anything else.

Who even am I? Since when does a warm washcloth and a kiss do more damage to my heart than anything that happened before it?

Because, yeah, the rest of it was *ruin me* hot, but this? Him holding me like I'm his.

That's the part I'll never recover from.

LUCY

I love my flat, but it just doesn't feel like home anymore. Home is starting to feel like the little house at the end of the lane, where Isla's laughter echoes in the evenings and Aidan's presence fills the rooms with a kind of warmth I'd been missing terribly.

I haven't moved in, but my toothbrush has taken up permanent residence in the bathroom, and my favorite mug sits on the shelf next to Aidan's.

He's only a few weeks into the new job with a local construction crew, but I can already see the change in him. He comes home with sawdust on his jeans and sun on his skin, that worn-out look in his eyes framed with peace. He jokes more, teasing me about the way I load the dishwasher or how I hum off-key when I think no one's listening.

He's happy.

I'm happy.

Every afternoon after closing the café, I take over for Aidan's mum, spending time with Isla until Aidan gets home. Dinner, a little playtime, then bedtime—it's second nature.

I'm at his place now, wiping down the kitchen counter, when a sharp knock on the front door pierces through the house.

I pause, frowning slightly. Aidan never knocks. His heavy boots usually announce his arrival long before I see him.

Another knock—louder this time, more insistent.

My stomach tightens as I dry my hands on a dish towel and head for the door. My fingers hesitate on the handle for just a second before I pull it open.

The woman on the doorstep is breathtaking. Tall and willowy, with golden curls that catch the evening light like spun silk. Her striking green eyes widen slightly as they meet mine.

"Oh, I'm sorry, I thought—" She trails off, glancing at the number on the door, her brows knitting together. Then her gaze returns to mine. "Is Aidan here?"

My heart pounds as I grasp for words. "He's... He's not home yet," I manage, my voice thinner than I'd like. She lifts her chin, and I can practically feel myself shrinking an inch.

She nods slowly. Her shoulders stiffen, and she presses her lips together. Her gaze shifts past me, sweeping over the house. "And Isla?" she asks, her voice tight, carefully measured, but I don't miss the way her fingers clench slightly at her sides.

I step into the doorway, blocking her view of the house. My pulse pounds in my ears, but I force my voice to stay even. "I'm sorry, but I can't share anything about Isla with someone I personally don't know. I don't think I caught your name?"

Her gaze snaps back to mine. If she's looking for weaknesses, she's probably already found a dozen.

"Emily. Isla's my daughter."

My stomach clenches. *No. No, no, no. This isn't happening.*

"I see," I reply as gently as I possibly can. "I think you'll need to talk to Aidan about it. He's not home right now, and it's not my place to speak for him. I'm sure you understand."

The tension coils tightly between us. My fingers curl around the doorframe, gripping it like an anchor, refusing to be the first to look away.

Finally, she exhales, the fight seeming to drain from her shoulders. "Fine," she mutters, stepping back. She rummages through her bag, pulling out a crumpled scrap of paper and a pen. With quick strokes, she scrawls a phone number and presses it into my hand. "I'll wait to speak to Aidan."

I nod. "That's the best thing to do." A beat of silence stretches between us before I add, "Have a good evening."

She doesn't respond. Just turns and walks away, her silhouette long and graceful against the fading light. I stand there feeling small in a way I haven't in a long time.

I close the door softly, locking it with trembling hands. Leaning against the cool wood, I shove the scrap of paper into my pocket and take a deep breath, trying to steady my racing heart. Isla's laughter spills from the living room as she watches whatever cartoon that has her attention, blissfully unaware of the storm brewing just outside.

I don't know what reason Isla's mother has for returning, but it really isn't my place to insert myself into that. I know one thing, though—I'll do everything in my power to protect that little girl.

Taking another deep breath, I shake off the unease and head back to the kitchen. My mind races, but I push those thoughts aside, focusing on the here and now. Isla needs her dinner, and I'm determined to keep things as normal as possible until Aidan gets home.

I keep my hands busy in the kitchen, but no amount of bustling can soothe my nerves. I can't help but wonder what this means for all of us.

Would Aidan want her back? The thought twists in my stomach like a knife, even though I know better. I've seen the steel in his eyes when he's mentioned her abandonment, heard the protective edge in his voice when he talks about keeping Isla safe. No, he wouldn't just welcome her with open arms.

But what if she's here to stay? What if she wants to be part of Isla's life again?

I have no claim here. I'm not Isla's mother. I'm just...Lucy. The woman who makes swirly butter toast and stays over sometimes. The woman who's fallen in love with a man and his daughter, building something that suddenly feels terribly fragile.

Life doesn't pause for doubts. Responsibilities and routines pull me forward, reminding me there's still a little girl depending on *me* right now.

"Isla, sweetheart," I call out, my voice only slightly shaky. "Dinner's almost ready. Can you come set the table?"

I hear the patter of her feet as she rushes into the kitchen. "Can I use the special plates?" she asks, her eyes wide and hopeful, filled with that innocent joy that always manages to melt my heart.

I nod, managing to return her enthusiasm with a smile of my own. "Of course. Just be careful with them."

As she cautiously carries the delicate dishes to the table, I take a moment to glance at the clock. Aidan really should be home any minute now, and the thought of how to bring up the unexpected visitor weighs heavily on my mind.

Just as I'm pulling the casserole dish from the oven, the familiar rumble of Aidan's truck fills the air, followed by gravel crunching under his tires as he pulls into the driveway. My heart quickens at the sound, a mix of relief and anxiety flooding through me.

"Daddy's home!" Isla announces, bouncing on her toes.

I swallow hard, determined not to let my nerves show. "He sure is. Why don't you finish setting the table and wash your hands while I go say hello?"

As Isla skips away, I step out onto the porch just as Aidan climbs out of his truck. He looks up and smiles when he sees me, but his expression quickly shifts as he approaches.

His brow furrows. "What's wrong?"

I take a steady breath, trying to find the right words, glancing back at the house to ensure Isla is out of earshot. "Someone came by the house just a little while ago, looking for you."

His brows knit closer together, confusion and concern etched into his handsome features. "Who was it?"

I hesitate for a moment. "It was Isla's mother."

The shock that registers on his face is immediate, quickly followed by a flash of anger. He runs a hand over his cheek, his jaw clenching.

"What did she want?" he asks, his voice tense.

"She was looking for you and Isla," I reply gently, trying to keep my tone calm despite the tension radiating off him. "I didn't let her in or tell her anything," I add quickly, sensing the need to reassure him. "I just said you weren't home and that she'd need to talk to you, not me."

His head tips back slightly as he exhales through his nose, and then he erupts. "Fuck!" The word tears out of him, loud and raw, and I flinch at the suddenness of it.

I've never seen him so visibly furious before. One hand rakes through his hair while the other flexes and clenches at his side. His movements are almost frantic, as though he doesn't know where to direct the anger simmering just beneath the surface.

"Aidan..." I begin, my voice soft, but he cuts me off.

"She doesn't get to do this." His voice is low, but no less

furious. "She doesn't get to show up out of nowhere and—" He breaks off, swiping a hand over his face again.

I take a cautious step closer, my heart aching at the sight of him so upset. "I didn't know what to do. I didn't want to make it worse, so I just...handled it the best I could."

He shakes his head, and the emotion in his eyes tugs at my heart. "You did the right thing," he says. "I just... I wasn't ready for this. I was never going to be ready for this."

I reach out, gently taking his hand in mine. His fingers reluctantly unclench, and I give them a reassuring squeeze. "I know. We'll figure this out together, okay?"

He nods, taking a deep breath, visibly trying to compose himself. "Isla," he says suddenly, his voice tinged with worry. "She didn't see Emily, did she?"

I shake my head quickly. "No, she was playing in the living room the whole time. She has no idea."

Relief washes over his face, but it's short-lived. Tension creeps back into his shoulders. "Did she say if she'd be back?"

"She just said she'd wait to speak to you," I reply, watching his reaction carefully. "She gave me her number." I pull the paper from my pocket and offer it to him.

He stares at it as if it might explode at any moment. The muscle in his jaw ticks, and for a fleeting second, I think he's going to crumple it up and throw it aside. Then he exhales a deep, weary sigh and tucks it into his pocket instead.

"I'll deal with that later," he grumbles, his voice strained. "Right now, I just want to see Isla."

I nod, reaching out to squeeze his hand one more time before we head inside. As we step through the door, Isla comes barreling toward us, launching herself into his arms.

He catches Isla effortlessly, lifting her high and pulling her close. "Hey, princess."

My heart twists as I watch him hold her. Aidan clutches

Isla like she's the only thing keeping him tethered to the earth. His large hands tremble slightly against her small back, and his eyes squeeze shut for just a moment too long. It's more than the usual welcome home hug. It's desperate, protective, as if he's afraid she might vanish if he loosens his grip even the littlest bit.

"Daddy, you're squishing me!" Isla giggles.

"Sorry, wee lass," he murmurs, but he doesn't immediately let go. Instead, he presses his face into her wild curls, breathing her in. When he finally sets her down, I catch the slight sheen in his eyes before he blinks it away.

Even though the circumstances aren't great, the sweetness of it squeezes something in my chest. Then, just as quickly, my stomach lurches. The smell of roasted chicken, warm and heavy in the air, turns sharp in my nose. What had made my mouth water minutes ago now ties my insides in knots. I draw in a deep breath, but it only makes it worse.

I grip the edge of the counter tightly, my knuckles turning white. My mind races, trying to process everything that's unfolded in the past hour, from the unexpected visit from the woman at the door, Aidan's visceral reaction, and now this sudden wave of nausea. It's too much.

Isla's laughter drifts in from the living room, where Aidan is undoubtedly putting on a brave face for her sake. I know I should be in there with them, helping to maintain this façade of normalcy. But at the moment, I can barely keep myself upright.

I close my eyes, willing the queasiness to subside, but it only grows stronger. It has to be the stress of everything happening all at once.

"Hey, are you okay?" Aidan's voice calls from behind me, breaking through my thoughts.

I turn to face him, forcing a weak smile. "I'm..." I begin, but the words catch in my throat as another wave of nausea washes over me. The kitchen suddenly feels too hot, too small.

I stumble slightly, and Aidan's strong arms are there in an instant, bracing me. His touch, usually so comforting, now feels like an unwelcome fire against my skin. The concern in his eyes is unmistakable, a deep furrow forming between his brows as he studies my face.

His fingers gently brush my cheek. "You're pale as a ghost."

"I think I'm going to lie down," I whisper. Dizziness clings to me, warping my surroundings.

He guides me up the stairs, his arm fixed around my waist. As we reach the bedroom, he gently eases me onto the bed. The cool sheets beneath me offer some relief.

I sink into the pillow, closing my eyes against the spinning room. Aidan's weight settles on the edge of the bed as he brushes a strand of hair from my forehead. "Can I get you anything?"

I shake my head, not trusting myself to speak. The nausea churns in my stomach, threatening to rise. I take another slow, measured breath, willing it away.

He hesitates, his gaze lingering on me for a long moment, before he nods. "All right." He brushes his thumb across my cheek one last time before standing. "If you need anything, I'm right here."

I hear his footsteps recede down the hall, followed by the muffled sound of his voice as he talks to Isla. I can't make out the words, but I imagine he's reassuring her, telling her I'm just not feeling well and need to rest.

It doesn't take long before I drift off.

AIDAN

The bloody storm that's Emily rolled in out of nowhere, and I wasn't prepared. Almost five years without one fucking word and she thinks she can just waltz back into our lives and turn everything upside down.

Does she even think about what it's been like for Isla? Does she know the weight of raising a child alone, day in and day out?

Anger coils tightly in my chest, my hands clenching into fists. I'm so damn furious. Why now? Why after all this time? I've fought tooth and nail to give Isla a normal, stable life, and now this...this *bullshit*. I won't let her come in and wreck all that. Not after everything I've done to shield my daughter from this kind of heartache.

She's not welcome here.

Lucy's been nothing but a steady rock for both Isla and me, and now I've dragged her into this disaster. She's been thrown right into the thick of it, and I can't shake this gnawing resentment toward myself for it. I hate that I can't protect her from this and keep her safe from the shitstorm that's just landed on our doorstep.

She doesn't deserve any of this. She shouldn't have to deal with the uncertainty, the tension, or the worry about Isla's mother popping up like the ghost from the past that she is. I feel like I've let her down. She should have been kept out of this drama.

The fire inside me flares hotter, morphing into rage. Emily has no idea what she's up against. I refuse to let anyone—especially her—rip us apart.

Lucy deserves better. Isla deserves better. I'll be damned if I let that woman ruin it all.

I'll handle Emily when I'm ready, but right now, I've got more important things to focus on. Isla's waiting for me to tuck her in. She's what really matters. I hang back for a moment, just watching her, letting the sight of her calm me.

When I step closer to the bed, my heart softens at the sight of her fighting off sleep, determined to stay awake just a bit longer.

"Hey." I lean down to place a gentle kiss on her forehead. "How's my girl doing?"

Her words are wrapped in sleep, but there's still that sweet smile on her face. "I'm good. Are you mad?"

I cover the storm brewing inside me with a soft smile, brushing a stray lock of hair from her face. "No, love, not at all. I'm just...figuring some things out, okay? Nothing for you to worry about."

She nods, her eyes fluttering shut, trusting me to make everything right. That's the part that cuts the deepest—her faith in me. She has no idea what's going on, and I want to keep it that way for as long as I can.

The house is too still as I make my way down the hall after saying goodnight to Isla. Every footstep seems to echo louder than it should. I pause outside my bedroom door, taking a long breath before pushing it open.

Lucy's lying on her side, her body curled into the blankets, her hair spilling across the pillow in soft waves. She looks peaceful. Beautiful.

It's hard to reconcile the image in front of me with the emotions she's probably wrestling with. I want nothing more than to protect her from the turmoil swirling around us.

I move toward the bed slowly, trying not to make a sound. As I sit on the edge, the bed creaks slightly under my weight and she stirs, her eyes fluttering open. I freeze, half expecting her to pull away, but instead, she looks up at me, her expression soft and unguarded.

"Hey," I whisper. "I didn't mean to wake you."

She blinks a few times, still groggy, but a small, reassuring smile creeps onto her face. "It's okay."

"Are you feeling better?"

"A lot better, actually." She takes a second before sitting up a bit straighter. "I'm sorry, Aidan. I didn't mean to react like that earlier. I don't know what happened."

"You have nothing to apologize for. That was a lot, and it isn't your mess to deal with."

She reaches out, her hand resting lightly on my arm. "Just remember, you have people who care about you. Who want to support you."

I let out a long breath, some of the tension easing from my shoulders at her touch and her words. She has this uncanny ability to make the weight on my shoulders feel a little lighter, a little more bearable. "I'm starting to see that."

She beams at that, a real smile that lights up her eyes and makes them sparkle in the dim light of the bedroom. "Good."

I sigh, pulling back slightly. "I don't know what she wants."

Her hand slides down my arm to grasp my hand, her fingers intertwining with mine. "Whatever it is, we'll handle it."

I stare at our joined hands, marveling at how her smaller one fits so perfectly in my larger, rougher one. It's a strange sensation, feeling her touch cut through the chaos. How is it possible that something so simple can soothe the raging storm inside me?

I lift my gaze to meet hers, and I find sincerity shining in those emerald depths. "I know I'm not the easiest person to deal with," I admit gruffly. "Especially with all this...baggage."

She tilts her head, a small, knowing smile tugging at the corners of her lips. "Aidan," she says softly, "I love you. All of you. Even the *baggage*." A tiny laugh escapes her, and her fingers give mine a gentle squeeze. "I don't mind carrying some of it if you'll let me."

Lucy. *My* Lucy. She's not running from my past. She's not afraid of it. And damn it, that means more to me than I could ever put into words.

"You really are something else, you know that?" I say, my voice a bit softer now. "I don't deserve you."

"Don't do that." She shakes her head. "Don't say you don't deserve me. You're a good man. A good father. You work hard, you love fiercely, and you'd do anything to protect the people you care about. That's exactly the kind of man I deserve."

The conviction in her voice hits me square in the chest. I stare into her eyes, searching for any hint that she's just saying what she thinks I need to hear. But there's nothing but truth there, nothing but that unwavering faith she has in me that I'm still trying to understand.

LUCY

I'm baffled by everything that unfolded today. When Aidan woke me up, I felt completely fine. In fact, when I opened my eyes and saw him sitting beside me, I felt a heat surge through my body, a wild impulse to pull him closer, to tear his clothes off right then and there. Totally inappropriate, given the heavy issue looming over us.

His scent is surrounding me, all woodsy and rugged, like the earth after rain, and it makes me forget everything but him. But there's a profound sadness etched into his features. It's as if something inside him has cracked open, revealing a deep well of confusion and fear that I'm not used to seeing.

I ache to reach for him, to take that weight from his shoulders. Seeing him so raw, so unguarded, hits me harder than I expect. I want to smooth away the lines of worry creasing his forehead, to kiss the tension from his jaw. At the same time, I also understand that what he needs right now isn't what *I* want.

"Talk to me," I whisper. "What are you thinking?"

He's quiet for a long moment. "I just keep thinking about

what she wants. Why now? Isla's five, Lucy. Five years of nothing, and suddenly, she shows up?"

The pain in his voice makes my chest tight. "Maybe she's changed. Maybe she realizes what she lost."

Aidan's gaze drops to our intertwined hands. His thumb traces circles on my skin. "When we found out Emily was pregnant, I was... I was happy about it." A sad smile settles on his face. "I thought we'd figure it out together, but she didn't want a baby. She didn't want any of it. And this might make me an asshole, but she doesn't get to just decide she wants to be a mother now," he says, voice rough with emotion. "What if she hurts Isla? What if she gets close to her and then leaves again?"

"You don't have to decide anything tonight. You can take some time to figure out what's best."

He looks at me then, really looks at me, with those storm-gray eyes that make my heart skip. "What do you think I should do?"

The question catches me by surprise. This is him letting me in, letting me help him through a major decision in his and Isla's lives. I take a deep breath, carefully considering my words.

"I think...you should hear what she has to say, but on your terms. Somewhere neutral, just the two of you. I think until you understand what she wants, you should keep Isla out of it."

"And if she wants to be in Isla's life again?"

That's the question that scares me, too. So instead of answering, I ask a question of my own. "What was she like? Before Isla."

Aidan's hand stills on mine. "Do you really want to know about her?"

The honest answer? "I don't know if I necessarily *want* to... It's more that I feel like I should."

He nods slowly. "She was charming when she wanted to

be." His voice is distant, like he's describing someone from another lifetime. "We met at a pub. I was working the rigs then, too, coming off a three-week stint. She was…vibrant."

I listen, doing my best not to picture this beautiful woman who once had his heart.

"It was good at first," he continues. "She was always restless, though. Always looking for the next thing." He exhales sharply. "When she got pregnant with Isla, I thought things would change. I thought she'd want to settle."

The muscle in his jaw works. "She tried, I think. For a while. Isla was four months old when I came home from being away for a couple weeks, and she was just…gone. Left a note saying she couldn't do it anymore. That she wasn't meant to be a mother and that she'd left Isla with my mum."

I feel physically ill imagining coming home to an empty house, a tiny baby, and nothing but a note. Forsaking both him and Isla like that makes my blood boil, but I keep my expression neutral, not wanting to add my anger to his pain.

"I don't know what to do," he admits. "I don't know how to fix this."

"You don't have to fix everything," I reply softly. "You're doing the best you can. And that's enough."

His eyes meet mine, a swirling mix of vulnerability and longing reflected in their depths. "I need you to know that what I had with Emily… It was nothing like this."

"What do you mean?"

"At the end, we were only together for Isla's sake." He shakes his head. "I cared for her, sure. But I never felt for her what I feel for you.

"When Emily left, I was devastated for Isla, angry at the situation," he continues, "but I wasn't heartbroken over her." His fingers tighten around mine. "With you, it's different. Everything is different."

"Aidan…" I whisper, not sure what to say.

"If I lost you, Lucy, it wouldn't just hurt. It would rip me apart. I wouldn't know how to put myself back together."

The words land so plainly, so honestly, that everything inside me goes quiet. All that prickly anxiety from Emily showing up is gone in one hit. I look up at him, and he's already watching me with a searching gaze. I know without a doubt he's not saying this to soothe me. He's saying it because it's true.

"Lucy," he says, his voice cracking slightly as he cups my face in his hands. "I love you. God, I love you so much it terrifies me. I'm so damn sorry you got pulled into this mess. You deserve better than—"

I press my finger to his lips, silencing him. "Don't you dare finish that sentence."

The protest barely leaves me before his mouth is on mine, fierce and hungry, as if he's been holding back for far too long. His lips press against my mouth, his tongue stroking mine, stealing every breath I have. I clutch at his shirt, pulling him closer until there's no space left. The kiss is a collision—tender and rough, apology and promise tangled together.

Aidan moves one hand to my back. Fingers skim down my spine, igniting sparks. They dip beneath the hem of my shirt, grazing the sensitive skin at my waist.

All of a sudden, it's as if my skin has become ultra-sensitive, every tiny movement and brush of his fingers stirring a restless ache within me. The sensation is overwhelming in the best way, sending shivers through me as my body responds to him in ways that feel almost too intense.

He cups my breasts through the thin fabric of my shirt, his thumbs grazing over my nipples. The sensation is powerful, almost devastatingly so. My nipples tighten and peak, achingly sensitive, yet still craving more.

What is happening right now? It's not just the heat

between us, though that's definitely playing a role here. No, there's this strange feeling like my skin has been ignited from within in the most exhilarating way. Is this normal? Is this what it feels like when someone completely shatters your self-control?

I don't get to wonder about it too long. His hands slide lower, skimming over my ribs and down to my hips.

"Lucy," he breathes against my lips, his voice low and rough with need. My name on his tongue sends another shiver racing through me.

I can only whimper in response, completely lost in the sensations overtaking my body. It feels like every nerve ending is heightened, hyperaware of his heat, the hardness of him pressed against me.

His hands find the hem of my shirt and tug upward. I lift my arms to help him, our lips parting only briefly as he pulls the fabric over my head. The cool air rushes against my heated skin, but he's right there, his warm palms gliding over my newly bared flesh.

I reach for him, my fingers fumbling with the buttons of his shirt, desperate to feel his skin against mine. He helps me, shrugging out of it impatiently until we're finally pressed together, chest to chest, heartbeat to frantic heartbeat.

"I need you," I plead, hardly recognizing the needy whisper as my own voice. "Please, Aidan."

A low growl rumbles in his throat as he captures my lips again. He trails hot, open-mouthed kisses down my neck, his teeth grazing the sensitive skin. I tilt my head back, giving him better access, a moan escaping my lips. His hands find my breasts again, kneading and teasing, sending jolts of pleasure straight to my core. I'm trembling, my body wound so tight I feel like I might combust at any moment.

His mouth travels lower, blazing a path down my chest. He

pauses to lavish attention on my breasts, drawing one aching peak into the wet heat of his mouth. I cry out, my back arching off the bed as he swirls his tongue around the sensitive bud. He gives the other the same treatment, sucking and licking until I'm writhing beneath him, my fingers tangled in his hair, holding him to me.

I'm going to come. Right here, right now. He hasn't even touched me *there*.

My fingers tighten in his hair as the tension builds, coiling tighter low in my abdomen. I'm trembling, my hips rolling unconsciously, seeking friction that isn't there. I'm dimly aware of soft, needy sounds escaping my throat, but I'm beyond caring. All that matters is the sweet torment of his mouth.

He seems to sense my desperation as he takes my nipple between his teeth, tugging gently before soothing the sting with broad strokes of his tongue.

"Aidan," I gasp. "Oh god, I'm so close."

He hums against my skin in response. Slowly, torturously, he drags his hand over my leggings, slipping his hand beneath the fabric of my panties. I press against his fingers, desperate for more contact. He groans low in his throat, the sound sending another wave of arousal crashing through me.

"Christ, Lucy," he groans. "You're fucking soaked."

His hands are suddenly at my waistband, tugging impatiently at my leggings. I lift my hips to help him, and he yanks them down along with my underwear in one swift motion. The cool air hits my heated skin, but I don't have time to register the feeling before he's nudging my thighs apart, his eyes darkening as he takes me in.

He doesn't waste a second before settling between my legs, his broad shoulders keeping me spread open for him.

The first touch of his mouth against me has me arching off the bed, a gasp tearing from my throat. His tongue slides up in one long, devastating stroke, and I have to bite my lip to keep from crying out too loudly. It's hard to remember to be quiet when he's doing...that.

"Oh my god," I breathe, my fingers tangling in his hair. He hums against me, the vibration sending shockwaves of pleasure through my body.

His hands grip my thighs, holding me open as he alternates between gentle licks and firmer strokes that have me writhing beneath him. I bite down on my lip to muffle the sounds threatening to escape as he finds that perfect spot, circling it with his tongue until my legs are trembling against his shoulders. The pleasure builds impossibly higher, coiling tightly in my core until I feel like I might shatter completely.

"Please," I whisper, not even sure what I'm begging for. More? Less? I can't think straight with his mouth doing wicked things that make my vision blur at the edges.

He slides two fingers inside me, curling them just right, and that's all it takes. The orgasm crashes over me, stealing my breath. I have to press both hands over my mouth to keep from crying out, my body shaking as wave after wave of ecstasy rolls through me.

Aidan doesn't stop, working me through it with gentle strokes until I'm boneless and gasping. When he finally lifts his head, his lips are glistening, and I can't take my eyes off him. He looks almost feral, his eyes burning with hunger as he moves up my body. The sight sends a fresh wave of desire through me.

I reach between us with the intent of undoing his jeans when he gently grabs my wrist. "Not tonight. This was for you."

"No," I whisper, tugging my hand free from his grasp. "I want to touch you, too."

"Lucy, you don't have to—"

"I know I don't have to," I interrupt, my voice surprisingly steady despite my trembling limbs. "I want to."

I place my palm against his chest, feeling his heart thunder beneath my touch. The confidence in my voice contradicts the nervous flutter in my stomach. I've never wanted someone like this before—never felt this overwhelming need to taste, to give, to watch someone come apart because of me.

"I want to make you feel as good as you make me feel," I admit, my cheeks burning with the confession.

His eyes don't leave mine as I slide my hand down his chest, over the ridges of his abdomen, until I reach the waistband of his jeans. My fingers work the button, then the zipper. He's hard and straining against the denim, and my mouth goes dry with anticipation.

"Lift your hips," I whisper, and he does, allowing me to tug his jeans down his thighs. His boxers do little to hide how much he wants this, the outline of him pressing insistently against the fabric.

I palm him, feeling the heat of his hardened length. His breath hitches, and a fresh wave of desire courses through me. I hook my fingers into the waistband of his boxers, pulling them down to free him.

He's beautiful—thick and firm, straining toward his stomach. I wrap my hand around him, marveling at the contrast between the velvet-soft skin and the steel underneath.

"Lucy," he groans as I begin to stroke him slowly.

I shift down the bed, positioning myself between his thighs. I glance up at him before I lower my head, pressing a soft kiss to his hip bone, then trail my lips inward. I can feel him holding his breath, the muscles in his thighs flexing beneath my hands.

When I finally take him into my mouth, his sharp intake of breath is the most satisfying sound I've ever heard. I start slowly, savoring the weight of him on my tongue. It's intoxicating.

"Fuck..." he moans. "Just like that."

His praise encourages me. I take him deeper, hollowing my cheeks as I work him with my mouth and hand together. His fingers tangle in my hair, not pushing, just holding on. I can feel him growing impossibly harder and thicker against my tongue, his breathing becoming ragged above me.

"Christ, Lucy."

I hum around him, the vibration making him curse under his breath. I increase my pace, taking him as deep as I can, wanting to give him the same pleasure he's given me.

"I should—" he starts, tugging gently at my hair in warning. "Lucy, I'm going to—"

But I don't pull away. Instead, I look up at him through my lashes, holding his gaze as I take him deeper.

His body goes taut as he reaches his breaking point. With a strangled groan, he comes, his release flooding my throat. I swallow everything he gives until he finally stills.

I press a soft kiss to his flushed tip before crawling back up his body.

"Come here," he murmurs, his voice rough and satisfied. He pulls me against his chest, holding me like I'm something he never intends to let go of. My cheek finds the curve of his shoulder, and I listen to the soothing rhythm of his heartbeat as it gradually slows.

There's still so much hanging over our heads, shadows waiting at the edges of this fragile peace. But right now, none of it matters. Right now, it's only this. Us.

thirty-seven
LUCY

I've been sleeping too much lately. More than I want to admit. Dragging myself out of bed to open the café feels like wading through wet cement, my body heavy, sluggish, refusing to cooperate. I keep blaming stress—there's definitely been enough of it to go around—but a little voice in the back of my mind whispers otherwise. Something's off. Maybe it's tied to what I already know lurks in my file at the doctor's office.

It's been days now, and Aidan still hasn't called Emily. I don't blame him. I wouldn't be in a rush to call her, either. Not after the way she just dropped back into his life. Honestly, she doesn't deserve for him to be in a rush. Not after leaving Isla, not after everything he's had to carry on his own.

He's been especially quiet today. His jaw set, his eyes distant as if he's been waging a war in his mind over what to do. I sit cross-legged on the couch, a mug of tea in my hands, trying to look like I'm focused on anything other than him. The weight of his decision is pressing down on both of us.

"I'm gonna call Emily." He exhales slowly, his fingers skimming down my arm before he pulls away.

He doesn't wait for me to respond. Just heads for the kitchen, shoulders drawn tight, head bent as he lifts the phone to his ear.

The moment he's out of sight, I press a hand against my stomach. That familiar ripple of nausea stirs low. It's subtle at first, but it builds, that uneasy churning that's become my constant companion these past few days.

It's definitely the stress. That would make sense, right? Things have been *a lot* lately. And I haven't been eating nearly enough. My appetite's been all over the place.

I wonder if...

No. I slam the door on the thought before it can finish forming, squeezing my eyes shut to erase it. But my heart's already racing and my mind is spinning out with possibilities I don't dare give shape to.

My body's just out of sorts because life's been one long storm lately. That's all it is. That's all it can be.

As the nausea twists in my stomach, my hand lingers there, almost on instinct. It's become a habit these past few days, like my body is trying to tell me something my mind refuses to accept. That thought—it's ridiculous. Impossible, even.

I can't be pregnant.

I press my lips together, swallowing the lump in my throat as my heart pounds faster. This is absurd. I've been on birth control. It should be, quite literally, impossible.

I close my eyes, taking a shaky breath as I fight a surge of emotions. Fear. Hope. Disbelief. It's all there now, a seed planted deep in my mind, and I know it's not going away.

Aidan's voice drifts in from the kitchen. I don't mean to eavesdrop, but his words cut through the silence, sharp and clipped. He sounds so...angry. Protective.

I strain to hear more. His voice rises slightly, the words becoming clearer.

"No, Emily. You don't get to just stroll back in like nothing happened."

There's a pause, and I can almost picture him running a hand through his hair, frustration etched on his face.

"I'm not keeping her from you. But we do this on my terms, is that clear?"

Another pause, longer this time. When he speaks again, his voice is tinged with a weariness that makes my heart ache.

"We can meet up." Another pause. "No, not with Isla. Not until we talk."

I purposely tune him out now. This is harder to listen to than I thought it would be. Isla feels like...*mine*. And I know she's not, but it would be impossible not to feel that way after I've spent months with her, watching her grow, loving her in a way I never thought I'd be able to.

She has no idea how she's saved me from the heartache that usually hits me when it comes to kids. The pain of *never* having what so many people take for granted, the ache of imagining what could've been. But Isla, with her little laugh and her curious eyes, has filled a space in my heart that was so empty. Even though it's complicated—*so complicated*—I can't help but feel protective of her, too.

I don't say anything as he walks back to me, though his expression softens the moment our eyes meet. He sits beside me again, pulling me close as if trying to recapture the calm we had before.

"Everything okay?" I ask, even though I already know the answer.

"Aye, as okay as it can be. I asked her to meet me at your café tomorrow. I hope that's okay."

I nod, pressing my cheek against his shoulder. "Of course it's okay."

And it is okay, in the way that I'll always support him, no matter what. At the same time, a small part of me is uneasy. I don't know if I want to see her again.

Though if she's here to stay, I might need to get used to it. I'm not ready for that, but I also don't have a choice.

thirty-eight
AIDAN

Emily's already there when I step into the café, tucked into a corner table. She doesn't see me at first, which gives me a beat to take her in. Her face is pale, shadows bruised beneath her eyes, like sleep hasn't touched her in days. She sits too still, as if holding herself smaller might make her less noticeable.

The difference between this woman and the one I used to know jars me. The one I trusted. The one who left.

I want to say I feel nothing when I look at her, but that's not entirely true. I feel *angry*. It's hot and crawls under my skin. I'm angry that she walked out and now thinks she gets to walk back in.

She looks up then, and her eyes flash with a surprise that quickly disappears behind a mask of indifference. She forces a smile, but it doesn't reach her eyes.

"I didn't think you'd come."

I don't answer right away, just stand there, staring at her.

I glance over to the counter, instinctively searching for

Lucy. She's moving around, doing her best to look busy, but I can see right through it.

When Lucy's eyes meet mine, her smile is a sucker punch to my chest. It's devastating in that sweet way that makes the knot of tension in my stomach loosen just a little.

It says everything without saying a word.

She gives me a subtle nod, encouraging me to take a seat and get this over with.

I turn back toward Emily, sitting down across from her before I say, "I show up when it concerns my daughter."

The silence stretches between us. I don't feel the need to make this easy for her.

"Thank you for agreeing to meet," she says finally, her voice softer than I remember.

"You didn't give me much choice." The words come out colder than I intend, but I don't apologize.

Her fingers fidget with a napkin, folding and unfolding the corners. "I suppose that's fair."

I lean back in my chair, crossing my arms. "What do you want, Emily? After five years of nothing, why are you here now?"

She takes a deep breath, her shoulders rising and falling with the effort. "I want to see her, Aidan."

There it is. The words I've been dreading since Lucy told me Emily had shown up at my door. I clench my jaw, fighting the urge to get up and leave.

"You lost that right when you walked out on her." My voice is low, controlled, despite the rage churning inside me.

She winces at my tone but doesn't back down. "Aidan, I know I've done things wrong—"

"Wrong?" I cut her off before she can continue, the words burning in my throat. "You didn't just do things *wrong*, Emily. You disappeared without a trace."

She flinches but doesn't say anything for a second. I honestly don't know what she expects from me. Maybe some semblance of understanding? I'm not sure I have that to give to her right now.

"I came back for Isla," she says. "I want a chance to know my daughter."

"*Our* daughter. The one I've raised alone since she was four months old."

Emily's eyes drop to the table. "I know that."

"Why? Just...*why*, Emily? What did I miss back then? I've been waiting for answers for five years."

Emily lifts her gaze, and for a second she looks...haunted.

"I panicked," she admits. "I didn't know how to be a mother, and I didn't want to be. I was selfish and didn't want to take care of a baby. And you...you were already so in love with her before she was even born."

So that really was it. I've beaten myself up for being angry all these years, wondering if Emily left because she was depressed, needed help, something—*anything*—other than just...not wanting the responsibility of a kid.

"I don't think I have anything to say to that, Emily."

She looks away, a muscle working in her jaw. "I know what I did. I know you'll never forgive me for it."

"This isn't about forgiveness." I lean forward, lowering my voice. "This is about Isla and what's best for her."

"I'm still her mother."

"You're her biological mother," I correct, fighting to keep my voice steady. "There's a difference."

She swallows, then meets my gaze again. "I've had five years to live with my choice and...the consequences. I wasn't ready back then. I couldn't do it, and I still truly believe Isla was better off. But now..." Her eyes soften, almost painfully. "I've changed. I won't lie, though. There will be no other children in my future, but I don't think I could live with myself if I didn't at least try to know the one I do have."

I'm...shocked. It's not some heroic story. It's just her, admitting the truth of who she was and who she is now. Five years of heartache and trying to be both parents, and it all comes down to this. Emily wasn't ready.

But Isla was still here. Needing someone. Needing everything.

I run a hand over my face, trying to process her words. "What exactly are you hoping for here?"

She shrugs, jerking her shoulders almost too quickly. "I don't know. Maybe just to see her sometimes. Get to know her a little. That doesn't seem so unreasonable."

Ah. The Emily I knew—the one who'd always been so sure of herself, so untouchable—hasn't fully disappeared. This version of her might be a bit more subtle, but there's still a stubborn edge, a sense that she's used to getting what she wants.

"I'm not asking to take her from you," she continues, her voice tight. "I know you're the only parent she knows. I'm not trying to...step on your toes."

She shifts in her seat, and I catch the way her eyes dart toward Lucy.

"If you're serious about this," I say, snapping her out of her trance, "then show up. Period."

She flinches again, but she doesn't back down. "I understand. Maybe I could come by this weekend. For a chance to fix things."

I want to say no. I want to shut it down right then and there, tell her she's too late and that Isla doesn't need her. This isn't about me, though, as much as I hate this. Isla deserves to know the truth, to see for herself that her mother is willing to try.

"Sunday. You come, and you show me you're serious. But if you screw this up, Emily…you won't get another shot."

I straighten, a knot tightening in my chest, my patience snapping. Enough. I've said what I needed to say, and I'm done negotiating.

"I'm serious," I continue. "If you're not all in, then don't waste our time. I never got a judge involved, but I will this time."

Emily's eyes widen at my words, and for a split second, there's a flash of panic. She clearly wasn't expecting me to throw down that kind of ultimatum.

I don't feel the need to linger. I stand before she has another chance to say anything else. My mind's already on Lucy. She's been watching us, and I can't leave without checking in on her, even if it's just for a second.

I walk over to the counter where she's still working and pretending to focus on wiping down the surface. Her eyes meet mine the moment I get close. There's a softness there, something that settles me just by looking at it.

I don't say anything at first, just stand there for a beat and take in the way the light catches the perfect, pouty curve of her lips. Then, I step in close, close enough to smell the sweetness of her perfume, and I don't hesitate. I lean over, pressing my lips to hers.

She pulls back slightly, her gaze searching mine. "You okay?"

I let out a slow breath, my shoulders sagging as the tight coil inside me unwinds. "I am now."

The corner of her mouth lifts in response.

"I'll fill you in tonight," I mutter, my thumb brushing gently over her cheek.

"Okay," she says quietly, but I see the understanding there. "I love you. I'll come by later?"

I let a small smile tug at my lips. "Aye...see you at home. Love you, too."

thirty-nine
LUCY

Aidan did fill me in on his conversation with Emily a few days ago, and as hard as I try to remain neutral about all of it, it's hard.

Now it's Sunday morning, and I'm staring at the unopened box on the bathroom counter at my flat. I've kept my little ritual of grocery shopping on the rare day off work, but today, I grabbed the test on a whim. The thought I've been ignoring for too long won't leave me alone, and with Emily scheduled to stop by Aidan's today, I can't pretend anymore. I need to know. I need some certainty before other people's choices impact my life again.

My thumb hovers over my phone screen. Finally, with a shaky exhale, I tap Juliette's name.

She answers on the second ring. "Hey, you! What's up?"

"I need a favor," I tell her, my voice cracking a fraction. "A big one."

"Of course," she replies without hesitation, concern threading through her tone. "What's going on?"

How do I even say it out loud? The words wedge in my

throat. The possibility has been whispering at the edges of my mind for days, growing louder with every wave of fatigue, every moment I caught myself wondering. To speak it makes it real. And the second I admit it, I'll have to face whatever comes next, whether it's the dream I've barely let myself hold onto or the crushing silence of being wrong.

And what if that's the case? What if the test is negative? I'll feel ridiculous for hoping, for daring to believe this could be possible. Or worse—will I feel broken all over again? I've spent so long convincing myself that I should tuck that particular dream into a box and shove it into some unreachable corner.

And yet...the hope has crept in, anyway.

"I think...I might be pregnant." The words hang in the air, strange and surreal. "I bought a test, but I can't...I don't want to do this alone."

There's a brief silence on the other end. "I'll be right there."

I haven't even hung up the phone before I start pacing the small bathroom, my reflection flashing past the mirror with each turn. My heart's hammering so hard I can feel it in my fingertips, in my temples, everywhere.

Fifteen minutes. That's how long it will take Juliette to get here.

The box sits there, taunting me. I pick it up, put it down, read the instructions twice more even though I already know them by heart. Two lines mean pregnant. One line means... Well, what it's always meant for me. A closed door.

I splash cold water on my face, trying to calm myself. What would I even say to Aidan if it's positive? With Emily suddenly back in the picture, the timing is awful. No, not just awful. Horrendous.

A soft knock at the front door nearly makes me jump out of my skin.

"It's me," Juliette calls, her voice muffled through the wood.

I open the door with shaky hands. She takes one look at my face and pulls me into a hug. I pull back, suddenly realizing what I've done. "Oh goodness, Juliette, I'm so sorry. I didn't even think—the girls. Did I pull you away from them?"

Juliette's eyes soften as she shakes her head. "Knox has them. They're fine. He's building some elaborate pillow fort that will probably take over the entire living room by the time I get back."

Relief washes over me, but the guilt lingers. "I shouldn't have called you like this."

"Stop it," she says firmly, taking my hands in hers. "This is important, and you can always call me. No, scratch that. You *better* always call me."

Her words bring fresh tears to my eyes. I blink them away, gesturing weakly to the bathroom. "The test is in there. Will you wait in the hall for a second?"

She nods, letting go of my hands to fall into step beside me. Together we move down the narrow hallway until we reach the bathroom. I step inside and close the door behind me.

I could swear the walls are pressing in as I fumble with the box.

I take a deep breath and follow the steps, each second stretching into what feels like hours. When I'm done, I place the test flat on the counter and open the door.

Juliette is leaning against the wall, her face a careful mask of calm, but I can see the concern in her eyes.

"Two minutes," I whisper, sliding down to sit on the floor, my back against the wall. She joins me, our shoulders touching.

"Whatever happens," she says softly, "I'm here."

I can't bear to watch time tick by, knowing that tiny piece of plastic holds answers that could change everything. "What if it's negative?" I finally ask. "I don't know if I can handle that disappointment again."

"I know," she murmurs. "I know you're scared."

The timer on my phone buzzes, making us jump. My heart hammers against my ribs, but I can't bring myself to move.

"Do you want me to look?" Juliette asks softly.

I nod, unable to form words. She stands, walking the few steps to the counter that might as well be miles. I watch her face, searching for any hint, any clue. She picks up the test, and for one agonizing moment, her expression gives nothing away.

Then her eyes widen. Her hand flies to her mouth.

"Lucy," she whispers, turning to me with tears already forming. "It's positive."

I push away from the wall, trying to stand, but my knees buckle and I end up right back down on the floor. "What?"

She kneels in front of me, holding the test where I can see it. Two pink lines. Clear as day.

"You're pregnant," she says, her voice breaking with emotion.

I take the test from her. Two simple lines, and yet, they feel impossibly monumental.

I'd made my peace with a life without the potential of little hands tugging at mine, without the chaos and wonder I've watched Juliette and Knox move through so naturally.

Now it's here. Somehow, impossibly, miraculously, it's *real*.

Tears prickle at the corners of my eyes. I want to scream, to laugh, to curl into a ball and cry all at once. The world feels impossibly vast, yet incredibly intimate in the same breath. I place my hand over my stomach, though there's nothing yet to touch but the promise of it. In that moment, I *finally* let myself feel hope. Pure, reckless, unbounded hope.

I stare down at the test again, like if I look long enough, the lines might disappear, leaving me empty handed. But they don't. They're stubbornly, defiantly there. My chest tightens with disbelief, relief, and...joy.

"I...I thought I'd never..." My words trail off, but Juliette doesn't let me finish. She doesn't need me to.

"I know," she whispers. "But look at you—you're going to have this." She swallows, voice breaking just slightly, and it's contagious. I can't help the hot, happy tears spilling freely down my cheeks.

This is terrifying. Exhilarating. This is every emotion I didn't even know I could carry at once.

Juliette pulls me into a hug, and I cling to her like a lifeline. "You're going to be so incredible, Lou," she murmurs. "No matter what, you've got this. You're never alone. Not for a second."

I pull back from her embrace, wiping my tears with the heel of my hand. My face feels hot, my mind still struggling to process what's happening.

"Oh my god," I whisper, staring at the test again. "I'm really pregnant."

Juliette's eyes crinkle with delight as a mischievous smile crosses her face.

"You know who's going to absolutely lose her entire mind when she finds out?" She raises a brow. "Bree. She's going to *freak*."

A laugh bubbles up through my tears. "You're right. I remember how she was with you and the twins."

I can already picture Bree shrieking and demanding every single detail, then immediately planning something elaborate and over the top. The thought makes me smile despite everything swirling in my head.

Then reality crashes back in, and my stomach drops. "Juliette, what am I going to tell Aidan?"

She tilts her head, studying my face. "You're going to tell him the truth. He loves you, Lucy. This is going to be—"

"Emily just came back," I interrupt, my voice rising. "She's trying to worm her way back into their lives, and now I'm pregnant?"

The fear tastes bitter on my tongue. I've seen how torn up he is about the whole Emily situation, how protective he is of Isla. What if adding a baby to the mix just complicates everything beyond repair?

"Lucy." Juliette's voice is firm, cutting through my spiral before I can work myself into a full panic. "Stop. Look at me."

I force myself to meet her eyes, though my heart is still racing.

"That man is head over heels in love with you," she says, her voice even and sure. "I've seen the way he looks at you like you hung the moon. And Isla adores you. You know that, right? You're not some complication in their lives."

"I...know that. But Jules, what if I'm not even capable of having a healthy pregnancy? Regardless of Aidan's reaction..."

The hallway suddenly feels too confining. I need air, space to think. Pushing myself up from the floor, I make my way to the living room.

Soft morning light filters through the curtains, casting a gentle glow across the room. Everything looks the same, and yet, nothing will ever be the same again.

I move to the window and push the pane open, letting the crisp Highland air rush in. The scent of heather and damp earth fills my lungs, grounding me, giving me something to hold on to when everything feels like it's shifting beneath me.

In the distance, I can see the misty outline of the mountains, solid and unchanging. It's comforting, somehow, to know that while my own universe has been turned upside down, the rest of the world carries on as always.

I press my hand to my stomach again. For a moment, I close my eyes, letting the cool air brush against my face. Even in the silence, my mind refuses to settle. I think about the doctor's words and how I'd walked out of that office feeling broken, like my body had betrayed me in the most fundamental way.

And now, against all odds, it's happening.

"Lucy?" Juliette's voice is soft behind me. "How are you feeling?"

I turn from the window and the familiar brush of fur winds around my ankles. Marmalade weaves between my legs, purring insistently, and for a moment, it's a small comfort in the whirlwind. "Scared. Thrilled."

"Totally normal." She smirks. "Were you planning on seeing Aidan today?"

I had stayed at my place last night because I wanted to give Aidan and Isla some space to get prepared for...*Emily*. The situation is already heavy enough without me being there and adding any more pressure.

"I'm not sure," I finally answer. "I need to wait to see what happens with Emily today."

Juliette winces at her name, a flash of discomfort crossing her face before she quickly masks it with a smile. She takes a deep breath, and her eyes suddenly light up with excitement.

"Well, regardless of what happens with...her," she says, deliberately avoiding Emily's name. "We have other things to think about now." She grabs my hands, squeezing them tight. "I'm going to be an auntie! Oh, just think—a little one with Aidan's eyes and your beautiful smile."

The image of a tiny baby with Aidan's fierce eyes makes my heart swell. "You're already planning their features?"

"Duh. Of course I am. But seriously, I'm here for whatever you need. Tips, tricks, pep talks, midnight panic calls. I know all the shortcuts."

I manage a shaky laugh, the tension inside of me easing some. "I just... I need to process this before I tell him. Figure out how I'm going to say it."

She nods, understanding in her eyes. "Of course. Don't wait too long, though, okay? This is good news, Lucy. The best news."

I let the weight of her words settle for a moment, and then the practical side of my brain kicks in. "I need to see a doctor," I say, forcing my voice steady. "I should probably get checked sooner rather than later. I don't even know how far along I am."

"Absolutely. We'll get you set up with the best doctor around. Someone who specializes in high-risk pregnancies, just to be safe."

The words "high-risk" make my stomach clench. I take a deep breath, trying to calm the fresh wave of anxiety. "Thank you. I mean it."

While Juliette's confidence is grounding, the next step is the one that feels more daunting than any appointment or morning sickness or sleepless night could ever be.

I have to tell Aidan.

AIDAN

I'm sitting down with Isla this morning, the weight of what's coming pressing down on me. She's too little to carry any of this, too innocent to even know what's coming. Yet here I am, about to place it in her lap.

"All right, little storm," I say, keeping my tone light, like this is nothing to be nervous about. "We need to talk about something."

She tips her chin up, those big, trusting eyes locking on mine.

"There's someone who wants to see you today," I manage, my throat tight as the words leave me. This is the part I've been dreading.

Her brows pull together, the question already forming. "Who?"

I draw in a breath that doesn't seem to reach my lungs. "Her name is Emily," I say carefully. Maybe if I speak slowly enough, it won't hit her as hard. "She's...your mum. Her name is Emily."

Confusion flashes across her face instantly. I watch it settle in as she attempts to grasp what I'm saying.

This is exactly what I wanted to avoid. It's not fair that I have to be the one to put that shadow in her eyes. I hate that I'm the one who has to watch innocence give way to doubt.

"But...Lucy takes care of me."

The words are so small, so certain, they cut straight through me.

Fuck. How do I explain this to her? How do I make sense of something so tangled when all she's ever known is me and the woman I brought in who's done nothing but show up all the time and love her?

We've never talked about this. Never needed to. Isla never asked, and I never had the heart to open the door. We've just... lived, day by day.

I shut my eyes. When I open them again, she's still watching me, wide eyed and waiting for me to give her an answer that won't hurt.

"Lucy loves you very much," I tell her, my voice unshakable even though I feel like I'm splintering inside. "And yes, she takes care of you just like a mum would. But...Lucy wasn't here when you were born. Emily was."

Her brows pinch tighter. "Why haven't I met her before?"

The question knocks the air out of me. How do you condense years of silence and poor choices into something a five-year-old can comprehend?

"Sometimes, sweetheart, grown-ups make complicated decisions," I manage, each word heavy on my tongue. "Emily... She wasn't able to be here with us."

"Why?"

God. I'm caught between the fury at Emily for vanishing and the ache of watching my little girl try to piece together something so far beyond her.

This conversation is all *wrong*. Isla should be running barefoot through the yard, giggling over bubbles, not sitting here with her tiny hands folded in her lap, waiting for answers to questions no child should ever have to ask.

"She couldn't be here," I say, my voice gruff despite my best effort to sound reassuring. "But just because Emily is coming to visit, that doesn't mean Lucy is going anywhere. You don't need to worry about that changing, okay?"

She nods slowly, but the doubt in her eyes guts me. I wish I could take it all away. Wrap her in enough warmth and certainty that she never even has to wonder.

I can't shield her forever. The only thing I can promise is that I'll fight like hell to protect what she does have.

And yet, in the back of my mind, a horrible thought gnaws at me. Did I just lie when I told her Lucy wasn't going anywhere? The idea of ripping that security from Isla makes me sick.

The knock comes at exactly two o'clock. Isla looks up from her coloring book, her crayon frozen mid-stroke.

"Is that her?" she whispers, so soft it nearly breaks me.

My throat works around the lump lodged there. I force myself to nod. "Aye. Remember what we talked about, okay? You don't have to do anything you don't want to do. If you're uncomfortable at all, you tell me."

She nods back, then slides off the couch. Her hand finds mine, her trust steadfast even when mine is anything but. I squeeze it gently before turning toward the door, every step heavier than the last as I reach for the handle.

Emily's standing there with a smile that's entirely too bright and forced, her shoulders wrapped in some cardigan that looks deliberately chosen—soft, homey, maternal. It's a costume, and my stomach twists at the effort she's put into playing a role she cast off years ago.

"Hello, Isla," she says, her voice pitched just a little too high, as if she's speaking to someone else's child in a grocery store aisle.

Isla shifts against my leg, pressing close. She peeks out from behind me, silent but watchful, studying Emily with curiosity.

"Come in," I say curtly. I step aside, keeping myself angled just enough between Emily and Isla.

She breezes past, her eyes looking everywhere but me. They skim over the mantle crowded with family photos, Isla's crayon masterpieces taped crookedly on the fridge, the shoes kicked off by the door. Our life is scattered across every surface. I swear I see a flicker of regret, longing, or maybe recognition of the life she almost had.

"Your home is lovely," she says, her tone too polished.

I don't bother answering. I'm not interested in polite lies.

Emily crouches down, her skirt pooling around her knees. "You've gotten so big," she tells Isla. "You're beautiful, just like I imagined."

Isla only presses tighter against my leg, her fingers fisting the fabric of my jeans. She doesn't say a word. Smart lass.

Isla eventually looks up at me, uncertainty written all over her face.

"You okay, kiddo?" I ask her. She gives me a small nod before she slowly releases her hold and makes her way to the couch. She perches on the very edge of the cushion.

Emily follows, sitting in the armchair close by, but I remain standing.

"I brought you something," she says, reaching into her bag and pulling out a small, neatly wrapped package.

Isla glances up at me, hesitation written all over her face before gingerly taking the gift. She peels back the paper, revealing a stuffed dog with floppy ears.

"Thank you," she mumbles. She doesn't hug it to her chest or squeal in delight. Instead, she balances it in her lap, testing the weight.

"Do you like dogs?"

Isla shrugs, her shoulders stiff. "They're okay. I like cats better, though. Lucy has a cat at her flat."

The mention of Lucy makes Emily's jaw tighten almost imperceptibly. "That's nice," she says, her voice tight. "Maybe you could tell me more about you? What's your favorite subject?"

Isla's brows furrow. "Subject?"

"You know," Emily replies. "Like at school?"

Jesus Christ. Does she really not know Isla hasn't even started school yet?

Isla blinks up at her, clearly confused. "I don't go to school yet," she admits, tugging at the hem of her shirt.

Emily's smile falters for just a second. "Oh...right," she says quickly. "Well... What do you like to do, then?"

"Art," Isla answers. "I'm really good at drawing. Lucy helps me with my letters sometimes."

Lucy. Every answer circles back to her, and I catch that subtle flash of irritation in Emily's eyes.

"What about your daddy?" Emily presses, shooting me a quick glance. "Do you two do fun things together?"

Isla's face lights up for the first time since Emily walked in. "We go fishing and make pancakes on Sundays. And we read stories before bed." She pauses, then adds, "Lucy reads with us, too. She does funny voices that make Daddy laugh."

Emily's hands clench in her lap. "That sounds...wonderful. I was thinking maybe you and I could spend some time together. Just the two of us. Would you like that?"

Isla shrinks back against the couch cushions. "I don't know," she whispers, eyes darting to mine for guidance.

"She doesn't have to decide anything right now," I interject. How dare she bring up *alone time* without speaking to me first.

Emily blinks, surprised, and I feel the anger rising, slow and hot in my chest. "If you want to spend time with Isla, you talk to me."

Her composure finally cracks. "Aidan, I'm trying here. Can't you see that?"

"I can see you're trying," I reply evenly. "But she doesn't *know* you."

The silence that follows is thick with tension. Emily's face flushes. "She's my daughter. I—"

"Isla," I cut her off. "Why don't you go get your drawing pad, love? Show Emily that picture you drew of the loch."

Isla nods eagerly, clearly relieved to have something to do, and scurries off to her room.

The moment she's out of earshot, Emily's mask drops completely as she stands. "This is ridiculous, Aidan. You're poisoning her against me."

"I would *never* poison her against anything or anyone. You've managed to do that all on your own," I shoot back, crossing my arms.

"She keeps talking about Lucy," she hisses, her voice dripping with resentment. "How *cozy*. You've replaced me with some café girl who's playing house."

My jaw clenches so hard I can hear my teeth grind. "I don't see how that's possible when there was no one here to be replaced."

Heat simmers behind her eyes. "I'm trying to fix things."

"Fix things?" I take a step closer, my voice dropping to a dangerous whisper. "Did you really think you'd be able to waltz in here and everything was going to be easy? That Isla was going to run into your arms like she knows you?"

"I knew it wouldn't be easy, but—"

"Did you?" I cut her off. "Because from where I'm standing, it looks like you expected to show up with a stuffed animal and have her call you mummy by teatime."

Emily's face goes pale, then red. "That's not fair."

"Fair?" I let out a bitter laugh. "You want to talk about fair? Fair would have been you being here when she had nightmares. Fair would have been you teaching her to tie her shoes or kissing her scraped knees. Fair would have been a lot of things other than you leaving her in the first place."

Her mouth opens and closes like she's searching for words that don't come.

"Daddy, I found it!" Isla's voice rings out as she comes running back into the room, clutching her drawing pad against her chest.

The tension in the room is thick enough to cut, and Isla's bright smile fades as she looks between us.

Emily immediately forces her smile back into place, but it's brittle now. "I'd love to see your drawing."

Isla doesn't move toward her. She steps closer to me, pressing against my side and using me like a shield.

"Why don't you show Emily the one with the mountains?" I tell her, hand brushing her shoulder.

She flips through the pad and finally holds up a picture. "This is the loch where we go fishing. And that's Lucy picking flowers by the water."

Three stick figures stand beside a blue oval. Emily's eyes linger. "That's very nice," she says, the words hollow. "Maybe next time you could draw one with me in it?"

Fucking hell. She's pushing way too damn hard.

Isla tilts her head, frowning. "But you weren't there."

I can't help it—a laugh sneaks out before I can stop it. Not at Emily's expense, but at Isla's sheer honesty. She just says exactly what she's thinking. My shoulders relax, and I find myself brushing a loose curl from her forehead, just because I can. God, I love that she's mine.

"Well, maybe we could make new memories," Emily finally says.

I watch Isla's fingers follow the edge of her drawing pad, and I can't stop the swell in my chest. She's *mine*. Mine to protect, and I'm so damn proud of her right now.

I'm proud that she's being cautious but open with a woman who has waltzed back in here like she'd just popped out for milk and forgot the way home.

My mind drifts to Lucy and how Isla talks about her so freely. To her, Lucy is just someone who loves her, who picks flowers and reads stories and doesn't need to be asked twice.

I press my hand against Isla's shoulder, grounding both of us. All I can think is—this is the life Emily left. The messy, beautiful, sticky-fingered life she walked away from. Now she wants back in, like this is some storybook redemption with a big emotional payoff waiting at the end.

I'll give her a chance, but I'm also not here to make her feel better about the choices she made.

I'm the one who tucked Isla in at night, who wiped away tears and held her through every storm. I've bled for this little girl in every way that counts.

Love isn't a fucking raffle you win just by turning up out of the blue. It's built. Earned. Day by day. Fish by fish. Flower by flower.

And right now, standing here without Lucy, I'd give anything for her to be at my side. We're not whole without her.

LUCY

Aidan asked me to come over after Emily left, and normally, I would have raced there the moment I could.

I waited instead, lingering in my flat until the glow of the setting sun signaled it was almost bedtime for Isla.

I'm just now pulling into his drive as the glow of the setting sun casts shadows over the hills. Isla's excited footsteps patter toward the door as soon as I step onto the porch. She pulls the door open with a flourish.

"Lucy!" she squeals, flinging herself at me. I catch her, lifting her into a hug and breathing in the sweet scent of her strawberry shampoo before setting her down gently.

"Hey, sweetheart. How was your day?"

Her nose scrunches up. "Weird."

Oh boy.

My heart drops a little. I open my mouth to respond when Aidan steps into view. He crosses the space between us in three long strides and pulls me into his arms. The tension I've been carrying all day melts away in a heartbeat.

"Missed you," he murmurs against my hair.

"I missed you, too."

He tilts my chin up gently, brushing his lips against mine in a soft, fleeting kiss. My stomach flips, warmth blooming through me, but before I can savor it, a small, outraged voice pipes up.

"Ew!"

I can't help the laugh that bursts out of me, and even Aidan grins. "Sorry, little storm. I did promise I'd warn you before we did that."

Isla just rolls her eyes which makes me laugh harder.

Aidan sends her upstairs to get ready for bed and fills me in on Emily's visit. My heart aches for both him and Isla. As much as I dislike the situation, I didn't wish for the meeting today to go poorly.

Now I'm standing by while Isla tucks herself into bed, her small frame curling up beneath the covers, looking every bit like an angel who has somehow found her way into my heart in the most unexpected of ways.

Aidan lingers in the doorway, watching as she drifts off to sleep. His shoulders are tight, the events of today weighing on him. I can't help the twist of sympathy that tightens in my own chest.

When her breathing evens out, signaling she's asleep, Aidan turns back to me, his expression tired. He leans against the doorframe, crossing his arms, and I take a step toward him.

"Emily wants to take Isla out next weekend," Aidan tells me. "Just the two of them."

My stomach clenches. "What did you tell her?"

"That it's too soon." His jaw tightens. "She didn't like that answer."

I don't need to see it to know. The woman who appeared at

our door carried a confidence that didn't take rejection lightly. "And Isla? How did she handle it?"

"Better than I expected, honestly. But before Emily got here today, Isla said..." he trails off. "I think she was confused on why you aren't her mum, Lucy."

He keeps his gaze just slightly averted, as if he's measuring my reaction, unsure of what I'll say or feel.

My throat tightens, and before I can stop it, my vision blurs. Tears well up in my eyes, threatening to spill over. I quickly swipe at them, embarrassed at how quickly they've come, but they don't stop. They fall, one after another, and I let them, even though I can't explain why this moment feels like so much.

"I—" I try to speak, but the words catch in my throat.

His eyes soften when he sees my tears, and he steps closer, reaching for me, his hand gently brushing my cheek. "I didn't mean to upset you."

I shake my head, tears still slipping down my cheeks.

"No, Aidan, you didn't upset me," I manage to say. "It's just... I never thought I'd hear those words. I love her so much," I whisper.

I never would have forced myself into that role for her. Not unless it was something they both truly wanted.

"What... What did you tell her?" I ask. "How do *you* feel about that?"

"I told her you take care of her like a mother would, but I didn't say more than that. I wanted to talk to you first."

"I'm not sure what to say to that," I admit softly. "I don't want to overstep..."

He doesn't look away, his eyes soft and patient, waiting for me to continue.

"I just don't want to do anything that might confuse her

when she's already going through so much," I add. "But I do care for her. So much."

"I know you do," he says, reaching out to touch my arm gently. "And she knows that, too. You've shown up for her in ways I could never have asked for."

I want to tell him that I'd love to be that person for Isla, that I can already picture us building a family. I want to tell him about the baby. The little one who's going to make Isla a big sister.

The words are stuck in my throat, tangled up in the fear of how he'll react and how everything will change. Because things *will* change.

That dreaded wave of queasiness hits me. My stomach churns violently, and I gasp for air, my hand flying to my mouth. The world tilts, my body betraying me with the unmistakable feeling of sickness that surges up my throat.

I stumble into the bathroom on unsteady legs. I almost don't make it in time, dropping to my knees as the wave of nausea crashes over me. I clutch the edge of the porcelain, my body trembling, but through it, I feel Aidan behind me. His hand lands gently on my back, rubbing small, soothing circles.

"Jesus, baby. Are you all right?" His voice is soft but thick with concern, the worry in it clear as day.

I nod weakly, too dizzy to speak, as another surge of nausea drags me down. I close my eyes, willing myself to breathe through it. When it finally eases, I reach up to flush before slumping against the wall, every muscle trembling with exhaustion.

I almost laugh. This is the second time today I've found myself sitting on the floor near or in a bathroom.

Aidan reaches for a damp washcloth and presses it into my hand, his touch lingering for a moment before he pulls back. I press the cloth to my forehead, the coolness against my skin a small comfort.

"Thanks," I murmur, my voice shaky.

He sinks to one knee beside me, eyes locked on mine, every line of his face etched with worry. The crease in his brow deepens as he studies me. "What's going on? You've been off for a while now."

I take a shaky breath. The cool tiled wall presses against my spine, supporting me as I try to find the words. This isn't how I imagined telling him.

His eyes search mine, pleading for an answer I'm not ready to give. My throat tightens as I swallow back the truth that's pushing to break free.

God, I'm terrified. He's already dealing with Emily, with Isla's confusion, and trying to keep their little world from falling apart. Now this?

I press the cool cloth to my neck, buying myself a few more seconds. I rehearsed this moment a dozen different ways in my head throughout the day, but never like this.

I can't bear the thought of watching shock and panic, or worse, disappointment wash over his face.

"Lucy." His voice is firm but gentle, pulling me from my spiral. "Talk to me."

I meet his eyes, finding nothing but love there. No judgment, no impatience. Just Aidan, waiting for me to trust him with whatever's weighing on me.

A bubble of hysterical laughter suddenly escapes my lips. It bursts out of me, *completely* inappropriate for the moment, and I can't seem to stop it. The laughter keeps coming, making my shoulders shake as tears spring to my eyes.

"I'm pregnant," I blurt out between gasps of laughter, the words tumbling out before I can stop them. "I'm actually pregnant."

Aidan stares at me in stunned silence. His eyes widen, lips parting as if to speak but finding no words. The seconds stretch into what feels like hours. I can't breathe, and yet, I can't tear my gaze away from him.

"You're..." His voice falters, the sentence dying on his lips as he searches my face for the courage to finish it.

I press my hand against my mouth, trying to stifle the laughter that's quickly turning to sobs.

"Pregnant?" he repeats. "Are you sure?"

I catch my breath and nod slowly. "I just found out this morning. I was going to tell you, I promise. I just...wasn't really sure how."

The color drains from his face. His hand instinctively runs through his hair, tugging at the strands as his gaze falls to the floor, distant and unfocused. He looks like a man who's just been hit by a swell of terror he doesn't know how to ride. All I can do is watch, completely helpless.

I hate how fast the silence fills the space between us, and just how loud that silence gets. I can hear the faucet drip. I can hear my own heartbeat pounding like it's trying to escape my chest. I can hear everything except *him*.

I wrap my arms around myself, wishing I could take back the words, wishing I could say them differently, gentler. Anything to soften it after the train wreck of a day he just had.

"Aidan," I whisper, almost afraid to break whatever trance he's trapped in. "Please say something."

His eyes finally lift to mine, and god, I wish I could read his mind.

"I thought you said..."

I swallow, my throat dry as sandpaper. "I did. I mean, that's what they told me. It was never impossible, just...unlikely." My hand instinctively moves to my stomach. "Remember when I had that awful sinus infection a couple months ago?"

Aidan nods slowly, recognition dawning in his eyes.

"The antibiotics probably affected my birth control. And all the...you know. We..." I gesture vaguely between us, embarrassed. "I didn't even think about it at the time. It seemed so improbable that I didn't consider..."

His expression shifts, the shock melting into awe. "A baby," he whispers.

I nod, tears welling up again.

He stares at me, silent. It's worse than if he'd yelled, or panicked, or walked away—because he's *feeling*, but I don't know *what*.

"I'm sorry," I blurt out, the words slipping out before I can stop them. "I'm so sorry. I didn't mean for it to happen like this. I had no intentions of hiding this, but I didn't know if you'd be okay, and I'm scared, too, and—"

"Don't," he cuts me off, his voice stronger now. "Don't apologize."

Suddenly, his hands are on my face, so warm, rough, trembling just a little. He looks at me like I've cracked open the whole universe and handed it to him.

"You don't get to apologize for a goddamn miracle," he says. "Not to me. Never to me."

I blink up at him, my lips parting to speak, but I don't know what to say. Not when his thumbs are brushing over my cheeks like he's memorizing the feel of me. Not when his eyes are full of something heavier than joy.

That's when I see it.

The flash of fear.

"Lucy," he says finally, his voice so quiet I can barely hear it. "I did it once. I raised a baby on my own, and it nearly destroyed me. I can't do that again. I just...can't."

My breath catches at the fact that he thought he might have to do it on his own. That after everything I've shown him, he still wonders if I'll turn into someone who walks away.

My heart twists with a mix of hurt and awareness. I want to say I understand, but hearing him question *my* commitment, the thought that I might be anything like Emily... It stings.

I take a steadying breath, reminding myself that this isn't a reflection of how he feels about me. It's about him, his past, his fears. Still, I can't just let that slide.

"I get that you're scared, Aidan," I say. "But I'm not Emily."

His gray eyes meet mine, a storm of emotions swirling in their depths. His jaw clenches, and I can see him struggling to find the right words.

"I know you're not her," he says, running a hand through his hair again, his voice thick with regret. "Fuck. I'm sorry. I just... I can't have you look at me one day and decide this isn't what you signed up for."

I reach for his hands, pulling them away from his hair and holding them firmly in mine.

"Look at me," I say, waiting until his eyes meet mine again. "I'm not going anywhere. Not now, not when things get hard, not ever. This is everything I've ever wanted."

His breath hitches, and I can see the walls he's built around his heart starting to crack.

"I love you," I continue, my voice growing stronger. "I love Isla. I already love this little one. We're a family, Aidan. All of us."

I know it'll take time for him to fully believe me, but every word comes from the depths of my soul. Slowly, his protective hand lifts, settling against my stomach.

"A baby," he breathes, wonder lacing every syllable. "Our baby... Christ, Lucy. Are you okay?"

The worry in his voice wraps around me, fierce and tender all at once.

I offer a small, crooked smile. "Can we get off the bathroom floor and talk about this somewhere else?" I tease, nudging his shoulder lightly.

His lips twitch in a faint smile. "Aye, fair point." Without another word, he sweeps me up into his arms. My arms go instinctively around his neck as he carries me to the bedroom.

Once there, he eases me onto the bed, keeping one arm wrapped around my waist until I sink into the mattress. He sits beside me, close enough that our knees brush, his hand lingering on my back.

"So," he starts. "How are you feeling? Really. You don't have to sugarcoat it."

I take a deep breath, letting myself relax. "It's a lot, I won't lie. I'm okay, though. I think I'm still processing it all, but I'm happy. Really happy." My hand instinctively drifts to my stomach, and his eyes follow, softening even more.

His throat bobs as he swallows, and he reaches out, resting his other hand lightly over mine. "I'll do whatever it takes to make this easier for you, for both of you. I just—" His voice cracks, and he clears his throat. "I just want you to be safe. That's all I care about."

Any lingering worries fall away with the tenderness of his touch. "We will be," I assure him. "We have you."

His eyes search mine, like he's trying to figure out if I really believe that. "Then come home."

My brow furrows. "I am home."

He shakes his head. "No, I mean…move in." His thumb brushes over the back of my hand. "Let me take care of you properly, Lucy. You shouldn't be going through this alone in your flat. I'll be worrying if the bathroom tiles are too slippery or if you've eaten enough. I want you here all the time. With us."

My heart stutters. "You realize this means that Marmalade has to come, too, right?"

Aidan's rich, deep laugh cuts through the heaviness that's been hanging over us. "The damn cat. Isla's going to lose her mind with excitement."

I open my mouth to throw back a smart reply, but the look on Aidan's face stops me cold.

His smile fades, but not in a bad way. It's as if he's seeing me all over again, noticing every curve and line for the very first time. His gaze drifts lower, catching on the gentle swell of my stomach beneath the fabric of my shirt.

And then he sinks to his knees.

He doesn't speak. His palm rests lightly over my stomach while the other slips to the small of my back, holding me.

"Aidan…"

He looks up at me, eyes shining with something fierce and tender. "You're carrying my child," he says. Then he leans in, pressing a soft, reverent kiss to my stomach, making a promise without words.

Air leaves my lungs in a shaky, stolen exhale, and all at once, the world narrows to just him.

My hand slides into his hair, fingers tangling in the strands as he rests his forehead against my stomach.

"Lucy… It's you. You, Isla, and this wee one. You're the ones I want waiting for me when the day is done."

I blink, the weight of those words folding around me like sunlight spilling through a window. It's not just about the baby, or the fear, or even the mistakes behind us. It's about choosing each other, day after day, no matter what else comes.

I don't even realize the tears are falling until his hands are on my thighs, slowly sliding upward, tracing the curve of my hips as he rises. He presses his lips to the hollow of my neck, and I wind my arms around him, holding him close.

He pulls back just enough to whisper, "Let me show you what this means to me. Let me take care of *you*."

When he lays me down, there's no rush or frantic urgency. Just devotion in every touch, every glance, every brush of his lips.

Just admiration.

Just love.

AIDAN

I'm wide awake, staring at the ceiling while Lucy sleeps next to me. She's here. She's safe. *She's carrying our baby.*

My first reaction should have been full of joy and pride... but what came first wasn't any of that. It was fear. A gut punch of panic. Instead of pulling her close, whispering it would all be okay, I froze like a damn coward.

She called me on it, and she was right to do it. She deserved better in that moment. She still does. Now, as I'm lying here, all I can think about is how to be the man she's already betting her whole heart on.

I turn my head, letting my eyes roam over her as she sleeps. She looks so damn peaceful, like the world has finally slowed down just for her. And when I think about a baby—*our* baby—it hits me.

This is right. Terrifying, but right. I want this.

I won't fuck this up.

Careful not to wake her, I tuck a stray chestnut lock behind her ear. My mind is racing. I think of the café, wondering if she'll need to bring in extra help so she doesn't wear herself out.

I imagine converting the spare room into a nursery, painting the walls a soft green that would mirror her eyes every time she stepped inside.

I think about Isla, who's going to be a big sister. How will she take it?

Then I think of the way Lucy's whole face lights up when she talks about the future. The patience she's shown me when I've been nothing but rough. She's going to be an amazing mother. Hell, she already is.

But...her family. I've been around long enough to know they're protective. If it were Isla, I'd be ready to take a swing at any guy who dared to touch her.

And now here I am. Older. With sweet, brilliant Lucy curled up in my bed. Pregnant with my kid.

Shit.

That age gap that never seemed like much before suddenly feels like a spotlight glaring down. I can already see the way her dad's going to look at me, like I'm the bastard who stole something precious from his daughter. Her mom, too. And her brothers? If they wanted to lay me out flat on the pavement, I'd let them. I get it. I'd be pissed, too.

What I'm mostly afraid of is that they'll look at me like I'm the last man that should be trusted with their daughter. Their sister. I know how it looks—I'm the guy fathers warn their daughters about.

Then there's the fact that Lucy wants *me*.

I'll do whatever it takes to make this easier on her. It might not be my first time walking this road, but it's hers, and she should get to feel every ounce of joy, every bit of excitement that comes with it. I won't let my own nerves steal that from her.

I want her to soak it all in. I want to soak it in, too, and if that means swallowing my pride and facing her family head-on...then that's exactly what I'll do.

I'M AN ASSHOLE. I did this to her. Lucy is sick—so fucking sick. This part is new to me. Emily had an easy pregnancy with Isla. I had no idea it could be *this* bad.

I think back to the past few days, to how quickly I'd moved her into this place the moment I found out she was pregnant. After a couple days, a few frantic calls, logistics sorted, and finding space for her ridiculous, overflowing mug collection, I had her safe and under my roof. Good thing, too, because I hadn't realized how fast her pregnancy could wear her down.

She's sick all day long, sunup to sundown. She stumbles out of bed in the mornings, clutching her stomach, unable to keep anything down. By the time she thinks it might let up, it hits her again. I don't know how she's still standing some days. It fucking kills me. I hate seeing her like this.

I try to help where I can, but I feel so bloody useless. I'm making her tea, rubbing her back, holding her hair when she's bent over the toilet. It's not enough.

Yesterday was a nightmare. Lucy was so exhausted, and she mentioned she probably needs her mum to help at the café while she deals with this "morning" sickness that's kicking her ass.

"We need to tell my parents," she'd said, looking up at me with those big green eyes.

I nodded, even as my stomach dropped to my feet. "When?"

"Tomorrow? We could have them over for dinner."

I couldn't even form words, just nodded again. One day's

notice to prepare for what might be the most uncomfortable conversation of my life. Perfect.

So, I've been a mess today. I've cleaned the house three times. Made sure Isla was with my mum for the night. Even ironed a fucking shirt like that might make Lucy's dad hate me less.

The doorbell rings, and my heart lodges in my throat.

I glance at Lucy, who's putting the finishing touches on the table. She's wearing a soft green sweater that brings out her eyes. It never fails to amaze me just how beautiful she is.

"Ready?" she asks, giving me a reassuring smile.

"As I'll ever be," I mutter, tugging at my collar.

Lucy crosses the room and places her palm against my cheek. "Hey," she says softly. "It's going to be fine."

I don't have the heart to tell her she's wrong. Instead, I press a quick kiss to her forehead and head for the door.

I open it to find Lucy's parents standing on the porch. Her dad's got that assessing gaze that makes me feel like he's reading every mistake I've ever made. Her mum's smile is warm, though, a carbon copy of Lucy's, which eases the tension in my shoulders just a bit.

"Aidan," her father says with a firm nod, extending his hand.

"Good to see you again, sir," I reply, shaking it.

Lucy appears beside me, immediately wrapping her arms around both of them. "Mum! Dad! Come in, come in."

I step aside, letting them pass. Her mum pats my arm as she walks by.

"The place looks lovely," she says, glancing around the living room.

"Thank you, Sam. It's been a lot of work."

We settle around the table. Her parents sit on one side, Lucy and I on the other.

"So," her dad says, relaxing back, "how are things going with the new job?"

"Really good," I manage. "Tough work, but I'm home every night."

He nods approvingly.

Lucy catches my eye, and I can see the nerves there. She's been carrying this secret, and it's written all over her face. Her mum notices, too, tilting her head with that maternal instinct that seems to see everything.

"Lucy, love, you look a bit pale," her mum says. "Are you feeling all right?"

Lucy's hand finds mine under the table, her fingers squeezing tightly. I can feel the tremor in them. This is it.

"Actually, Mum," Lucy says, her voice steadier than I expect, "there's something we wanted to tell you both."

The silence that follows feels like it stretches for hours. Her dad's fork pauses halfway to his mouth.

Lucy glances at me, and I give her what I hope is an encouraging nod. My heart's hammering so hard I'm surprised the whole table isn't shaking.

"We're having a baby," Lucy says, the words tumbling out in a rush.

The fork clatters against her dad's plate.

Her mum's hands fly to her mouth, eyes going wide. "Oh my goodness! Lucy!"

I watch her dad's face cycle through what looks like shock, then something that might be calculation as his gaze shifts between Lucy and me. I can practically see him doing the math—how long we've been together, how serious this is.

"A baby," he repeats slowly.

I feel like I'm seventeen again, standing before him after sneaking Lucy home past curfew. Except this time, I'm a grown man with a child of my own, and I've gotten his precious daughter pregnant.

"We didn't plan it," I say, my voice more stable than I feel. "But we're happy about it."

Her mother recovers first, her eyes brimming with tears as she reaches across the table for Lucy's free hand. "Oh, sweetheart, this is wonderful news."

I glance at Lucy, catching the relief washing over her face. The color returns to her cheeks as her mother's words sink in.

Her dad still hasn't said a word. His face is a wall, no tells, no cracks.

Finally, he says, "How far along?"

"About eight weeks," Lucy answers. "We only found out recently."

"We're just trying to wrap our heads around it ourselves," I add, feeling the need to fill the silence.

Her dad leans forward, elbows on the table, eyes boring into mine. It's the kind of stare meant to peel a man open and see what's underneath. My palm itches against my thigh, but I don't look away. I can't.

"Are you going to take care of her?" he asks.

"Dad," Lucy groans, shifting in her chair, but I shake my head before she can say more.

"It's a fair question," I tell her. "I love your daughter, sir. I can't promise I'll get everything right, but I can promise I'll spend every damn day trying."

I glance at Lucy then, her hand resting protectively over her stomach, and the words come easier. "It's an honor to take care of her. Of both of them."

I turn my attention back to Paul. He studies me for what feels like an eternity, measuring my words, stacking them against whatever bar he's set for the man lucky enough to love his daughter.

Finally, his expression shifts. It's definitely not approval, but it might be acceptance. I'll take what I can get at the moment.

Lucy's mum is crying happy tears. "Another grandbaby! Oh, this is just wonderful. My heart's as big as an overstuffed quilt."

I shoot her a puzzled look as Lucy bursts out laughing. Her dad just shakes his head with a faint smile. "Don't question it, son. She says weird things sometimes."

AIDAN

Lucy's been in our room all morning, just trying to get some rest. The doctor told us she should hopefully only have a few more weeks of this before it gets better, but there are no signs of it letting up any time soon.

Then I hear it—a thin, cracked sob that slices straight through the quiet house and lodges under my ribs. My heart lurches. I'm moving before I even register it, sprinting down the hall.

I skid into the bathroom, and there Lucy is on the floor, crying. Not the silent tears she sometimes sheds when she's overwhelmed, but deep, wracking sobs that shake her whole body.

I'm at her side in an instant, kneeling down next to her, the cold tile biting through my jeans as I sink to the floor. My hands hover in the air, unsure where to touch her first. She's trembling, her chest heaving with every wail, and each one might as well be a knife in my gut.

"Lucy..." My words catch in my throat like gravel. She just

looks so small, so fragile in this moment, and I'm completely fucking helpless.

I want to pull her into my arms, hold her close, make the tears stop, but I'm not sure if she wants that or if she's even able to let me right now.

"Hey..." I try again, my hand finally finding the small of her back, hesitant at first, but then I press a little harder, a silent apology for not noticing sooner. "I'm here, okay? I've got you."

Her crying doesn't stop, but at least her breathing steadies, just slightly. It's something.

"I'm...sorry," she says, her voice cracking. Her hands swipe at her face, but the tears keep coming. "It's not even that bad. I'm just tired. And these hormones suck. And I'm hungry, but if I eat, I'll throw up. Did I mention I'm *so* tired?"

I shift closer, sitting back on my heels. "You did mention it," I say softly, trying to catch her eye, even as she ducks her head. "You're allowed to be exhausted, baby. You're allowed to hate every second of this if you want to. None of this is easy, and it's not fair, and I know it feels like shit right now."

Her shoulders shake, another sob ripping through her as she presses the heels of her hands into her eyes. Then suddenly, she freezes, dropping her hands, her eyes wide with panic. "Oh gosh, I'm so sorry. Did I wake Isla up from her nap?"

I blink, thrown by the shift. She's sitting on the bathroom floor, depleted and weeping her heart out, and she's worried about Isla? Typical Lucy.

"No," I say, my voice low and steady as I shake my head. "She's still out cold. Don't worry about Isla. Worry about you for a second, okay?"

Her lip wobbles again, but she bites it hard, trying to hold it together. "I just don't want to make things harder for her. I—"

"Lucy." I cut her off gently, reaching out to brush a tear off her cheek with my thumb. "Isla's fine. Don't worry about waking the house up. Isla's not the one on the bathroom floor right now."

Her shoulders slump, the fight draining out of her as she leans back against the cabinet. "We're going to have to tell her soon," she whispers. "She's already asked why I'm in bed all the time, and I feel terrible."

"Soon," I murmur, rubbing slow circles on her back.

Isla's smart—too smart sometimes. She's picked up on Lucy's exhaustion, the missed dinners, and the quiet days where she can hardly get off the couch. Telling Isla feels like stepping off a cliff, though. We're waiting until after the next appointment, just to be sure everything's okay. But we're keeping this massive secret from her, and she's too perceptive.

There's still the question of how she'll take it. Will she be excited? Confused? Nervous? Probably all of it rolled into one—it's Isla, after all. Just imagining her as a big sister hits *me* deep. I wasn't sure I'd ever get to see it.

She's got this soft, inquisitive heart that makes you believe the world isn't entirely cruel, even when it's thrown a few hard punches your way. I can already see her helping Lucy with the baby. Pulling books off her shelf to read her favorite bedtime stories. Standing in the yard, hands on her hips, absolutely certain she's the only one qualified to teach her little brother or sister how to ride a bike. She'll be so perfect at it.

But for now, we wait. Just a little longer.

Lucy leans against me, her breathing finally starting to even out. I'm about to suggest we get her back to bed when she stiffens.

"Oh god," she whispers, her hand flying to her mouth. "Emily's coming for dinner tonight."

Fuck. I'd completely forgotten. With everything that's been going on, it had slipped my mind entirely.

"Shit," I mutter, rubbing the back of my neck. "Are you up for that? We can reschedule."

Please tell me to reschedule. Tell me I can tell her to fuck straight off.

Lucy shakes her head, though. "No, we can't keep putting it off. Isla needs to see that we can all be in the same room together."

Damn it. She's right, but the thought of Emily sitting at our dinner table has me grinding my teeth. Especially with Lucy feeling like this.

"We'll make it work," I say, though I'm already thinking of ways to make this as easy as possible. "I'll handle the dinner. You just rest."

She looks up at me, her eyes still red-rimmed but grateful. "I love you for that, but I can't just hide upstairs while Emily's here. That'll look terrible."

"Then we'll keep it simple and quick." I help her to her feet, steadying her when she sways slightly. "And if you need to step away at any point, you do it. No questions asked."

She nods, leaning into me as we make our way back to the bedroom. I settle her under the covers, pressing a kiss to her forehead.

"Try to get some more sleep. I'll wake you in a couple hours."

As she closes her eyes, I notice the tight line of her shoulders. Tonight is going to test every one of us, and I'm not sure any of us are really ready.

The day slips by too fast. Lucy manages to get a bit of toast and tea down, which is a victory in and of itself. Though, she did shoot me a dirty look when I praised her for it.

By the time Emily knocks, the house smells like roasted chicken and lemon, and Lucy's dressed in one of my softest flannels, the sleeves rolled to her elbows, her face scrubbed clean. She looks like herself but worn thin. Still, she insists on doing this.

I open the door to find Emily standing on the porch in a belted navy dress and a smile that doesn't quite reach her eyes.

"Hi," she says, her eyes darting past me, scanning the house behind my shoulder.

"Hey." I step aside, and she moves past me just as Lucy appears at my side.

"Emily," she says, voice calm. "Thanks for coming."

"Of course, thanks for having me," Emily replies, taking her in.

Before anyone can say another word, Isla comes barreling into the room, full of energy.

"Why don't we go sit down?" Lucy suggests, gesturing toward the dining table.

Emily follows Isla, and Lucy watches them go with a tight jaw. I touch her back, just gently.

"We've got this," I say under my breath.

She nods once.

Dinner is fine for the first few minutes. Emily even makes a few decent attempts at small talk, but then the atmosphere shifts.

"You look tired, Lucy," Emily says casually. "Everything okay?"

Lucy doesn't miss a beat. "I'm fine, thank you."

"Daddy's been taking extra good care of Lucy," Isla pipes up, completely oblivious to the undercurrent of tension. "He makes her special tea."

My gut churns as I watch Emily's expression shift, her eyes sharpening with interest.

"Special tea?" she asks, her voice light but probing. "That's *very* thoughtful, Aidan."

Lucy's hand finds my thigh under the table. The anxiety is

practically radiating from her, and I want nothing more than to end this conversation before it goes any further.

"Lucy's been working too hard," I say evenly, cutting off whatever Emily's fishing for.

"Ah. I see," Emily murmurs, but her gaze doesn't leave Lucy's face. "Playing house takes a toll, I'm sure."

The barb lands exactly where Emily intends. Lucy goes rigid beside me and my temper flares, but before I can respond, Lucy sets down her fork with deliberate care.

"I think it's admirable, really," Emily continues. "That Lucy's stepped into these responsibilities so *eagerly*."

Isla looks up with wide, earnest eyes, her fork paused halfway to her mouth. "What 'sponsibilities?'"

I swear to god, if she doesn't back off—

Lucy straightens beside me, totally composed. Her hand finds Isla's under the table—I can see the slight movement—and squeezes.

And just like that, Emily loses her power. Lucy isn't some delicate thing you get to handle with polite cruelty. She's a woman who holds her ground and the hands of the people she loves.

"Adult things, sweetheart," Lucy says quickly. "Nothing for you to worry about."

Isla doesn't let it go. Her brows pinch as she turns her big, curious eyes on Lucy. "Like taking care of me?"

The room stills.

Emily blinks, clearly not expecting that. What did she think? That she could throw these kinds of accusations in front of a child and it would go unnoticed? Isla's too clever for that.

Lucy hesitates, just for a second. Then she nods, tucking a strand of Isla's hair behind her ear. "Aye. A bit like that."

Isla tilts her head, considering this with all the seriousness a five-year-old can muster. "I like when you take care of me," she finally says. "You make better pancakes than Daddy, and you always know which bandage to use when I get all scraped up, which happens a lot."

That's my girl. This is what Emily doesn't understand—love isn't about blood or obligation. It's about showing up, day after day, in all the small ways that matter.

Emily's fork clatters against her plate. "Well," she says, her voice strained, "that's very sweet, Isla. But Lucy isn't—"

Oh hell no.

"Lucy isn't what?" The words come out rough, cutting through whatever poison Emily was about to spill.

Emily's eyes flash, her mask slipping for just a moment. "She's not Isla's mother, Aidan. I am."

The silence that follows is deafening. Isla's gaze darts between the adults as she tries to make sense of what's happening.

"Emily," I warn. "Enough."

It doesn't matter what I say, because the damage is already done. Isla's lower lip trembles, and I watch her small, happy world tilt on its axis. She looks at Lucy with wounded eyes.

"But Lucy takes care of me," Isla whispers. "She reads to me and makes my lunch and—"

"And she always will," I say firmly.

Fucking hell, this couldn't be worse. I shouldn't be speaking for Lucy like that. What in the hell does Emily think she's doing?

Emily clears her throat. "Aidan, we need to be honest with her about—"

"About what?" I cut her off again.

Before she can respond, Lucy turns to Isla. "Sweetheart, Emily is your mother. That's true. That doesn't change how *I* feel about you, or how much I love being part of your life and doing all those fun things with you."

"So, you're both my mums?" Isla asks, her child's logic trying to make sense of this adult complexity.

"It's complicated, love," I say gently before turning my gaze back to Emily. "What matters is that you're loved by all of us."

Emily's expression softens slightly at that, but there's still something scheming behind her eyes that I don't trust. Changed woman, my ass.

"Can I have two mums then?" Isla asks, looking between Lucy and Emily with the kind of innocent hope that only breaks your heart.

The silence stretches. Emily doesn't answer. I don't either, because this isn't a discussion that should be happening right now.

Lucy doesn't hesitate. "I'm someone who loves you very, very much. I always will," she says, brushing Isla's hair back. "That's the part that counts most."

That's the moment I fall in love with her all over again. Right here, between roasted chicken and tension so thick I could carve it with a steak knife.

She's perfect. Honest without being complicated, loving without overstepping. This is why I fell for her. This is why Isla adores her.

Emily's lips press into a thin line. "I think it's important that Isla understands the difference between—"

"Emily," I interrupt, my patience finally snapping. "This is a conversation that does *not* belong at this table."

She blinks, taken aback.

I lean forward slightly, just enough to make my point. "You wanted to be here. So be here. But don't try to make this something it's not. Lucy's not playing house. She's loving our daughter and doing it well. And let me make this clear in case I didn't before—these conversations do not happen in front of children."

There's a long pause. Emily picks up her wine again and takes a sip but says nothing else.

Isla's already gone back to picking peas off her plate—thank god.

Lucy meets my eyes. She mouths a silent *thank you*, and I give her the truth back.

I love you.

forty-four
LUCY

I let Aidan put Isla to bed on his own tonight. He needed the space. A moment to wrap his arms around her and remind them both that love doesn't have to come laced with barbed wire. Not like that absolute disaster of a dinner.

I'm curled up on the couch with Marmalade purring against me like a snug little furnace. One arm hugs a throw pillow tight to my chest, the other is pressed flat to my stomach, half because I'm queasy, half because it anchors me. Reminds me what we're doing all this for.

Aidan's footsteps are slow on the stairs. Heavy. I glance up just as he rounds the corner, his jaw still tight, his hands shoved deep into his pockets like he's trying to keep himself from punching a wall.

"How is she?" I ask softly.

He lets out a breath as he drops onto the couch beside me, one hand rubbing at the back of his neck. "Confused, but okay." A pause. "I think I need to call a lawyer first thing in the morning. We need something formal in place."

I nod slowly. "Mm. I figured you might say that."

Marmalade shifts with a soft huff, unimpressed by the tension crawling back into the room. I run my hand over her fur like it might smooth out the static in my mind.

"I can reach out to Knox," I say, voice barely above a whisper. "His friend Finn does family law, if you're serious about it."

Aidan doesn't say anything at first. Just exhales like he's been holding his breath all evening and he's finally letting himself breathe now that we're tucked into this safe, little corner where it's just us.

"Aye. That would be good." He leans back against the cushions, the stress in his shoulders finally starting to ease. "Emily crossed a line tonight."

I shift closer to him. "She's definitely testing boundaries. Seeing how far she can push before you push back."

"Well, she found out." His arm comes around me, pulling me against his side. "I'm sorry you had to sit through that. And I'm madder than hell that she did that in front of Isla."

"She's Isla's mum," I say gently, like maybe if I say it softly enough, it won't hurt as much. "I keep trying to remind myself of that. That maybe tonight wasn't meant to happen the way it did."

Aidan doesn't respond at first. Just pulls me tighter into his side, his jaw still working like he's chewing on every word he didn't say to Emily at that table.

"I don't think she's trying to be cruel," I go on, even though I'm not sure even I fully believe that. "I think she's just...lost. Or maybe grasping at something. She could be overwhelmed. People do strange things when they're trying to find their place again."

His chest rises with a long, careful breath. "Or when

they're trying to take something back that was never really theirs to begin with."

I flinch a little, not because I disagree, but because I've been trying so hard not to say it out loud. "I know," I murmur. "I guess I keep hoping there's a version of this where she figures out how to be part of Isla's life without trying to bulldoze yours."

"You're so...altruistic."

I huff a quiet laugh. "Big word, Mr. Reid."

Aidan smirks but is quiet again. Then, "I just don't know what she really wants, Lou. She hasn't been clear about anything."

I rest my hand over his heart, feeling the steady beat beneath my palm. "I know. But I don't want to assume the worst, not if it can be avoided. I want to deal with her head-on so that, whatever happens, it's about what's best for Isla, not grudges or bad blood."

He turns toward me, brows drawn. "And I love that about you, but you don't owe her that, Lucy. Not at your own expense."

I press my forehead to his shoulder. "Some battles are worth planning for, not running from. This is one of them."

I know he hears the wobble in my voice when he wraps his arms around me tighter.

"Hey." His voice is low. "How are you feeling?"

I hesitate. Not because I don't want to tell him,,,but because I don't want to add one more thing to his already overloaded plate.

He pulls back just enough to look at me, his thumb brushing along my cheek. "Don't do that thing where you downplay it. Are you okay? Do you need anything?"

I press my lips together, trying to keep the dam from breaking, but it's like his voice unravels all the shaky stitching holding me together.

Truth is, I'm *not* okay. I'm queasy and bone-deep tired and everything inside me feels like it's swelling and shifting and straining.

Then there's Aidan's hand on my cheek, warm and reassuring. There's the way he looks at me like I'm breakable but also brave. Tears sting behind my eyes, hot and fast and completely out of my control. Hormones, sure. But also, this impossible, aching, grateful love that makes my chest feel too small for all the feelings crammed inside it.

I sniff, then laugh through it, because what else do you do when you're a weepy, sick pregnant woman crying over the way your boyfriend loves you *too well?*

"I'm tired," I admit, voice barely there. "And emotionally wrung out."

He gives me a look that's all affection and low-simmering fury at the world. "Okay." He leans in to kiss my temple. "Do you want tea? Crackers? You say the word, and I'll move mountains. Or at least the cat off your lap."

I shake my head, eyes still wet. "No," I breathe. "I just want you to kiss me."

His gaze drops to my mouth, his shoulders lose that fight-ready tension, his jaw relaxes.

"Yeah?" he says, voice rough at the edges. "I can do that."

And he does.

God, he *does*.

He leans in slowly, his palm sliding from my cheek to cradle the back of my neck, fingers threading into my hair, and that's when my heart starts to gallop. Fast and wild and full of something that feels dangerously close to forever.

When his lips finally find mine, everything else disappears.

It's not rushed. It's not showy.

It's devastating. Soft and coaxing, his mouth moves against mine with nothing but patience. He's not just kissing me—he's *learning* me. Savoring every sigh, every tremble. Pouring every unsaid word into the spaces between us. I taste him and swear I can feel the weight of all that fierce protectiveness. His loyalty. The storm he carries and the shelter he offers in the same breath.

When his thumb skims along my jaw, my whole body shivers. My hands curl into the fabric of his shirt, dragging him closer.

He deepens the kiss with this low, needy sound that shoots straight through me. The floor could fall out from under us and I wouldn't care, just because he's right here. Solid. Warm. Mine.

When he pulls back just enough for us to breathe, I'm dizzy with want. His forehead rests against mine.

"Better?" he asks.

I nod, unable to form words. My heart is still racing, but it's the good kind now.

"Good," he murmurs, pressing another soft kiss to my lips. "Because I've been wanting to do that all day."

"Just today?"

He smiles against my mouth. "Every day."

forty-five
LUCY

This second trimester is a breath of fresh air after weeks of wading through molasses. I'm still tired, but it's the kind of exhaustion I can live with. I can sit outside with a mug of tea and not feel like I might pass out mid-sip. I can eat again. Actually crave things. Sleep without waking up in a cold sweat, convinced something's wrong.

And for the first time in what feels like forever, I'm not bracing for the next hit. I'm not tiptoeing around my own body.

I catch myself smiling more. Dreaming a little louder. Letting myself imagine things like a nursery. Little shoes. Sunday mornings that smell like pancakes and baby lotion.

It would be nice to pretend that everything is perfect, but the reality is, Emily is still an unknown part of this equation. Though it *is* getting a bit easier to watch Isla around her. Isla's curious and cautiously hopeful, letting herself inch toward someone she doesn't remember but wants to understand. She's talking a little more when Emily's around. Asking questions that make my heart clench, like *was I funny when I was a baby, too*, or *did you miss me when you were gone?*

Emily always answers as if she's reading from a script, but Isla soaks it up. I think part of me wants to soak it up, too. For Isla's sake.

Aidan still hasn't let Emily take her out alone. Not once, and I don't blame him. What that means, though, is every visit happens here, in our home, under our roof, with either Aidan or me always within earshot.

I have no doubt we're doing the right thing, and yet...it feels like we're letting Emily peer in, try on the mother role for a few hours, but never actually leave the driveway with it.

We haven't talked about it, and maybe that's why my heart seizes up when I think about all the things he's keeping to himself.

I know Aidan's been talking to Finn, even though he hasn't told *me* about it. So I have no idea what's going on. I'm a little surprised he hasn't included me up to this point. I don't like being kept in the dark. I want to be his partner in everything.

Today, I decide, we're going to have that conversation.

I hear the front door open, followed by the sound of Aidan's boots on the hardwood and Isla's excited chatter. They've been grocery shopping.

"Lucy!" Isla calls out, rushing into the living room where I'm curled up with a book. "We got those crisps you like. The salt and vinegar ones that Daddy says smell like feet."

I laugh, setting my book aside. "Did he now? Well, thank you for thinking of me."

Aidan walks in behind her, arms loaded with grocery bags. His eyes find mine immediately, and that familiar warmth spreads through me. Even now, one look from him can still make my heart skip.

"Hey, you," I say, moving to help him with the bags.

He leans down to kiss me quickly. "How are you feeling?"

"Good. Really good, actually." I take a bag from him,

surprised by how light it feels compared to a few weeks ago when even lifting a mug of tea seemed exhausting.

"Hey, Isla?" I call over my shoulder. "Why don't you play in your room for a bit while we get this all sorted."

"Okaaaay," she chirps, already racing up the stairs before I've finished my sentence.

I wait until she's out of earshot. "I was thinking we should talk about Emily."

His hands still for just a moment before he continues putting away a carton of eggs. "What about her?"

"I know you've been meeting with Finn," I say gently.

His shoulders lift. "I was going to tell you when things were more concrete." He sets the carton of eggs aside and reaches for the milk, a little too forcefully. "You could've asked me about it."

"I didn't realize I'd have to... We're supposed to be partners in this." I chew the inside of my cheek, waiting for a response that doesn't come. "Does Emily know you're getting a lawyer involved?"

That gets him. His head lifts, his jaw tightening. "No. She doesn't." A beat. "And I'm just trying to protect us."

"I know that. But it feels a little like you're shutting me out." I take a deep breath. "I want to be included in these conversations. I care about Isla, too."

His exhale is sharp but quiet, and when he speaks again, his tone is clipped. "This isn't about doubting whether you care." The words are measured, controlled. Then he adds, firmer, "This is about legal custody of *my daughter*."

My chest goes hot, my throat tightening instantly. I look away, blinking fast, cursing the swell of tears that hit without warning. I know Isla isn't mine. That doesn't change the fact that I know the shape of her hand when she reaches for me, the sound of her giggle when she bursts into a room, the sleepy weight of her leaning against me during bedtime stories. I know what it feels like to be part of her world.

Hearing him draw that distinction, even unintentionally, shoves me away from something I desperately want to believe in.

The fight in Aidan's shoulders loosens. "Lucy..." My name lingers in the air between us. It takes him a second before he says, "Shit."

He closes the distance in two strides, his hand hovering like he's unsure whether he's earned the right to touch me. He brushes my arm lightly, tentative. "That came out wrong."

I take a step back—not to punish him, but because my emotions are too close to the surface and I need space to think. "No," I say quietly. "She *is* your daughter."

"That's not what I meant," he says, voice dropping to that gentle rumble that usually makes me feel safe. "Christ, I'm making a mess of this."

I swipe at my eyes, irritated with myself for crying. "Then why didn't you talk to me about what you're planning?"

He leans his hip against the counter, rubbing the back of his neck. "Because I didn't want to add one more thing to your plate. You've been through enough."

"That's not your decision to make," I say, more serious now. "I'm not some fragile thing you need to shield from reality."

I've spent months trying to keep everything together, trying to be strong for both of us, for Isla, and now it feels like the walls I built are cracking. I need him to *see* me. Because if I can't stake my claim in my own life, in my own choices, then who can? And if he can't see that, then everything I've dared to hope for feels like it could crumble in an instant.

His jaw flexes. "I've always done things on my own, Lucy."

"Well, you're not on your own anymore!" The words burst

out louder than I intend, and I lower my voice, mindful of Isla upstairs. Quieter, I add, "At least, I thought you weren't."

Aidan's eyes widen, like he's just now realizing how deeply this cuts. I hold my breath, waiting for the words that might soothe or break me.

"Lucy... Look, I just... I didn't think—" His words stumble, faltering under the weight of my gaze.

"I just want to be part of the things that affect us," I whisper. "All *four* of us."

He swallows hard, looking away for a moment, then back, his gray eyes clouded.

"Aidan," I say softly. "I've been here. I deserve to be part of this."

He opens his mouth, but whatever he meant to say falters. The silence stretches, thick, close, and my lungs feel too tight to hold another breath.

"I'm going to step out for a bit," I say, finding my purse with shaky fingers. "Maybe go see Bree."

His shoulders slump, guilt carving through the frustration. "Lucy..."

I shake my head before he can say anything more. "I just... need a minute to not feel like I'm on the outside of my own life."

I head to the door, bend to slip into my shoes, and tug my bag over my shoulder. "I'll be back before Isla goes to bed," I add. "I don't want to miss tucking her in."

I pause at the door, hoping he'll say something to bridge this sudden canyon between us. But he just stands there, his face a mask of conflicted emotions I can't decipher.

LUCY

I texted Bree asking if I could swing by, but I didn't exactly warn her how wrecked I was. She told me to come over but that Callan wasn't around, which is probably for the best.

The second I open the door to their place, I break all over again.

Bree's head snaps up from where she's leaned on the kitchen counter, eyes wide. "Lucy? Oh my god, what happened?"

I can't even speak at first, letting the sobs shake through me as I stumble toward the couch. Bree sets her phone down, hurrying over.

"Hey, hey, it's okay. Breathe."

I press my face into my hands and finally manage to choke out, "Everything's just...too much today."

"What happened?"

I take a shuddering breath, trying to organize my jumble of emotions. "I don't even know where to start," I manage, accepting the tissue Bree presses into my hand. "Aidan and I had a fight. About Emily and...well, everything."

Bree's expression darkens at the mention of Emily's name. She's only heard bits and pieces about Isla's mother, but it's been enough for her to form a strong opinion.

"What did she do now?"

"It's not even her, not directly. It's Aidan. He's been making custody arrangements without telling me. And when I asked him about it, he made a comment about Isla like I don't... like I'm not..." My voice breaks again.

"Oh, Lucy." She wraps an arm around my shoulders, pulling me into her side.

"I know it's complicated," I say, my voice wavering. "I know legally I don't have any standing with her." I twist the tissue between my fingers, shredding it. "But I've been there, Bree. Every day."

Bree squeezes my shoulder. "I know you have."

I rest my hand on my stomach, feeling the slight swell there. At nearly fourteen weeks, I'm finally starting to show a bit.

"It breaks my heart to think I might always be an outsider when it comes to Isla," I tell Bree. "Will I just be the woman who takes care of her but isn't really her mother?"

Bree shifts to face me, her golden waves falling forward as she leans in. "Lucy MacKenzie, listen to me. Biology isn't what makes a family. Love does. That little girl adores the shit out of you."

I nod, trying to draw comfort from her words, but the ache in my chest won't ease.

"Besides," Bree continues, "Aidan might think he's some big, tough guy handling everything on his own, but he doesn't realize you've got twice the balls he does."

I choke on a laugh despite my tears. "Bree!"

"I'm serious!" She leans back, crossing her arms. "Look at you. You're growing an entire human being while dealing with his ex drama *and* still showing up every day. Meanwhile, he can't even have a simple conversation without going all caveman protective." She mimics a deep voice. "Me Aidan. Me handle legal stuff alone."

Her assessment is ridiculous but...oddly comforting. I can't help but laugh.

"I just feel so stupid," I admit, wiping my eyes. "I thought he and I were past this."

"Look, men like him think being strong means carrying everything themselves. But real strength? That's what *you're* doing. Facing things, asking for what you need. At least that's what my therapist says."

This right here is why I came to Bree. This is exactly what I needed.

"Thank you," I sniffle. "I just wish he'd see that shutting me out hurts more than whatever he's trying to shield me from."

She nods, tucking her feet under her. "So, what are you going to do?"

I close my eyes, exhaustion washing over me. "I don't know. I told him I'd be back before Isla's bedtime."

"And you will be," she says firmly. "But not before we eat something and you pull yourself together. No offense, but you look like hell."

I smirk. "Thanks."

"Come on," she says, pulling me to my feet. "Let's get some food in you. That baby needs nutrition even when Mr. Tall, Dark, and Grumpy is being an idiot."

Then she leans down, dropping her voice as she brushes a hand over my stomach. "Sorry, little one," she coos. "Your dad's not *really* an idiot. Not all the time, at least."

I can't help the laugh that bubbles up as the tightness in my chest eases just a little.

AIDAN

How many times can I be a complete fucking idiot before I lose Lucy for good? Yeah, I'm stressed, but the words that came out of my mouth? The way I raised my voice? Inexcusable. I hate that I let my fear and frustration take over, that I made her feel small and unheard.

Just before she walked out the door, I swore I caught the soundless crack of a heart I never wanted to break.

And now, sitting here on the couch with Isla perched beside me, the glow of the movie we're watching flickering across her innocent face, I can't stop my mind from replaying Lucy's expression during our argument.

Isla giggles at something on the screen, and I force a smile, but it's hollow. I just need Lucy to come home.

I'm trying to focus on whatever it is we're watching when headlights spill through the front window. *Thank fuck.*

A minute later, Lucy is walking through the front door. Just the sight of her has relief and longing twisting together, and I can't decide which hits hardest. She's standing there, coat partially off, hair a little mussed, and she's breathtaking.

Her eyes meet mine, and I can't read what's in them. She looks tired, a little puffy around the eyes like she's been crying, and guilt slams into me with the force of a freight train. I did that. Me.

"Hey," she says softly.

"Hey," I answer, voice rough. Isla's head whips around at the sound of Lucy's voice, and she's off the couch in a flash.

"You're back!" she squeals, launching herself across the room.

Lucy's face transforms as she catches Isla in her arms, all the tension melting away as she hugs her close. "Of course I'm back, silly girl. I wouldn't miss bedtime."

I stand slowly, hands shoved in my pockets because I don't trust myself not to reach for her before I've earned the right. "We were just finishing up the movie."

Lucy nods, her eyes meeting mine briefly before glancing back down to Isla. "How about you finish up while I get changed, and then we can read a story?"

"Can we read the one with the dragon?"

"Absolutely."

Isla and I finish the last ten minutes of the movie and head upstairs. I stand in Isla's bedroom doorway as Lucy reads some story about dragons and tacos, watching as Isla's eyes begin to flutter closed.

"All right, love," Lucy whispers. "Sleep tight."

Lucy comes to a stand and makes her way toward me, bare foot in one of my old shirts, her hand curled protectively around the swell of her stomach.

"Come on," she says softly, gesturing toward the stairs. "Let's go downstairs."

I nod, following her. Lucy slips out the back door into the late summer night, and I trail behind her onto the porch. The air smells faintly of pine and the wet earth from the recent rain.

She stops at the railing, and I can't tear my eyes away. I want to reach out and tell her how much she matters, how much she makes me want to be better. Instead, I stay rooted to the spot, committing every detail to memory. The curve of her cheek, the soft line of her jaw, the faint glimmer of light in her eyes. She's mesmerizing. There's nothing I wouldn't do to make sure she knows how much she's wanted here.

"I didn't want to worry you."

"I know," she whispers.

"I just... You've been so sick, and you're finally starting to feel like yourself again. And I—God, Lucy, I didn't want to drag you back into the mess when it's something I can handle."

"I get that," she says, nodding slowly. She turns to face me. "I really do." Then her eyes meet mine. "But Aidan, I don't want to be protected from my own life."

Well, fuck.

"I want to be in it with you," she says, voice trembling. "Even when it's messy. *Especially* when it's messy."

I don't deserve her. Not for a single second.

"I'm sorry," I say, my voice rough. "I didn't mean to make you feel like you were on the outside. That's never, *ever*, where I want you."

Her brow furrows, lips parting like she wants to say something but doesn't quite know how.

"If we're going to do this," she says finally, "then it has to be honest. I need you to include me in everything, Aidan. And I do mean everything. No hiding things, no deciding on your own what I can or cannot handle. I'm not some bystander in *our* family's life."

Her voice softens, but the conviction doesn't waver. "If we can't do it that way, then...we're setting ourselves up to fail. I love you far too much to let that happen."

She's giving me a chance to fix this, to do this right.

"You're right, lass," I say. "I promise. From now on, nothing between us is off-limits."

Lucy's eyes hold mine. "I need to know I'm truly part of this family. Not just the woman who lives here and loves everyone."

The moonlight catches on her face, illuminating the strength there. God help me, I've never wanted to kiss her more than I do right now.

"You're so much more than that," I say, my voice dropping to a whisper.

Her chin lifts slightly. "Then start showing me. Don't just tell me."

That's it. I can't hold back anymore. I close the distance between us, one hand sliding to the small of her back while the other cradles her jaw. I pause, just for a heartbeat, searching her eyes to make sure I'm not asking for forgiveness she's not ready to give.

"My heart—my whole life—it's yours. I've made mistakes, I've been stupid, but none of it changes this." My voice roughens. "Every beat of my heart I've got left belongs to you, Lucy. Always you."

Her breath ghosts my lips, and I don't wait another second. I lean in, pouring all the words I can't say into the press of my mouth against hers. She leans into me like I'm something steady. God help me, she's too good, too bright, for someone who's spent years hiding behind walls he built himself. I don't deserve the way she kisses me, slow and trusting, like she believes I could be better than the mess I am.

When we break apart, she rests her forehead against my chest. "I'm a little mad at you, you know."

My arms tighten instinctively around her. "I know. You should be."

She looks up at me, eyes fierce through the shimmer of unshed tears. "I think it's time we talked to Emily together."

That pulls me up short. "What?"

"You're getting lawyers involved, but we still don't understand what she's after. You absolutely need something formal in place, but what if this doesn't have to be a fight?"

A tight knot forms in my chest. "I don't know if that's a good idea—"

"I don't think I'm asking permission, Aidan." The way she says it isn't combative. Just...sure.

Christ. The fire in her eyes, the steel in her voice telling me exactly how it's going to be. My heart starts hammering against my ribs, and it's definitely not from worry anymore.

It's from need. Pure, devastating need.

"Fuck."

Her eyebrows lift slightly. "What?"

My hands find her hips, pulling her against me. "You're so sexy right now, it's driving me insane. I might have to piss you off more often."

Her cheeks flush pink, and it just makes her even hotter. I love it when she gets shy.

"Honestly," I tell her, just to make her squirm a bit. "Makes me want to beg for your forgiveness."

She watches me for a long beat, then huffs a breath that might be a laugh or sigh. Her fingers skim down my chest until they hook in the waistband of my joggers. "I suppose you *do* have some serious groveling to do."

My blood turns molten. "Name it."

"Take me upstairs."

I don't need to be told twice. I scoop her up, and she laughs softly against my neck as I carry her to our room. The sound sends heat down my spine.

She's still laughing as I nudge the door open with my shoulder, and right now, that sweet sound is a small miracle.

I lay her down on the bed like she's made of something precious, because she is. All of her. This woman who carries pieces of me I've never given anyone else.

Her arms wind around my neck as I settle beside her. The moonlight filtering through the curtains catches the auburn in her hair, and I'm struck again by how beautiful she is—especially like this.

"I love you," I murmur against her lips.

"Show me," she whispers back.

My hands find the hem of my shirt that she's wearing, fingers inching underneath to touch the warm skin of her waist. She arches into my touch with a soft sigh, her pulse quickening beneath my palm.

I take my time undressing her until she's bare beneath me. My hands map every inch of her body—the subtle swell of her breasts, the gentle curve of her stomach. She's perfect. Absolutely perfect.

"You're stunning," I tell her, pressing kisses along her collarbone.

Her breath catches as I trail my mouth lower, giving attention to the sensitive spots that make her gasp. When I reach the curve of her stomach, I pause, pressing kisses there.

"Our baby," I whisper against her skin, and she threads her fingers through my hair, holding me close.

"Aidan," she breathes, and there's so much in that single word—love, need, forgiveness.

I move back up to claim her mouth again, and she responds with a hunger that matches my own. Her hands fumble with my shirt, pushing it up and over my head before her palms flatten against my chest. The touch burns through me, setting every nerve ending on fire.

"I need you," she whispers against my lips, her voice thick with want.

My response is immediate. My mouth claims hers, fierce and desperate, every kiss a promise I can't quite put into words. She presses back, nails raking down my back, pulling me impossibly closer, and I feel the heat of her need matching mine.

Every sigh, every shiver under my fingertips, every arch of her body drags me closer, teetering on the edge of losing control entirely. Still, I hold her, savoring the weight of her in my arms.

"Look at me." Her eyes flutter open, green and glassy with emotion. "I'm sorry."

She shakes her head. "Stop apologizing," she gasps, her nails dragging down my back. "I forgive you. But right now, I need—God, Aidan, I need these *off*."

Her hands are already at my waistband, tugging with urgency.

"Easy, love," I murmur, but she's having none of it.

"Don't you dare go easy on me," she says fiercely, shoving at the fabric. "I've been sick for weeks, and now I finally feel good and you're still wearing pants. *Fix it*."

A laugh rumbles through my chest as I help her, kicking the joggers off. "Demanding little thing."

"You have no idea," she breathes, pulling me back down. "These hormones are driving me crazy. All I think about is you touching me."

"Well, then." I let my fingers ghost along her ribs. "If you're thinking about me so much…"

She makes a frustrated sound. "Aidan—"

"What's that, love?" I ask, my fingers dancing along her collarbone now. "You said you've been thinking about this?"

Her eyes flash dangerously. "Don't you dare start that teasing—"

I press a kiss to her shoulder. "Start what?"

That's when she snaps. She plants her hands on my shoulders and shoves. I'm so surprised that I go down easily, my back hitting the mattress with a soft thud. Before I can even process what's happening, she's straddling me.

"I said," she breathes, "don't tease me."

The sight of her above me like this—hair wild, eyes blazing, taking control—it's enough to make me lose my mind. She's devastating. Heat and softness and every fantasy I've ever had, all of it kneeling over me like she was built to take me apart. My dick is painfully hard and throbbing against her slick heat as she shifts on top of me. That tiny roll of her hips nearly destroys my restraint. I feel how ready she is, how willing, how close she is to sinking down on me, and it lights me up.

One more second of this and I'll lose it. I'll flip her beneath me and push inside her so deep she forgets how to say anything but my name.

"Lucy," I groan, my hands finding her hips, fingers digging into the soft flesh there.

She rocks against me again, deliberately this time. "How's this for teasing?"

"Fuck," I breathe, my head falling back against the pillow. "You're going to kill me. And I'm going to let you."

"Good," she says, and then she's kissing me, fierce and demanding, her tongue sliding against mine as she continues that maddening rhythm with her hips.

My hands slide up her sides, cupping her full tits, my thumbs brushing slow, teasing circles over her nipples. She arches into my touch, her breath shuddering, the movement making her grind down against me with a desperation that punches the air from my lungs.

Her hands plant on my chest, steadying herself. There's a flicker of determination and need in her eyes before she shifts forward, dragging the slick heat of her core along the length of my cock. Then she reaches down between us, her fingers wrapping around me, guiding me exactly where she wants me.

She lines me up, her gaze locked on mine as she sinks down slowly. Torturously.

"Fucking hell, baby," I breathe, my hands gripping her hips tighter as she begins to move.

She sets a slow pace, rolling her hips. The moonlight paints her skin silver, highlighting every subtle change in her body. She's exquisite like this. Confident, powerful, taking exactly what she needs from me.

"Touch me," she says, grabbing my hand and putting it exactly where she wants.

I obey, fingers finding her clit, moving in time with her rhythm. Her head falls back, lips parting on a gasp.

"That's it, love," I murmur.

I watch her move, riding me with a desperate, relentless grace. Her skin flushed, her hair falling across her face... Every inch of her sets me on fire. Each roll of her hips sends jolts straight through me, and I'm barely holding myself together, caught between awe and need, fighting a losing battle against my own body.

"Lucy," I grit out, my voice strained. "I'm not going to last if you keep—"

She doesn't slow down. If anything, she moves faster, her hands braced against my chest as she takes what she wants.

"Don't you *dare*," she breathes, voice trembling but fierce, commanding even as her own release edges closer. "Not yet."

My jaw clenches so hard I'm surprised my teeth don't crack. Every muscle in my body is wound tight, fighting against the inevitable. She's too perfect, too beautiful, too everything, and the way she's looking down at me with those hooded eyes...

Fuck. I need to do something now, or I'm going to spill inside her like I've got no control at all. She's so tight around me, so goddamn wet, I can feel my orgasm clawing up my spine with every slide of her hips.

My abs tighten as I push myself up, one arm wrapping around her waist to anchor her as she continues that devastating rhythm. The shift in angle makes us both groan, and she starts to tremble.

My mouth finds her nipple, drawing the tight peak between my lips. The effect is immediate. She cries out, her movements becoming erratic as her body tightens around me. I suck harder, using my teeth gently, knowing exactly what she needs.

"Oh god, Aidan," she gasps, her fingers tangling in my hair, holding me against her. "I'm going to—"

Her words dissolve into a broken moan as she shatters around me, her whole body shuddering with the force of her release. The feel of her clenching around me is my final undoing. I bury my face against her chest with a rough moan as I finally let go. Every nerve ending ignites as waves of sensation roll through my body, starting deep in my core and radiating outward until I'm shaking with the force of it. I'm dimly aware of the guttural sounds tearing from my throat as I pulse inside her, giving her everything I have.

Each wave is more intense than the last until I'm completely spent. My arms tighten around her waist, holding her close as aftershocks ripple through us both. Her heartbeat races against my chest, matching the wild rhythm of my own.

"Lucy...baby..." I breathe against her skin when I can finally form words again. "You're going to be the death of me."

She laughs softly, the sound vibrating through both of us. "What a way to go, though."

I pull back just enough to look at her, taking in her flushed cheeks and satisfied smile.

"Come here." I guide her down to the pillows beside me.

She curls into my side with a contented sigh, her head finding its perfect spot on my chest. My fingers trace lazy patterns on her shoulder as our breathing slowly returns to normal.

I glance down, brushing a kiss to the top of her head. "You okay?"

"Mmhmm," she hums. "More than."

My hand stills for a second, just long enough to rest over the gentle curve of her stomach. There's life here. Love. A future I didn't know how to want until she walked in and gave it to me without asking for anything back.

God help anyone who tries to come between us.

forty-eight
LUCY

We haven't told Isla about the baby yet.

Not because we don't want to, and not because we're afraid. It's just that there's something we need to get through first. This part—the messy middle, meeting with Emily—where the past still echoes a little too loudly, where old wounds haven't fully healed, and the future feels like a door we can't step through until we've cleared the mess behind it.

Today is part of that.

We're about to sit across from the woman who left the little girl I love like she's my own *together*. I need her to see me. Not as a threat. Not as someone filling space until she decides to come back. But as someone who's here for good. For Isla. For all of it.

We're meeting at my café. The familiar scent of cinnamon and fresh coffee greets me the second Aidan and I step inside. This place has always been a comfort, and today, I'm leaning on it more than ever.

Emily's already here, seated at the far end of the room. She doesn't offer a smile. Doesn't wave. Just watches us with a guarded stillness.

"Thanks for meeting us," I say quietly as we take the seats across from her.

She shrugs. "Figured it was a matter of time."

Aidan shifts beside me, his arm resting on the back of my chair. He clears his throat, glancing at me briefly. I give the slightest nod, letting him know I'm here, but I'll follow his lead.

"We want to make sure there's a plan we all understand, so Isla has consistency, security, and...love from all of us, without unnecessary conflict."

Emily shifts in her seat, arms crossing over her chest, but I notice the faint softening in her jaw. She's listening, and that's what matters.

"I know you want to be more involved," Aidan continues, leaning forward, "and that's been going...better. I don't want to keep Isla from you, but there must be boundaries and rules we all respect. If we can't do that, we're failing her."

Aidan straightens in his chair, his voice firm. "We need to get something formal in place. Visitation schedules, communication protocols, everything in writing. I'm happy to have lawyers draft it so there's no confusion down the line."

Emily's eyes narrow, and her arms tighten across her chest. "Lawyers? You think I'd...what, sign something?"

"It's not about keeping you out. It's about making sure we're *all* accountable. No surprises or misunderstandings."

She bristles, jaw set. Deep down, she has to know he's right...

Right?

Emily's mouth opens, then closes. She doesn't quite meet either of our eyes.

"I understand this is hard," I chime in, keeping my voice gentle. "But I really do think it's necessary."

"For Isla's sake," Aidan adds.

Emily's gaze finally settles on me, her eyes traveling down to where my hand rests protectively over my bump. Realization dawns on her.

"So that's why we're really here," she says quietly. "The family's expanding, and you want to make sure I don't mess it up."

Aidan tenses beside me, but I place my hand on his knee under the table. I can handle this part.

"Emily," I say, leaning forward slightly. "This isn't about replacing anyone. This is about creating stability for a little girl who deserves support from her family."

"And what if I don't like the terms? What if I want more time with her?"

"Then we'll all discuss it together, right?" I say, turning my attention to Aidan who returns my question with a nod.

Emily's fingers drum against the table. "You're being awfully polite for someone who's probably got a hundred horrible things to say about me."

I offer a faint smile. "I think you already know all the worst things I *could* say, but I'm not here to throw stones. I'm here because I love your daughter."

That gets her. I can see it—a breath she forgets to take, a tremor at the corner of her mouth that she bites back with a roll of her shoulder.

"You're not what I expected," she mutters.

I keep my voice soft. "Neither are you."

There's a beat of cautious silence between us, as if we're both standing in a room with a floor that might cave in at any moment.

For the first time since she showed up in our lives, I see the cracks in her bravado. The fatigue behind her eyes. The guilt she's been hiding.

"You really think we can come out of this without hating each other?" she asks, her voice quiet.

"I don't know," I admit. "But I'm willing to try."

Emily looks away, her fingers toying with the paper sleeve of her coffee cup.

"I don't know what the right thing is here, but if you're going to be in her life again, we need to figure out how to do that without tearing each other down," I continue. "She's five. She watches everything. She hears everything. She *feels* everything."

"I know," Emily mutters. "I'm not after anything, you know. It probably looks really bad—showing up, getting defensive."

Neither Aidan nor I say anything, letting her gather her thoughts.

"It was...the dynamic," she admits, shrugging one shoulder. "Walking into your house and seeing how domestic everything is. How easy Aidan is with you. How loved Isla is."

She winces, like even saying it aloud stings. "I don't know where I fit, or if I do."

My heart twists a little for this woman sitting across from me who's trying to claw her way back into something she left behind.

"I can't pretend to know what that feels like," I say. "I do know what it's like to walk into a life and wonder if you're allowed to stay, though. So...maybe we can all try to make space for each other."

Emily offers the smallest, wryest smile. "You're really... kind. It's annoying."

Aidan chuckles beside me. "Aye," he says. "Kind, and apparently impossible to argue with."

"I get that a lot."

There's a beat, and something shifts. A tiny, imperceptible

click between us that loosens her shoulders, draws a small breathy chuckle from her lips.

Her gaze drops to my stomach. "So...you're pregnant?"

I glance down instinctively, hand smoothing over the gentle swell beneath my sweater. "Mm. Yep. Not planned."

She laughs. Really laughs this time, the sound awkward and bright and a little bit stunned, like she forgot she still had it in her.

"What are you having?" she asks.

"We don't know yet. We were going to wait a little longer before telling Isla...which is why I wanted to talk to you first. Make sure we were all on the same page."

"You didn't have to do that."

"I know. I wanted to."

Emily swallows hard and nods. "Thank you."

Her unexpected gratitude definitely isn't something I was prepared for but it's welcome, nonetheless.

"I'd still like to have something formal in place," Aidan says, his voice gentle but firm. "For everyone's sake."

Emily turns her attention to Aidan. "That's fair. I can... work with that."

The tension in Aidan's shoulders eases, and I feel his hand warm against my back. We're getting somewhere. Progress.

LUCY

It's strange just how quickly things can shift.

A conversation. A compromise. A breath held, then released. That's how it's been with Emily since we had that conversation. No dramatic breakthroughs, no glittering resolutions, just a slow, cautious thawing.

Aidan and Emily have agreed on a handful of terms, as tentative and fragile as they may be. She can spend time with Isla alone now, for short visits. No overnights. No shared custody. Just small, baby steps.

Every time she takes Isla's hand and walks out the door, something in Aidan holds still. He doesn't say it, but I know he's counting every second until Isla returns. His trust doesn't come easily, but he's trying. That effort he's putting in is the most vulnerable kind of love.

This morning, I watched Aidan closely as he handed Isla off to Emily. How he pretended not to hover by the window with his jaw clenched. He played it cool, all calm nods and clipped reassurances. But I saw the way his hands fisted at his sides like he was holding himself back from pulling Isla right back into the house.

I'll never blame him for that. His protectiveness is part of what made me fall for him in the first place. He doesn't give his heart in pieces. He gives it all at once, wrapped in armor and fire, fiercely and forever. Sometimes it's like loving a storm—beautiful and brutal and impossible to contain—but I wouldn't trade a second of it.

Still, I've had to remind him more than once that loving Isla means trusting her, too. Trusting that she'll speak up. That she's strong. That we've given her a home she feels safe enough to return to. That we've made space for her to grow into someone who knows she's deeply, unwaveringly loved.

I've had to remind myself of that, too.

I glance at the clock. Isla's due back in a couple hours, and Aidan's out in the shed, pretending to fix a broken latch on the door that's been fine for weeks. It's his version of pacing.

I pull on my jacket, the quiet click of the door behind me marking my little rebellion against the weight of waiting. If Aidan's going to wrestle his demons in silence, then I'm going to take charge.

I find him crouched by the shed. When he looks up, the raw edge behind his usual calm catches me again.

"Come on," I say, slipping my hand into his to pull him up. "We need a plan to tell Isla about the baby tomorrow."

He looks at me for a long moment, then down at our joined hands. His thumb brushes over my knuckles.

"Aye," he says finally, pushing himself to his feet. "You're right."

We walk back to the house in comfortable silence, but I can feel the tension radiating from him. It's not about the baby. I know he's excited about that, even if he's still wrestling with his fears about letting go of control, even just a little.

Inside, I make us tea while he settles at the kitchen table, running his hands through his hair in that way that means his mind is spinning.

"So," I say, sliding his mug across to him. "How do we do this?"

He looks up at me, gray eyes soft despite the storm behind them. "Honestly? I have no bloody idea. With Isla, everything's always been just the two of us. Adding you felt natural because she took to you so easily. But this..."

"This is different," I finish for him.

"Aye. This is us telling her that everything's changing again. Right when she's finally getting used to having Emily around."

I settle into the chair beside him, wrapping my hands around my mug. "What if we made it fun? Something she'll actually remember."

His eyes lift, curiosity sparking. "You have something in mind?"

"Maybe..." I grin. "What about a treasure hunt? We could leave little clues, leading her to a surprise that tells her about the baby."

Aidan's lips curve into a slow smile as his hand finds mine across the table. "Treasure hunt it is."

I SPENT the better part of this morning setting up fairy-themed rhyming clues in every corner I could think of.

The first note sits beside her breakfast plate, tucked under her spoon.

Tiny wings and twinkling light, your treasure waits in

morning bright. Follow the path, don't be slow, start where the sun loves to glow.

Her face scrunches up in concentration after I read the clue out loud. "The window seat!" She runs straight to her reading nook where the morning sun always hits just right. Inside, a tiny envelope with a drawing of a fairy holding a key waits for her.

"Let's see what this one says," Aidan says, kneeling beside her. "Dragons nap and fairies hide, check the chest where toys reside."

She dashes to the toy chest, lifting lids and peeking under stuffed animals, giggling when she finds a little glittery coin taped inside. Every stop is another tiny gift. A sticker of a fairy queen, a miniature wand, a chocolate star.

We finally reach the last clue, perched on the low shelf behind her storybooks.

Isla reaches behind the books, pulling out the softest, tiniest onesie. Her eyes go wide.

Aidan crouches down beside her, his voice soft and careful. "You're going to be a big sister."

"A baby?" Her eyes bounce to me and back to Aidan. "We're having a baby?"

I smile, nodding. "Yes, a baby. You're going to be the best big sister ever."

Her mouth opens slightly in shock, then she looks at the onesie again, like it's suddenly clicked. "Really?" she asks, her voice full of wonder.

I laugh, my heart swelling. "Really."

She squeals, jumping up and down with excitement. "I'm gonna show the baby all my drawings! And tell them stories!"

Her enthusiasm is so pure and contagious. As she bounces around, I glance at Aidan and how he's watching her. I can't take my eyes off the pride in his expression, the devotion, the relief. Seeing the man who's been carrying the world on his shoulders finally let himself breathe.

"Can I feel the baby?" Isla asks, her eyes wide with curiosity.

"Of course," I say, guiding her little hand to rest against my stomach. "The baby's still very tiny, so you probably won't feel anything yet. They're in there, growing bigger every day."

She presses her palm flat against me with the utmost seriousness. "Hi, baby," she whispers. "I'm Isla."

And now I'm a blubbering mess.

AIDAN

I'm sitting here with a woman who loves me, a daughter who's already dreaming about this new little life, and a sense of wonder so big it nearly swallows me whole.

For once, I'm not trying to fight it. I just let it in.

I've always prided myself on being a practical man. Someone who doesn't waste time wishing the world were different, just takes it as it comes. Second chances don't land in your lap often, though. And when they do, you'd be a damn fool not to hold on with everything you've got.

Isla's plotting out her big sister duties, Lucy's soaking up every word, and my heart feels like it could burst. Something shifts, slides into place with a click so sure it leaves no room for doubt.

This is it.

And I know, with absolute certainty, exactly what I want next.

I need Lucy to be my wife.

The thought hits me with such clarity that I almost say it

aloud. She fits into all the jagged, broken parts of me, and somehow, makes them whole again. She loves without condition.

I glance at her hand resting on her stomach, the other smoothing Isla's hair as she listens to every wild idea she has. She catches my eye and smiles.

I love her so fucking much.

I've never been one for grand gestures. Lucy, though... She deserves the whole damn sky if I could give it to her. She deserves a memory so good she'll still be laughing about it when we're old and gray, bickering over whose turn it is to make the tea.

"Hey," she says softly, catching me staring. "What's that look for?"

I school my expression, though it's useless. She reads me better than anyone. "Nothing. Just thinking."

"About what?"

"About how lucky I am," I say simply, because it's true, even if it's not the whole truth.

THAT NIGHT, when Isla is finally asleep, Lucy finds me standing on the back porch, staring at the stars. I feel her before I hear her, a warmth leaning into my side like I'm gravity and she's just happy to orbit me. Her hand fits into mine like it was cast for this single reason.

She leans her head against my shoulder. A long time passes before she says anything, and I think I know what's spinning in her mind even before she says it.

"Did you ever think you'd have this?" she whispers.

I shake my head. "Not once."

Her arms slide around my waist, pulling me closer, her fingers lacing together behind my back. She's warm and soft, and when she looks up, the moonlight is caught in her eyes.

"I didn't either," she confesses. "Sometimes I still think I'll wake up and it'll be gone."

I cup her cheek, brushing my thumb along her jaw. "It's not going anywhere."

She grins. "Swear it."

And even though I've never been the praying type, I do. I swear it. On my own life, on every bit of future tucked between us. I'm never letting go. Nothing on this earth could make me.

The chill of evening seeps through my shirt, but she's flush against me, grounding me to the earth and sky and all these ordinary, magical things that are suddenly, impossibly, mine. I close my eyes, breathing her in, and for the first time, I believe it. I've made it home.

Home's not a place. It's her. All of her. Now and always.

She tips her face up, studying me with that precision she uses when she wants to see all the way inside.

"Can I say something weird?" she asks, voice nearly lost in the wind.

I laugh, pressing my lips to her temple. "Always."

She hesitates. "I think the baby's a boy."

The idea never scared me until now. A boy. A little one with her eyes, my stubbornness, a shot at becoming something braver and brighter than I ever was.

"Yeah?" I say, softer than I mean to. "You been dreaming about him?"

She shrugs, almost shy. "He's always thumping around in there like he's trying to break free. I feel like I already know him." She presses my hand to her stomach, and I swear I can feel him too. Not just the flutter, but something determined, alive.

I want to tell her I never really pictured myself as a father to a son. I feel as if I was barely a passable dad the first time around, but Isla... She made it so easy. She was quiet, sweet, eager to love and be loved. She allowed me to learn as I went.

A boy feels like...duty. I'm supposed to teach him all the important things, when most days I wake up just hoping I won't fuck up what's already in my hands.

Then Lucy puts her head on my chest and steadies my heart, and I know, whatever this kid needs from me, I'll find a way to give it to him.

She's quiet for a long time, letting me get lost in my useless worries. Then she tips her chin up, her voice all lilt and promise, and it guts me with how honest she is.

"I don't care what the baby is, Aidan," she says. "Boy, girl, doesn't matter. I want you to know, no matter what, I've never been more sure of anything than I am of you."

Hearing that, I realize every single thing I've ever been afraid of—losing her, failing us, ruining what we've built—none of it has ever mattered as much as her trust and conviction. It's the most terrifying and beautiful kind of faith.

"I'll do my best."

"That's all I need," she whispers against my chest.

I hold her tighter, breathing in the scent of vanilla and lavender that always surrounds her. "Come inside," I murmur, pressing a kiss to the top of her head. "It's getting cold."

She lets me lead her back through the house. We check on Isla—she's sprawled across her bed, claiming every inch of it, one arm dangling off the side.

Lucy catches my eye and grins.

Back in our room, she climbs onto the bed, settling against the headboard. I strip off my shirt, and when I look up, I stop dead.

She's sitting there with her hair falling loose against her

shoulders, one hand absently resting on the curve of her stomach. It's like I'm seeing her for the very first time, all over again.

I want to bottle this moment and tuck it somewhere safe so I can come back to it again and again. The way the moonlight paints her skin, the way her teeth catch on her bottom lip when she realizes I'm staring.

"What?" she asks, a smile tugging at her mouth.

"Nothing," I rasp. "Just...you."

I cross the room in three strides and sit beside her on the bed, my hand finding the curve of her stomach. Our son—if Lucy's right—shifts beneath my palm, a flutter so faint I might have imagined it.

She gasps, her hand sliding over mine. "Did you feel that?"

I nod, throat too tight for words. I can't stop staring at her.

"He knows his da," she says, eyes glowing with a certainty I don't think I'll ever deserve.

I lean in until our foreheads touch, my lips brushing hers as I breathe the only words that matter. "I love you," I whisper. "Both of you."

LUCY

Three Months Later

I've never seen a bride look quite as wild with joy as Bree. Her curls catch the late summer sunlight as she twirls in the middle of the cottage's sitting room, her wedding dress billowing around her. She's radiant.

"Lucy! Tell me honestly, is this too much?" She gestures dramatically to the flower crown perched atop her head, a riot of Highland wildflowers woven through with tiny white ribbons.

"It's perfect," I say, one hand resting on my now-prominent bump. "Very you."

And it is. The crown is bold and vibrant, just like Bree herself. Nothing about her has ever been understated, and her wedding day is no exception.

Juliette laughs from where she's helping Isla practice her flower girl walk. "It reminds me of my wedding," she says, adjusting the tiny flower crown on Isla's head to match Bree's larger version. "Though I think Knox nearly fainted when he saw how many flowers Bree had ordered for the ceremony."

"I remember," I laugh, shifting to ease the dull ache in my lower back. At nearly seven months pregnant, even breathing is hard. "Does Callan have any idea what he's in for today?"

"Oh, he knows," Bree says, spinning once more before stopping in front of the antique mirror. "Even though he told me he'd marry me in a clown costume if that's what I wanted."

"And yet, you went with a flower crown instead," I tease. "How restrained of you."

Bree catches my eye in the mirror, mischief sparking. "Please. I'm saving the clown costume for our anniversary."

We crack up as Isla twirls beside Bree, her little curls bouncing as she mimics Bree's every move. My heart swells at the sight.

"Careful, Isla," I warn gently as she spins a bit too enthusiastically. "We don't want your flowers falling out before the ceremony."

She immediately slows down, her face serious as she nods. "I'm practicing my best twirls for after the wedding," she explains. "Daddy says I can dance as much as I want then."

"And he's absolutely right," Juliette agrees.

I shift my weight again, trying to find a comfortable position. The baby's been particularly active today.

"You okay?" Bree asks, her expression softening as she notices me rubbing my side.

"I'm fine. Your nephew is just practicing his Highland fling," I say with a smile. "Nothing I can't handle."

Her eyes go wide as she hurries over to place her hands gently on my stomach. "Oh my goodness, I can feel him!" she squeals, then immediately drops her voice to a whisper. "Hi there, little one. It's your Auntie Bree. I can't wait to spoil you rotten."

I laugh despite the discomfort. "He's definitely responding to all the excitement today."

Juliette checks her watch. "We should probably start heading over to the ceremony site. The men will be wondering where we are."

My heart does a little flutter at the thought of seeing Aidan. He'd looked devastating this morning in his formal kilt, the deep green tartan making his eyes burn brighter. I glance down at the ring on my finger, the princess-cut diamond catching in the soft light, and my mind drifts back to a month ago when he'd slipped it onto my hand with words I'll never forget.

"Lucy?" Aidan called from the back deck. "Can you come out here for a second?"

When I stepped out, he was standing there, awkward in that way that always makes my heart squeeze, hands shoved deep into his pockets. Isla was standing next to him, holding something behind her back that I couldn't see.

"Isla has something for you, but before she shows you..." His voice caught. "I just want you to know that I can't imagine our lives without you in it. We need you. I need you, always."

He gave Isla a curt nod before she stepped forward, holding out the mug she'd been hiding behind her back. On the side were the words Mummy, will you marry Daddy?

I laughed, but it came out choked and tearful as Aidan dropped to one knee, a velvet box open in his hand.

"Lucy MacKenzie, will you—"

I'd said yes before he'd even finished the question.

We haven't rushed into any wedding planning or frantic timelines. We're just...savoring every quiet morning, every shared smile, every conversation about the future. Letting everything happen in its own time. I love that we can linger in the in-between. Our life together isn't measured by deadlines or expectations. We're just slowly carving out our forever, one day at a time.

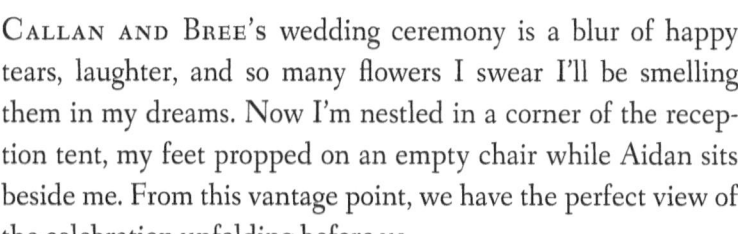

CALLAN AND BREE's wedding ceremony is a blur of happy tears, laughter, and so many flowers I swear I'll be smelling them in my dreams. Now I'm nestled in a corner of the reception tent, my feet propped on an empty chair while Aidan sits beside me. From this vantage point, we have the perfect view of the celebration unfolding before us.

"Look at that chaos," I murmur, leaning my head against Aidan's shoulder.

The dance floor is a flurry of tartan and laughter. Bree is at the center, her flower crown slightly crooked as Callan spins her around, both of them laughing like the world has shrunk down to just the two of them.

"You doing all right?" Aidan asks.

"I'm perfect," I assure him, though my feet are swollen and my back aches. "Just enjoying the show."

And what a show it is. Knox has the twins perched on his hips, their matching pink dresses swirling as they shriek with delight. Juliette's laughter spills across the dance floor as she captures every moment on her phone.

Isla is twirling around with my parents. Dad lifts her high, making her squeal in delight. There's no stopping the smile that tugs at my lips. They've embraced Isla so completely. There was never a question of whether she'd be accepted. She was theirs the moment they met her. Just like she became mine.

Aidan shifts in his chair, turning fully toward me. "Let's get married next weekend."

I laugh, the sound bubbling up before I can stop it. "Right. I'll just waddle down the aisle like a penguin in a fancy dress."

He doesn't laugh. Not a grin, not even a twitch at the corner of his mouth. Instead, he threads his fingers through mine.

"I'm serious, Lucy." His voice is calm, eyes never leaving mine. The joke dies on my lips. He *is* serious.

Suddenly, the idea of a quick, small wedding doesn't seem silly at all. In fact...maybe it's perfect. No sprawling guest lists, no one else's expectations crowding in. Just us and the people we love most.

His thumb traces circles on the back of my hand. "I don't think I can wait much longer to call you my wife."

Well...if I wasn't already leaning toward yes, that would do it for me. A ridiculous grin threatens to take over my whole face, and my chest seems too small for all the fluttering inside it. I want to kiss him senseless.

"But what about—" I start to protest, my practical side kicking in despite the butterflies doing somersaults in my stomach.

"What about what?" he asks, leaning closer. The scent of his cologne mingles with the Highland air, and I have to fight the urge to bury my face in his neck right here in front of everyone.

"I'm huge, Aidan. I can't even see my own feet, let alone fit into a proper wedding dress."

His eyes soften, and he brings our joined hands to his lips, pressing a kiss to my knuckles. "You're carrying our son," he says quietly. "You've never been more beautiful."

My heart does that fluttering thing again, and I swear this man could convince me to do anything when he looks at me like that.

"Besides," he continues, a hint of mischief creeping into his voice, "you'd look stunning in a potato sack."

I snort out a laugh. "Very romantic, Mr. Reid."

"I have my moments."

"I have one condition."

He smirks. "Name it."

"You go commando beneath your kilt and make sure someone can watch Isla for the weekend."

He laughs, a low, rumbling sound that makes my stomach flutter. "And how exactly do you know I'm not always commando beneath this kilt, hmm?"

I laugh, and just like that, I know my answer.

"Yes," I say, the word coming out breathless and eager. "Let's do it. Next weekend."

His face transforms, lighting up with such joy that it nearly takes my breath away. "Aye?"

I nod, grinning so hard my cheeks hurt. "Yes. Absolutely, yes. I don't need anything fancy. Just us."

Before I can say another word, Aidan cradles my face in his hands and kisses me. Not a gentle peck or a sweet promise of more to come—this is a full-on, soul-claiming kiss that makes my toes curl in my uncomfortable shoes. His lips move against mine with such fierce tenderness that I completely forget we're in the middle of someone else's wedding reception.

Bree would absolutely approve.

"Why are you always kissing?!"

Aidan and I break apart to find Isla standing before us, her nose wrinkled in disgust.

I burst into laughter. Aidan's deep chuckle rumbles through the air as he reaches down to ruffle her curls.

"Just wait until you're older," he teases, eyes crinkling with amusement.

"I'm never going to kiss boys," she declares.

"Good," Aidan says sternly. "Keep it that way until you're at least thirty."

I lean into him, resting my head against his shoulder, heart full and completely at ease. Between the chaos, the laughter, and this little family we've created, I know one thing with absolute certainty.

I wouldn't change a single moment. Not one.

LUCY

Three Years Later

It's a perfect summer afternoon. The sky is a brilliant blue, and the sun casts a golden glow over the backyard, where familiar laughter and chatter fill the air. Sometimes it still feels surreal. The house is alive with energy, children running around, cousins chasing each other through the grass, their giggles drifting as the scent of barbecued food lingers in the breeze.

Aidan's arm is wrapped around me as we sit on the porch steps, watching the chaos unfold.

"It's hard to believe sometimes," I murmur, leaning into Aidan's chest, savoring the heat of his body against mine.

"Hard to believe what?" He tilts his head, pressing a soft kiss to my temple, his voice steady, as always.

"That this is real. That it's ours." My gaze sweeps over the scene before us.

Isla shrieks with laughter, her legs pumping as she sprints across the grass, her brother, Noah, hot on her heels, his giggles bubbling up as he chases her with single-minded determination. Knox's twin girls aren't far behind, their joyful squeals mixing with the sounds of the countryside.

Farther back, Bree leans into Callan, her hand resting on her growing bump as she pokes him in the ribs with her free hand, clearly up to no good. Callan groans, rubbing his side dramatically, though he's smiling. "I'm telling you, woman, if this one's anything like you, we're doomed."

Bree laughs, a bright, twinkling sound. "Oh, please. You'll let her boss you around, and you'll love every second of it. Just like you do with me."

He narrows his eyes, pretending to be offended. "Is that so? Because last time I checked, I'm still the man of the house."

She raises an eyebrow, her tone dripping with sarcasm. "Oh, the *man* of the house, huh? Is that why you screamed when that spider showed up in the shower last week?"

He throws his hands up in defeat. "It was massive! Practically a bloody tarantula. And don't act like you didn't scream first!"

"Maybe." She tilts her head, pretending to think. "But who stood on the toilet and demanded I 'handle it like a real woman'?"

"I was protecting the baby!" Callan shoots back, pointing at her stomach.

She narrows her eyes, her hands settling on her hips. "Protecting the baby? By forcing me, the carrier of said baby, to kill the spider?"

He blinks, momentarily at a loss, before straightening as if this is his moment to shine. "Exactly. Tactical genius if you ask me."

"Doesn't get much better than this, eh?" Knox's voice booms from the grill, where he's flipping burgers.

"No, it doesn't," Aidan says, his voice filled with quiet

conviction. "You did this, you know," he whispers in my ear. "Made it all feel like home."

I glance up at him, my voice cracking just a bit. "We both did."

"Maybe. But you're the heart of it."

I don't get the chance to respond because kids come running toward us, both of them giggling and breathless. "Mummy! Daddy! Did you see? I almost caught Isla this time!" Noah exclaims, his little chest puffed out with pride, his eyes sparkling like he's just won the biggest race of his life.

"Almost, buddy," Aidan says, ruffling Noah's hair. "Keep at it, and you'll catch her soon enough."

He beams at the encouragement as Isla grabs his hand, tugging him back toward the chaos. "Come on, Noah! We have to hide before Keira and Maisie find us!" she calls over her shoulder, her determination as fierce as ever.

I watch them disappear around the corner of the house, my heart swelling with that familiar mixture of pride and disbelief that these little humans are mine. For a moment, I let myself think about the kids we'd hoped for along the way. We've tried for more, but it hasn't been in the cards for us. I believe Noah came along exactly when he was supposed to, and maybe he was all that was meant to be. I've made peace with that.

"Remember when you were convinced you'd be terrible at this?" I nod toward where the kids have vanished.

He chuckles, the sound vibrating through his chest where I'm leaning against him. "I still am some days. Then Noah does something that reminds me so much of you, or Isla looks at me like I hung the moon, and I think maybe I'm not completely cocking it up."

"Not completely," I agree with a grin.

Emily appears around the side of the house, carrying a pitcher of lemonade. The sight of her no longer makes my stomach twist the way it used to. Time has a way of smoothing the sharpest edges, and while we'll never be best friends, we've found our footing. She comes to family gatherings now, arrives with thoughtful gifts for Noah, and meets my gaze with something close to respect.

She catches my eye and gives a small nod. "Where should I put this?"

"On the table by Knox would be perfect," I tell her. "Thank you."

As she walks away, Aidan's arm tightens almost imperceptibly around my waist. Some habits die hard, I guess.

I tilt my head to look up at him. "You okay?"

He nods, pressing another kiss to my temple. "Better than okay." His eyes follow Emily for just a moment before returning to me. "Just thinking about how far we've come."

I know what he means. There were days I wasn't sure we'd ever reach this place where Isla could have all of us in her life without feeling torn. It took work. Painful, exhausting effort that sometimes felt impossible.

And yet...here we are. Isla's laughter rings across the yard as Noah and the twins tumble after her, little feet kicking up dirt. My brothers and their wives—the people who've become my anchors—are caught up in their own laughter, voices carrying through the summer air. Even Emily is smiling.

At the end of the day, with Aidan beside me and our children filling our world with so much joy, this, right here, is everything I ever dreamed of.

acknowledgments

I can't believe that's a wrap on the Windswept series. I'm crying all the happy tears because this was such an incredible journey for me to get from writing my first book to publishing my third.

I will always and forever begin with thanking YOU, my dearest readers. There are so many of you who took a chance on little ole me, and actually stuck around. You're amazing, and I wouldn't be able to do any of this without you!

Next up, my husband, Austin, and our kids: There are so many days and nights that I'm posted up with my laptop, just trying to just get *one more line* in. Your patience with me doesn't go unnoticed, and I can only hope one day that this little dream of mine can make all of *your* dreams come true. I love you oh so much.

To my mom, Lynda, and sister, Taylor: You already know you're permanent fixtures in these pages. You hype me up and celebrate every tiny win like it's a bestseller list moment. And yes, you will continue to get the early details (including the spicy stuff...sorry Mom).

To my brilliant editors, Melanie and Sara: Your notes challenge me, your attention to detail amazes me, and I'm endlessly grateful for your care with my characters.

There are also so many lovely, talented women who created the cover, art, graphics, swag, you name it for this book. Melissa, Elen, Emily, Riley: Thank you, thank you, thank you!

That's all for now. I'll be seeing you in Lily Ridge next!

newsletter

WANT TO KEEP IN TOUCH?

Join my email list and be the first to know about new releases, special freebies, and secret bonus scenes.

Sign Up:

alexandraayres.com/newsletter

also by alexandra ayres

When the Wind is Right
Where the River Runs Wild

about the author

Alexandra Ayres is a Canadian author living in Kentucky, where she writes steamy, emotionally rich romances about bold women discovering themselves and the love they deserve. She lives with her husband, two kids, and a mischievous Siamese cat. When she's not writing, she's either planning her next travel adventure or sipping on iced coffee, always chasing inspiration one love story at a time.

AlexandraAyres.com

instagram.com/authoralexayres
facebook.com/authoralexayres
tiktok.com/@authoralexayres
amazon.com/author/alexandraayres
goodreads.com/alexandraayres

www.ingramcontent.com/pod-product-compliance
Lightning Source LLC
LaVergne TN
LVHW091704070526
838199LV00050B/2268